MURDER BETWEEN THE TIDES

A British Murder Mystery

MICHAEL CAMPLING

Shadowstone
Books

Published by Shadowstone Books
ISBN: 978-1-915507-03-7

It is not often that someone comes along who is a true friend and a good writer.

— **E.B. WHITE**

This book is dedicated to the memory of my dad, Herbert Campling. He excelled at solving puzzles, and I think he would've enjoyed this story immensely.

PROLOGUE

NEWQUAY

I t's quiet here. But not silent. Never silent.

Far below, the freezing sea hisses, spitting its angry venom against the unforgiving cliff face. It's getting dark now, but the white flecks of spume are starkly visible, spattering over the black rocks.

I take a step closer to the edge, and the rumbling call of the waves grows louder. A sudden sense of emptiness rushes up from the gathering gloom, an icy gust of air swirling around me, tugging at my clothes. I'm light headed, and the stony path that had seemed so solid shifts beneath my feet. My shoes scrape over the damp gravel, but the sound belongs to someone else, someone brave enough to step to the brink.

Specks of sea spray settle on my skin and gather on my eyelashes. I blink, wiping my eyes with the backs of my cold hands, but not all the salt water on my cheeks has come from the sea.

A seabird, a European herring gull, slides into my field of view then glides away, its wings unmoving, the perfect white feathers of its sleek body unruffled. I watch the gull for a moment, following it with my eyes until it dives and disappears beneath the cliff's edge. In the distance, the bright lights of the town twinkle cheerfully, the drab winter streets temporarily brightened by garish strings of Christmas lights.

Even so, I know that the pastel colours of the painted houses are jaded and careworn, the gift shops and cafes empty and desolate. But soon, for one hotel at least, there will be an influx of visitors. I will no longer be alone.

And if everything goes according to plan, I will be avenged.

I take one last look at the hungry sea. *Soon, you will have what you desire*, I tell the churning waves. *You will have your sacrificial offering*.

Then I turn toward the town, and I start walking.

SATURDAY

CHAPTER 1

EMBERVALE

In the front room at The Old Shop, Dan stood back from the window to admire his handiwork. Until a couple of days ago, he'd never owned a single Christmas decoration, but Alan, his neighbour, had assured him that most of the residents of Embervale brightened the village at Christmas by displaying lights on the front of their houses. Sure enough, in recent weeks Fore Street had taken on a cheery glow as more and more houses were adorned with strings of lights.

Eventually Dan had joined in, purchasing a modest set of multicoloured LEDs, and he'd spent the last ten minutes stringing them backward and forward across the inside of his front-room window.

He tested the suction-cup hooks that held the wire to the glass and, satisfied that they were secure, he plugged the lights in. The LEDs sparkled into life, and Dan smiled. Perhaps Christmas in Embervale wouldn't be so bad.

There was to be a Christmas fair in the village hall, a festive-themed quiz evening in the pub, and the local school children were staging a pantomime. Dan had protested that the school event would be for parents only, but Alan had insisted that everyone was welcome, and the matter was settled.

For Dan, a lifelong Londoner, Christmas meant crowded streets, frantic shopping trips and a kind of stifling urgency that crept in at around the twentieth of December. In Embervale, they did things differently. Alan had the bit between his teeth, and it looked as though Dan was to be dragged into the festivities whether he liked it or not.

Time to tackle the tree, Dan thought. The fir tree stood, undecorated, in the corner. It was too big for the room, but he'd bought it on impulse, carried away by the moment.

He'd gone with Alan to buy the tree, but instead of heading into Newton Abbot or Exeter, Alan had driven them along winding lanes until they'd reached a farmyard. There they'd been greeted by a young man in overalls who'd ushered them into a cavernous barn. A row of freshly cut fir trees leaned against the wall, and they'd taken their pick. The price had been ludicrously low, so when Alan handed over his cash, Dan had grabbed a tree for himself.

The deal done, there'd been none of the usual fussing about with nylon nets. As soon as Alan had folded down the rear seat of his car, the young man had simply stuffed their chosen trees into the back. The whole process had taken only a matter of minutes and was entirely painless. And if anyone except Dan noticed the dead leaves and strands of straw dragged into the car by the trees' lower branches, they hadn't mentioned it.

In the past, Dan would've been annoyed if his purchases had come accompanied by debris. But since moving to the countryside, he'd learned that whatever he did and wherever he went, a certain amount of mud and dirt would be inevitable; it was part of life.

It's amazing what you can get used to, he thought. He looked pointedly at the large toolbox that lay open at the side of the room, and at the spirit level propped beside the door.

Although the redecoration of The Old Shop had been nearing completion for some months, Dan's decorator, Jay, always managed to find one more thing that needed doing, and evidence of his activities was everywhere. Once Jay started a job, he was reluctant to let it go, and even though it was a Saturday, he was upstairs, working away.

As if to prove the point, a dull thud boomed from the ceiling. Jay had persuaded Dan that all the carpets should be removed, and the fine old floorboards stripped back and polished. At the time, Dan had been all in favour of the idea, but since then the noise of the floor sander and the inevitable dust and disruption had stretched his patience almost to its limit.

A muffled curse came from the room above, and Dan's heart sank.

Another thud and Jay muttered a few terse sentences, though Dan couldn't make out what was said. Either Jay was making a call, or he was grumbling to himself; both were equally likely.

What's the problem this time? Dan wondered. His money was on something to do with wiring. According to Jay, the fuse box was one short step away from bursting into flames. Dan knew how it felt.

Jay's heavy footsteps thumped on the stairs and, when he appeared in the doorway, his expression said it all.

"Go on," Dan said, "tell me the worst."

Jay winced. "You're not going to like this, but we've hit a snag."

We? Dan thought, but all he said was, "What kind of snag?"

"I'm not going to lie. It's bad. The boards in the main bedroom were okay, but when I got to the landing, it was a different matter. It's riddled with woodworm, and from what I can see it's got into the staircase too. It's a wonder you haven't fallen through it."

Dan scraped his hand down his face. "How much will it cost to put right?"

"We'll have to strip out a lot of the old boards and replace them, but that's not the only problem. The joists are full of holes. You'll need to have the whole place professionally treated, and that's not something I can do. We're going to need a specialist."

"I suppose I'll have to wait until after Christmas, but it can't be helped. It'll have to be done."

"As it happens, I've got a mate in this line of work," Jay said with a wolfish smile. "For him, this'll be a small job. And you're in luck. He can fit you in right away."

"You've called him already?"

Jay nodded. "No point mucking about. He can start the day after next. Monday. That's perfect because I can come in early and rip out the boards. My mate only has a few days free, so he'll have to tackle the bedrooms, the landing and the stairs all at once."

"But I'm supposed to be sleeping in the spare room until—"

"You'll have to move out," Jay interrupted. "He'll be spraying chemicals all over the place. You can't be around when he starts. You'll have to find somewhere to stay for a few days."

Dan shook his head in disbelief.

"Why don't you ask Alan?" Jay said.

"He won't be there. He's going away for some kind of writing event or other."

"There you are then. You can probably stay at his place while he's away."

"Perhaps."

"Right, that's sorted then. I'm glad we've got that fixed up. I may as well leave my tools here." Jay headed for the door. "I'll see you on Monday," he called over his shoulder. "Bright and early."

"Right," Dan said to the empty room. "It looks as though I haven't got much choice."

∾

"Woodworm?" Alan said, ushering Dan into his kitchen. "That's bad news."

"Tell me about it. The thing is…"

"You'll be needing somewhere to stay." Alan nodded as though deep in thought. "Mm. I suppose that might work."

Dan's expression brightened. "Really? I can stay at your place while you're away?"

"No, that wasn't what I was thinking. Don't take this the wrong way, but I'm not keen on people being in the house while I'm not here. Anyway, my idea is better. Much better."

"Oh? Are you going to offer me the use of your shed or something?"

"Of course not. I was thinking you could come with me, to Newquay."

"But I thought you were going on some kind of writing holiday."

"It's a writing retreat, not a holiday," Alan said pointedly. "I'm hoping to get a lot of work done."

"Fine, but I'm not a writer."

"That needn't matter. You'll get a place to stay with bed and breakfast, and you can please yourself during the day. Have you ever been to Newquay?"

"No, and I'm in no great rush to go to the English seaside in the middle of winter."

"There are some lovely coastal walks," Alan said. "And the town is quite nice. I'm reliably informed that there are even some good places for vegans to eat out."

Dan raised an eyebrow. "You were looking for vegan restaurants? Have I tempted you to convert?"

"Certainly not, but since I booked, I've been sent

information on every possible kind of dietary requirement and lifestyle. I happened to notice the vegan options, that's all."

"Fair enough," Dan said. "The point is, I can't invite myself along to your event. Anyway, I expect it's all booked up, isn't it?"

"I know someone who's pulled out at the last minute. He's trying to offload his room, so I'm sure you could get it for a knock-down price."

"I see. I suppose, in the circumstances, I'll have to think about it."

"Well, you'd better be quick," Alan said. "I'm leaving on Monday morning, so if you want that room, you'll need to book it as soon as possible."

Dan hesitated.

"Think of it as a holiday," Alan went on. "I'm happy to give you a lift. I was driving there anyway. All you need to do is sit back and relax. You'll have a few days by the sea, away from all the noise and the dust of Jay's Herculean labours. I mean, you must be getting sick of it. He's taking forever to get the job done."

"Jay is something of a perfectionist." Dan weighed his options for a second, but in all honesty, he had little choice. "All right, I'll come along. If you could tell your friend I'll take the room, that would be great. Just let me know how much and where to send the money, and I'll take it from there."

Alan smiled. "Excellent. We'll go first thing on Monday morning. It won't take long to get there, but I'm meeting the others for lunch and I want to be there in plenty of time. In the afternoon I'll be doing some work, but after that we could meet up for something to eat."

"Won't you be busy discussing the relative merits of the three-act structure or something?"

"This is a hotel in Newquay were talking about, not some

MURDER BETWEEN THE TIDES

swanky literary reception. I think you'll find that most jobbing writers like a trip to the pub as much as anyone else." Alan chuckled under his breath. "But now that you come to mention it, I might need to escape from the others for a while. They're a nice bunch, but one or two of them like to talk shop all the time, and it can get a bit tiresome."

"Ah, so you have an ulterior motive for inviting me."

Alan shrugged. "I prefer to call it enlightened self-interest. Anyway, you're getting a cheap holiday out of it, so I think you're doing pretty well. It's win-win. A tide in the affairs of men, which taken at the flood, and all that."

"Mm. Julius Caesar. That didn't work out too well for him." Dan stood. "I'd better go and pack. Tell me, what's the dress code for a gathering of writers?"

"Comfortable. And don't forget, bring plenty of warm layers. When the wind comes blasting over the Atlantic, it takes your breath away."

"Now he tells me. I'll be sure to bring a decent coat." Dan crossed to the door, but he paused before opening it. "Thanks for this, Alan. It is a good idea. You're right, I could use a few days away from the house."

"Well, you'll get plenty of peace and quiet at Newquay," Alan said. "I can guarantee it."

SUNDAY

CHAPTER 2
NEWQUAY

E dward Hatcher breezed through the doors of the Regent Hotel at 9 am precisely, and that was exactly as it should be. But almost immediately his expression darkened; there was no one waiting to greet him.

Pulling himself up to his full height and removing his grey fedora with a flourish, Edward stalked toward the reception desk and delivered a sharp tap to the gleaming brass bell. *An unnecessary contrivance,* he thought. *Surely the desk should be staffed at all times.*

Edward stood motionless, waiting. The bell's chime echoed through the empty lobby and faded away, but still no one arrived to welcome him.

Someone barged through the hotel's main door, but it was only the taxi driver who'd brought him from the station. And he didn't look happy.

"All right, mate," he said. "Are you going to come and get these bags or what?"

"In a moment. I have summoned assistance, and I'm sure that a porter will arrive presently."

The driver rolled his eyes. "I can't wait all day. I've got another call. Now, you've paid your money, and I've stopped the meter, so we're done. I'll put your bags outside."

Edward bridled, flaring his nostrils. "You'll do no such thing. You may bring my bags into the hotel, and if you're quick about it, you may get a tip."

"You what? Who the hell do you think you are?" The driver didn't wait for a reply but turned on his heel and marched out.

"Wait," Edward called. But a moment later, he heard the grumbling rattle of a diesel engine as the taxi sped away. "Of all the nerve," Edward muttered. "I should have taken his number."

"What was that, sir?"

Edward turned with a start, staring at the stout, middle-aged man who'd appeared behind the counter. "Where did you spring from? And more importantly, where were you when I arrived?"

The man offered an apologetic smile. "Very sorry about that, sir. I was just in the porter's cubbyhole, answering a call from one of our valued residents." He hooked his thumb over his shoulder, and Edward noticed, for the first time, the small compartment tucked away behind the reception desk. The cubbyhole was separated from the lobby by panels of polished oak, and no doubt it was an original feature of the hotel. Little larger than a broom cupboard, it would have been a place for the night porter to stay warm while keeping an eye on the lobby.

Edward noted the computer screen sitting on a narrow counter inside the cubbyhole, the display filled with the unmistakable image of playing cards. *Online poker*, Edward thought. *Oh well, it could have been so much worse.*

"My name is Matthew," the receptionist went on, "and may I take this opportunity to welcome you to the Regent hotel."

The man's smile was genuine, his tone sincere, and

Edward's mood mellowed. "Very well, Matthew. Perhaps you could start by retrieving my luggage from the pavement outside. My driver was less than helpful."

"Certainly, sir. First, could I just check that you have a reservation?"

"Of course. My name is Edward. Edward Hatcher." He smiled expectantly. His name wasn't always recognised, but it was important to be ready. One never knew when one might run into an avid reader, and it paid to make the right impression.

But Matthew showed no flicker of recognition, and he lowered his head to study yet another computer screen. "Hatcher," he muttered. "Hatcher, Hatcher, no, no." He flicked an anxious glance at Edward. "If you could just bear with me for a moment, sir, I'm sure I'll be able to... Ah! Edward Hatcher. Five nights. You upgraded to the Regency suite."

Edward inclined his head in acknowledgement. "That is correct."

"Of course! You're here for the writers' group."

"Once again, Matthew, you've hit the nail on the head. Now, perhaps you would be kind enough to bring my luggage inside."

"Be right with you. I'm just activating your keycard." Matthew began typing on the computer's keyboard, his fingers jabbing inexpertly at the keys. "Just one minute." Matthew's face fell. "This machine is taking its time, but it won't be long. Probably." He pushed the keyboard aside and smiled at Edward. "So, what kind of books have you written? Anything I might have read?"

Edward's expression froze. "That's hard to say," he began, but before he could explain further, a booming voice rang out across the lobby.

"Max Cardew!"

Edward and Matthew gazed at the man who'd called out:

an imposing figure marching toward them from the entrance, a sense of authority in his every step.

"You're Max Cardew?" Matthew asked, his voice hoarse with suppressed excitement. "I love your books. The wife likes them too. Even my kids read your stuff, and they never pick up a book otherwise. We must have read everything you've ever done. And that series on the telly was fantastic." Matthew licked his lips. "Is it true what they say about *The Seventh Cipher?* Are they going to make it into a film?"

The new arrival let out a bellow of laughter as he joined them at the reception desk, then he gestured toward Edward. "You'll have to ask my friend here. He writes under the name Max Cardew, not I."

Matthew frowned at Edward. "But you don't look anything like him. I mean, I'm sorry, sir, I don't mean any disrespect, but this gentleman is pulling my leg, isn't he? Because, as I say, we've got all the Max Cardew books at home, and the photo on the back—"

"Was taken some time ago," Edward said. "You have to remember that I've been writing for many years, and my publicist insists that I keep the same photograph. It's a question of branding, apparently." Edward recovered his composure. "But thank you for your kind words about my work. If you'd like me to sign any of your books, please do bring them along. I'd be happy to oblige."

"Right," Matthew said. "Thanks. I might do that."

Edward cast a sidelong glance at the man who stood beside him. "Nice to see you again, Brian. I didn't know you were joining us this week."

"Yes, I checked in last night. I wanted to get a feel for the place, get my feet under the table."

"I see. I hope this means that your book sales have taken an upturn. I was sorry to hear that you parted ways with your publisher." Then, to Matthew, Edward said, "I'm sure you've heard of the famous Dr Brian Coyle. His books made quite a splash when they came out. Tell me, Brian, was it three years ago or four?"

"Five," Brian replied from between clenched teeth. "But I've got a whole new series coming out. This one's going to be great. It'll blow the roof off the bestseller charts, you'll see."

"Ah, that is good news. You've found another publisher?"

"Not yet. Actually, I'm thinking of going independent. I can take care of the whole thing myself. It's the way forward."

"Self-publishing. Interesting." Edward favoured him with a benevolent smile. "Good luck with that, Brian. And I mean that sincerely. I hope it works out for you."

Brian watched Edward carefully as though waiting for the other boot to drop, but finally he nodded. "Thanks, Edward. I appreciate it." He hesitated. "And when I came in, I wasn't laughing at you. I didn't mean any disrespect."

"Think nothing of it," Edward said. "I'm very aware that I don't live up to my pen name's glamorous image, but there we are. We work with what we have."

"Very true." Brian chortled quietly. "Still, all those years in intelligence — your old career gives you a certain aura of mystique. That kind of authenticity is gold dust. I can't compete with that."

Edward tapped the side of his nose. "Hush, hush, old chap. You know I never talk about those days."

"And that only adds to your image. The quiet man with a secret past. I've got to hand it to you, you've got it all worked out." Brian gestured at the reception desk. "I'll leave you to get checked in. I've been out for a bracing walk along the clifftops, and I'm ready for a coffee."

Matthew, who'd been turning his head to follow their conversation, was suddenly roused into action. He grabbed his computer's keyboard and typed with renewed vigour. "Right. Before I get your key, Mr Hatcher, I just wanted to check something with your friend if that's all right."

"Be my guest," Edward replied.

"Thank you, sir. *Dr* Coyle, is it? I have you down on my system as *Mr* Coyle. Is that incorrect?"

"Yes. I prefer to go by my proper title. And before you ask, no, I'm not a medical doctor. I have a PhD."

"In that case, I need to update the system." Matthew scowled at the screen. "I'll do it later. Now, Mr Hatcher, you wanted a hand with your bags. I'll fetch them in."

"Oh dear," Brian said. "Edward, I hope those weren't your cases I saw outside."

"Why?" Edward asked.

Brian stifled a smile. "A small dog was passing by, a scruffy little terrier, and I'm afraid he cocked his leg against your suitcase."

Edward's cheeks coloured. "What?"

"Sorry to be the bearer of bad news. I'd have stopped the little brute, but I was too late. There was nothing I could do."

"Oh my God!" Edward pointed at Matthew. "This is your fault, you idiot! If you'd done your job properly, this wouldn't have happened. If anything's been damaged, I'll expect full compensation."

"But—"

"I don't want to hear any excuses," Edward snapped. "Just get out there and fetch my bags then bring them up to my room."

Matthew nodded unhappily. "Certainly, sir. I'll see to it straight away."

Edward held out his hand. "Key."

"Yes. Of course." Flustered, Matthew hunted through the items on his desk, his fingers made clumsy by his haste. At last, he produced a plastic keycard and slid it across the counter toward Edward. "You're on the fifth floor, sir. The views from up there are fantastic. They're our best rooms."

"Is there a lift?"

"I'm afraid not, sir. It's being renovated over the winter.

But we're very proud of our grand staircase. It's an original feature."

"I'm sure it is," Edward said. "And assuming I survive the ascent, where will I find my room?"

"That's easy, sir. Turn right as you leave the stairs, then head to the end of the corridor. You can't miss it."

"Thank you." Edward scooped up the card, then he nodded to Brian. "Nice to see you again. I'm sure we'll have time for a chat later."

"Definitely," Brian said. "I'll look forward to it."

Edward sent a stern glance at the beleaguered receptionist, then he strode toward the stairs. *Not an auspicious start*, he thought. *But surely, things can only get better*.

MONDAY

CHAPTER 3

NEWQUAY

I n his room on the fifth floor of the Regent Hotel, Dan set his holdall on the floor and glanced around his room. As well as the double bed, which looked okay, there was a small desk and chair, a wall-mounted television and a narrow wardrobe, but that was pretty much it. He checked the bathroom; while it was small, it was clean and functional.

Returning to the bedroom, he crossed to the window and pushed the slats of the vertical blind aside. The tall sash window let in plenty of light, but the view was uninspiring: a steady stream of traffic trundled past in both directions, and over the road an odd assortment of small shops was sandwiched between a supermarket and a pharmacy. Dan spotted a coffee shop, but it looked as though it was closed.

At this time of day? It was mid-morning, and a prime time to dispense cappuccinos to those in need of caffeine. But there was little in the way of passing trade: the hotel seemed to be some distance from the town centre, and precious few pedestrians graced the wintry pavements.

Dan sat on the edge of the bed, pleased that the mattress was reasonably firm. Beside the bed there were four separate light switches, all of which looked as if they'd been added on separate occasions. Briefly, he experimented with the switches in various combinations, but discovered the purpose of only three of them.

He cast his eye over the TV's remote control, but it was unlikely to hold any surprises, and anyway it was time to go and explore.

Alan's room was only a little way along the corridor from Dan's, but the contrast between the two bedrooms was stark. "Very posh," Dan said, taking in the polished oak desk and the king-sized bed.

"I had the same room last year, so I made sure to book it in plenty of time," Alan replied. "Is your room okay?"

"It's fine. Shall we go out and grab a coffee, or do you have an official event to attend?"

"Some of us are meeting for lunch in the restaurant downstairs. I'm free until then, so I'm sure we'll be able to scare up a decent cup of something."

Downstairs, Alan halted at the entrance to the hotel's bar. "This place is open, and there's a distinct aroma of fresh coffee."

"I'm happy to give it a go," Dan said. But when they stood at the bar, he frowned at the automated bean-to-cup coffee machine on the counter. "Maybe we should try somewhere else."

"Why trudge all over town looking for somewhere better?" Alan asked. "This will be fine, and the conservatory is nice. You get a great view of the sea."

Alan indicated an archway in the far wall, and when Dan peered through to the conservatory, he caught a glimpse of the sea, the winter sunlight catching the white-crested waves.

"Why don't you find a table?" Alan said. "I'll get the coffees. I know what you want."

"Are you sure about that? Perhaps I might take a sudden fancy for a skinny soy latte with a shot of hazelnut syrup."

The barman appeared to take their order, and Alan said,

"Two large Americanos, please. One black, and one with cold milk on the side."

"Certainly, sir," the barman said. "Anything else?"

"No thanks," Dan said, then he offered Alan a smile. "You win. But I'll pay for the coffees, and you can choose the table."

"Done." Alan headed to the conservatory, and a couple of minutes later Dan found him relaxing on a sofa by the window, a slender woman with long red hair sitting at his side.

Alan waved him over, and Dan joined them but remained standing, unsure whether he was intruding.

"Roz, this is the friend I was telling you about," Alan said. "Sit down, Dan. Make yourself comfortable. This is Roz Hammond. Roz is an old friend, and a very talented lady indeed."

Roz smiled and patted Alan gently on the arm, a multitude of colourful bangles rattling on her wrist. "You mustn't flatter me, Alan, it'll go to my head. But you're so charming, I can't help but forgive you."

Alan and Roz laughed at the same moment, and Dan shifted his weight from one foot to the other. "They're bringing the coffees over, but it looks as though you two have a lot of catching up to do, so I'll leave you to it."

"Don't you dare," Roz said with a twinkle in her eye. "I've been dying to meet the infamous Daniel Corrigan. Alan's told me all about your adventures, and I want to see if you live up to the legend."

A young woman arrived bearing a tray of drinks. "Two Americanos, one with milk?"

"Yes, thank you," Alan said.

The drinks were placed on the low table, and the decision was taken from Dan's hands; he had to stay. He took an armchair facing Alan and Roz, and as he took an experimental sip of his coffee, Roz leaned forward, focusing her attention on him. And Dan couldn't look away.

Roz had the kind of natural beauty that came from fresh air and clean living. Dressed in a unique style, she wore an eclectic mix of flowing fabrics in bold patterns. Her silky scarf and dangly enamelled earrings were a dazzling shade of turquoise, and the colour emphasised the deep blue of her eyes.

There was something otherworldly about Roz, and although her voice was soft, Dan found himself listening with rapt attention. "So, Dan, tell me about *you*. What makes you tick?"

Dan's expression froze. "I'm not sure how to answer that. Who could?"

"What do you mean?" Roz asked.

"It seems to me that we all have our own ideas about what we're like as individuals, but we can never see ourselves as others see us."

Roz held his gaze. "So when you look at me, what do you see?"

"Well, if I had to guess, I'd say that you're an artist, or rather, an illustrator. You work with children. You're from somewhere in the London area, but you now live in Cornwall. You're a local. You enjoy walking, but you cycled here today. You cycle regularly, partly for the exercise, but mainly out of concern for the environment."

"How did you know all that?" Roz turned to Alan. "Have you told him about me already?"

Alan chuckled. "Not at all. I knew you were coming today, but I haven't mentioned you to Dan. It's just a knack that he has."

"It's not that difficult," Dan said. "You have some small ink stains on your fingers, and judging by the bright colours, it seemed likely you're an illustrator. Being from London myself,

I recognised the cadence in your voice, but your accent has changed, and your vowels have taken on a distinctly Cornish note. Your shoes are sturdy, waterproof and built for walking, but I think you cycled here this morning. There's a tiny mark on your forehead that looks like the impression left by a cycling helmet. Apart from your shoes, your clothes are not from high street stores, and they're all made from natural fibres. I'd say they were fair trade cotton and, taken together, your concern for the environment is fairly obvious."

Roz stared at him. "But how did you know I worked with children?"

"That's harder to explain," Dan said. "There's something in your manner and in the disarming way you ask such frank questions. Most adults shy away from saying anything too personal when they first meet someone, but children are refreshingly honest when it comes to finding things out. When they want to know something, they simply ask, and it seemed to me that you may have picked up the habit from working with children regularly."

"I'm extremely tempted to tell you that I'm an accountant from Edinburgh and I've never ridden a bike in my life," Roz said. "But the truth is, you're pretty close. You didn't guess that I practise tai chi every morning as the sun rises, but then, how could you know? And, of course, you missed out the important detail that as well as being an illustrator, I'm a writer."

"I didn't think it was worth mentioning," Dan replied. "After all, you're at a writers' retreat. Why else would you be here?"

An awkward silence fell over the group, but then Roz laughed, leaning back in her seat and chuckling, her hand on her stomach. "I can see that we'll all have to be on our best behaviour or you'll find us out, Dan."

"I don't think you have anything to worry about," Alan said. "You're one of the kindest people I know, Roz."

Roz laid her hand on Alan's arm. "That's very sweet of you."

"I mean it. The work you do in schools is an inspiration. I was a teacher myself, remember, and I know that what you do makes a real difference."

"I enjoy it," Roz said. "I wish I could say that it pays the bills, but with all the cuts these days, there isn't enough money to go around. And I don't like to charge too much or the schools won't be able to afford it."

"It's a damned shame. There should be proper funding." Alan lowered his voice. "Speaking of money, I was sorry to hear about that business with the Max Cardew books. Did you ever get paid properly for that?"

Roz shook her head. "I wasn't getting anywhere, so I've stopped chasing them. It was all my fault. I should have looked at the contract more carefully." She hesitated. "Did you know that he's here this week?"

"Yes, I saw Edward's name on the list."

"Max Cardew himself," Roz said.

"You've lost me," Dan admitted. "Who are you talking about, someone called Max or someone called Edward?"

"They're one and the same," Alan explained. "Max Cardew is the pen name of a man called Edward Hatcher. His books are very popular and they've even been made into a TV series. A few years ago, Roz did some great work for him, creating character art for his book covers, but she was never properly paid."

"They used my work on all kinds of merchandise," Roz said. "Pencil cases, posters, you name it. I did get some money, but the publishers, not to put too fine a point on it, screwed me over. For a while, I hired a lawyer to fight for my rights, but now the publishers have dropped all my artwork. They offered me a small lump sum if I agreed to draw a line under the whole thing. That's when I gave in."

MICHAEL CAMPLING

"That's a shame," Dan said. "It must have been very upsetting for you."

Roz shrugged. "I've let it go. Since the TV series came out, everything was rebranded using the actors from the show, so as far as I'm concerned the whole affair is over. I don't hold grudges."

"Speak of the devil," Alan said, "and he shall appear." He nodded toward the doorway, and Dan turned to see a smartly dressed man in his late fifties marching into the conservatory, scanning the room as if searching for someone. His gaze lit on Roz and his step faltered, but he carried on walking toward them, a broad smile plastered across his face.

"Roz!" he called out. "How lovely to see you. I'd heard that you were joining us, and I wanted to say personally how sorry I am about the way my publishers treated you. I did my best to intercede on your behalf, but the bean counters wouldn't listen to me. The only thing they care about is profit."

"That's all right," Roz said. "I quite understand."

Edward bowed his head. "You are most gracious, my dear. I hope we can put the whole sordid business behind us. And who knows, perhaps we may be able to work together again in the future, under different circumstances."

Roz did her best to return his smile, but the tight lines around her mouth told a different story. "Perhaps. But my work has taken a different direction, Edward. I much prefer to work with a younger audience. They're so engaged, so open. You can't put a price on that kind of sincerity, and I wouldn't swap it for the world."

"Well said," Alan chipped in, attracting an appraising glance from Edward.

"I don't believe we've met." Edward extended his hand. "I'm Edward Hatcher, but you may know me by my pen name, Max Cardew."

Alan shook his hand. "I'm Alan Hargreaves. Actually,

we've met before, Edward, but only briefly. It was at a conference. I don't suppose you remember. You must meet a great many people."

"My apologies, Alan. This is my first time at this little retreat, and I know some of the people on the list, but I have no memory for names, I'm afraid." Edward turned to Dan, offering his hand. "Are you a writer as well?"

"No, I'm a friend of Alan's." Dan shook Edward's hand, surprised at the firmness of the older man's grip. "I'm just here for a few days' holiday."

"Really?" Edward raised his eyebrows. "You must be a glutton for punishment. We writers are an odd bunch, and we're probably not fit for normal company. But you must come along to our little dinner tonight. Some of us have planned to eat at the Thai restaurant along the road, and it would be nice to have at least one normal human being in the mix."

"I might do that," Dan replied. "I enjoy Thai food, so long as they do tempeh or tofu or something."

Roz sat up straight. "Oh, are you a vegan, Dan? Me too."

"Almost," Dan said. "I still eat fish, I'm afraid."

"There's no need to sound so apologetic about it," Roz replied. "We are each of us on a journey."

"How charmingly New Age," Edward said. "Anyway, I understand the restaurant is thoroughly modern, so I'm sure they'll be able to cater for your needs. But, naturally, it's entirely up to you to decide. The table is booked for 7:30. I hope to see you there." Edward flashed a smile around the group. "I must go and find a quiet spot to work. I've grown used to the stillness of the countryside: the fresh air, birdsong, the gentle peal of the bells of Saint John's, and in the summer, the scent of lavender drifting in from the fields while a train chuffs away into the distance. It's most conducive to work. But I was getting stuck on a crossing of the first threshold, and I thought the change of scene would do me good, so here

I am. And it's working already! There are some notes I want to make, and I must get them down before they vanish from my mind completely. Forgive me, but when the muse calls, I must obey." He smiled once more, then he headed for a door that gave onto the garden. A moment later, Dan saw Edward pacing back and forth across the lawn, staring straight ahead and speaking into a small device in his hand: a dictation machine perhaps, or a mobile phone.

"What the hell is a crossing of the first threshold?" Dan asked.

"It's when the hero gets committed to the journey," Alan said distractedly, his attention on Roz. "Are you all right?"

Roz shrugged.

"I thought you handled that very well," Alan went on. "He's insufferable, isn't he?"

"Forget about it," Roz replied. "Edward's a bit of a stuffed shirt, bless him, but as I said before, I don't bear him any ill will. I've moved on."

"Good for you," Alan said.

But Roz did not appear to have heard him. "It's all forgotten," she went on. "Water under the bridge. I'm not going to let that man spoil my week. Whenever I see him, I'm going to smile and be friendly. Just you watch me."

"Right," Alan said slowly. "Roz, what are you doing between now and lunchtime? Because I'm happy to keep you company. I'd love to hear what you're working on at the moment, and maybe we could talk about some of the sessions you've been doing in schools. I really should be doing some of those myself, so it would be good to hear your take on it."

Alan cast a meaningful glance at Dan, and it was instantly understood.

Dan drained his coffee cup. "I think I'll take a walk into town and get my bearings. I might even scout out a nice place to grab some lunch. We could meet up later, and if you like, we could go to this dinner with Edward and his cronies. What do you say?"

"Good idea," Alan said. "I'll see you later."

Dan stood. "It was nice to meet you, Roz."

"You too," Roz replied. "And you do, by the way."

"Pardon?"

Roz smiled. "You do live up to the legend. I thought Alan must have been exaggerating, but if anything, he downplayed your abilities. I look forward to talking to you later, and who knows, I might be able to work out a thing or two about you. After all, no one looks quite as keenly at the world as an artist. When you have to express an emotion with a few lines and some blobs of colour, you really have to understand your subject matter."

"I never thought of it like that before," Dan replied, and rapidly revising his opinion of Roz, he took his leave.

CHAPTER 4

D an enjoyed the brisk walk from the hotel into town, but a brief tour of the local shops convinced him that he needed something else to occupy his mind. He had no real need of artistically designed greetings cards, and though he glanced at a few shops as he passed, he couldn't muster much interest in the artfully displayed knick-knacks attempting to pass themselves off as retro chic. Besides, he didn't have enough money to spend on fripperies. *I really need to find some work*, he thought as he marched through the town, ignoring the festive displays in the shop windows.

His bank balance was kept afloat by a small income from the start-ups he'd invested in over the years, and there was still some money left over from the sale of his flat. He could get by, for a little while at least, but the future was a different matter, and there was a spreadsheet on his laptop that he hardly dared to look at anymore.

Turning away from the town, Dan found a footpath that led across a stretch of grass, and he followed the path without knowing where it led. The grass was short, the path well maintained, and in the summer months the area would probably be crowded with kids playing football, families enjoying picnics, and teenagers lolling with a practised air of nonchalance. But now it was deserted, and as Dan left the town behind him, he seemed to be turning away from the world.

Dan took a deep breath of cool air, tasting salt and detecting the faint aroma of damp sand and seaweed. And the smell of the seaside took him back to childhood holidays, simpler times. *I need to unwind*, he told himself, and he rolled his shoulders, lengthening his stride to get his heart and lungs going. He had his running gear back at the hotel, so perhaps he could work out a suitable route for a quick 5K. He might even be able to drag Alan along.

The path forked, and Dan stopped to weigh up his options. On his left, the path looked as though it led along the clifftop and that would surely be an inspiring route to run.

Dan turned left and strode onward with a new sense of purpose. Soon, he was following the ragged line of the coast, separated from the cliff's edge by a waist-high chain-link fence. He leaned against the fence to peer down to the sea. The tide was freshly out, the damp rocks still gleaming wetly in the winter sunlight. How far was the drop to those jagged rocks? Perhaps twenty metres or so, but it was hard to judge: the vertical cliff face gave no reference point, and beyond the rocks the sandy beach was empty. Perhaps he could run on the beach. He couldn't see a way to climb down to the sand, but there had to be a path or some steps. Surely, he'd find a way down if he followed the clifftop path, so he turned away from the sea view and walked on.

After a while, the path led back toward the road, and Dan spied the Regent Hotel in the distance. There were a few more walkers strolling along, some with the aid of walking sticks, and all swaddled in winter coats and hats. One man threw a ball for his dog: a slender greyhound that leaped and raced across the grass at breathtaking speed. And as Dan followed the dog's progress, he caught sight of a familiar figure wandering dreamily along the path, heading in the same direction as him. Roz. There was no mistaking her long red hair, her untamed ringlets streaming out behind her, caught by the breeze. And the long winter coat she was wearing was, of course, a distinct shade of turquoise.

Dan watched her for a moment. Roz moved in an oddly theatrical way, her back straight, her head held high and her arms swinging at her sides as if she were on stage in a West End musical. Had she suddenly spun around and begun singing a song about bluebirds, Dan wouldn't have been entirely surprised.

And there was something else. With a start that made him hold his breath, Dan realised that Roz was not, as he had first thought, walking on the same path as him; she was on the wrong side of the fence. She must have found a way through or climbed over, but she was strolling along the very edge of the cliff, marching along the narrow strip of earth which could surely crumble beneath her feet at any second.

Dan started running, his legs kicking into action before he even had time to think about what he was doing. He dashed along the path at full speed, his feet pounding against the unforgiving gravel path. He was gaining on Roz now, and he called her name, but she did not turn around, did not slow her strangely energetic progress.

Dan pushed himself to run faster. He called again, shouting her name, although his instincts made him hold back from yelling at full volume. What if he startled her? What if she turned at the sound of her name and slipped, plummeting to her death?

As he ran, Dan felt for his phone in his pocket. He might need to call for help.

But Roz had stopped walking. She'd turned away from the edge, and now she was clambering over the fence, stepping over the wire as if oblivious to the danger.

Dan slowed to a jog, unsure what to do. Roz was safe now

and heading back toward the street. Dan had only just met her, and he had no right to question her actions, so he halted, catching his breath as he watched her stroll across the grass. She did not look back.

"Did you see that?"

Dan turned to see a man watching him from the comfort of a park bench.

"Yes." Dan studied the fence where Roz had climbed over. The wire sagged, the top curled over as if damaged deliberately. "This fence is ridiculous. Anyone could climb over. It isn't safe."

The man considered the fence for a second, then he looked at Dan. "I saw you this morning. At the hotel. Are you one of us?"

"I'm sorry?"

"A writer," the man explained. "Are you here for the retreat? Only, I saw you with Alan Hargreaves, so…"

"No, I'm not a writer. Alan's a friend."

The man raised his eyebrows. "I see. People don't usually bring their… friends to these things. Enemies, yes, but friends, never."

The man studied him as if expecting an explanation, but Dan simply smiled.

The man stood, stepping closer and extending a gloved hand. "I'm Brian Coyle. Dr Brian Coyle. The writer."

"Dan Corrigan." Dan shook hands. "I don't remember seeing you at the hotel. When did you arrive?"

"Yesterday. And I keep myself very much to myself during these things. I know most people like to mingle and gossip, but when I'm on a writing retreat, I retreat and I write. That's what I'm here for. The clue's in the name."

"You probably get tired of answering this question," Dan began, "but what kind of thing do you write?"

"There are two things I have to say to that, young man. The first is that a writer *never* gets tired of being asked about his work. The second is that I'm surprised you haven't heard of my award-winning YA series, *Department Seventeen*."

"Erm, no. I can't say I have."

Brian stared at him for a moment. "Ah, would I be right in guessing that you don't have any kids yet?"

"That's right." Dan made to leave. "Nice to meet you, Mr Coy—"

"*Doctor*," Brian corrected him. "And it was interesting to make your acquaintance, Dan. Any friend of Alan's is a friend of mine. But I must say, I'm a little surprised. I never knew that he was… that is to say…"

"To say what?" Dan asked.

Brian waved his hand in the air. "Sorry, I'm a bit of an unreconstructed old fart, and you never know where you are these days. The terminology is forever changing, and I worry I'll say the wrong thing and offend someone."

"In that case, you're going the wrong way about it. The word you're looking for, *Doctor* Coyle, is *gay*, and though it's none of your business, I'm not, and though I probably shouldn't speak for him, neither is Alan."

"Oh. Right. Sorry. Forgive me, I didn't mean…"

Dan was tempted to let Brian flounder, but instead he said, "Never mind. It was a simple misunderstanding. Forget about it."

"Thank you." Brian sighed in relief. "Anyway, what do you make of Roz? I couldn't quite believe it when she appeared in front of me, climbing over the fence like that. She was quite the sight, her flaming hair flowing in the wind. She put me in mind of a pagan goddess. Brigid, perhaps, the patroness of poetry, medicine, and arts and crafts." He chuckled. "Quite appropriate when you think about it, given her line of work."

"I wouldn't know about pagan gods," Dan said. "But she had me worried for a minute. The cliff edge isn't stable. There are signs all along the fence."

"What you've got to understand about Roz is that she's not quite—" Brian broke off suddenly, pressing his lips together.

"Not quite what?"

"Nothing. I spoke out of turn." Brian offered a genial smile. "Roz is great. She's very talented. She's won more prizes and awards than I care to think about. If there was any justice, she'd be loaded, too. But she's not had an easy time of it, and though literary prizes can be nice, they're not all they're cracked up to be. I've known plenty of prize-winners who spend their days working in an office to fund their writing habit."

Dan studied Brian Coyle. The man liked the sound of his own voice, but he had some skill as an orator. After a shaky start, he'd recovered quickly, taking control of their conversation and steering it in a direction of his choosing. And he'd done it with a certain flair, throwing in titbits of information to capture Dan's attention and lead him by the nose. But Dan was not to be so easily distracted. "Dr Coyle, I wouldn't normally interfere, but frankly I'm concerned for Roz's well-being. If you know of some problem she's having, you should tell someone — if not me, then talk to Alan. He and Roz are friends, and I'm sure that Alan would be very discreet."

Brian shook his head. "It's nothing. Least said, soonest mended." He glanced from left to right, then he took a step closer to Dan and, when he spoke, his voice was a guttural whisper, his tone emphatic. "This conversation is at an end."

Dan held his gaze, refusing to be intimidated. And when it came to a staring match, he won.

Brian turned on his heel and stomped away, his steps rapid but his posture stiff and his shoulders hunched.

What a pompous jerk, Dan thought. But there was more to Brian Coyle than an overinflated ego. His parting words had contained a thinly veiled threat, and his glare had told Dan all he needed to know. The man was brimming with repressed rage. And anger, when it was constrained for too long, could break out in any number of ways. Unless the good doctor changed his state of mind, then sooner or later he'd give vent to his fury. It was only a question of time.

Dan looked back toward the hotel, but he'd no desire to follow in Coyle's footsteps. And anyway, Alan would still be busy so there was no reason to head back. Turning away, Dan retraced his steps and headed for the town. There was one thing that he did need to buy, and that was a decent lunch.

As the welcoming lunch drew to a close, Alan cast his eye around the table. New friendships had formed, old ones had been renewed, and already the writers had formed into two distinct cliques. At Alan's end of the table, Roz, Brian and Edward had congregated around the retreat's organiser, Dominic Rudge. And they'd been joined by another writer, Tim Kendall. Alan didn't know Tim well but decided he was good company. Tim had been around the literary circuit for years, and he had a rich seam of anecdotes to mine, each one enlivened with the artfully dropped names of the great and the good.

At the far end of the table, the Johnson twins held court. Margaret and Pansy Johnson were quietly self-effacing sisters who, in their sixties, had discovered a talent for creating the kind of contemporary romance stories that sold in huge numbers. But as well as being commercially successful, their hardworking no-nonsense attitude had earned them the respect of their peers. And now an eclectic mix of admiring writers hung on their every word.

Marcus Slater wrote epic tales of fantasy, and he was a young man on the make. Dressed in an impressively white shirt and a grey suit that was slightly too large for his slim frame, his intense gaze never left the Johnson twins, and it looked as though he was peppering the conversation with searching questions. Opposite Marcus, Albert Fernworthy had heard of the stereotypical image of the science-fiction writer and was keen to conform. Although only in his forties, his extravagant beard and his full head of unkempt curly hair were grey. His glasses had a heavy black frame, and his checked shirt was open to reveal a black T-shirt emblazoned with the Starfleet logo from Star Trek. Marcus would happily explain which series this particular variant of the logo was from, and Alan made a mental note not to ask. Sitting next to Marcus, Lucille Blanchette listened attentively but did not join in the conversation. Lucille was in her late twenties, petite and with her hair styled in an elegant bob. She was the only person of colour in the group, and she was, by far, the most prolific. An intensely serious and studious person, Lucille tended to remain quiet during the social gatherings, but she'd written a bestselling time-travel series that needed its own shelf in any bookshop. Teenagers spent their free time arguing over her books, and some even dressed as the characters she'd created. Teachers praised her for encouraging their students to read, and parents read her books as soon as they could wrest them from their kids. Hollywood had come calling many times, but according to rumour, Lucille wasn't interested. She preferred to get on with writing her next book.

As Alan watched, Lucille giggled at something Marcus had said, and her mask of seriousness slipped away for a moment. She caught Alan looking at her and sent him a shy smile. But before he could say anything, Dominic Rudge rose to his feet, and Alan sighed inwardly.

Standing tall, Dominic surveyed the group, one eyebrow raised in patient expectation, and one by one the assembled writers fell silent, their eyes on Dominic, their expressions blank. Across the table from Alan, Roz caught his eye and grimaced.

Dominic bowed humbly, then he cleared his throat and beamed around the group. "My fellow scriveners," he began, "it is my distinct pleasure to welcome you all, once again, to our annual writing retreat here in Newquay. As winter's gloom draws ever closer, we writers do not allow the darkness to oppress our spirits. No, we hunker down with renewed vigour, working to express ourselves through our art, honing our craft.

"I believe that most of you have attended our retreats previously, and for that I'm grateful. But for those of you who are new to us, or those who would appreciate a reminder, the arrangements are simple. Breakfast is provided in the hotel, but the days are yours to do with as you please. In the evenings, we have tables reserved at a variety of local hostelries so that we may meet to share a meal. A list of those venues, along with the dates and times, has been emailed to you already. Attendance at any of these events is completely optional, and you should not feel obliged to come along if you prefer to make your own arrangements. However, many of us find that after a hard day tapping at the keyboard, we enjoy some downtime in which we can reflect on our day's work, share our experiences with our peers, compare notes and perhaps enjoy a drink or two in like-minded company. The first of these events is this evening, when we convene at the Temple Garden Thai restaurant just down the road from the hotel. Our table is booked for 7:30 pm, and if you are intending to join us, we would appreciate prompt arrival.

"For the remainder of this afternoon, please make use of the amenities at the hotel, or find a place of your own to work. You might favour a trip to one of the town's coffee shops where, at this time of year, you should be able to find a quiet corner where you can write. A list of suitable venues has already been emailed to you in your welcome package.

However, if you prefer not to venture out, but you don't wish to be confined to your room, I find the conservatory at the hotel to be a pleasant place to while away a few hours, especially on an afternoon such as this, when the sunshine has made a welcome appearance. The view over the sea provides an ever-changing vista that seems to ease the mind while keeping the creative juices flowing.

"Now, I know that many of us think of ourselves as introverts, so please bear that in mind when chatting among yourselves. Not everyone appreciates company, but some do. I'm more than happy to chat with you at any time, so even if you see me working at my laptop, please feel free to interrupt and ask any questions you like.

"So, with a final note of thanks to you all for attending, I will stop boring you and let you get on with your work. I wish you a rewarding and productive afternoon, and indeed a great week, and I hope to see some of you this evening."

He beamed around the table once more as if expecting a round of applause, but since no one made a sound, he added, "Thank you." Then he bowed his head in an overly formal gesture and, still smiling, he retook his seat.

The writers glanced at each other, exchanging wry grins, then almost as one, they rose to their feet, studying their surroundings. They looked, Alan thought, like newborn lambs discovering for the first time that there was an entire pasture to explore.

"I need a walk," Roz said. "Do you fancy coming with me, Alan?"

"Another one?" Alan asked. "You went for a walk this morning, didn't you?"

She shrugged. "I need fresh air and space; they're my inspiration. And the sea air is terrific today. It makes you feel glad to be alive."

"It's certainly bracing." Alan offered an apologetic smile. "I'll happily go for a walk another day, but right now I have a few ideas I want to start work on. While Dominic was making his speech, my mind wandered, and I pictured a whole scene. You know how it is. If I don't get it down soon, I might lose it."

"No worries. I expect you're going to the dinner this evening."

Alan nodded. "Yes, and I think Dan will come along too."

"He's a brave man. Well, good luck with your work. I'll see you later." Roz gave Alan a warm smile, then she headed for the exit.

Alan stood still for a moment. *I wonder if I made the right choice*, he thought, picturing a stroll in the sunshine in Roz's charming company. But he'd have plenty of time to catch up with her in the evening, so he steered his thoughts back toward his work.

Retrieving his laptop bag from beneath his chair, Alan made for the conservatory. It looked as though most of the other writers had hit on the same idea, but there were still several tables free by the window. Alan passed Brian Coyle, and the two men exchanged a nod in greeting.

"I met your friend this morning," Brian said. "Dan. An interesting character."

"Yes." Alan paused for a moment, glancing at the untidy stack of papers laid out on Brian's table. "You still write longhand? I thought those days had gone."

"I still like a decent pen and a thick pad of good quality paper, but just at the outlining stage. After that, I resort to my trusty Chromebook." He patted the messenger bag taking pride of place on the only other chair. "It's small and light, but the battery lasts for ages. It's a real workhorse."

"Speaking of work, I must get down to mine." Alan made to move away, but Brian beckoned him closer.

"A word to the wise," Brian murmured. "That windbag, Rudge, is ensconced in the corner. Don't sit near him, whatever you do. The man never does a stroke of work. He just sits there, looking like he means business, but all he wants to do is pounce on the nearest unsuspecting fool, and then he'll talk until the cows come home."

"I know what you mean," Alan admitted. "I know that he puts a lot of effort into organising these events, but he does like to chat."

"That's putting it mildly, Alan. But then, you always were a gentleman." Brian gestured toward his papers. "I'd better tackle this lot. There's a fight scene in here, somewhere, and I can't for the life of me find it. Maybe I left it in my room. I'll have to go and look. I'm stuck without it." He stood, stuffing his papers into the messenger bag, and Alan took the opportunity to slip away.

Dominic Rudge had made himself at home in a corner, his leather satchel spewing papers across the table while his widescreen laptop took up the rest of the surface. Alan acknowledged him with a smile, but he steered clear, finding a comfortable chair beside the window and pulling the small table toward him. It didn't take him long to lay out his own laptop, and a minute later he was scanning through the notes he'd made on his work in progress: a new adventure for the hero of his books for children, Derek, International Explorer. *So far, so good*, he thought. The new scene he'd pictured would dovetail perfectly into the story, providing a welcome chunk of action for Derek and his resourceful nephew, Jake. In the hunt for an ancient Inca amulet, Derek would lead Jake into a tropical rainforest, but they'd find themselves captured by a lost tribe. Thrown into a rough wooden cage, they'd be held captive while the tribe's leader performed a long and drawn-out ritual. *I can't think where that idea came from,* Alan thought, smiling at the memory of Dominic's rambling speech. Of course, Derek and Jake would escape unharmed, and Jake would provide the plan. Perhaps he'd astound the tribe by showing them something they'd never seen before: his trusty Swiss Army knife, perhaps.

Working quickly, and without bothering to even think about punctuation and spelling, Alan typed the scene down as he saw it in his mind's eye. It was thin on detail, but that could be added in the next draft. Thirty minutes later, the bare bones of the chapter had emerged, and Alan sat back to read it through. *That makes the middle section more interesting,* he decided. He often had trouble with a book about halfway through the first draft. *The saggy middle* was what some writers called it, but Alan generally thought of it as a *soggy centre.* Like an under-baked cake, the middle section of a manuscript could be distinctly unappetising, failing to live up to the promise of the early chapters. But just as a cake couldn't be baked a second time, an ailing manuscript couldn't be fixed by adding a few extra sentences. When the story lost its narrative drive, it was time to get creative and work in extra scenes and characters to liven it up. Hopefully, Derek and Jake's dramatic capture and escape would fit the bill.

Alan tweaked the text a little as he read it through, but for a first draft it was good enough. He sat back and saw that while he'd been immersed in his work, Brian had returned to his table and was busy scribbling on a pad.

On Alan's right, Tim had set up his laptop on a table at the centre of the room, and anyone could see that the man was lost in his work. Tim was perched on the edge of his seat, craning his neck to peer intently at his laptop's screen, while his fingers performed an elegant dance over the keyboard as he worked.

I should have learned to touch-type, Alan thought for perhaps the thousandth time in his career as a writer. And Tim looked up, meeting Alan's gaze.

"Hello," Tim said. "How's it going? Are you stuck?"

"No, it's going well," Alan replied. "But I don't think I could keep up with you. You look like you're on a streak."

Tim smiled modestly. "I always work this quickly. It's the

way my mind works. I see the blank page and I just have to fill it. I've always been the same, ever since I found my niche."

"Historical romance, isn't it?"

"Historical drama. There's a certain romantic element, but nothing between the sheets if you know what I mean. Once the hero and the heroine get together, it's very much a question of drawing the curtains around the four-poster bed. It's all very *wholesome*, very *clean*." Tim offered a saccharine smile. "You should see the morality clause in my contract. I've written shorter novellas. But these books have been good to me. They pay the rent. So when my lovely publisher lays down the law, I obey."

"I know exactly what you mean." Alan was about to say more, but he was cut short by a yell from across the room.

"Coyle!"

Alan and Tim swivelled in their seats to see Edward Hatcher storming into the conservatory, his cheeks white with rage. He stopped in front of Brian, waving a sheet of paper in front of his nose.

"What the hell do you mean by this?" Edward demanded. "Come on, man. Explain yourself!"

Brian held up his hands. "Edward, I have absolutely no idea what you're talking about."

"Don't you dare," Edward snarled. "Don't even think about trying to play the innocent. You know damned well what I'm talking about. This!" Screwing the sheet of paper into a ball, he hurled it at Brian's head.

Brian ducked. "What the hell! Edward, there's no need—"

"Don't take that tone with me," Edward spluttered. "I know it was you. You were the only one who knew I was resting after lunch, so you slipped your little note under my door while I was asleep. You're too much of a coward to face me, so you resorted to a childish prank."

Brian retrieved the crumpled sheet of paper from the floor,

opening it out. "But I've never seen this before. What does it even mean?"

"You know what it means, Coyle."

Brian shook his head, bewildered. He opened his mouth to speak, but Edward didn't give him the chance.

Lifting his chin in haughty gesture, Edward said, "My lawyers will make mincemeat of you, Coyle. They'll crucify you." Then he stalked from the room, almost colliding with the hotel's receptionist. "Out of my way!" Edward cried.

Matthew jumped back, and Edward swept out into the lobby.

All eyes turned to Brian.

"Don't look at me," Brian said. "I can honestly say I haven't got the faintest idea what he was going on about. And this note — I don't know what it means."

"What does it say?" Alan asked.

Brian squinted at the sheet of paper, holding it at arm's length. "The writing is on the wall. Your secret is about to be revealed. Very soon you'll get what you so richly deserve, and the world will see you for what you are." He looked at his unwanted audience. "It sounds like something from *The Times* crossword, and I never was any good at that kind of thing."

"I don't think it's a crossword clue." Alan pushed his table aside and stood. "I'd better go and see if he's okay. Dominic, do you know what room he's in?"

Dominic blinked as though waking from a daydream. "Yes. Erm, let me see." He tapped at the keys on his laptop. "Edward is in 501."

"No, that's my room," Brian said. "Look again."

"Oh dear." Dominic's cheeks coloured. "I'm sorry, I, er…"

Alan turned his attention to Matthew. "You must know which room he's in."

Matthew nodded. "Of course, sir, but I can't give out personal information like that. It's more than my job's worth."

"Found it," Dominic said. "He's in the Regency suite. He upgraded his room a few days ago, and I forgot to update the spreadsheet."

"Right. I'll go and find him." Alan hurried into the lobby, but he hadn't made it as far as the staircase when Roz ran in from the hotel's entrance.

"Alan! What's wrong with Edward?"

"We're not sure. Have you seen him?"

"Yes. I was coming back along the coastal path, and I... I happened to glance over the edge, and that's when I saw him. He was going down to the beach, and I knew something was wrong because he didn't even have a coat, and there's a bitter wind blowing in from the sea."

"He's not himself," Alan said. "He had a run-in with someone, and it's knocked him out of kilter."

"That explains it. He was charging down the steps like a man possessed, and they're steep. It's a miracle he didn't fall."

"Which steps were these?"

"If you turn left when you leave the hotel, the steps are just down the street. You have to cross the road, then they're the first steps you come to. You can't miss them. They're right next to an ice cream kiosk." Roz hesitated. "He won't go too far, will he? The tide's coming in fast, and if he's not careful, he could easily get cut off at this time of year."

"He's in no mood for being careful. I'd better go and find him and bring him back."

Roz took hold of Alan's sleeve. "You don't think he'd do something stupid, do you?"

"Not if I can help it," Alan said. Then, taking Roz's hand from his arm, he dashed for the door.

CHAPTER 6

D an gave the town another chance, and with the help of his phone, he discovered a vegan cafe and enjoyed a good lunch of chilli and rice, washed down with a decent coffee. *This place isn't so bad*, he thought. Newquay wasn't a large town, but compared to Embervale it was a bustling metropolis. There were more bars than he'd expected, and he guessed that in summer the place would be filled with young people seeking sun and surf.

After lunch he sauntered back toward the hotel, taking deep breaths of sea air. The road took him up a slight incline, and as he gained height he caught a glimpse of the sea. As a lifelong London-dweller, his idea of a waterfront property was an apartment beside the lugubrious Thames, but here, the restless energy of the Atlantic ocean created a different atmosphere: a sense of movement and relentless change.

He crossed the road to get a better view, then he paused for a while, enjoying the warmth of the weak sun. Behind him there was a bench, but though he was tempted to sit in the sunshine for a few minutes, the bench was occupied: partly by a young woman, but mainly by the guitar case that lay on its side across the wooden slats.

Seeing him looking at the case, the woman sat up straight. "Sorry. Do you want to sit down? I can move the guitar."

"Thanks, but I'm all right here," Dan replied. The young woman had an earnest expression, but when she met Dan's gaze, there was an intensity in her stare that struck Dan as odd. Maybe it was just the way the light caught her hazel eyes, but there was something unsettling in the way she looked at him, almost as if she was afraid.

Should he ask if she was all right? Dan wasn't sure. Perhaps, like him, she'd been enjoying a quiet moment of solitude, and he'd startled her. He tried a reassuring smile. "Thanks anyway. I didn't mean to disturb you."

"No problem. I'm leaving, anyway." Wearily, the young woman hauled herself to her feet and grabbed her guitar case, then she trudged across the road. There was a bar opposite, and taking a second to straighten her posture, the young woman disappeared inside.

Dan resumed his journey. Soon, the grand frontage of the Regent Hotel loomed in the distance, and a familiar figure emerged from the entrance, hurrying toward the road. Dan raised a hand in greeting and called out: "Alan! Where are you going?"

Alan's step faltered, then he changed direction to join Dan. "Do you remember Edward?" he asked. "Edward Hatcher. We met him this morning."

Dan nodded. "Why? What's happened?"

"He's just stormed out of the hotel in a terrible mood. He had a blazing row with Brian. I'm not sure what it was about, but someone slipped him a note, and it seems to have upset him. He barged in, blamed Brian, then he stomped off. Roz said he headed for the beach, and the tide's coming in. I don't think Edward knows the coast. He could easily get himself into trouble."

"You're going to look for him?"

"Yes. I want to make sure he's all right."

Dan saw the concern in Alan's eyes, and without hesitation he said, "I'll help. Which way do you think he went?"

"Roz says he took the nearest steps down to the beach. Come on, I'll show you."

They hurried across the road, Alan leading the way, and a minute later they arrived at a wooden kiosk, its serving hatch firmly closed for the winter. Beside the kiosk, a set of steep stone steps led downward to the beach, and the narrow strip of bare sand was already much smaller than Dan had expected. The waves were small but coming thick and fast, racing up the beach. Dan and Alan paused to look along the coast, but Edward could've been concealed in any one of a dozen small coves, and he was nowhere to be seen.

"Quick," Alan said, and they climbed down as fast as they dared. Dan ignored the steel handrail built into the cliff's face, although the steps had been made for feet smaller than his, and the stone was made slippery by a thin layer of sand.

At the bottom, Alan said, "There's a lot of ground to cover. We'd better split up. I'll head back toward the town, and you take the other direction. But be careful. Keep an eye on the route back to the steps, unless you can see another way back up to the top, that is. It's no good if we're the ones who end up stranded."

"Sure. We'll find him. He can't be far away."

"Yes, but if you do find him, tread carefully. Edward was very irate when I last saw him, and I'm not sure how he'll react to someone chasing after him."

"Understood," Dan said. "Let's go. If I find anything, I'll call you."

They parted ways, and Dan broke into a jog, staying close to the cliff face. As he rounded a rocky outcrop, Dan spotted a tall young man, moving just as quickly as him and in the same direction. And from the young man's shoulder dangled a camera; a camera with a long lens.

Dan had noticed a few keen birdwatchers during his morning walk, but somehow, this man didn't fit the mould. Rather than wearing waterproof gear in sombre colours, the man was dressed for an afternoon in town: a fashionable silvery coat that caught the light, mustard-yellow trousers and a pair of red canvas shoes.

As Dan watched, the young man suddenly increased his pace, and Dan found himself matching his speed. There was something furtive in the way the man moved, darting forward then pressing his back against the cliff face. It was possible that he was trying to photograph an elusive specimen of the local wildlife, but Dan didn't think so. Naturalists tended to keep to their hides or creep slowly from place to place, whereas this man moved like a predator. And that meant that his target was almost certainly human.

The man ducked behind a ridge in the cliff face, disappearing from sight, and when Dan followed he saw that his instincts had been right. The line of the cliffs fell back to form a wide cove, and in the distance Edward Hatcher trudged along the beach, heedless of his surroundings, his head down and his shoulders hunched.

The young man had seen him too, and he paused to aim his camera's lens squarely at Edward. Seizing his opportunity, Dan dashed toward the photographer, the sound of the waves masking his footsteps.

The young man was intent on his task, and he didn't react until Dan stood in front of him. Then he flinched, lowering his camera and pressing his back against the rocks.

"What are you doing?" Dan demanded.

"Mind your own business," the man snapped, twisting his rat-like features into a scowl. He was in his twenties, but he bore the scars of acne from his teens, and frown lines that hinted at an education from the school of hard knocks. But along with the powerful lens, he was sporting a Canon 5D, a pro-level camera, and as he sidestepped past Dan, lifting his camera to reacquire his target, he looked as though he knew what he was doing.

He fired off a few shots then paused to glare at Dan. "Are you still here? What do you want?"

"Why are you taking pictures of that man?"

"Mind your own business. I'm working, all right?" He looked Dan up and down, then he sniffed. "Do you know him? A friend of Edward Hatcher, are you?"

Dan held his gaze. *A journalist*, he decided, then he turned away, striding across the sand to catch up with Edward. Dan glanced back, but the journalist had gone. Perhaps he'd seen enough, but more likely, he'd seen the waves rushing in and retreated to a safer place; the sea's salty spray would not have been good for his gear.

Dan reckoned he had just a few minutes to retrieve Edward and guide him back to the steps, so he broke into a run, covering the distance between them in seconds.

As Dan approached, Edward turned with a start. "You! What are you doing here?"

"I was looking for you." Dan jogged to a halt beside Edward, and the older man stepped back as though fearing contagion.

"What's going on?" Edward demanded. "Why are you haring after me like some kind of maniac?"

"You may not remember, but I'm Dan Corrigan, a friend of Alan's. He said there was an incident at the hotel, and he was concerned about you."

"Well, really!" Edward stood tall, straightening his jacket. "I've never heard anything so foolish in all my days. Incident, indeed!"

"So, you're all right, then?"

Indignant, Edward stared at Dan for a moment, but then his expression softened. "Listen, I'm sure you mean well, but there's no need to worry on my account. The whole thing was a storm in a teacup." He smiled uncertainly. "I just needed a minute to cool down, that's all. I needed some space, some fresh air. I ought to be used to Brian and his little jokes by now, but I'll admit, I lost my temper. It was silly of me."

"What happened, exactly?"

"Nothing much. Brian sent me a snide little note. It was all very childish, the sort of thing a schoolboy might do. But I'm afraid I let it upset me. His note hit a nerve, and I found it rather hurtful."

Dan thought for a moment. If what Edward said was true, then why had Alan been so concerned? It didn't make sense. But Alan didn't tend to overreact — quite the opposite — and when it came down to it, Dan would place his trust in Alan over Edward every time. From what he'd seen of Edward Hatcher, the man could be suave when it suited him, but his manner came across as forced and artificial: every word was chosen for effect, every mannerism executed as though perfectly rehearsed.

"I see," Dan said. "In that case, I'll call Alan and let him know you're all right."

"Thank you. I'm sorry to have caused an upset. I dread to think what they're all saying about me now. I expect Dominic is having palpitations. I'll head back to the hotel and put everyone's mind at rest."

"Good idea. We can walk together, but we'd better get a move on. The tide…" He pointed and Edward grimaced.

"Oh dear me, I have been a silly fellow. It's easy to see that I'm a landlubber."

"You and me both."

They headed back toward the steps, and Dan took out his phone, sending a quick text to let Alan know they were on the way. He kept half an eye on the nooks and crannies of the cliff's craggy face, but no one lurked among the shadows.

As if guessing Dan's concern, Edward tapped his arm. "I say, you didn't happen to see anyone following me, did you?"

"There was a photographer, or maybe he's a journalist. A young man in a silvery coat."

"I knew it! That damned paparazzo! He's been dogging my steps for weeks."

"Really? No offence, Edward, but I thought they were more interested in TV celebrities and the royal family."

"If only. Unfortunately, it appears I've been added to the menu, and that young man has made it his personal mission to pursue me. He's followed me here, all the way from Fulham!"

"You live in Fulham? Which part? I'm from London myself."

"I have a pied-à-terre off the Fulham Road. It's nothing fancy, and I generally find I'm undisturbed when I'm there. But that Fleet Street rat has ruined it for me."

"Why? What's his interest in you?"

Edward's lips twitched as though he was having difficulty restraining his words. "I'm not supposed to say anything. There's a project in the offing, but I've signed a non-disclosure agreement, and I've been warned in no uncertain terms what will happen if I let the cat out of the bag."

"I know all about NDAs," Dan said. "In my old line of work, they came with the territory."

Edward perked up. "Oh, were you a lawyer? Perhaps you could help. You could send that young man a cease and desist letter or something of the sort. I'd happily pay for your time."

"No, I wasn't a lawyer. I was a consultant on a lot of high-tech projects. A kind of trouble-shooter."

"Pity. Ah well, I suppose he'll be lying in wait. There's nothing for it but to ascend and face the music."

Edward suddenly looked tired, and Dan couldn't help feeling sorry for the man. Whatever Edward's faults, he didn't deserve to be hounded from place to place, and he was obviously finding it a strain. That probably explained why he'd lost his temper; his nerves had been stretched to snapping point.

"I can't advise you formally, but perhaps I can help," Dan said. "I could talk to the journalist, tell him to back off. I know enough legalese to make it sound official."

"You'd do that? He's a nasty little piece of work. I've argued with him myself, but he's like a dog with a bone."

"I'll certainly try. I'm nothing if not persistent."

Edward brightened. "You could be my minder for the week. I was looking forward to this retreat, but it'll spoil the whole thing if I can't set foot outside without being photographed. If you could get that particular monkey off my back, I'd pay you a daily rate, plus expenses, of course."

"Erm, that's an interesting idea, but I'm not—"

"Please say you'll consider it," Edward interrupted. "It won't be an onerous task. When I go out, you'd accompany me and keep that pest at arm's length. I'm not expecting you to indulge in a fistfight, but you have a certain physical presence, and you look as though you can handle yourself. I dare say you can look intimidating when you want to."

Dan shrugged modestly. "I like to keep fit. I'm a runner."

"There you are then. Perfect. You've already proved that you're a resourceful chap, and I know a bright spark when I see one." Edward grinned. "You can name your price. So long as you can knock up an invoice, I can write the whole thing off against tax."

"I'd like to help." Dan looked away for a second. He had difficulty seeing himself as some kind of bodyguard, but he needed work, and an opportunity had just landed in his lap. Sometimes, you had to take whatever came your way; you never knew where it might lead. If Edward wanted to pay him for his time, why not let him? After all, judging by the quality of the man's clothes, he could afford it.

But there was something holding Dan back. He looked

Edward in the eye. "I could only work for you if you're completely honest with me."

"Naturally."

"I'd need to know why you're being chased by paparazzi. You don't have to go into the details, but I need an overview. If I don't like what I hear, I won't be able to work for you."

"Fair enough." Edward considered the matter, then he came to a conclusion. "Okay. My books have been made into a TV series over here, but I've never cracked the US market. That's all about to change. I've been in talks with a top Hollywood producer, and after a lot of negotiations, things are finally heating up. If it comes off, the franchise will be worth a fortune. We have some big names on board for the cast. Household names. Hollywood legends. One of them, the leading man, invited me out when he was in London. We got along famously. He wants to know all about the books and the background to the stories. He's one of those actors who like to get beneath the skin of each character, find out what makes him tick. So we met several times for a chat, sometimes over lunch and sometimes over a few drinks in the evening."

"And that's when the paparazzi picked you up."

"Unfortunately, yes," Edward said. "My relationship with this actor is purely professional and above board. For him, it's part of his job, and as for me... to be honest, I was enjoying a moment in the limelight, rubbing shoulders with the rich and famous. But I wasn't prepared for the price tag that came with the experience. The fame tax, that's what they call it." He shuddered. "All I can say is, it's a beastly business and an intrusion of my privacy."

"I imagine it is." They were nearing the steps now, and Dan glanced upward. The journalist was probably waiting for them above, lining up his next shot. Was Dan happy to be snapped alongside Edward? Was he ready for his picture to appear in the tabloids?

It's no skin off my nose, he decided. *And the money would definitely come in handy.* He shrugged out of his coat. "Here. Wear my coat. Turn the collar up to shield your face, but walk at your normal speed and keep your back straight. Hopefully, the collar will spoil his shot, but we don't want it to look like you've got something to hide. I'll go up first, and if he's there, I'll make sure he backs off. That'll give you a head start, and once I've had a word with him, I'll catch up with you. We'll head back to the hotel together, and I'll position myself between you and him at all times."

Edward smiled as he accepted Dan's coat. "Excellent. It's a little big for me, and it's not quite my style, but it's a good idea. I can see you're cut out for this. I take it that you're accepting my offer?"

"Yes, for the moment. We'll talk details later. In the meantime, are you ready?"

Edward nodded firmly, then they set off, Dan leading the way. At the top of the steps, Dan spied the photographer skulking on the other side of the road. He was leaning against a wall and speaking into his phone, but as Dan headed straight for him, he pocketed his phone and raised his camera.

"You can forget that," Dan called out. "No more photos."

The journalist hesitated, but only for a split second. He sidestepped, aiming his camera past Dan. But Dan moved to block his view.

The young man lowered his camera to glare at Dan. "Back off! Stay out of my way."

"I can't do that," Dan replied. "No more photos. The man has a right to his privacy."

"No he doesn't. I know my business. He's in a public place, and for another thing, Hatcher is a public figure, so what he does is a matter of public interest. You, on the other hand, are harassing me for no reason, so back off, or you'll be the one who's in trouble."

Dan's only reply was a cold stare. He glanced over his

shoulder and saw that Edward was following the plan, marching away with his face hidden but his back straight. The journalist swore under his breath, then he took a moment to size Dan up. "What's your game? You're not personal security. I know the type, and you ain't it."

"I've made the position clear. Stay away from my client."

"Oh yeah? Is that a threat?"

"A warning," Dan said. "You're right, I'm not a hired thug. But I have a lot of contacts, and I know how to pull strings. I can make life difficult for you."

The journalist met his stare for a full second before he looked away. "Whatever." He pulled a pack of cigarettes and a disposable lighter from his coat pocket, and Dan took that as his cue to leave.

"I'll be seeing you around," the journalist called after him. "A story this big doesn't go away — not until it's done."

Dan didn't look back as he strode along the path to catch up with Edward. But the journalist's words stayed in his mind. *A story this big.* That sounded like so much more than a few meetings with an actor. Had Edward lied to him? *But he was so convincing*, he thought. The more he considered Edward's explanation, the more convinced he was that the whole thing was an elaborate fiction. After all, that was precisely what Edward did for a living.

CHAPTER 7

Dan paced the length of the hotel lobby.

From a padded seat in the reception area, Alan watched him. "Dan, are you going to prowl up and down for the whole evening?"

"No. Only until Edward arrives. Maybe I should try calling him again."

"You could try, but it looks like he's not answering his phone. You must've called him five times already." Alan checked his watch. "We'll have to head out to the restaurant soon, so I'm sure he'll be here any minute. And if not, he might've changed his mind about going out."

"Then why didn't he let me know?"

"He's probably working; that's what he's here for. When I'm writing, I put my phone into airplane mode and leave it in another room."

"Belt and braces," Dan muttered. "Why am I not surprised?"

"Better safe than sorry." At a sound from the grand staircase behind him, Alan turned in his chair. "This could be him."

Dan paused to watch the stairs, and a moment later a small group bustled into view.

Brian Coyle was engaged in earnest conversation with Tim Kendall, Brian gesticulating to add emphasis to his words, while Tim nodded thoughtfully, his hands behind his back. Behind them, Roz Hammond walked at Dominic's side, the pair of them very close as they descended the stairs.

Edward was not among them.

Dan's phone buzzed, and he pulled it out, frowning at the notification on the screen. Earlier, he'd exchanged numbers with Edward, and this text message was from him. Dan opened the message and read: *Go ahead without me. I'll come when I'm ready.*

Alan went to his side. "Have you heard from Edward?"

"Yes. He's going to join us at the restaurant."

Brian and the others approached them.

"What's this?" Dominic asked. "Who's going to join us?"

"Edward," Dan replied. "He said to go ahead without him."

"He's probably too embarrassed to show his face," Brian said. "After his tantrum this afternoon, I can't say I'm surprised."

Dominic wagged a finger at Brian. "Come on now. No more falling out. I expect everyone to be on their best behaviour."

"Including Edward?" Roz asked.

"Definitely." Dominic checked his watch. "Right, come along everybody. The Johnson twins and their entourage are dining elsewhere this evening, so apart from Edward, we're all here. Let's head to the restaurant. Chop chop."

Exchanging rueful glances, the group started forward, but Dan hung back. "I should go and check on Edward."

"Nonsense!" Dominic looked down his nose at Dan. "You don't know Edward. He wants to make a dramatic entrance.

He'll come when he's good and ready, and not a moment before. Now, come on everybody. Move along like good boys and girls or I'll have to make you walk in pairs and hold hands." He grinned expectantly, but when no one appreciated his impersonation of a jovial schoolmaster, he let out a dismissive grunt. "We'd better go or they'll give our table to somebody else."

Dominic marched for the door.

Behind his back, Brian sent a mischievous smile around the group, and lowering his voice, he said, "I blame public school."

"I went to public school," Tim said. "Eton. Not that it matters, but which one did Dominic attend?"

"He didn't," Brian replied. "But he feels as though he ought to have done, and he's never quite got over it."

Outside, the winter evening was bitterly cold and dark as pitch, but the walk to the restaurant was short, and Dan passed the time chatting to Roz. She was reticent at first, perhaps a little wary in case he was analysing her every word, but once she got on to the topic of her work, her reluctance vanished.

"I'd love to see some of your illustrations," Dan said.

Roz grinned. "I'd invite you to my boudoir to see my etchings, but we've only just met."

"You have a boudoir?" Dan asked. "I'm impressed."

"It's more of a shed at the end of my garden. On a good day, you could call it a log cabin, but it's nothing glamorous."

"And you live locally, yes?"

Roz nodded. "On the other side of town. I have a little place that stands out on its own. It's small, but it's right by the sea, and the light is fantastic."

"It's very handy for you that the retreat is so close to home," Dan said.

"Yes."

In front of the group, Dominic halted outside the restaurant. "Here we are. Right on time."

He strode inside and the others followed, standing in an awkward group as Dominic talked to the young woman behind the counter.

"We've been here before," Alan said to Dan. "You'll like it."

Brian sidled up to them. "If you like a bit of spice, have the jungle curry. Very hot but very good. You can thank me later."

"I might just do that," Dan replied.

The young woman plucked a set of menus from the counter, tucking them under her arm. "This way please. Your table's all ready. Florence will be your server, and she'll come and take your order in a moment."

"Excellent," Dominic said. "And how appropriate to be waited upon by someone named after such a city. Ah, Firenze! A place that has inspired so many great artists."

The young woman smiled uncertainly. "I'm sorry?"

"Never mind," Dominic said. "Let us take our places." He looked back at the door. "Still no sign of Edward. Ah well, he's being true to form."

Their table was large and circular, and they took their seats quickly, Alan sitting on Dan's left and Roz on his right. Menus were handed around, and Dominic, Tim and Brian all reached into their pockets and produced reading glasses.

"Alan, I see you haven't succumbed to myopia," Tim said as he cleaned the lenses of his glasses on a soft cloth. "You must tell us your secret."

"No secret," Alan replied. "I'm just a bit younger than you."

Tim laughed. "As always, you're refreshingly honest. But it'll catch up with you. When you stare at a blank page for a decade or so, something's got to give."

"I might get away with it," Alan said. "My parents still have excellent eyesight, and my grandparents were the same: sharp eyed into their sixties."

Tim smiled appreciatively. "You have me beaten there. My father donned specs on his fortieth birthday, and he scarcely took them off until he passed away. Mind you, in his line of work, short-sightedness was an occupational hazard. He was in the House of Lords, you know. And before that, he was a High Court judge, so he was forever poring over one legal tome or another. The man had his head in a book from morning until night."

"Perhaps that's where you got your love of literature," Alan said.

"That's kind of you to say, but he didn't see any connection between my work and his. I'm afraid Papa was unimpressed with my literary ambitions. In his eyes, the only good thing I ever did was to marry well."

"Did he live to see how successful you became?"

"Oh, yes." Tim smiled, but here was a gleam of sadness in his eyes.

Time to change the subject, Alan thought, but he was saved by the arrival of a young woman bearing a tablet computer and a welcoming smile.

The young woman's hair was fashioned into a neat bun, and she was dressed in a brightly patterned silky dress that could've come straight from Thailand. Her make-up tried valiantly to suggest an almond shape to her eyes, and though it didn't quite succeed, the effect suited her, perhaps because it drew attention to her most striking feature: her irises were a distinctive shade of hazel.

"Hello, I'm Florence," she began, beaming around the group. "Can I get any drinks for—" She stopped abruptly, lowering her gaze, her chest heaving as she took a shaky breath.

"Are you all right?" Roz asked.

"No," Florence murmured without looking up. "I'm sorry, I... I've got to go." She hurried away, almost stumbling as she rushed between the tables. Then she disappeared through a swing door at the back of the restaurant.

Brian raised his eyebrows. "The poor thing. We must look like an awful bunch."

"Perhaps she heard Dominic banging on about Firenze," Tim said. "That's enough to make anyone head for the hills."

"I didn't say a word to her," Dominic replied. "I was busy studying the wine list. But this kind of thing is typical of young people these days. They have no attention span, no work ethic, no spine." He grew more irritated as he spoke, slapping the table with his palm to punctuate his words. "And another thing — where's Edward? That's what I'd like to know. This really isn't good enough. It's appalling behaviour!" Turning in his seat, he raised his voice. "I say, can we have some service over here, please? Hungry people. Thank you."

Dan shook his head in disbelief. Generally, he tried not to take an instant dislike to anyone, but in Dominic's case, it was hard to see an alternative. The man was arrogant, rude and consumed with self-importance. It would be good to get away from him for a while.

To Alan, Dan said, "Can you order me the jungle curry with tempeh and some jasmine rice? Oh, and a beer. Whatever you're having."

"Sure," Alan replied. "But why?"

"I'm going to pop back to the hotel. I probably won't be long."

"Did you forget something?"

Dan stood, grabbing his coat. "No. But I want to check on Edward." To everyone else, Dan said, "I'll be back soon." Then he headed outside.

As he walked, Dan called Edward's phone, redialling

when it went to voicemail. And on the third attempt, the call was picked up.

"Hello?" Edward said, his voice faint and strained.

"Hi. It's Dan. I'm on my way back to the hotel."

"Don't do that. There's no point. It's too late."

Dan walked faster, taking longer strides. He was almost back at the hotel. "Edward, where are you? Are you still in your room?"

He waited. He could hear Edward breathing.

"Edward, don't do anything. Wait until I get there." Dan was running now, dashing into the hotel lobby. But then he heard something on the phone, and he skidded to a halt. It had sounded like a wave crashing against a beach, but it might've been a rush of air hissing across the microphone. "Edward, are you outside?"

But the only reply was a murmured shush that could've been the breeze or a sigh of despair. And then silence.

"Oh my God!" Dan breathed.

"Is there a problem, sir?"

Matthew was watching him from behind the reception desk. "Are you all right, Mr Corrigan? Do you need anything?"

"Yes. I need to find Edward Hatcher. Did you see him go out?"

Matthew shook his head firmly. "No, sir. I've been on the desk for a few hours, and I saw him go up to his room this afternoon, but I don't think he's been out again, although…"

"What?"

"He could've slipped past without me seeing. I've been quite busy with one thing and another."

"Right. In that case, I might need you to let me into his room. But first, let me check something. Don't go away." Dan hurried outside. The street was deserted, and Dan cursed under his breath. But as he turned back to the hotel, a figure edged into view, a pale face peeping around the hotel's corner. *Got you!* Dan sprinted to the corner, and as he'd hoped the figure did not disappear.

The journalist leaned against the wall, his camera on its strap and his phone in his hand.

"How long have you been here?" Dan demanded.

"I dunno. Hours. Why?"

"Because…" Dan hesitated. "Listen, what's your name? What paper do you work for?"

"I don't have to answer your questions. What's going on?"

"We'll get to that. If you help me, I might be able to help you. But first, I want to know your name."

"All right. I'm Charlie. Charlie Heath. And I'm freelance."

"Okay, Charlie, this is important. I need to know if Edward Hatcher has left the hotel."

"Of course he hasn't. If he'd gone, I wouldn't be standing around here freezing my nuts off. He's still inside."

"Oh God!" Dan breathed. Edward had sounded as if he was outside. Had he climbed out of a window?

Dan ran back to the entrance, his mind a whirl of unwanted images.

"Hey!" Charlie yelled. "You said you'd give me something."

But Dan didn't look back.

Inside, he jogged to the reception desk. Matthew stood in front of the desk, a woman in her twenties at his side, their heads together as they talked, their voices hushed and urgent. But when Matthew saw Dan, he broke off his conversation, stepping smartly back like a child caught standing too close to a tray of freshly baked cookies.

"Mr Corrigan, you really must tell me what the problem is."

"I don't know," Dan replied. "But I'm worried about Edward Hatcher. I'm pretty sure he's still somewhere in the hotel, but we'll start with his room. Let's go."

"I have to stay on the desk, but Daphne will take you up."

Matthew indicated the woman. "Daphne's one of our housekeepers, and she'll have to be the one who goes into the room. I hope you understand."

"Fine. Whatever. But we have to go right now."

Matthew nodded to Daphne. "Off you go. But remember what I told you." He sent her a warning look.

"All right, I know," Daphne said. "This way, sir."

She led Dan up the stairs to the fifth floor, and picking up on his sense of urgency, she hurried along the corridor until they reached a wooden door marked, *The Regency Suite*.

Daphne knocked on the door. "Mr Hatcher. I need to service the room. Can I come in?"

"Open it," Dan said.

"I have to ask first. He could be doing anything."

Dan forced his voice to stay calm. "Just open it. Please."

"All right. You'll have to stay out here though." Daphne knocked once more, calling out Edward's name, then she slid her keycard briefly into the slot, and very slowly she pushed the door open. "Mr Hatcher? Are you there? Mr Hatcher?" She stepped into the room, and Dan caught the door before it swung shut, then he followed her inside.

"You have to wait!" Daphne hissed.

But Dan shook his head. "He's not here. He's cleared out."

"Mr Hatcher is very neat and tidy. His room always looks like this. And anyway, I've got to check the bathroom."

"Go ahead."

Cautiously, Daphne opened the bathroom door and peered in. Then she let out a sigh of relief.

"Is he there?" Dan asked.

"No. And I'm glad he isn't. There's nothing worse than walking in on a man when he's in the bathroom."

"Yes, there is." Dan crossed to the nearest window. The sash window was tall, but it was closed, and the catch was still in place. He checked the second window, but although the catch was undone, when he tried to lift the window, it moved only a little then it stopped, halted by a short length of white cable locked to the frame. "Are all the upstairs windows locked like this?"

Daphne nodded. "Health and safety. We don't want anybody falling out, or…" her hand went to her mouth. "You don't think he's done something like that, do you?"

"I don't know. Is there a fire escape?"

"No. There are fire doors, and we've got emergency exits on the ground floor, but if anyone opens a fire exit, the alarm goes off."

"He must've slipped out a back way," Dan said. "He could've gone out through the kitchens or something."

"Why would he do that?" Daphne asked. "He could walk out the front whenever he wanted." She looked at Dan wide eyed, but it was an affectation; she had something to conceal.

"What do you know, Daphne?"

"Nothing."

"That's not true, is it?" Dan said. "Come on. Tell me. It could be important."

"It's nothing really, but I know there's a reporter hanging around, and Matthew reckons he's here on account of Mr Hatcher. I can't see what all the fuss is about. I mean, I'd never heard of him until he turned up."

"I want you to call down to reception. Ask everyone to be on the lookout for Mr Hatcher. I have to find out how he left the hotel and when."

"Hang on." Daphne went to the wardrobe and opened it. "His suitcases were in here this morning. I saw them when I cleaned the room. Now they're gone, and they were big. Matthew strained his back lugging them up here, and he didn't even get a tip. He wasn't happy about that, I can tell you."

"Then Edward can't have gone through the kitchen, he'd have been too conspicuous." Dan ran his hands through his hair. This was becoming ridiculous. Edward had said he'd meet them for dinner, and now he'd disappeared, luggage and all. And his voice on the phone had been heavy with despair, all trace of his usual ebullience gone.

Dan tried calling Edward again, but his call went straight to voicemail.

Edward was gone. And something was wrong. Something was very wrong indeed.

CHAPTER 8

Dan waited in the hotel's lobby, sitting calmly on a leather sofa and using the time to gather his thoughts. He'd already called Alan, and it wasn't long before his neighbour arrived, a plastic carrier bag dangling from his hand.

"Thanks for coming so quickly," Dan said. "I'm sorry to spoil your dinner, but I need your help."

"It's all right. I got our food to go." Alan laid the bag on the coffee table as he sat down on a sofa facing Dan. "You said it was important, so here I am."

"What did you tell the others?"

"As instructed, I told them very little. I said you weren't feeling well, then I left as soon as I could." He looked at Dan expectantly. "This is the point at which you explain."

"It's Edward. He's gone."

"You mean, he's checked out?"

Dan shook his head. "He's just disappeared. He took his luggage, but he didn't tell anyone he was leaving, and somehow he managed to leave the hotel without being seen. It would've been relatively easy for him to slip past the receptionist, but that journalist was outside, and he swears Edward didn't leave the hotel."

"All right. That's odd, but I get the impression that Edward tends to be a bit dramatic. It's a strange way to behave, but it isn't sinister."

"There's something else," Dan replied. "I called Edward when I left the restaurant, and when I said I was coming to the hotel to find him, he said, 'Don't do that. It's too late.' Something like that, anyway."

"How did he sound?"

"Depressed, as if he was resigned to his fate. And I'm pretty sure he was outside. I thought I heard the waves, but maybe it was something else."

Alan ran his hand along his jaw. "This isn't good. It's getting cold out there." He hesitated. "Has anyone called the police?"

"I have, and they said they'd make a note and watch out for him. But as far as we know, Edward isn't at risk. They thought he'd probably decided to leave for some reason of his own, and they said I should call again if he doesn't turn up."

"We should go and look for him." Alan stood, grabbing the bag of food. "We can ditch this, get something later. Let's go."

Dan pushed himself to his feet. "I thought we could try the beach where I found him earlier. I don't know how he could get there without being seen, but it's the only lead I've got."

"It's a start," Alan said. "And that's better than nothing. Let's go."

They headed out together into the darkness, shoulders hunched against the cold, the wind chill made worse by the damp sea air. If Charlie was still outside with his camera, Dan didn't spot him. *Just as well,* he thought. *He's the last person I want to see.*

They left the streetlights behind as they neared the

clifftops, and in the darkness the ceaseless rhythm of the waves seemed to come from every direction, each boom and splashing rush followed by the crackle of pebbles rolling over the rocks like a drawn-out death rattle.

Dan took his rechargeable torch from his pocket and sent the bright beam searching through the misty air.

Alan pointed. "Look. There."

"What?" Dan aimed his torch. There was no one in sight, but his torch's beam picked out the boarded-up kiosk that stood near the steps leading down to the beach.

"Over here." Alan jogged over to the kiosk and pulled something from the shadows.

Hurrying to Alan's side, Dan shone his light. And his heart sank. Alan was studying a large suitcase, and though Dan had never seen Edward's luggage, the case was a brand-new Samsonite: exactly the kind of bag he'd own.

"There's no label," Alan said. "Shall we open it?"

"We'll have to."

"What about fingerprints? We don't know what's happened here."

"I'll be careful, but we have to see inside. It might help us find him." Dan handed his torch to Alan. "Hold this."

Alan held the light steady and Dan kneeled down, flipping the latches, handling them as carefully as he could. The case wasn't locked, but Dan was suddenly reluctant to open it. He took a breath, then he lifted the lid.

For a moment, neither of them spoke.

The case was almost full: shirts neatly folded, a cotton pyjama jacket, a soft woollen cardigan.

"These could belong to anybody," Alan said.

Dan picked out the cardigan and turned the label around. "Cashmere. It's his. It has to be." He closed the case, then he stood, crossing to the top of the steps. The beach was lost in the darkness, but he could make out the white tops of waves in the distance. At least the tide was out.

"I'm going down," Dan said. "Do you want to stay here, or—"

"I'm coming with you," Alan interrupted. He held Dan's torch out to him. "Here. I'll use my phone's flashlight. But we can't go far from the steps. If we don't find him soon, we'll have to come back up."

"Agreed." Dan picked his way down the steps, one hand on the handrail, the other holding his torch at shoulder height. Alan followed close behind him, but they didn't speak.

This is madness, Dan thought. *We'll never find him.* But he had to hope. There was always a chance.

Dan stepped onto the beach, but the mist hung heavy in the air, swallowing the light from his torch. The sea was louder now, the sound whirled around by the wind, waves raking the shore with a spluttering hiss like spiteful laughter.

"Edward!" Alan called out. "Are you there?"

But Dan touched his arm then played his torch's beam on the damp sand. "There are no footprints. No one's been down here since the tide came in."

"Even so, we should still look," Alan insisted. "In case he… fell from the top."

"All right. But we'll stick together."

They trudged across the sand, peering at each strange shape that emerged to taunt them: driftwood, clumps of seaweed, a length of rusted chain.

Alan called Edward's name several times, but to no avail, and after a few minutes they halted.

"We're getting too far from the steps," Alan said. "We'd better head back."

"You're right." Dan took a last look around, then they turned back, staying close to the cliff. They found the steps quickly, and Dan shone his torch upward.

"After you," Alan said.

But Dan didn't move. Something on the cliff's face had

caught the light, and he shifted his torch, making the beam retrace its path. There. Caught on a clump of plants, a piece of wet cloth fluttered feebly in the updraught.

"Is that…?" Alan began.

"A jacket. It's Edward's. He was wearing it this afternoon." Dan heaved a sigh. "We have to call the police again. Something's happened to Edward. I'm sure of it."

TUESDAY

CHAPTER 9

After a quiet breakfast in the hotel, Dan and Alan sat in one of the hotel's function rooms, Dan nursing a mug of black coffee, Alan sipping from a cup of tea. There'd been no news of Edward, but Dominic had taken charge of the situation, insisting that as the retreat's organiser, he'd be the one to liaise with the police.

Since then, Dominic had kept his cards close to his chest, fobbing off all enquiries with a sympathetic smile and a murmured reassurance that everything would be all right. Dan had offered to help, but Dominic had assured him that everything was already in hand.

This morning, Dominic had called a meeting of everyone on the retreat, and Dan had decided to gatecrash. After all, he'd been the one to raise the alarm.

Tim Kendall arrived promptly at 8 o'clock, followed by Brian Coyle and Roz Hammond.

"Morning," Tim said, sitting next to Alan. "I don't suppose there's any news."

"Not yet," Alan replied. "Dominic should be here any minute, and then we'll find out if anything's happened."

"Fingers crossed," Brian said. He took the seat next to Tim, and Roz sat beside him. She acknowledged Dan and Alan with a sad smile, but she didn't speak; she sat slumped in her chair, staring into space.

A moment later, Marcus Slater and Albert Fernworthy arrived, both men looking tired and distracted. Sombre greetings were exchanged, then they took their places, sitting quietly.

A tense silence crept across the room, and Dan leaned closer to Alan. "Maybe I should get things started."

But before Alan could reply, Dominic Rudge entered the room, his face pale and his expression pained, his battered satchel clasped tightly across his stomach as though he feared it might be snatched away.

"Is this it?" Dominic asked as he took a seat. "Where's everyone else?"

Albert cleared his throat. "Margaret and Pansy have gone home. They were quite upset. Edward was, I mean *is*, a friend of theirs, and they couldn't stand the idea that something might've happened to him. And then there was some journalist—"

"What?" Dominic interrupted. "Already?"

"He was here before Edward disappeared," Dan said. "He's been following Edward for some time."

Dominic scraped his hand down his face. "My God. That's all we need." He took a breath, lifting his chin and shaking his head as if bucking himself up. "What about Lucille? I'm sure she won't have cut and run."

"Actually, I think she might well have gone home," Marcus said. "I haven't seen her this morning, but last night she talked about leaving. She seemed... downhearted."

"Very well, since it looks like no one else is going to turn up, we'll make a start." Dominic scanned his audience to make sure they were paying attention, then he began. "There's not much to tell. As of this morning, no one has heard from Edward. The police have been informed, but I'm afraid they've been almost useless. They say that Edward is not yet officially a missing person, but I convinced them to send someone out to take a look around."

"That doesn't sound like a proper search," Dan said.

Dominic sent Dan a stern look. "Alas, I fear you may be right. But the matter is out of my hands. The sergeant claimed that they'd done all they could, and at least they recorded everything. If Edward isn't found, the case can be escalated appropriately."

Marcus raised his hand. "To be honest, I've been thinking about heading for home. That's okay, isn't it?"

"Yes, you *can* go if you really want to. It's entirely up to you. You can all run out on me if you feel so inclined." Dominic wrung his hands. "Unfortunately, if you choose to go, I won't be able to offer you a refund. Technically, the retreat hasn't been cancelled."

An embarrassed silence filled the room until Brian broke it. "For myself, I'm staying put, but only because I'm still harbouring a faint hope that Edward will turn up. Failing that, I want to be ready to help the police with their enquiries. I think we all feel the same. But as for the retreat... I'm sure we all have more pressing matters on our mind right now."

"Yes, of course," Dominic said. "I'm sorry. I didn't mean to diminish the significance of what's happened. I misspoke. I'm exhausted. I didn't sleep a wink."

"I don't suppose any of us slept well," Roz said. "I kept thinking about Edward, out there on his own. It was such a cold night."

Dominic nodded wisely. "It's sad. Very sad. But unfortunately, there's nothing much we can do. If there are further developments, I'll make sure you're all informed."

"But what exactly did the police say?" Tim asked. "Do they think he might've jumped?"

"They're keeping an open mind. Since he hasn't been

found, there's not a lot they can do, but they have contact details for all of you, and I'm sure they'll be in touch."

"You haven't really answered my question," Tim said. "Do they think that Edward might've taken his own life?"

"They're not sure," Dominic replied, "but sadly, they can't rule out the possibility."

"I can," Dan said.

Dominic stared at him, blinking. "I'm sorry?"

"I spoke to Edward earlier that day," Dan replied. "He was positive, energetic, making plans for the future. He's making a deal with a film company, and he was thrilled about the whole thing."

"Daniel, with respect, you're not even meant to be at this meeting," Dominic said. "Of course, none of us want to think the worst, but Edward's behaviour was very erratic yesterday. And then there was the suitcase he left behind. I'm sorry to say this, really I am, but it doesn't look good."

"I agree with Dan," Brian said. "I've known Edward for years, and he's not the suicidal type. He might've come across as a bit effete, but underneath it all, he's tough. That stuff about him working in intelligence wasn't made up for publicity; it was real. He'd spent time in the field, all across Eastern Europe. He's done things that'd turn your hair white, and he lived to tell the tale. There's no way he'd top himself."

Roz touched Brian's arm. "We can't always know what goes on in someone's inner life. Maybe all those years of secrecy took their toll. It's not good for someone to live under pressure. We all have our vulnerabilities."

"Not him." Brian shrunk from her touch, folding his arms. "The man had a core of steel. I mean, look at this note." Fumbling in the breast pocket of his jacket, he produced a folded sheet of plain paper. "I found this in my room." He donned his glasses, and read: "Your energy and drive know no bounds, and soon, I'm sure, you'll receive the acclaim of your peers."

"That was from Edward?" Dan asked.

"Yes. At least, I assume so. He didn't sign it, but I'm sure he meant it as an apology for the way he lost his temper yesterday." Brian smiled around the group. "I'd have thought that was obvious."

Dan leaned forward. "Can I see that?"

"Of course." Brian handed him the note, and Dan studied it carefully. It was typewritten, the indentations of each character clearly visible in the thick writing paper. Dan held the paper up to the light. It was ivory in colour, and although the paper was perfectly smooth on one side, it had a distinctive ribbed texture on the back, and there was a watermark: the single word *Conqueror*.

"When did you find this?" Dan asked.

"Last night, when we came back from the restaurant. It was in my room. He must've slipped it under my door before he… left."

"Interesting," Tim chipped in. "I also found a note in my room. Like yours, it was unsigned, but I had no idea who it was from, so I didn't attach much importance to it at the time."

"I had one too," Dominic said. "What did yours say?"

"I don't have it with me, but I have a good memory for this sort of thing." Tim took a breath as though about to make a speech. "The breadth of your vision spans the centuries, and your work will live on for years to come." He sighed. "It was rather sweet, so I thought it might've been from Roz."

Roz shook her head. "No. It was nothing to do with me, so perhaps it was from Edward. Dominic, do you have yours?"

"Yes. It's here somewhere." Dominic rifled through his bag, muttering under his breath. "Ah! Here it is." He plucked a sheet from the mass of papers, and it looked to Dan as though it was typed on the same paper as Brian's note.

"It was in my room last night. I must say, I guessed it might be from Edward at the time, and you'll see why in a minute, but it slipped my mind entirely." Dominic cleared his throat then read, "When sorrows come, they come not single spies, and mistakes are even more common. But soon, you'll have a new horizon."

"What made you think it was from Edward?" Dan asked.

"The reference to spies, of course. Edward always enjoyed playing with words, and he probably thought I'd enjoy the way he repurposed the quote from Hamlet."

"I had a note," Albert said. "I left it in my bag upstairs, but it was something about boldly venturing to new realms." He shrugged. "I thought it was nice, but I had no idea who it had come from."

"Mine was similar," Marcus added. "It said, *May your quests be ever more epic.*"

"It seems as though everyone had a note except me," Alan said.

"I didn't get one," Roz said quickly. "But then, I'm not staying at the hotel." Her cheeks flushed a little. "What about the people who've gone home? I wonder if any of them had notes."

"I could find out," Dominic suggested. "I've got email addresses for everybody."

"Good idea," Dan said. "But we're forgetting the most important note. Edward received one himself, didn't he?"

"Yes. He thought his note was from me," Brian replied. "But as I've said before, I didn't write the blasted thing. And whoever did, they have a lot to answer for. They might as well have pushed him over the edge." He winced. "Sorry, that was an unfortunate turn of phrase, but you know what I mean."

"Do you still have it?" Dan asked.

Brian frowned. "Did you know that he hurled it at me? Looking back, you wonder if the strain was already starting to show."

"But do you have the note or not?" Dan did his best to keep his tone level. "It could be important, Brian."

"I might have it. I rarely throw anything away. Let me see." Brian wore a tweed jacket, and he rummaged through the pockets in turn, producing a wad of receipts, two small notepads, a beermat and several sticky notes. "It doesn't seem to be here. I wonder if I was wearing my other jacket."

"You weren't," Alan said. "I remember."

"Mm. I'll have another look. The pockets in this old thing are somewhat capacious. That's why I like it." He delved into the pockets again. "Ah! Here it is." He produced a ball of crumpled paper and uncurled it carefully.

Dan held out his hand. "Can I see it?"

"Sure." Brian handed it over.

The note matched the others in that it was typewritten on the same paper, but its tone was altogether different. Dan read it aloud: "The writing is on the wall. Your secret is about to be revealed. Very soon you'll get what you so richly deserve, and the world will see you for what you are."

The room was silent, and Dan looked at each of them in turn. Someone had threatened Edward, and either they'd driven him to despair, or they'd made good on their threat and done him harm. The person who'd sent that threat must've been close to Edward, so they were almost certainly in the room. All that remained was to find the culprit.

CHAPTER 10

After the meeting, Dan and Alan stood in the hotel lobby.

"Where shall we start?" Alan asked.

"Start what?"

"Looking into Edward's disappearance, of course. And don't tell me you're not going to do it, because I won't believe it for a second."

Dan raised an eyebrow. "I was thinking about asking a few questions. After all, Edward asked me to help him, and I feel as though I let him down."

"You did nothing wrong, but there's something strange going on, and I'm sure we could help if we put our minds to it." Alan eyed Dan for a moment. "Do you want to start with the notes?"

"Not yet. The notes are interesting, but I'd prefer to start with a more direct line of enquiry."

"Such as?"

"Edward's room. It was pretty empty when I last saw it, but even so, I'd like to take a look around."

"Good idea," Alan said, "but I don't think they'll let you in."

Dan smiled. "I have an idea about that. Let's go and see what we can do."

They climbed the stairs quickly, but Dan halted on the fourth landing.

"Edward's room is on the next floor," Alan said.

"Yes, but the housekeeper is on this one." He indicated a glazed door, and through its window they could see a large laundry trolley stacked with a mound of clean white towels.

Dan pulled the door open and strode up to the trolley. Nearby, a room door stood ajar, and sounds of activity came from within.

"Hello," Dan called out. "Could I have a little help out here?"

"Coming," a woman's voice said, and a moment later, Daphne appeared. She smiled politely, but there was something guarded in her expression, and she looked from Dan to Alan, measuring them up. "Can I help you with something, gentlemen?"

Dan smiled warmly. "Yes, Daphne, I hope so."

"Oh yes?"

"This will only take a minute. You see, I lent something to Mr Hatcher, something of a personal nature, and I'd very much like to retrieve it. I was hoping that I'd be able to pop into his room and see if he's left it there."

Daphne's brow furrowed. "I'm sorry, sir, but I really don't think that's possible."

"It'll only take a minute," Dan said. "And you could be with me the whole time."

"But you've already been in that room. It's empty."

"I know," Dan replied. "But everything was a bit fraught when we were in there yesterday, and it didn't occur to me to look properly. In the heat of the moment, I completely forgot that Edward had something of mine, and as I say, it's a personal item. I'm sure you understand."

"Oh. Personal." Daphne looked down, her hands clutched

together. "What kind of thing are we talking about? Was it jewellery, for instance, or… an item of clothing, maybe?"

"I prefer not to say any more," Dan replied. "But listen, Daphne, I can see your heart's in the right place. And it would put my mind at rest if I could take a quick look in that room. Will you help me out?"

Daphne pursed her lips, but then she gave him a small smile. "I can't see the harm, especially since the room's empty." She glanced back into the room she'd been cleaning, then she pulled the door shut. "We'll have to be quick. With all those people checking out early, I've got a lot of rooms to sort out today."

They followed Daphne to Edward's room, and she entered first, looking around before she beckoned them in. "As you can see, it's empty, but where do you think this personal item is likely to be? If it was in the bed, then you're too late, because I've changed the sheets already."

"I'm not sure," Dan replied. "We'll just have a look around." He gestured to the desk. "Alan, if you could have a good rummage through there, please. I'll start over here."

"Right."

Alan sat down and began going through the desk drawers, while Dan turned his attention to the small cabinets that served as bedside tables. He checked thoroughly, running his hands around the empty spaces in case anything had been tucked into a corner out of sight. But he found nothing on either side of the bed.

Finally, he kneeled on the floor and peered into the narrow gap beneath the bed.

"There's nothing under there," Daphne blurted. "I moved the bed and vacuumed the carpet."

Dan stood, eyeing Daphne closely. "Do you always clean beneath the bed when someone checks out?"

Daphne shook her head, reluctantly. "No, but I was told to do a thorough job."

"By who?" Dan asked.

"I don't remember. It must've been the manager. I'm always getting told to do something or other. I've got a list of jobs as long as your arm. So, if you can't find what you're looking for, I'll get back to work."

"Give us a minute," Dan said, crossing to the wardrobe and opening the door. There was a high shelf inside containing spare blankets and pillows, and Dan reached up, pushing his hand as far to the back as he could. "Nothing. Alan, are you having any luck?"

"Not yet," Alan replied. "I've got one more drawer to—" He broke off suddenly. "This could be interesting."

Dan strode over to the desk, and Alan rose from the chair, a small hard-backed book in his hands. "Look at this," Alan said, handing the book to Dan.

"*The Forgetful Fox Goes on a Picnic,*" he read. "Well done, Alan."

"That's strange," Daphne said. "You find all kinds of funny things when you're cleaning out a room, but I never noticed that book."

"It was under some sheets of paper," Alan replied. "Neatly tucked away."

"What kind of paper?" Dan asked.

Alan shook his head. "Ordinary white paper with the hotel's letterhead. I expect it's in all the rooms."

"It is." Daphne peered at the book, her arms folded. "A children's book — it's not what I'd call personal."

"It has sentimental value." Dan flipped through the pages. "It was signed by the author."

"Roz Hammond," Alan added. "She's staying at the hotel."

"Oh, I see," Daphne said. "So you've found what you were looking for. Good. I'll get back to work."

Dan and Alan exchanged a look.

"Yes, I think we're done here," Alan said.

"Thank you, Daphne," Dan added. "I appreciate your help."

"All right. No problem." Daphne ushered them toward the door. "Happy to help."

In the corridor, they watched Daphne bustle away.

"We didn't achieve much," Alan said.

"I don't know. We have this." Dan held up the children's book.

"Yes, I can't help but wonder why a man of Edward's age would have one of Roz's books in his desk. I'm pretty sure Edward didn't have children. Perhaps it was a gift for a niece or nephew."

"It could be," Dan replied. "But what really interests me is the fact that the ever-helpful Daphne had made such an effort to clear out the room. And she was definitely twitchy about something. She has something to hide."

Alan looked doubtful. "I'd say she was keen to get back to her work. If she was a bit on edge, it was probably because we'd made such an odd request. I expect you see a lot of strange things when you work in a place like this. As far as she's concerned, we're just another example of men behaving oddly."

"We'll see," Dan said. "But I'm sure that someone in the hotel has been trying to cover something up, and when we find out what that is, we'll be on our way to finding out what happened to Edward."

CHAPTER 11

Matthew looked both ways along the corridor before he ducked into the laundry room, closing the door firmly behind him.

Daphne, busily sorting through a pile of towels, looked up with a start. "Oh, it's you. You made me jump." She went back to her task, but said, "Everything all right?"

"You tell me," Matthew replied. "Did everything go all right? Did you get the money?"

Daphne stopped what she was doing. "Not yet. He said he'll pay if the story pans out and not before."

"Typical." Matthew scowled, chewing on his thumbnail. "We've got to strike while the iron's hot. With Hatcher running away, this could be bigger than we thought. Maybe *I* should have a word with Charlie. He won't mess *me* about."

"He didn't mess me about, Uncle Matt. He said he has to sell the story first, then the paper will pay him, and he can pay us. He said that's how it works."

"He would say that, wouldn't he? I knew we should've gone straight to the *Sun* or the *Daily Mail*."

"With what?" Daphne asked. "A pair of lady's knickers? It's not exactly earth shattering."

"Yeah, it is. They love all that kind of thing. *Panties*, that's what they always call them. It shows Hatcher was up to something, doesn't it? He must've had a girl in there, and there's no way those lacy little things belonged to a woman his own age."

"Hm. I might be able to help you there."

Matthew's eyes grew bright. "Tell me."

"This morning, a couple of blokes, Dan something-or-other and Alan Hargreaves, asked if they could look for something in Mr Hatcher's room. Something *personal* they said."

"What? You didn't let them, did you?"

Daphne shrugged. "Yeah. So what? I'd already been through everything. It was clean."

"Right." Matthew puffed out his cheeks. "Okay. So they didn't find anything."

"I didn't say that. They found a book, a children's book. And guess who must've given it to him."

"I dunno. Who?"

"Roz Hammond. That woman with the weird clothes. I always thought she was a bit odd, and now we know. She might come across all save-the-planet or whatever, but she's not above finding herself an older man with a bit of cash."

"A book? That doesn't prove anything."

"But that's not all. I was on an early shift this morning, and when I went down to get ready for breakfast, I saw her creeping about in the corridor. It can't have been much after six, so she must've stayed the night."

Matthew grunted under his breath. "Bloody hell. It goes to show, doesn't it? You never can tell."

"I know the type. Butter wouldn't melt, but it's all for show. Underneath, she'll be as hard as nails and looking out for number one."

"She's always been friendly to me," Matthew said. "I'd never have put her with Mr Hatcher. I thought…"

MICHAEL CAMPLING

"What?"

"Never mind." Matthew made to leave. "I'll do a bit of earwigging. If I can find out a bit more, we can take it to Charlie. But we'll only give him the info if he pays up front. Got it?"

"It's worth a try." Daphne lowered her gaze to the trolley stuffed with unwashed towels, its cloth sides bulging. "Anything's worth a try."

"Good girl," Matthew said, then he let himself out.

The corridor was empty, and he saw no one as he made his way to the lobby. Even with the writing retreat, most of the bedrooms were empty, and now some of the writers had already packed their bags. If he was going to dig up enough dirt to make a decent story, he'd have to move fast, before it was too late.

It was late morning, so there'd be a few guests hanging around in the conservatory, slurping tea and coffee like it was going out of fashion. They'd be talking, gossiping about Hatcher, and it wouldn't be hard to eavesdrop on their conversations. He was good at it.

It's a shame it had to be Hatcher, Matthew thought as he headed for the conservatory. He really did like the Max Cardew books. But truth be told, Hatcher had brought this on himself. You could misbehave all you liked when you were a nobody, but if you wanted fame and money, you had to pay the price. That journalist wouldn't have turned up unless Hatcher was up to something. The man had misbehaved, and now the chickens were coming home to roost. *It's nothing personal,* Matthew told himself. *Business is business.*

CHAPTER 12

Dan and Alan found Roz in the conservatory. She was sitting alone on a sofa facing the windows, a sketchpad on her lap. But although she held a pencil in her hand, she wasn't drawing. Her gaze was fixed on something in the distance, or perhaps on nothing at all.

She looked up as Dan and Alan approached, offering them a smile. "Join me," she said. "I can't work today and I need some company."

"Thanks," Dan replied, and he pulled up a chair.

Alan sat next to Roz on the sofa. "You're worried about Edward?"

Roz nodded sadly. "Poor Edward. I wonder where he can be."

"Actually, that's what we'd like to talk about." Dan had brought the book they'd found, and he placed it carefully on the coffee table in front of Roz. "This was in Edward's room."

Roz stiffened, then she leaned forward to pick the book up. "Why were you poking around in his room? Wait. Don't answer that. I assume you were playing detectives."

"We're concerned for Edward, that's all," Alan said.

"Hm." Roz opened the book to the title page, tracing a

circle around the inscription with her fingertip. "He asked me to sign it just yesterday. He'd brought it with him, and…" Roz blinked away a tear, wiping her eyes on the backs of her hands. "I'm sorry, but Edward said some lovely things about my work. He could be very sweet when he wanted to be. It was as if he understood."

"Understood what?" Dan asked.

Roz looked him in the eye. "Me. It was as if he could see through to the person underneath, to who I really am. That kind of intuition is a rare gift, especially in a man."

"I'm not sure I believe that," Dan said.

"No?" Roz sighed. "You might be right. I've known one other man with that level of empathy and understanding, but that was a long time ago." She shook her head as if dismissing a thought. "Sorry, I'm rabbiting on. Are you guys having a drink or anything?" She peered across the room. "I ordered coffee, but it hasn't turned up yet."

"Maybe later," Dan replied. "If you don't mind, I'd like to talk some more about Edward. When did you last see him?"

"Yesterday, in the afternoon," Roz replied. "I know he had a bit of a temper, but that row with Brian really upset him. I went up to his room to see if he was all right."

"And was he?" Dan asked.

"I thought so at the time," Roz said. "He seemed calm. He said that he'd been doing some thinking and come to a decision. When you look back at it, that sounds awful, but while we were talking, he was happy. Genuinely happy. It was like he was lighter somehow, like a weight had been lifted from his shoulders."

"That's a good sign, isn't it?" Alan asked.

"It could be," Dan replied. "It depends on what kind of decision he'd made."

"I don't think he'd—" Roz broke off abruptly, and when Dan followed her gaze, he understood why. Matthew was advancing on them, bearing a large cup of coffee on a tray.

"Sorry for the delay, madam," Matthew said. "It took me a while to find the oat milk you requested."

"That's all right, Matthew."

Roz smiled, but Matthew did not return it. Instead, he turned to Dan and Alan. "Can I get you anything? You take your coffee black as I recall, Mr Corrigan. And perhaps a pot of Earl Grey for you, Mr Hargreaves?"

"A black Americano would be great, thank you," Dan said.

"The same for me, please," Alan added.

"Certainly, sir. I'll get those in a jiffy." Matthew rocked back on his heels, but he didn't move away.

"That's all, thanks," Dan said. "We don't want anything else at the moment."

"Right. Erm, if you're sure. I'll be back with your drinks presently."

They watched as Matthew strolled away.

"Is it just me, or was he a bit off with me?" Roz asked.

"I think he's like that with everyone," Alan replied. "He's an odd character. He seems to do everything around here. If we looked in the kitchen, I wouldn't be surprised to find him wielding the pots and pans."

"But he's usually so helpful and kind," Roz insisted. "And I really don't like the way he called me madam. That was very strange."

"He was being plain nosy," Dan said. "Anyway, he's gone for the moment, so let's get back to the subject. Roz, it sounds as though you had a heart-to-heart with Edward. Would you say you were close friends?"

Roz shook her head. "Not especially. That conversation was an exception. We'd worked together, but until yesterday, he'd often been quite distant with me, aloof, even."

"I have the impression that he was that way with most people," Alan said. "Don't get me wrong. I have nothing against the man, but he wasn't the easiest person to get to know."

"He didn't remember that you'd met before," Dan said. "Does that affect your opinion?"

"Certainly not," Alan replied. "But you must admit, he came across as aloof, like he was holding something back. Maybe it was all those years working for MI6. He lived with secrecy for so long that it became a habit."

Dan nodded thoughtfully. "I've been thinking about that. It occurred to me that an ex-spy would have no difficulty in finding a way to leave the hotel without anyone noticing."

"You think he was a master of disguise?" Alan chortled. "I can't see that myself."

"There are subtle ways of going unnoticed," Dan said. "And anyway, you'd be surprised at how little people actually notice the world around them. Have you ever done the selective attention test?"

Roz frowned. "No, but I have a feeling I'm just about to."

"Why not? I'm sure that someone as intuitive as you will pass with flying colours." Dan took his phone from his pocket, and after a brief search he handed it to Roz. "Press play on the video, then follow the instructions."

"Okay." Roz tapped the screen. "It's just some people playing basketball, and it says I have to count how many times people in the white shirts pass the ball. Is that it?"

"Concentrate," Dan said. "Make sure you count all the passes. You mustn't miss a single one."

Roz watched the screen carefully for a minute, then she smiled. "Fifteen passes. I got it right. But... What? What gorilla?" Roz stared at the phone, then her eyebrows shot up her forehead. "Oh my God! Someone in a gorilla suit walked through the middle of the game, and I didn't even see them. I was so busy counting the passes, but... I can't believe it."

She handed the phone back to Dan, and he smiled as he pocketed it. "Our brains can only concentrate on so many things at once, and we tend to be influenced by the context. We see what we expect to see."

"Do you think Edward created a distraction and then slipped out?" Alan asked.

"No," Dan replied. "A distraction would have worked inside the hotel, but don't forget, he slipped past the eagle-eyed journalist outside. Whatever Edward did, I suspect it was something quite subtle. After all, he was lugging a heavy suitcase at the time."

"I can vouch for that," someone said.

Dan turned to find Matthew standing right behind him, a tray in his hand. "Sorry, sir. I didn't mean to startle you." Matthew nodded toward the tray. "Your coffees." As he placed the steaming cups on the table, he said, "Yeah, those bags of Mr Hatcher's weighed a ton. I don't know what he had in there, but it was certainly heavy." He placed a receipt on the table. "Would you like to charge those drinks to the room, gentlemen?"

"Yes, put them both on my bill," Dan said quickly. "But hang on a minute, Matthew. You said *bags*."

"Yes, sir."

"How many bags did Mr Hatcher have?" Dan asked.

"Two large suitcases, plus a suit carrier and one smaller bag." Matthew held out his hands to indicate the size. "It was the kind of thing you might keep a laptop in. The suit bag was light, of course, but the other two! I almost put my back out."

Dan narrowed his eyes. "We only found one suitcase outside, Matthew. As far as you know, has anyone found any trace of Mr Hatcher's other bags in the hotel?"

Matthew's face fell. "Mr Corrigan, I hope you're not suggesting that anyone on the staff would've taken it. Because I can assure you that no one would ever dream of doing such a thing."

Dan held his gaze for a long second, then said, "I wasn't

accusing you of anything, Matthew. But we're trying to find out what happened to Mr Hatcher, so it's essential for everyone to be open and honest, and sometimes that means asking difficult questions. Okay?"

Matthew nodded. "Yes, sir. It's a troubling business. The staff are all quite upset by it, I can tell you. But I can honestly say that no one has come across Mr Hatcher's luggage. He must've taken it with him, though I've no idea how he slipped out with it. It's a puzzler."

"Okay," Dan said. "Thanks, Matthew."

Matthew inclined his head then strolled away, making a slow circuit of the room, pausing to rearrange the chairs around a nearby table.

Lowering his voice, Dan said, "I can't decide if the missing luggage is good news or bad. It could mean that Edward has taken it with him, but it could just as easily mean that someone stole it. Maybe they couldn't make off with both bags, so they took one, threw the jacket away and then ran off."

"We could try searching for it," Alan said. "It was heavy, so someone might've been tempted to ditch it. We could retrace our steps from last night. In daylight, we might spot something that we missed."

"Maybe later," Dan said. "For now, I'd rather start with what we have."

"Such as?" Roz asked.

"The notes," Dan replied. "Who would want to threaten Edward, and why?"

"Professional jealousy?" Alan suggested.

"It's a possibility. It was interesting that Edward assumed his note came from Brian. Have they clashed in the past?"

"They bickered over silly little things," Roz said. "Sometimes they behaved like a couple of grumpy old men, but that's because they were too much alike. Underneath it all, they were friends."

"I didn't know that," Alan admitted. "Maybe that's why it rankled so much when one of them had more success than the other. A few years ago, Brian was riding high, but now the tables have turned. Maybe Brian isn't happy about that."

"But Brian swore he never sent that note to Edward," Dan said. "And I believe him. From what Roz has just said, it sounds as if they weren't afraid to vent their feelings face to face. Is that right?"

Roz nodded firmly. "They knew how to wind each other up, but I always thought that, secretly, they enjoyed the cut and thrust."

"There you are then," Dan said. "People who can argue in person have no need to slip each other sly notes. It wasn't their way. If they were straight with each other, it's because they shared an understanding. They may not have shown affection for each other, but I believe they were firm friends."

"That's plausible, I suppose." Alan looked at Roz. "What do you think?"

Roz tilted her head on one side. "Dan's right. They fell out all the time, but they also stood up for each other. If Brian had known that Edward was in some kind of trouble, he'd have done anything to help him."

"Anything?" Dan said.

"You know what I mean," Roz shot back. "The point is, I'm positive that Brian did not send that note."

"That leaves Tim, Dominic, Marcus, Albert and the people who've left." Alan paused. "I wonder if Lucille and the Johnson twins received notes."

"Dominic could find out," Roz said. "But you've missed one of the suspects. I'm sure you trust each other, but surely I'm still in the frame, aren't I?"

Dan examined her expression, then he said, "Yes. Your book was the only thing Edward left behind. That may or may not be significant, but at this stage I can't rule you out."

Roz pushed out her lower lip. "I see. Maybe you should

keep this." She still had the book in her lap, and she held it out to Dan. "You could dust it for fingerprints or check it for bloodstains and DNA."

Dan offered a tight smile. "I don't want to upset you, Roz, but you asked, and I answered honestly."

"If you think that's okay, then there's nothing more to say." Roz tossed the book onto the table, then she stood. "I might see you later, Alan. I'm going for a walk. I need some air." She strode from the room, and Alan turned on Dan.

"That was totally uncalled for. You can't just go around accusing people. Roz is a friend. I've known her for years, for God's sake. Sometimes, Dan, I despair of you, I really do." Alan ran his hands through his hair. "You know what? I'm going up to my room. I need a break from all this." He stood stiffly.

"Hang on a sec," Dan began, but Alan held up his hand to rule out further discussion.

"I'll catch up with you later. In the meantime, you might consider finding Roz and apologising. If not for her sake, then for mine."

"But—"

"I don't want to hear it," Alan said, then he walked away, leaving Dan on his own.

But she is *a suspect*, Dan told himself. *Otherwise, why was she so defensive?* There was no doubt in Dan's mind: Roz knew more than she was prepared to admit.

CHAPTER 13

Alan stomped up the stairs and along the quiet corridor, but as he neared his hotel room, his anger at Dan's behaviour was already starting to fade. There were times when Dan didn't filter his words before he spoke out, and though he sometimes caused offence inadvertently, he didn't usually set out to hurt anyone. He could be blunt, but he wasn't malicious.

Sooner or later, he's going to get thumped, Alan thought. *But I don't suppose he'll change his ways.* And maybe that was as it should be.

Reaching his room, Alan slid his keycard into the lock, but as he laid his hand on the handle, voices echoed through the corridor.

A door opened and a woman murmured something and then giggled, the lilting notes of her laughter sounding familiar. But before Alan could decide where he'd heard that voice before, a man backed into the corridor. And there was no difficulty in identifying him.

Dominic turned toward Alan and, for an instant, he froze. Then he smiled, sauntering in Alan's direction with a swagger in his step. "Alan, how are you holding up, dear boy?"

"Fine." Alan peered past Dominic, but no one else emerged from the room, and the door clicked firmly shut.

Following Alan's gaze, Dominic glanced over his shoulder, then he sent Alan an obsequious smile. "I've been doing the rounds, checking in on everyone, making sure they're all right."

"Was that Lucille I heard?" Alan asked. "I thought she'd left."

"Ms Blanchette is staying with us for the moment. She prefers to keep herself to herself, but she's quite a brave little thing." Dominic smirked. "She has more spirit than you might imagine."

Alan kept his expression blank. "I'm glad to hear that she's all right. And I'm fine too, so there's no need for me to hold you up. Perhaps I'll see you later." Alan pressed on the door handle but it wouldn't budge, and he realised he'd left the key card in its slot. Grabbing the card, he tried the handle again, but the door remained stubbornly locked.

"They're a bit temperamental some of these locks," Dominic said. "There's a knack to them. You have to slide the card in just so, and then whip it out again. If you leave it too long, the damned things lock themselves. Would you like me to try?"

Alan shook his head. "Thanks, but I've got it." He performed the necessary routine, and this time the lock disengaged with a click. "Right. Goodbye, Dominic."

Pushing the door open with more force than was necessary, Alan hurried inside. But he froze in the doorway, still gripping the handle tight.

Behind him, Dominic said, "Alan? What's wrong?"

"That." Alan pointed. And there, lying on the carpet, was a sheet of neatly folded, ivory-coloured paper.

Dominic stepped over the threshold, standing

uncomfortably close. "Good Lord!" he breathed. "How strange. Has that only just arrived?"

Alan nodded. "It wasn't there this morning."

"Aren't you going to read it?"

"Yes. Of course. But there could be fingerprints or something."

"Mm. On the other hand, if it concerns Edward, it could contain valuable information as to his whereabouts."

"Maybe I should fetch Dan," Alan said. "He's good with this sort of thing."

Dominic looked doubtful. "I've heard your friend fancies himself as an amateur detective, but do we have time for that? Every second counts."

"That's true. Maybe, if I handle it carefully…" Alan picked up the note, holding it only by its edges, then slowly he unfolded it.

Like the others, this message had been typewritten, the letters pressed deep into the thick paper. And it contained just two short sentences.

Dominic leaned even closer to Alan, reading over his shoulder. "From one literary explorer to another. Don't worry – Edward has nothing to fear." Dominic grunted. "Is that it?"

Alan checked the other side of the page, but it was blank. "There's nothing else."

"That's all she wrote, eh?"

"She?" Alan asked.

"Just an expression. Anyway, it looks as though it's not much help after all. The part about Edward isn't exactly reassuring, and it doesn't really tell us anything, does it."

"Yes it does," Alan said. "It tells us that whoever sent the other notes, including the threatening message given to Edward, they're still here. They're still in the hotel."

Dominic raised his eyebrows. "You could be right. But when I tried to tell the police about Edward's note, they weren't interested. They seemed to think it was irrelevant, a tiff between friends."

"Even so, we ought to keep them informed."

"Very well," Dominic said wearily. "If I must, I can go and phone them now." He held out his hand for the note, but Alan shook his head.

"Thanks, but I'll hold on to this. I want to show it to Dan." He paused. "He doesn't always make a favourable impression, but whatever you may think of him, Dan has a first-rate mind. I value his opinion."

Looking distinctly put out, Dominic lowered his hand and stepped back. "Have it your own way." He glanced up and down the corridor, then he lowered his voice. "But whatever you do, try not to alarm the others. They're skittish enough as it is, and I really don't want them upset any further. All right?"

"We'll do whatever it takes," Alan replied. "We're going to do our best to find out what happened to Edward, and if that means stepping on a few toes, then so be it."

Dominic fixed Alan with a scolding stare. "I don't know what's got into you, Alan. You used to be such an easy-going chap. I'm not sure that your new friend is a good influence."

Alan bridled, squaring his shoulders and taking a swift step closer to Dominic, forcing him back. "I trust Dan. And right now, that's more than I can say for you, Dominic. You might want to bear that in mind."

"Is that so? Then I have nothing further to say." Dominic turned on his heel and marched away, heading for the main staircase.

Alan looked down at the sheet of paper in his hands. It was true that it didn't give much away, but he'd see what Dan made of it. And if that meant eating a slice of humble pie, then so be it.

CHAPTER 14

D an was still in the conservatory, sitting in exactly the
same place, when Alan arrived.

He listened carefully while Alan explained exactly what
had happened, then he took the note from Alan and read it,
holding it up to the light to check the watermark. The paper
was identical to the other notes, and although Dan couldn't
be sure, it looked as though this message had been written
with the same typewriter as the others.

Dan re-folded the note and handed it back to Alan. "You'd
better keep this. But I wouldn't worry too much about
fingerprints and such. Whoever wrote these notes, they'll
have been careful. They'll have worn gloves."

"That wouldn't surprise me," Alan replied. "But that
reference to Edward proves something. It shows that the
person sending these notes is still around, so that rules out a
few suspects, doesn't it?"

"Yes. It also begs a question: was the typewriter already
here or did they bring it with them?"

"A portable machine would be reasonably light," Alan
said. "I have an old Olivetti at home, a Lettera 32. It has its

own carry case, so something like that would be easy enough to carry."

"Yes, but it would have to be concealed. The culprit wouldn't want to be seen lugging a typewriter case around."

Alan clicked his fingers. "Edward's second suitcase. Matthew said it was heavy. Now we know why."

"That's an interesting theory. Unfortunately, it looks as though your note was written *after* Edward and the second suitcase disappeared."

"Simple. Someone took the case, typewriter and all, and brought it back to the hotel. Or perhaps it never left. Someone could have stolen the suitcase and hidden it in their room."

"You're forgetting that it was Edward who received the threatening note. I really don't think he typed it himself. Still, you're right about one thing: the typewriter could have been hidden inside a larger bag."

"Hm. I wonder if anyone heard anything."

"What do you mean?" Dan asked.

"The typewriter in use. Even a portable is quite noisy, and the walls in this hotel are pretty thin. There's a chance that someone will have heard the notes being typed." Alan frowned. "I wonder why I didn't receive my note at the same time as everyone else."

"My guess is that someone happened to come along just as your note was about to be posted under the door. The culprit had no choice but to walk away. But there's something else."

"What?"

"Did you notice the gap between the two sentences? It's a little wider than you'd normally expect, wouldn't you say?"

Alan unfolded the note to study it. "Yes, I think you're right. It's certainly wider than standard double spacing."

"And what does that tell you?"

"It was added afterwards," Alan said. "Someone fed the

paper back into the machine, and added the line about Edward."

"Correct. And interestingly, the second line is perfectly level with the first. I haven't used a typewriter in years, but from what I remember, it can be quite tricky to get the paper lined up properly. This person knew exactly what they were doing, and once more we can see how careful they are."

"The more modern, electric typewriters are fairly easy to line up — they can load the paper automatically." Alan held the paper closer to his eyes. "But I think this was done on an older machine. Some of the letters are darker than others, and that happens when the ribbon starts to wear out."

Dan tutted under his breath. "I'm a fool. When we were talking to Daphne, we should have asked her if she'd seen a typewriter in any of the rooms. Or she might have noticed a lot of paper in a waste bin."

Alan stood. "There's no time like the present. Let's go and find her."

"Why not?" Dan pushed himself to his feet. "We'll ask at reception."

From behind the reception desk, Matthew looked up as Dan and Alan approached. "Good morning, gentlemen. How are you today? Can I help you with anything?"

"We're fine, thanks." Dan leaned his elbows on the counter. "But yes, there is something you can do for us. We'd like to have a word with one of the housekeepers, preferably Daphne. Can you tell us where she is?"

"If there's a problem with the cleanliness of your room, I'll be happy to resolve the issue."

"There's no problem," Alan said. "We just want to ask a couple of questions in relation to Edward's disappearance."

Matthew's smile vanished. "Oh. Oh dear. Has something… happened?"

Dan shook his head. "It's nothing to worry about. We

thought one of housekeepers might've spotted something, that's all."

"I see. I'm sorry, but with things being so quiet at this time of year, Daphne's managing the housekeeping on her own, and she's gone home. But she's on a split shift today. She'll be back again this evening, in the restaurant." Matthew offered a nervous smile. "If there's anything I can do to help…"

"We want to know if anyone has a typewriter in their room," Dan said. "We thought someone might have noticed it when they were cleaning the rooms, or they may have heard it being used."

"Or one of the other guests might've heard it," Alan put in. "Has anybody complained about the noise of somebody typing?"

Matthew shook his head. "There haven't been any complaints about that kind of noise. Classical music at all hours, yes, but typing, no."

"Who's been playing music?" Dan asked.

"I really shouldn't say, sir. Please, forget I mentioned it." Matthew smiled. "But if it's a typewriter you're after, I'm sure I can lay my hands on one. We have a couple of old machines in storage."

"Where?" Dan asked. "Why didn't you mention this before?"

"I'm sorry, sir, but I wasn't entirely clear about your question. You asked about Daphne, not a typewriter."

"Yes, yes," Dan said, "but where are these typewriters?"

"In one of the storerooms. In the basement. I can have someone fetch one of them up for you, if you like."

Dan forced himself to speak slowly. "Matthew, I need you to take us to these typewriters right now. And I don't want to hear any arguments about rules and regulations or health and safety. This could help us find Mr Hatcher. His disappearance could be ruinous for this hotel's reputation, so I'm sure you'd like the situation to be resolved as soon as possible."

"We'd appreciate your help, Matthew," Alan added. "I'm sure it'll only take a couple of minutes."

Matthew studied each of them in turn, then he nodded. "All right. I don't quite see what you're getting at, but if it helps to find Mr Hatcher, I'll see what I can do." He picked up a handset and tapped a couple of buttons before pressing it to his ear. "Sheila, could you pop down and cover me on reception for ten minutes? I've got a little errand to run."

He listened, then said, "Thanks. You're a star."

Smiling, Matthew replaced the handset. "I'll be right with you, gentlemen. Happy to help."

THE DOOR that led down to the hotel's basement had a combination lock, and Matthew tapped in the code quickly and without having to think about it.

"Is this the only door to the basement?" Dan asked.

Matthew nodded cheerfully. "The only one we use. There's another at the back of the hotel, but it's kept locked and I don't have the key. I don't know who has, come to think of it. The owners must have one, but they're hardly ever here."

"How many people know the combination?" Alan said.

"Most of the staff. We keep all kinds of things down there. There's outdoor furniture, cleaning equipment, even a couple of chest freezers."

Dan and Alan exchanged a look, but Dan shook his head. There was no earthly reason to presume Edward had ended his days nestling among bags of frozen cod.

Matthew opened the door with a flourish. "Here we are." He flipped a switch and a set of fluorescent lights flickered on, revealing a modern concrete stairwell. "I'll lead the way. There's plenty of light but watch your step."

Matthew set off, Dan and Alan following close behind.

"Would somebody really go to all this trouble to write a few notes?" Alan asked.

"If they were driven by a sense of purpose," Dan said. "If they had a deep need to twist the world until it fitted into their vision of reality, then there's no telling what a person might do."

"Bloody hell," Matthew muttered. "Pardon my French, sir, but do you really have to say that kind of thing while we're going down here? It's giving me the creeps."

"Pay no attention," Alan said. "Dan has a vivid imagination."

"Me too," Matthew replied. "Me too."

They reached the bottom of the stairs, and Matthew led the way along an almost featureless corridor. The walls and ceiling were painted white, but the floor was bare concrete and there was a faint aroma of damp and decay.

"I'm told that this part of the hotel was renovated a few years back," Matthew said. "On account of a flood."

"How long have you worked here?" Alan asked.

"I started in March. It feels like a long time ago to me, but compared to most of the staff, I'm still the new arrival."

"I thought as much," Alan said. "I came on the retreat last year, and I'm sure I'd have remembered you."

"Very kind of you to say, sir." Matthew halted beside a door. "If memory serves, the old office equipment is in here."

He opened the door, and they followed him into a small room, its walls lined with heavy-duty shelving. Tangles of cable spilled from plastic crates, dusty printers sat atop beige desktop towers, and CRT monitors stared blindly from the lower shelves. Dan spotted every conceivable type of electronic till, and there were even a couple of mechanical tills, the large round buttons thick with dust and laced with cobwebs. But he couldn't see any typewriters.

As if reading his mind, Matthew said, "Give me a sec."

Then he bent down and grunted as he dragged a large plastic crate from a shelf and laid it on the floor. Lifting the lid, he grinned. "There we are, gentlemen. As promised."

Dan and Alan huddled around the crate.

"What do you think?" Alan asked.

"I'm not sure," Dan replied. "They look like they haven't been used for years."

The two typewriters were sturdy office machines bearing the name *Olympia*, but they were coated with grime, and dust lay thick between the keys.

Alan pressed a key, and though the correct letter leaped up to hit the roller, he said, "No ribbon." He tried the other typewriter, but the keys refused to budge. "The carriage lock must be on. If I can find it, I might be able to—"

"Don't bother. These aren't the ones we want. You only have to look at them to see that." Dan straightened his back, and the others followed suit.

"Oh dear," Matthew said. "This is all we've got. I don't know of any others."

Alan sighed. "Back to the drawing board."

"Sorry not to be more help, gentlemen. I was hopeful for a minute, there. I thought you were on to something."

Dan watched Matthew for a moment. The receptionist was excited about something; he was almost bouncing on the balls of his feet. He was generally eager to please, but that didn't explain the greedy glint in his eyes. Why had he gone out of his way to bring them down to the basement? Dan had expected him to put up more of a fight, but Matthew had changed his tune as soon as Edward's name had been mentioned. Did Matthew really care so much about the hotel's reputation, or did he have an ulterior motive for wanting Edward to be found?

"Shall we go back up?" Matthew asked. "Perhaps there's some other way I can help."

Dan nodded, his eyes still on Matthew. "We'll see."

Matthew set off cheerfully, but as they trooped back along the corridor and up the stairs, Dan didn't say a word.

CHAPTER 15

Cycling back toward the hotel, Roz took a detour across the park. Strictly speaking, she wasn't supposed to cycle on the footpath, but the afternoon was cold and there was no one else around. She had the entire park to herself. Perfect.

She'd popped home for a while, partly to take a break from the strained atmosphere in the hotel, but mainly to check if Shona had dragged herself out of bed and had something to eat. Roz had felt her stomach tightening as she'd approached the house, but there'd been no one home except for the cat. Whether Shona had actually made it into college was another matter entirely, but at least she was doing *something*, and that was a start.

The house had been quiet: no loud music, no one stomping up the stairs, no one chatting to friends online. Roz had learned to savour these moments of stillness; they didn't last for long.

Things might've been different if she'd stayed with Shona's father, or rather, if he'd stayed with her. But it was no use wishing for the impossible. Some things could never be. Some things were best forgotten.

But as Roz cycled through the park, familiar memories came back to haunt her. She tried to focus on the beauty of the perfect winter's day, but it eluded her. And she was plunged into the past. *He wanted me to get rid of her*, she thought. *He wanted me to snuff her out before she'd taken her first breath.* He'd cared more for his reputation than for anything else, and she'd never forgive him for that. Never.

Men.

She'd never let herself be snared by their lies again.

But at least she still had her daughter.

Shona was a sweet girl at heart, and if she sometimes let her fiery temper get the better of her, it was only because she was so passionate about so many things. *I was exactly the same at her age*, Roz told herself. In time, Shona would learn to channel her emotions, to use them, to make herself stronger. *Just like me.*

Roz rode over to the coastal path and dismounted, leaning her bike against the fence and removing her helmet, letting the wind have its fun with her hair. She breathed deeply, taking in the view, staring out across the endlessly fascinating rise and fall of the waves; the pattern ever changing, never faltering or ceasing in its labours.

And it helped. It calmed her mind, and she needed that right now. She thought of the time bomb in her backpack. The letter had been waiting for her at home, the ivory-coloured envelope sitting on the kitchen table. The post didn't arrive until ten, so Shona must've left the house sometime after that.

I'll call her later, Roz decided. *See how she's doing.* She'd be accused of fussing but so what? She was a mother, and she wasn't afraid to show her concern. It came with the territory.

Her thoughts went back to the letter in her bag. It must be connected in some way to Edward, but she didn't know what to make of it. She'd have to show it to someone, but who? Dominic had organised the retreat, so it probably ought to be him. *No*, she told herself. *Not him.*

Roz closed her eyes for a second, made her mind blank, pushed down the surge of revulsion rising from her stomach. *I am full of light. I feel. I exist. I am full of light.*

The mantra worked; it usually did. But not always. That would be too much to expect.

After a while, Roz hooked her helmet's straps over the handlebars and started walking, pushing the bike at her side. There was something relaxing in the tick-tick-tick of the rear hub as the rugged wheels rolled easily over the gravel. She'd stay on the marked path this time; she was in no mood to enjoy the exhilaration of scrambling along the clifftops, and besides, she'd be reluctant to leave her bike unattended even for a short while. There may have been no one in sight, but her trusty Trek hybrid was the most expensive of her personal possessions, and when it came to bikes, scooters and skateboards, the park seemed to be some kind of Bermuda Triangle.

It's a damned shame, she decided. *There's not enough trust in the world. It shouldn't be like this.* Unbidden, an image of Daniel Corrigan came to mind, and she forced herself to exhale slowly, releasing her pent-up tension. Who the hell did Dan think he was? He had no business accusing her of anything. He had absolutely no idea what she was going through; no concept of what she had to deal with every day.

"Sod him!" she whispered. And she smiled. She wasn't going to let an arrogant man ruin her precious time with her friends. Life was too short.

Roz turned away from the path and struck out across the park, still pushing her bike. She was starting to feel the cold now, but it wasn't far to the hotel, and she could get a cup of herbal tea and find a cosy corner to get warm and unwind. She might even get some work done.

Roz was almost at the hotel when the man walked toward her.

"Excuse me, love," he called out. "Could you help me out for a second?"

Roz knew she should keep walking, but her heart overruled her head. *Trust in others*, she told herself. *Be the change that you want to see in the world.*

She halted at a safe distance from the man. He was young, but he was too well dressed to be asking for money. Anyway, she felt sorry for him. His face had the pinched look of someone who'd been out in the cold for too long.

"Possibly," Roz said. "What's the problem?"

The man smiled and moved a little closer. "I've seen you coming and going over the last couple of days, and I'm sure I know your face from somewhere. Maybe I saw it in a magazine or something. I hope you don't mind me asking, but you're a writer, aren't you?"

"Author and illustrator. But I don't think you'll have seen me in a magazine, unless you're a fan of the *Times Educational Supplement*, that is."

The man laughed, showing a row of perfectly white teeth. "I'll have you know that I've had pieces published in both the *TES* and the *TLS*. I've even had a handful in the *Guardian*."

"Ah, I didn't realise you were a journalist. You should've said. Anyway, I'm sorry, but I can't help you."

Roz pressed her lips tight together and started walking, but the man fell in alongside her.

"Don't be like that. I'm not doing anyone any harm." He paused. "My name's Charlie, by the way. Charlie Heath."

"I'm not listening, Charlie," Roz said without looking at him. "Goodbye."

"Are you having an affair with Edward Hatcher?"

His question came so unexpectedly that Roz stopped and stared at him. "Are you… are you serious?"

Charlie held her gaze. "Deadly. I know he's been having a little fun since he's been here. Are you the lucky lady?"

"That's the stupidest thing I've ever heard. Edward is a

decent man – he doesn't behave like that. You need to get your mind out of the gutter."

"Is that so? And here's me trying to help you out. I can get you a decent payout if the story's strong enough, but this opportunity won't last forever. Hatcher has a week, maybe two, in the spotlight, then he'll be forgotten. If you come to me too late, I won't be able to get you a penny."

Roz turned her head away from Charlie, but she felt her cheeks tighten, her jaw clench.

"Ah," Charlie said. "In need of a little injection of capital, are we? You and me both, love. But luckily for you, it's not my money I'm throwing around. I know an editor with a bee in her bonnet about Edward Hatcher, and she's willing to pay to get a good story." Charlie's tongue flicked out to moisten his cracked lips. "But this isn't a hatchet job we're talking about. There's no grudge, no bad blood between them. She reckons Hatcher is the man of the moment. He's a symbol of the shift from the old world to the new. He's an old-school MI6 guy who writes stories for a living. He literally *is* the spy who came in from the cold. We just want to show his softer side, to make him seem human to the readers."

Roz halted. She looked Charlie in the eye. "I've given you my answer. Now leave me alone or I'll call the police."

"Look, if I laid it on a bit thick, I'm sorry." Charlie held up his hands. "To tell you the truth, I'm getting a bit desperate. I'm a freelancer, and I've already spent a lot of my own money chasing this story. If it comes to nothing, I'll be seriously out of pocket. And you know what that's like. We both know what it feels like when you get the rough end of the deal. I mean, we're both writers, aren't we Roz?"

"I didn't tell you my name."

"No, but I do my research. I didn't want to freak you out, but I know who you are." Charlie stepped closer, his hand going to his pocket.

"What are you doing?" Roz demanded, hating the hint of fear that crept into her voice.

"Take this." Charlie held out a business card. "My mobile is on there. When you change your mind, when you realise that you don't owe Edward Hatcher anything, and you remember that, in a fair world, he'd owe you a great deal, call me. I can make the arrangements, get you some cash very quickly. But it has to be soon, Ms Hammond. It has to be very soon."

Roz kept her eyes on the card: a simple rectangle of white cardboard. What harm could it do to take it? She wouldn't be betraying a friend. She wouldn't, couldn't, tell him anything about Edward. There was nothing to tell. But there was something else that might interest a newspaper. And it hadn't escaped her attention that Charlie had used female pronouns to refer to the editor. Roz took a breath, felt her chest muscles shaking with repressed emotion. And then the card was in her hand, her fingers snatching it from Charlie before she knew what she was doing. She turned and walked away, putting some distance between her and Charlie before she had time to change her mind.

I don't have to call him, she told herself. *I can throw his damned card away.* But she wouldn't do that. She needed the money. When you were a single parent with a teenage daughter, you *always* needed money. And with one thing and another, she was behind with the payments on her mortgage. Whatever she did to try and keep her head above water, she kept slipping below the surface. It took all her strength to keep going. She'd needed the writing retreat as a respite, as a time to get her new book together, and it was all going wrong, falling apart. She needed something to change.

Can I trust a journalist? she thought. But she had to pay for her cottage somehow. It wasn't just her home, it was her studio, her place of work. It was her world. If she lost that…

I don't have a choice, she decided. She'd have to talk to the reporter. And she'd have to let the world know the truth of the secret she'd been carrying for far too long. Whatever the consequences. It was time.

CHAPTER 16

Alone in his hotel room, Dan stood by the window, gazing out at the dark streets. A sea mist, tinged orange by the streetlights, clung to the shadows at street level, but above the shops and houses the sky was clear and the stars shone bright. It wasn't yet seven in the evening, but it looked freezing outside. He opened the window to get some air, but an ice-cold breeze blasted in, and he slammed the window shut.

Sod that, he thought. *I'm going nowhere.*

But he needed to get out of that room.

Alan had spent the afternoon working, and Dan had spent the last few hours running through his thoughts on Edward's disappearance, trying to sort the facts into a logical order. He'd made dozens of notes using Google Keep on his phone, tagging each item and hoping to see some kind of pattern emerge, but it hadn't worked.

Dan had tossed his phone onto the bed, but now he snatched it up and placed a call.

Alan answered almost immediately: "Hi, Dan. What's up?"

"Time to eat. I was thinking about staying here and trying the restaurant."

"I thought you didn't approve. You said the vegan options were dated and unimaginative. You said, if you had to eat one more veggie burger, you'd go mad."

"Hm. I've changed my mind."

There was a pause before Alan replied. "You want to see if you can collar Daphne and ask her a few questions."

"The thought had crossed my mind. But anyway, even if she's not here, I'm not keen on venturing out. It's freezing outside, and it's only going to get colder."

"Okay. I'm almost done for the day. I'll meet you in the restaurant. What time is it? I've lost track."

"Almost seven."

"Right. Let's say quarter past. And if you're there first, get me a pint."

"Fair enough. I dragged you down to a damp basement to look at a load of old junk today, so I reckon I owe you one. What do want, a pint of Tribute?"

"Whatever looks good," Alan said. "I trust you."

"I'm honoured. I must've graduated from the Hargreaves school of fine ale. Is there a certificate?"

"Not until you swear to relinquish lager in all its forms."

Dan sucked air over his teeth. "Even if it's artisanal?"

"Especially if it's artisanal, has the word *craft* on the label or comes in a flip-top bottle."

"I still have much to learn," Dan said. "I'll see you downstairs."

"Right. And by the way, I found something out. Listen to this."

Dan frowned. A quiet hiss came from his phone, then he detected the faint strains of orchestral music.

Alan came back on the line: "Did you get that?"

"Yes. Classical music. Which room is it coming from? I can't hear it from mine."

"It's Tim Kendall. He's in the next room, and I gather he's fond of German opera. Very fond."

"Don't tell me he joins in," Dan said.

"He sings both the male and the female parts, and he has a fair stab at the chorus too. Quite an accomplishment."

"And I thought you had a much better room than me." Dan chortled. "I wouldn't trade places for all the lager in the world."

"It's not so bad. He's in tune most of the time. And I'm oblivious to it while I'm working. In some ways, the background noise is quite motivational."

"I'll take your word for it," Dan said. "See you later."

He ended the call, then he headed for the bathroom. He only had a few minutes to get ready, but that was long enough to smarten himself up. As well as Daphne, he was hoping to bump into Roz, and he may as well try to make a good impression. When he'd last spoken to Roz, he'd been crass and insensitive, and Alan was right, he owed her an apology; he had to hope she'd hear him out.

He hadn't meant to upset her, but Roz had plainly taken his words to heart. He'd grasped that she was a highly intelligent woman and an independent spirit, but he'd totally misjudged her and made a fool of himself into the bargain. *I should've been more aware*, Dan told himself. *I can't believe I was so stupid.*

Dan washed and dried his face then decided it was time for a clean shirt. In the bedroom, he sorted through the meagre selection hanging in the wardrobe and selected his white Brooks Brothers cotton shirt. He changed quickly, and as he buttoned his cuffs, his mind went back to Roz. It was odd that he'd misread her so completely. That wasn't like him. It wasn't like him at all.

CHAPTER 17

S itting in the hotel's restaurant, Dan pushed a pint of beer across the table to Alan.

"It's Doom Bar," Dan said, then he sat back to await the verdict.

"Thanks." Alan examined his pint, holding it up to the light before taking a sip. But his expression gave nothing away.

"Well?"

"Good choice. I've had it before, but not for a while. It's like meeting an old friend."

"I'm having the same." Dan sampled his pint, enjoying the aromatic bitterness of the hops. "Weird name. I hope it's not an omen of the evening to come."

"It's named after a sandbar. A notorious place for wrecks, so I believe." Alan smacked his lips. "Mind you, it's a bit moreish, so the name could easily turn out to be prophetic in the morning."

A young man approached the table, a notebook in his hand and an expectant gleam in his eye. "Good evening. Are you ready to order?"

"Yes," Dan said. "I'd like the grilled fillet of sea bream, but could you make sure it's cooked without butter or cream?"

"Certainly, sir. If you have any allergies, please let me know and I'll check for you."

Dan smiled. "Thank you. It's dairy products that I need to avoid."

"No problem. Although thinking about it, the bream usually comes with creamed potatoes. Can I offer you a substitute?"

"Chips?" Dan asked hopefully. "Unless they're cooked in animal fat."

"Rapeseed oil," the waiter said. "Is that okay?"

"Perfect."

"And I'll have the cod and chips with minted peas," Alan said. "Nice and simple." He plucked Dan's menu from the table, then passed it, along with his own, to the waiter.

"Thank you, sir." The waiter gave them an appraising look then hurried away.

"I know people have allergies and that's no laughing matter," Alan began, "but I remember when you could walk into a restaurant and order what you wanted without all this fuss. A meal should be a relaxing thing, but it's been turned into a game of twenty questions."

"Times change," Dan said. "People like to know what's in their food and where it comes from. There's nothing wrong with that."

"There is if it makes everyone obsess over every mouthful. All that stress and anxiety, it can't be good for you."

"This, coming from a man who rejects lager on the grounds that it's untrustworthy."

"Touché," Alan said. "I'll give you that one."

They paused to enjoy a few mouthfuls of beer, then Dan turned to survey the room. "There's no sign of Daphne. Perhaps she's working in the kitchen."

"She's probably poisoning your dinner as we speak. You

might be getting too close to the truth. You'll have to be eliminated." Alan chortled. "You should see your face. Priceless."

Dan joined in the laughter. "So, how was your friendly neighbourhood opera singer? Still performing?"

"He was in fine voice when I came down. At least, he was trying. You'd have to give him full marks for effort."

"You should have a word with him," Dan said. "I'm sure he'd stop if you asked him. Tim came across as nice enough."

Alan shrugged. "Let him have his fun. He's not doing me any harm."

"I'm not sure I'd be so tolerant. You're a very patient man."

"It comes in handy now and then." Alan glanced across the room. "Oh, I didn't notice Brian sitting over there."

"He came in just before you. He said hello, but I think he wants to be alone."

Brian was occupying a small table near the wall. He sipped from a large glass of red wine without looking away from the book he was reading: an old hardback with gold lettering on a faded blue cover.

"He said there's a hard frost," Dan added. "The pavements are quite treacherous, apparently."

"I'm not surprised," Alan said. "I looked out when I closed the blinds, and the sky was crystal clear, but there was a halo around the moon. They say that means snow."

"That's an old wives' tale. Or should that be, old partners' tale?"

"It doesn't have the same ring to it. We'll have to call it a superstition and leave it at that."

They chatted for a while, but after quarter of an hour or so, they lapsed into companionable silence, sipping their drinks, each content to be alone with their thoughts.

This beer's going to my head, Dan decided. *I need to eat.* Checking the other tables, he tried to figure out which customers had ordered before them, and how many of them had already been served. But before he could come to a firm conclusion, the kitchen door swung open. Briefly, he hoped Daphne might emerge, but instead, their waiter made his way through the door, a heaped plate in each hand.

"I don't want to get your hopes up," Dan said, "but I can spy some chips. This might be for us."

"Excellent." Alan grinned, craning his neck to see. But the waiter halted in the middle of the restaurant, his brow furrowed and his gaze fixed on something across the room.

Dan turned in his seat. A lone man stood in the centre of the restaurant's main entrance. He wore a smart Berghaus coat, but his grey trousers were soaked from the ankle to the knee. The man ran his hand through his dark hair, restoring his neat side parting. Then, keeping his expression blank, he scanned the room. He was looking for someone, but not in the way that one friend might search for another. His stare was cold and hard; the look of a professional assessing the scene.

Dan lowered his voice and, catching Alan's eye, he said, "Police. I'd put money on it."

"I wouldn't bet against you," Alan whispered. "It must be something to do with Edward. I hope he's all right."

As if hearing them, the man's head snapped around, his gaze sliding from Alan to Dan. His expression didn't change, but he began walking toward them, his stride measured.

At the same time, the waiter overcame his surprise, hurrying forward to meet the new arrival. "Sir? Can I help you? Do you have a reservation?"

The man barely glanced at the waiter. "No. I'm Detective Sergeant Firth. Devon and Cornwall Police. I'm looking for anyone who knew a man called Dominic Rudge."

"Knew?" Dan said. "We know Dominic. Has something happened to him?"

DS Firth pulled a small wallet from his pocket and presented his warrant card. "I understand that Mr Rudge was here with some sort of writing group. Are either of you gentlemen in that group?"

"I am," Alan replied. "Is everything all right?"

"I need a word," Firth said. "If you wouldn't mind stepping into another room for a few minutes, that would be most helpful."

"I'd better come too." Dan stood, returning Firth's stare. "I may have some information that could be of use to your enquiry."

"No one said anything about an enquiry," Firth replied. "Your name, sir?"

"Daniel Corrigan. I was employed by Edward Hatcher, the man who disappeared."

"I'm aware of the report on a missing person, Mr Corrigan, but I'm here in relation to Mr Rudge."

"Even so, I might be able to help," Dan said.

"All right." Firth gestured toward the door. "Let's go through. There's a room we can use."

"But, what about these?" The waiter indicated the plates he was carrying.

"Could you keep them warm for us?" Alan asked. "We'll be back soon. I hope."

"I'll try, sir."

"Thank you." Alan looked longingly at the pile of golden chips on his plate, then he nodded to DS Firth. "Let's go."

Firth led them through the lobby to a wide doorway, and opening one of the double doors, he ushered them inside.

The room was probably used for private functions, but the tables and chairs had been stacked and pushed against the walls, revealing an expanse of brightly patterned carpet.

Firth plucked a couple of chairs from the nearest stack and arranged them next to each other, then he added a seat for himself. "Please, sit down. This shouldn't take too long."

Dan and Alan sat uncomfortably, their hands in their laps,

while Firth recorded their names, addresses and contact details in his pocketbook.

"Mr Hargreaves," Firth said, "how would you describe your relationship with Mr Rudge?"

"Reasonably friendly. I didn't know him well, but we got along. Dominic organises these writing retreats every year, and I usually attend. I'd describe him as a professional acquaintance."

"I only met him on Monday," Dan put in. "But my first impressions were that he was once married, but now he lives alone. Divorced rather than separated. He's short of money, but he's held back by his refusal to let go of the past."

Firth narrowed his eyes. "You said you only just met the other day. Did he tell you all this?"

"No, but it was obvious to me. You can tell a great deal by the clothes people wear, their choice of words, the way they deal with others. Dominic had success once. He carries around a laptop that, in its day, was top of its class. But it's due for the scrapheap. I'm surprised it still works. But that's not all he's clinging on to. He's still dining out on past glories, or trying to, but they don't bring him enough to live on. There's a small hole in the front of his jacket, and it looks like moth damage. He knows it's there — he keeps holding his hand in front of it, trying to cover it up — but he hasn't had it repaired or bought a new one. All his clothes are looking a little jaded."

"You're right about him being divorced," Alan said. "How did you know?"

Dan hesitated. "Have you seen the way he looks at women? There's something disturbing about it, something hungry and hateful at the same time."

"You might have something there." Alan chewed on his lower lip. "I saw him coming out of Lucille's room, and I knew something wasn't right. He gave me the creeps, but I couldn't put my finger on it. Thinking back, it was just as you say. That look in his eyes…"

Firth pursed his lips as he consulted his notebook. "Lucille. I don't have a guest by that name."

"Her surname is Blanchette," Alan said.

Firth frowned. "No. Could she have registered under another name?"

"It could be a pen name," Alan replied, "but I've always thought Lucille was her real name."

"Could you describe her, sir?"

"Twenties, petite, short hair, Afro-Caribbean."

Firth made a note. "Right. Let's get back to Mr Rudge. When did you last see him?"

"It was probably around eleven o'clock this morning," Alan replied. "He was coming from Lucille's room. Whatever her real name is, her room is on the same floor as mine."

"And I saw him a couple of hours before that," Dan said. "He'd called a meeting to let everyone know what was happening about Edward Hatcher. Which, as it turned out, was precious little because the police hadn't taken it seriously. Perhaps now that someone else is in some kind of trouble, there'll be a change in the official attitude."

Firth remained impassive, but Dan saw the way his nostrils flared.

"At this point," Firth began, "I should inform you that Mr Rudge was found a short while ago, and sadly, he is deceased."

Alan gasped, and Dan sat very still, staring at the policeman. "What happened?"

"We're doing our best to piece that together, but I can tell you that just before seven o'clock this evening, Mr Rudge was found on a beach nearby, and he'd sustained injuries consistent with a fall."

"Do you think he might've… done it deliberately?" Alan

asked, his voice faint. "Maybe, with Edward going missing, it put the idea into his head."

"That's unlikely," Firth said. "Mr Rudge's hands were tied behind his back. We're treating his death as suspicious, and I fully expect that this will become a murder enquiry."

"My God!" Alan murmured. "Someone pushed him off a cliff. That's... I don't know what to say."

Alan paled, and Dan said, "Are you all right? Do you want a glass of water?"

"Something stronger," Alan replied. "I've never fainted in my life, but I don't feel too good."

"You need to eat something." Dan turned to Firth. "Is there anything else or can we go?"

"You're free to leave. We'll be in touch, but if you think of anything that might help us to establish Mr Rudge's movements during the day, please contact me." Firth swapped his notebook for a business card and, when he offered the card, Dan took it.

"We'll talk again soon," Firth went on. "My colleagues are already speaking to the other guests, but we often need to follow things up, so we'll give you a call."

"Right," Alan said. "Can we leave the hotel? Can we go home if we want to?"

Firth considered this for a second. "The short answer is yes, but if you and Mr Rudge's associates could stay until, say, tomorrow evening, it might be more convenient for all concerned."

"That's no problem," Dan said.

"Good. Thank you. I'll let you get back to your dinner." Firth stood, and Dan and Alan followed suit.

But as Firth made to leave, Dan said, "What did they use?"

"Sorry, sir?"

"To tie Dominic's hands," Dan replied. "You didn't say, but what did they use?"

Firth narrowed his eyes. "Why do you ask?"

"Because it's significant. It's the weapon, isn't it. If Dominic had simply been pushed, he might've fought back or managed to save himself. But his hands were tied, and that's what makes this a deliberate murder. Planned. Cold blooded." Dan locked eyes with Firth. "The murderer had one choice to make: how to tie Dominic's hands. That decision is critical, and in the murderer's mind, that makes it significant."

"Ninety-nine times out of a hundred, you'd be wrong," Firth replied, a note of anger creeping into his voice. "Most murders are simple: brutal, but simple nevertheless. It's a crime committed by people who are vicious, mean and ignorant. They're too lazy to work for what they want, but when they see an opportunity, they take it, using whatever comes to hand. And generally, they're too stupid to notice they're on CCTV the whole time."

"But in this case, I'm right, aren't I?" Dan said.

Reluctantly, Firth nodded. "He was tied with some kind of ribbon."

"Like a decorative thing?" Alan asked.

"No. We think it came from an old-fashioned typewriter."

"The one from the basement," Dan blurted. "The ribbon was missing." He moved closer to Firth. "There's an old typewriter in a storeroom downstairs. Matthew, the receptionist, can show you. The ribbon was missing. That must be where it came from."

"We'll look into it. Did either of you touch this typewriter?"

"I don't think so," Dan said. "But…" he glanced at Alan.

"There were two, and I touched both of them," Alan admitted. "Sorry. I had no idea…"

Firth allowed himself a small sigh. "We'll need you to come over to HQ at Bodmin so we can take your fingerprints. That way, we can eliminate your prints and see what's left.

I'll need both of you. It's about a thirty-minute drive from here."

"Now?" Alan asked.

"No, sir." Firth's smile couldn't have been more patronising. "Contrary to what you've seen on TV, forensics is a slow business. They have to be extremely careful, and there's only so much they can do at any one time. Tomorrow will be fine. I'll set it up, then I'll give you a call and arrange an appointment. In the meantime, I'll track down this typewriter, and you can go back to your fish and chips." He gestured toward the door. "After you, gentlemen."

They trooped through the lobby where Matthew was waiting at the reception desk, his habitual smile replaced by a sickly grin. DS Firth marched toward him, but before he could say a word, Roz burst in through the outer door, her cheeks flushed and her eyes rimmed with red. In her long coat, her hair wild from the damp night air, she cut quite a figure, and they all stared at her in undisguised fascination.

Roz halted, her chin raised in defiance, but her gaze darting from one man to the next. "What? Why are you looking at me like that?"

"It's Dominic—" Alan began, but Roz cut him short.

"That *man*," she growled. "Don't even mention his name. Not to me. Not tonight."

"Why?" Dan asked.

"Because I'm sick and tired of Dominic bloody Rudge, that's why." Roz let out a burst of bitter laughter. "They'll all be talking about him tomorrow. But I won't have to put up with his smug bullshit any more. You'll see. It'll all come out now. I've taught him a lesson — one he'll never forget."

"Oh my God!" Alan said. "Roz, what have you done?"

"Never mind what I've done," Roz replied. "It's what *he's* done, that's the point. But he's finished now. History."

"Excuse me, madam." Firth stepped close to Roz, producing his warrant card. "I'm Detective Sergeant Firth,

Devon and Cornwall Police. I need to ask you a few questions."

Roz's triumphant expression slipped away. "Why?"

"It will be best if we talk in private," Firth said. "There's a room we can use. It's right here."

"No." Roz backed away. "I don't want to."

"I'm afraid you have no choice. I'd prefer to do this with your help, but if you make things difficult, I have reasonable grounds to make an arrest."

Roz's hand went to her chest. "What are you talking about? You can't arrest me."

"I can and I will." Firth sidestepped around her, heading for the space between Roz and the main door. "What's it to be? Are you prepared to help me out voluntarily, or do I need to use handcuffs?"

"Roz, listen to him," Alan said.

But she shook her head. "No. This isn't right."

"I see." In one stride, Firth was at Roz's side, taking hold of her upper arm.

Her reaction was instant. Roz's body went rigid, and she opened her mouth wide to let rip with a yell at the top of her voice: a roar of anger and defiance.

Alan started toward her, but Dan grabbed hold of his sleeve. "Leave her, Alan. Give her some space."

Roz tried to shake her arm free, but Firth held tight, his feet planted firmly on the floor and his expression implacable. "Have you finished?" he asked, and Roz stopped struggling.

Her shoulders slumped. "You don't understand," she muttered. "You just don't get it. None of you."

"Then why don't you explain it to me?" Firth said. "Let's start with your name."

"Roz Hammond."

"Thanks, Ms Hammond. Now, it's best for all concerned if we get you out of here. We'll take a short drive to the local station. It's quiet there and you'll be safe. Then, when you're ready, we can sit down and have a chat. Okay?"

Roz nodded, then she hung her head. "It's all going to come out anyway. We may as well get it over with."

"Can I come with her?" Alan asked.

"Not right now," Firth said. "Okay, Roz. My car's right outside, and I'll call my colleagues and have someone sit with you in the back to make sure you're all right." Still holding Roz's arm with one hand, Firth fished in his pocket with the other, producing a phone and thumbing the screen. "Anisha, I need you in the lobby right now. We're taking one Roz Hammond down to the station for questioning. Thanks." Pocketing his phone, he looked Roz in the eye. "DC Kulkarni is a female officer. I thought you might prefer that."

"Yes," Roz replied. "Thank you."

They waited in silence.

Roz kept her gaze on the floor. "Maybe I shouldn't have done it," she mumbled. "But he deserves it. He has it coming."

Dan frowned at the word *has*, but Roz was distraught, confused. And before Dan had a chance to ask Roz what she'd meant, a harassed-looking woman hurried down the stairs and marched across the lobby. Judging by the way she cast a stern eye over the odd little party, this was DC Kulkarni.

"All right, boss," she said. "Ready when you are."

"This is Roz," Firth replied as if introducing a casual acquaintance. "She's got lots to tell us, so we're going to pop down to the local nick for a chat." He paused, studying his colleague. "How far did you get? Anything interesting?"

"We covered most people," Kulkarni said. "Most of the rooms are empty, thankfully, so we're almost done. I've left Tom to finish up the last few. And, yes, I've had one very interesting conversation. I think you'll be pleased."

"What was the name?"

Kulkarni glanced at Dan and the others. "I'll fill you in later."

"The name isn't confidential, Anisha. They're all staying in the same hotel."

"Ms Turner," Kulkarni said. "She gave me lots of background on the victim."

Roz lifted her head, her features reanimated. "Who? Who's been talking about me? What have they been saying?"

"Don't worry about it," Firth said. "Let's go."

Kulkarni went to Roz's side, and they escorted Roz through the doors and out into the night.

"Bloody hell," Matthew breathed, his hand on his chest. "I don't know if I can take much more of this. I really don't." He stared at Dan and Alan. "She was always so nice. I can't believe she... she did for Mr Rudge."

"She didn't," Dan said. "I'm certain of it."

"I'm with you one hundred percent," Alan replied. "But you heard what she said. She more or less admitted it."

"No, she didn't," Dan said. "What she actually said... it didn't add up at all. Something's very wrong here, but unfortunately, Roz has dug herself into a hole. It's up to us to dig her out again."

"How?"

"Simple. We'll find the real murderer."

WEDNESDAY

CHAPTER 18

Alan woke early, but he had no desire to stay in bed. He got up and dressed, and as soon as the restaurant opened, he headed downstairs for breakfast.

He presented himself at the restaurant and was met at the door by a waiter, the young man looking a little pained, as though he was harbouring a headache. *Hangover*, Alan decided as the waiter squinted at the list of names on a clipboard.

"Hargreaves," Alan said. "Room 509."

"Thank you, sir." The waiter crossed through Alan's name with a highlighter pen, and Alan noticed that one other name had been marked: *Turner*. The name rang a bell, then he recalled that DC Kulkarni had referred to it the night before.

"Right, Mr Hargreaves, can I bring you some tea or coffee?"

"Tea, please."

"No problem. Please take a seat and I'll bring your tea and take your order in a moment."

"Thanks." Alan felt a thrill of anticipation as he stepped through the door; there was a chance he might meet the mysterious Ms Turner. But there was only one other customer present, and he knew her already.

Lucille Blanchette sat by a window, sipping from a large cup, but she replaced her cup on its saucer and offered Alan a warm smile.

"Good morning." Alan wandered over to the table next to hers. "Do you mind if I sit here?"

Lucille gestured to the chair opposite her own. "Please, join me if you like."

"Thank you." Alan sat at her table. He smoothed down his hair and glanced down at his shirt to check it wasn't too crumpled. He'd dressed hurriedly while half-asleep, whereas Lucille looked as though she'd just stepped from a beauty parlour. Dressed in a stylishly cut white cotton shirt, her hair was perfect, and her make-up was subtle and immaculate.

"I thought you might prefer to be alone," Alan went on.

"Not today," Lucille replied. "After everything that's happened, I'm glad of the company."

Alan nodded. "It's a terrible business."

"Yes. But sadly, I wonder if it wasn't inevitable."

Alan raised his eyebrows, a flurry of questions vying for attention in his sleep-deprived mind. But before he could speak, the waiter arrived bearing a bowl of porridge for Lucille and a pot of tea for Alan. Looking a little paler and faintly nauseous, the waiter scribbled while Alan ordered poached eggs on toast, then he left more swiftly than he'd arrived.

Alan poured a cup of tea and sipped even though it was still too hot. "You're here early."

"Up at five, on the dot, rain or shine. I like to start the day with meditation, then I write, I eat breakfast, I write some more. That's the shape of my mornings."

"I'm impressed. It's no wonder you're so prolific. You've got time-management down to a T."

Lucille tilted her head to one side. "It's not complex. I

divide the day into blocks, that's all. Around midday, I go for a walk or a workout, then I grab a light lunch. In the afternoons, I edit, then I eat a healthy dinner and relax before an early night. It started out as a routine, but now it's a ritual."

"Is that why you don't come along when we go out in the evenings?" Alan asked.

"It's one of the reasons." Lucille set about her porridge, stirring it thoroughly before scooping up a spoonful and tasting it. "Not bad. I asked for oat milk, but they'd run out, so they made it with soy."

"You should talk to my friend Dan, you'd get along famously."

"Oh? Is he lactose intolerant too?"

"No, at least, I don't think so. It's a matter of principle for him. He's almost a vegan."

Lucille wrinkled her nose. "Maybe we wouldn't get on so well. I'm having the full English breakfast after this. Bacon, black pudding, the works."

"Ah." Alan chuckled. "I must admit, I was tempted by the fry-up, but I'm cutting down on the fatty stuff." He patted his stomach, at the same time tightening his abdominal muscles and sitting a little straighter.

"You don't have to worry. You look like a man who keeps himself fit."

"Well, I walk a lot. Living in the country, it's easy to hike for a few miles. All I have to do is step out of the door. And I've recently started running. Dan got me into that." Alan gulped down a mouthful of tea. *Stop babbling*, he told himself. But as soon as he put down his cup, he found himself describing his cottage in Embervale, the valley in particular, and Dartmoor in general.

Lucille listened intently, watching him while she ate, taking in his every word. Alan had thought Lucille was a shy and retiring person, but this morning she seemed different. Her expression was open, her manner forthright, and when she focused her gaze on Alan, he couldn't help but feel flattered.

"It sounds lovely," Lucille said. "I don't know Devon at all, but I'd like to see it sometime."

"If you're ever in the area, pop in. You'd be welcome any time."

Lucille smiled. "Thank you. I might do that."

"You live in London, don't you?"

"Yes. Primrose Hill. But I get around quite a bit for book signings and school visits. I don't drive, but I can always hop on a train."

"They're quite slow when you want to go cross country," Alan said. "Devon isn't the best-connected place in the country."

"No problem. I've got an app, and I'm good at negotiating the railways. You can save a fortune if you plan carefully and buy your tickets in advance. On the way here, I came a day early, and I cut the standard fare in half. Plus, I shaved half an hour off the journey."

"Well done. Our nearest stations are Exeter and Newton Abbot, so if you're ever passing through, I'd be happy to meet you from the train, show you the sights."

"Does Newton Abbot have sights?"

Alan laughed. "Not many, admittedly, but Exeter might be more to your taste. The cathedral's worth a visit, and they have a Christmas market in the grounds. It'll be opening soon — the market, I mean."

"Hm. Not really my thing." Lucille arched an eyebrow. "Any decent pubs?"

"Plenty."

They shared a smile, and Alan relaxed. Lucille was certainly good company, and she'd taken his mind off the awful events of the evening before. There'd been something he'd intended to ask her about that, hadn't there? But what was it?

The waiter arrived with their breakfasts, and Alan cut into a perfectly poached egg, suddenly realising how hungry he was. The previous night, after Roz had been taken away, he and Dan had returned to the restaurant, but though they'd been provided with fresh meals, neither had felt much like eating. Now, he tucked in with an enthusiasm that Lucille seemed to find entertaining.

"You needed that," Lucille said.

"Very much so. Last night, Dan and I were just about to eat when DS Firth came along. And, well, you know what happened next."

"Yes. Poor Roz."

Alan hesitated. "Earlier, you said it was inevitable. What did you mean?"

"Ah, I wasn't talking about Roz. I meant Dominic. He…" She closed her lips tight, shook her head. "Never mind. I don't want to speak ill of the dead."

"Lucille, if there's something you know about Dominic, you should tell the police. It might help Roz."

"I've done that already. I talked to someone last night. DC Kulkarni. She seemed okay. She listened to what I had to say, and she took it seriously."

Alan stared at Lucille. "You're Ms Turner, aren't you?"

"Yes. Didn't you know?" Lucille grinned. "I often use my pen name; it's so much more impressive than my real one."

"Oh, I don't know. There's nothing wrong with Turner. It makes me think of J.M.W. Turner. It didn't do him any harm."

Lucille regarded him levelly. "He wasn't a writer, and his first name wasn't Paige."

Alan's mouth formed an O.

"Exactly," Lucille said. "You can imagine what fun my school years were. And putting my surname first doesn't help; it's still a dreadful pun."

Alan tried hard not to laugh, but he didn't quite get away with it. "I'm sorry, Lucille, or would you prefer me to call you Paige?"

"Lucille is fine. My mum and my brother call me Paige, but that's about it." She hesitated. "Except for that note."

"You had an anonymous note?"

Lucille nodded.

"What did it say?"

"Nothing much. It said, 'Turn the page, a fresh sheet is waiting for your story.' That was it."

"So whoever wrote it, they knew your real name," Alan said.

"Yes, but it's not a secret. It's just that, to most people, I'm Lucille, the studious writer. I still use my legal name for anything official, but that's okay. I like to keep everything compartmentalised." She paused. "Also, there are times when it's good to have an alternate identity to fall back on."

She fixed Alan with a look, and he had to ask: "Such as?"

Lucille pursed her lips. She studied Alan for a moment as if weighing him up, then she made a decision. "You asked me about Dominic Rudge. It's like this, Alan. Lucille laughed at his jokes, listened to his stories and pretended to be impressed with his award. But Paige... she thought he was a creep. And the last time I saw Rudge, he was getting very close to meeting Paige. Do you see what I'm saying?"

Alan nodded, the smiles and laughter they'd shared a moment ago instantly forgotten. "And that's what you told the police?"

Lucille nodded firmly. "You're damned right. I'd always known Rudge was an idiot. He fancied himself, and he seemed to think we all shared his high opinion. I mean, it's a joke, right? A middle-aged lump like him, hitting on a woman half his age." She shook her head. "It's a joke until it isn't."

"That's terrible." Alan clenched his jaw. "You shouldn't have to put up with that!"

Lucille laid her hands on the table, her fingers pointing toward Alan. "It's okay. You don't have to worry about me. I know how to take care of myself."

"He didn't...?"

"No way. He came up to my room, but I kept my distance. I know I shouldn't have let him in, but he said he had something important to tell me, something about Edward. So I said it was okay." She sucked air over her teeth. "As soon as I closed the door, he started spouting his crappy lines. I went along with it for a couple of minutes, then I showed him the door."

"I saw him leave," Alan admitted. "My room is just along the corridor. At the time, I thought you'd already gone home."

There was a pause before Lucille replied. "You look embarrassed, Alan. I suppose you must've heard me laughing and put two and two together."

"No. Not exactly. I did hear you laughing, but I knew something wasn't right. I didn't like the way Dominic talked about you, but in a way, it was good that I heard you. It let me know you were okay. Well, not okay, but... you know what I mean."

Lucille nodded sadly. "I had to get him out of my room, so I made a joke out of it and laughed along. I don't know if it was the right thing to do, but it worked. He lapped it up and went off like a lamb. Otherwise, he'd have seen a different side of me. Lucille might live in a big house on Primrose Hill, but Paige grew up in a council flat in Tower Hamlets, and she knows a thing or two."

"Even so, it makes me sick to think he was harassing you just a few metres away from me." Alan's fingers found the table's edge and gripped it tight. "If only I'd known, I'd have come to help."

"You know what? I believe you. You're a decent bloke, Alan. There's not many like you."

"I don't know about that." Alan took a long drink of tea, draining the cup, then he refilled it from the pot. "Do you think Dominic tried it on with Roz? If he did, it could look bad for her."

"I honestly don't know, but even if he did, Roz wouldn't lash out. She hasn't got it in her. She's such a gentle person and so kind."

"You sound as though you're friends," Alan said.

"We've only met a few times," Lucille said. "But we get on really well. She's been teaching me tai chi, or trying to, and I know she could never hurt anyone."

"I totally agree, but…"

"What?"

"I'm probably being stupid," Alan replied. "But I can't help wondering. What if she was pushed into it, tormented until she lost her temper? When I saw her last night, she was like a different person."

"I heard about it," Lucille said. "And what I said to the police… I hope it'll help her. They'll see what Rudge was really like."

Alan froze, his cup halfway to his lips. Roz had said something very similar about Dominic before she was taken away. DS Firth had taken her outburst as an admission of guilt, but what if her words could be interpreted another way?

Alan took a mouthful of tea and swallowed it down without tasting it. He needed to talk to Dan. But when the subject was as sensitive as this, he'd have to wait until he could explain in person. And that could wait until he'd finished breakfast with Lucille.

CHAPTER 19

After a fitful night, Dan was glad when the alarm on his phone sounded at seven. He silenced it, then promptly fell asleep, dreaming of the tide racing toward him. His legs heavy, he clambered onto an outcrop of rock, but the sea still surged over his shoes. Searching for an escape, he looked up to the cliffs towering above him. There was no path, no escape route. But there, standing on the very brink of the cliff, stood a dark figure. A man. Dan called up to the man, asking for help, but his voice was drowned out by the waves. And a moment later, the man stepped forward and fell, tumbling through the void, his piercing cry of despair carried by the wind.

Dan woke, gasping for air, his mouth dry and his head throbbing. He rubbed his eyes, but he could still hear the keening wail from his dream. "Bloody seagulls," he mumbled. "Don't they ever stop?"

He checked the time on his phone and saw that he'd missed a message from Alan: he wanted to talk as soon as possible. Dan sent a quick reply, arranging to meet Alan in the lobby in half an hour. *Make that an hour*, he thought, changing the text. Then he pressed send and flopped back against his pillows. He needed a moment to regain his equilibrium, then he needed a hot shower and some breakfast before he met with Alan.

Dan replaced his phone on the bedside table. Roz's book still lay beside his watch, and thinking of Roz, he plucked the book from the table and flicked through the pages.

The pictures were beautifully drawn, and the story was simple but engaging. Led by Freddie the fox, the cast of forest animals planned a picnic. On the way, they encountered a stream that they could only cross with the help of Olly the otter. After that, they became lost in the woods, but Pippa, a pied wagtail, flew ahead and found the right path. Freddie managed to get his feet stuck in a patch of deep mud, but Timothy the toad used his strong legs to pull him free. Nelly the newt showed them how to wriggle under a gate that barred their way, and finally they found the picnic spot they wanted.

Of course, Freddie had forgotten the picnic rug, but they all decided that they preferred to sit on the soft grass in the sunshine, and they had a wonderful time. Until, that is, a weasel appeared, emerging from his secluded castle on the hilltop. Named King Hurlnot, the cruel weasel owned the land they'd wandered onto, and he chased them off, wielding a fearsome stick that looked more like a club. Working together, Freddie and his friends escaped unhurt, and they decided to have their picnic closer to home. At this point, Freddie remembered where he'd put the picnic rug, and they had a great time after all. The next time they went on an adventure, they decided, they'd be more careful where they chose.

Dan put the book down. It was odd. There was something about the names of the characters that nagged at his mind. He flicked back through the pages. Freddie, Olly, Pippa, Nelly, Timothy. They all had friendly, sing-song names, and each was alliterative. But not King Hurlnot. The weasel's name ought to have begun with a *W*. But then, he was the villain of the piece, so perhaps it was deliberate that he didn't fit the rule.

But what about the others? Were they random, plucked from Roz's imagination? Dan didn't think so, though he wasn't sure why.

Nelly, he thought. *Why pick a name that's so strongly associated with an elephant?* There had to be a reason, but the only other reference that came to him was little Nell from *The Old Curiosity Shop*.

"That's it," Dan whispered. Olly was Oliver Twist, Pippa was Pip from *Great Expectations*, Timothy was tiny Tim from *A Christmas Carol*. But what about Freddie?

Grabbing his phone, he opened a browser and ran a quick search. Fred was Scrooge's nephew. That left only the weasel, but although Dan tried every variation of King Hurlnot that he could think of, he drew a blank.

There has to be some kind of logic to it, Dan told himself. *And I know who to ask.*

He made a call, and it only took a few seconds for Alan to answer.

"Change of plan?" Alan asked.

"No. I want to ask you something."

"Go ahead."

"The name King Hurlnot," Dan said. "Does it mean anything to you?"

A pause. "No. Should it?"

"Yes. It's a character from one of Roz's books."

"Ah. I must confess, I haven't read them all. There are quite a few. But why do you ask?"

"In the book Edward left in his room, all the characters come from Dickens. All except one. There's an evil weasel called King Hurlnot, and his name doesn't fit. I want to know why."

It sounded as though Alan was suppressing a yawn. "All

right, but I don't see the relevance."

"Edward made a point of bringing that book with him, and when he asked Roz to sign it, she said they had a heart-to-heart. Remember?"

"Yes. She said Edward understood her."

"Right. And now we have to understand Roz, figure out what makes her tick. The book could give us an insight."

"By the work one knows the workman," Alan said. "One of my favourite quotes. La Fontaine. A French poet."

Dan smiled. "I knew I'd called the right person. Listen, could you have a think about this name? You're better at solving crosswords than I am."

"Flatterer. Go on then. Spell it for me, and I'll see what I can do."

Dan spelled out the name, then he thanked Alan and promised not to be late. But before he could hang up, Alan said, "Are the other names really all from Dickens?"

"Yes. Too many to be a coincidence. Roz altered them all slightly. Little Nell becomes Nelly, Oliver Twist becomes Olly, Pip becomes Pippa, and so on."

"And Scrooge's nephew was called Fred," Alan said thoughtfully.

"I had to look that up. But you're the writer."

"I try." Alan sighed. "It's quite common for an author to play games with names and places. Some people like to plant obscure references in the text, like Easter eggs for eagle-eyed readers. But I wouldn't have had Roz down as that kind of person. She never struck me as someone who enjoyed playing games with words. And there's something else."

"What?"

"Well, it's funny you should mention Dickens, because there is a connection with Dominic."

"Did he see himself as a modern-day Dickens? I wouldn't put it past him."

"Yes and no," Alan replied. "He was pompous enough to

compare himself to the great man, but that's not the point. His surname is decidedly Dickensian. I always thought Dominic had chosen it as a pen name, after the novel, *Barnaby Rudge*. But no. He was born a Rudge. He used to say that was why he became a writer."

"Interesting. I wonder… Is it possible, do you think, that Roz based her characters on real people, people she knew?"

"It's more than possible," Alan said. "It's likely. All writers steal, and every good character is based on something taken from a real person."

"And what about the bad characters? The villains?"

"They're even more interesting. The villains are where a writer can take revenge."

Dan scratched at the stubble on his chin, a picture of Dominic Rudge as a weasel coming to mind. He blinked the image away. "We'll talk later, but wasn't there something you wanted to tell me?"

"It can wait," Alan said. "I'd rather not discuss it on the phone. We'll take a walk, somewhere where we won't be overheard."

"No problem. See you in a bit."

Dan hung up, then he headed for the bathroom. His mind was filled with a tangled web of possibilities, and if he was lucky, a hot shower would help him to tease the threads apart. And if he was very lucky, he might begin to see some connections. Because as things stood, he was completely stumped.

CHAPTER 20

D an wolfed down a bowl of cereals and fruit for breakfast, washing it down with a cup of strong coffee, then he made for the lobby where, as arranged, Alan was waiting for him, his coat already on.

"Are you ready?" Dan asked.

"Always."

Dan donned his coat, then they headed outside to talk, pacing along the coastal path, their hands in their coat pockets and their heads together.

"Did you come up with anything on the weasel?" Dan asked.

"Give me a chance," Alan protested. "I found a list of Dickensian characters online, but there are hundreds, and although Hurlnot sounds like a name Dickens might've conjured up, it wasn't on the list."

"Okay, let's put that to one side and go back to the human angle. How long have you known Roz?"

"About five years. We met at the Cheltenham Literary Festival. I was just getting started. I'd had my second book published, but I was still getting to know the ropes. I gave a little talk in a side room, but Roz was putting on a show in one of the main tents. I went along to see how it was done."

"When you say *a show*, you mean she was performing a reading?"

"More than that," Alan said. "She was in full costume, and she had a whole cast of supporting characters. It was amazing. The place was packed with young kids and their parents, and Roz raised the roof. In a different life, she could've been an actor. Her show was hilarious. Lots of slapstick and pratfalls."

"Which character did she play? Pippa?"

"No. Who else would she be but Freddie the forgetful fox? He's the main character. She put so much effort into her performance, she made her stories come alive. She had those kids in the palm of her hand. And it suited her too. With her red hair, she really looked the part. The transformation in her was magical."

"I see," Dan murmured. "That makes me wonder. Maybe I was wrong about Roz. People who can easily step outside of their personality can be dangerous, divorced from reality, unstable."

"What? You don't believe that. Being a good actor doesn't make you a sociopath. You're clutching at straws."

"Maybe, but I saw a different side to Roz when Firth grabbed her. I'm supposed to be good at reading people, but I didn't see that coming. Like you, I thought she was a gentle person."

"She is."

"Not last night," Dan said. "When she was talking about Rudge, there was a hard rage in her eyes. And after what Lucille told you about the man, we have to ask exactly what Rudge had done to upset Roz. If he'd pestered her, she might've snapped."

"No. Roz hasn't got a mean bone in her body."

"I wouldn't be so sure. Victims of harassment can carry

the scars for years, like fault lines buried deep in solid rock. The ground seems solid, and you'd never know the fault was there. But if the pressure builds and becomes too great, you get an earthquake."

Dan stopped to lean against the low fence, looking out to sea. Alan stood at his side.

They watched the waves in silence for a minute, then Dan said, "You know what it's like to be hauled in for questioning. How do you think Roz will stand up to it?"

"Don't remind me. It may have been six months ago, but I can still smell the stale air in that room." Alan shuddered. "Roz will find it even harder than I did. She was overwrought when they took her in, so she must be desperate by now. She can't stand being cooped up. She might say something, anything, to get out of there."

"At least she'll be able to give her side of the story," Dan said. "If Rudge harassed her in some way, she can explain that. Unfortunately, they could easily throw that back at her, claim she was provoked."

"Agreed. She could be getting herself even deeper into trouble."

"Then we need to work fast. What evidence do we have that Roz is innocent?"

"None," Alan said. "As far as we know, she was outside at the right time, she was angry at Rudge, and she could've found a way to get into the basement and take the typewriter ribbon. Plus, we have what she said about Rudge. We might *think* it was about something else, but our shots in the dark won't help her. We need to prove it."

"Right. But let's talk about what Roz actually said. She said that Rudge was going to get what he deserves. She didn't use the past tense, so unless she thinks he's going to be punished in the afterlife, she clearly didn't know he was dead."

"So what did she mean?" Alan asked. "She must've done something she regretted, because she said as much."

"Let's pursue that. Roz said that everyone would find out what Rudge was like. *Everyone.*" Dan thumped his fist against a fencepost. "It's obvious! She wanted to expose Rudge, and she couldn't have had it much easier. There was a journalist right outside the hotel, and he was getting desperate for a story. Any story."

"Yes! And if we can find him, he might be able to back Roz up. He might even be able to give her an alibi. But he wasn't there today, was he?"

Dan shook his head. "He's probably scurried off to file his story, but he'll be back, sniffing around. He wasn't expecting a murder. He must be straining at the leash."

"In the meantime, maybe we can track him down online. You said he's freelance, so his details should be easy to find."

"You could take charge of that," Dan said. "I need to be free to look into other lines of enquiry."

"What does that mean? We haven't got anything else to go on."

"I'll come up with something." Dan moved away from the fence. "I need to get moving, get the gears turning. Let's walk into town."

As they pounded the pavement, Dan quizzed Alan on each of the attendees at the retreat, trying to gather as much background information as possible. The writers were an oddball bunch, that was for sure, but there was nothing to suggest there was a murderer among them.

"Could it have been Edward, do you think?" Alan asked.

"It's possible," Dan replied. "He could have staged his own disappearance, even sending himself a note. From what you told me, he made quite a drama out of the note he supposedly received. He could've done that deliberately, making sure everyone knew he'd been threatened, planting an image of himself as a victim in our minds. That way, we'd be unlikely to think of him as the perpetrator. Having placed himself in the clear, all he had to do was lie low for a while. We know he has a background in intelligence, so that would have been no challenge for him."

"Yes. And it would've been easy for Edward to lure Rudge out of the hotel. After such a dramatic disappearance, all Edward had to do was get in touch somehow, and Rudge would've come running."

"It's certainly a compelling scenario," Dan said. "Unfortunately, we don't have a shred of evidence to support it, and unless we find Edward, we're unlikely to get it. Having gone to all that trouble, Edward wouldn't have left any obvious clues lying around."

"The police will have Rudge's phone records. If he was called just before his death, that trail could lead somewhere."

"There's no way we can get access to that kind of material. We'll have to come up with our own data."

"Easier said than done," Alan said.

"We've done it before. And don't forget, we have an advantage. We're here, on the ground, and we know everyone involved. People will talk to us more openly than they would to the police."

"It's certainly worth a try. Until Roz is released, we've got nothing better to do."

"Good." Dan rubbed his hands together. "I don't know about you, but my fingers are freezing. It's about time I wrapped them around a large mug of coffee."

"Good idea. And, as usual, I'm sure you already have a place in mind."

"You know me too well. There's a nice little cafe not far from here. It's tucked down a side street. If you didn't know it was there, you'd never find it."

"And is this wonderful cafe, by any chance, a vegan establishment?"

"It might be. I can't say I noticed." Dan grinned. "They

have triple chocolate brownies, carrot cake, banana nut muffins..."

"Consider me on board. Let's go."

It was a short walk to the Horizon Cafe, and as they approached, Dan was sure he could smell the aroma of freshly roasted coffee drifting along the narrow side street. They rushed to the door, eager to get out of the cold. But as Dan yanked the door open, he almost collided with the young woman hurrying to leave. She stepped back smartly, and the large guitar case she was carrying collided with a nearby table, rattling the crockery.

The young woman turned to the astonished customer. "Oh my God, I'm so sorry. I hope I didn't spill your drink or anything."

"No problem, my dear," the man said. "No harm done. No harm at all." He was seated with his back to the door, but Dan recognised Brian's voice instantly.

The young woman glared at Dan. "Excuse me. I need to get past."

"Of course." Dan stood aside, and Alan did the same.

"Sorry about that," Alan said. "Our fault entirely."

"No worries." She muttered something under her breath, then she stormed out through the door and was gone.

Looking around, Brian saw them and beckoned them over. "Come in, come in. Please, feel free to join me. There's just about enough room."

"Thanks," Alan said, shrugging out of his coat and taking a chair at the table. "The place is packed."

Dan slipped his coat off and squeezed himself onto the remaining chair, fitting his knees under the table with some difficulty. "The harder it is to get a table, the better the coffee shop. If you can get a seat at 11 o'clock on any given morning, it's a sure sign that the coffee is no good."

"Or it might be too expensive," Alan argued.

Dan shook his head. "If the coffee is good enough, people will pay."

Brian chuckled. "Is it always like this with you two? You're quite the double act. And you certainly know how to make an entrance." He hooked his thumb over his shoulder. "She was a feisty little thing, wasn't she?"

"She said something as she went by," Dan replied. "I'm sure it was meant as an insult, but I didn't quite catch it."

"She called us emmets," Alan said. "It's a Cornish word for ants, but it's often applied to tourists. In Devon, we say grockles, but it's much the same thing. Outsiders, strangers, pests."

"That's just rude." Dan frowned. "Actually, I've seen her before. On Monday, when I went for a walk."

"Dear me!" Brian said. "I thought you were supposed to be some sort of Holmesian figure, a man with extraordinary powers of observation."

"I've never said any such thing," Dan protested.

"Don't take offence," Brian replied. "I don't mean anything by it. It's funny, that's all. Your modern man doesn't like to stare, and maybe that makes me a middle-aged lech, but I know a pretty face when I see one. And that young lady was the waitress at the Thai restaurant. Sure, she had her hair done up, and she was made up to the nines, but it was her all right. She has very pretty eyes."

Dan struggled to his feet, extricating himself from his seat with some difficulty.

"What are you doing?" Alan asked.

"I'm going to see if I can catch up with her."

Alan started to rise, but Dan waved him back.

"I'll explain later." Dan raced outside, but the streets were almost empty, and there was no sign of the young woman. She could have gone into any one of a number of shops, but while it was one thing to catch up to someone in the street, it was quite another to pursue them into a building.

Defeated, Dan went back inside and sat down.

"I ordered you an Americano," Alan said. He didn't ask for an explanation, but his expression showed that he expected one.

"Do you remember the way she behaved in the restaurant?" Dan asked. "At the time, we didn't think much of it, but now, we have to wonder what horrified her so much that she had to run away. Did she recognise someone? Did she see someone do something? We have to know."

Brian shrugged. "Maybe she was having one of those days. A busy restaurant, she gets in a muddle, then she realises her mistake and dashes off to put it right."

"No," Dan said. "She was genuinely shocked. You could hear it in her voice. She apologised before she disappeared into the kitchen."

Alan nodded. "She was definitely upset about something. I suppose we might run into her again. She's obviously local. Where was she when you first saw her?"

"She was sitting on a bench by the coastal path. I'd stopped to look at the view—"

"Of the landscape or the pretty girl?" Brian chuckled, then he held up his hands. "Joke. Sorry. Carry on."

"She was sitting on a bench. She offered to move her guitar case so I could sit down. I told her not to worry about it, then she said she was leaving anyway." He paused. "She went into a bar. I wonder if she plays there."

"We could ask," Alan said. "They might not want to give out her details, but they'd probably pass a message on."

Brian sat back, his hands on the table, palms flat. "Sounds like a wild goose chase to me, but how you spend your time is your business. I'm just glad it puts me in the clear."

"How so?" Dan asked.

"Well, as you were coming in, you saw how the young lady spoke to me. She was perfectly nice, apologetic even. So if there's a bogeyman in our midst, it isn't me."

Dan watched Brian, taking in the laughter lines around his eyes, the indentations on his nose from the habitual wearing of glasses, the frayed edge of his shirt collar. On first meeting, Dan had thought the man had a temper, but now, he saw another side to Brian; if he was a rogue, he was a likeable one. There was a spark in Brian's eyes and a lightness in his gaze, as if he found the world to be a perpetual source of entertainment. And he was clearly an intelligent man. Was he clever enough to try and pull the wool over Dan's eyes?

A waiter arrived with their drinks, and while they all said thank you, Brian's grateful words were the warmest, the most heartfelt.

Dan sipped his coffee, then he leaned his elbows on the table. "Brian, what field is your doctorate in?"

Brian wiggled his eyebrows. "Aha! Am I about to be interrogated? Gawd bless you, Mr Holmes, I'm an honest man, I am. I never done nothing, and anyway, nobody saw me."

Alan had been taking a drink, and he struggled to suppress a snort of laughter. Wiping his mouth with the back of his hand, he said, "Come on, Dan. That was funny. Admit it."

"All right," Dan replied. "Maybe I take myself too seriously, but one man has disappeared, and another has been murdered. Meanwhile, one of our friends is being grilled by the police, and I fear for her state of mind."

Brian made a show of straightening his face. "Quite right. If you want to help Roz, then count me in. I'll help if I possibly can."

"Thank you," Dan said. "I'm sorry if I came across as a bit heavy handed, but I'm genuinely interested. What's your field of study?"

"Regrettably, I'm no longer active in the world of academia."

"I thought you lectured," Alan said. "I've heard you talk about it."

Brian sighed. "Oh, they wheel me in from time to time. In a world of dry talks and draughty lecture halls, I'm something of a minor celebrity: the boffin who became a well-known author. So I turn up and waffle on for an hour or so, reliving past glories. And they laugh politely at my old jokes, then they clap and make a fuss, but..." Brian smiled. "Time moves on, and I'm yesterday's news. I'm not doing any research, so I've got nothing new to publish in the journals. The young Turks fill the lecture halls because I'm a novelty, but half of them have never heard of me, and the other half are laughing up their sleeves. But it pays pretty well, and my publisher likes me to do it; so as long as the universities keep asking, I'll dust off my material and give it my best shot. The show must go on."

"I can imagine you'd be good at public speaking," Dan said. "It's a skill that not everyone has. But I can't help noticing that you didn't answer my question."

"Aha! Rumbled! I share my interest with that great criminal mastermind, Moriarty. Mathematics."

"That must be fascinating," Dan replied. "I've often wished I was better at it."

"It's a broad field," Brian said. "Most people don't understand that. They think of the maths lessons they sat through in school, but there's a lot more to it than that. There's not this one thing called mathematics that you can study for a while and then say, there, I've done that. It's more like a science. In many ways, it's *the* science, the fundamental study that underpins all the others. It's the framework by which we can investigate the universe."

Dan tilted his head to one side. "Interesting. I've never thought of it like that."

"You should write a non-fiction book," Alan suggested. "There's a big market for that kind of thing."

"I've kicked the idea around more times than I care to remember, but I want to move on. I prefer to spend my time dreaming up adventures." He looked Alan in the eye. "Would you go back to teaching?"

"No, not now," Alan said. "Once a teacher, always a teacher, but I'm a scribbler now, and that's that."

"Quite right." Brian turned his attention to Dan. "So, is my interrogation over? I must say, as grillings go, I feel I've got off rather lightly."

"I do have one question," Dan replied. "But I think you'll appreciate it, because it's a fundamental one."

"Intriguing. Go on then. Let's hear it."

"On the night Rudge was killed, you'd been outside for some considerable time. Why?"

Brian's smile remained fixed, but the spark of humour faded from his eyes. "What makes you so sure I was outside?"

"I saw you in the restaurant, and when you came in, you were still cold. You were pale, and your shoulders were hunched. When you passed, I remarked that it was a cold night, and you told me that the pavements were slippery. The word you used was *treacherous*."

"Yes. That's right." Brian took a drink from his coffee. Lowering his cup to the table, he stared at it for a while, and when he looked up, he seemed to have aged ten years, his cheeks sagging, his mouth downturned. "I'm supposed to have kicked the caffeine habit. The booze too. Fatty food, sugar, red meat: you name it, I'm supposed to have given it up."

"Oh dear," Alan said. "Are you unwell?"

Brian patted the left side of his chest. "Dodgy ticker. Aortic aneurysm. I'm scheduled for surgery in the new year. They gave me the date and told me I had to use the time to get myself back in shape. No stress. Strict diet. Plenty of fresh air and exercise." He paused. "That's one reason I was keen to come on this trip. I thought a few days by the sea would help. I even asked for a sea view, upgraded my room, but it hasn't exactly been restful so far, has it? If anything, I feel in worse shape than when I arrived."

"I'm sorry to hear that," Dan said. "Is that why you were outside? You wanted some exercise?"

"Sadly, no." Brian let his words hang in the air, then he took a breath. "I used to smoke, all right? Heavily. That's one of the reasons my heart is in such a bad way. But as soon as the doctors told me, I gave up, just like that. And I was doing so well. But this week..." He hung his head. "If my cardiologist knew about this, he'd probably kick me off the waiting list. But when Edward disappeared, and we all feared the worst, I couldn't hack it. I caved in. And that night, I needed to get out, to grab a pack of cigarettes and light up. It was the only way I could cope."

Dan sniffed. "I can't smell it on your clothes, and I can usually tell a smoker straight away."

"I only had a couple. Well, maybe it was more like five or six. I lost track. When I finished one, I lit another. Chain-smoking. The old habit came back. It was as if my fingers knew what they were doing. But after a while, I managed to get a grip. I threw the whole pack in the bin, lighter and all."

"Where did you walk?" Dan asked.

"I can't really tell you, not for sure. I was mooching through the streets, not really looking where I was going, thinking about Edward." Brian paused. "We were never friends, at least, not what you'd call close friends. But we've known each other a long time. And I know him well enough to be worried about him. Very worried."

"What do you think might have happened to him?" Alan asked.

Brian massaged his brow with his fingertips. "I really have no idea. No idea at all. I've turned it over in my mind time and time again, but I can't get anywhere. He had so much to live for, *has* so much to live for. The idea he might have harmed himself in some way… it doesn't make sense."

Dan fixed his gaze on Brian, then he said, "Do you think Edward could have killed Dominic Rudge?"

Brian stared at Dan, then he turned to Alan. "Is he serious? Does he expect me to dignify that ridiculous question with a reply?"

"It's something we've been considering," Alan said. "Edward could have staged his own disappearance, and then—"

Brian slammed his palm against the table. "Nonsense! I've never heard anything so stupid in my entire life. I don't know what you two think you're doing, but you have absolutely no idea what you're talking about. And as for you, Alan, all I can say is that I expected better from you."

Brian stood, the legs of his chair juddering across the floor.

"Please, calm down," Dan said. "In your condition—"

"Condition be damned!" Brian snapped. "I'll not sit here while you besmirch Edward's reputation. For all we know, the man may be suffering right now. He may even have been killed. And all you can do is wander around dreaming up crackpot theories! Well, I won't stand for it. Goodbye. I've got nothing more to say to you." With that, he marched to the door, his back straight. And a moment later, he was gone.

"Ah," Alan said. "That didn't go well."

"No. It didn't." Dan glanced at the coffee shop's clientele, most of whom were staring at him with frank amazement. Dan offered a reassuring smile, but the woman stalking toward them did not look as though she'd be so easily appeased.

She halted in front of their table. "I'm Nikki, and I'm the owner. Is there a problem, gentlemen?"

"Nothing serious," Dan replied. "A misunderstanding."

"Hm." Nikki pursed her lips. "A lot of our customers are regulars, and we try to keep a positive atmosphere. Restful.

We don't want any rowdy behaviour, thank you very much. So if you could finish your drinks quietly, it would be best all around."

"Of course," Alan said. "Sorry about all the fuss. And by the way, this really is excellent coffee. The best I've had in ages. We were just saying that, weren't we, Dan?"

"What? Er, yes. Definitely. Five stars. On TripAdvisor *and* Google."

"That would be appreciated," Nikki said. "Now, I understand that your friend didn't pay his bill before he left, so I presume you'll be settling it for him."

"Yes. No problem," Dan replied.

Nikki placed a slip of paper firmly on the table, and Dan scooped it up. "Oh." Dan tried to conjure a smile. "I'm sorry, but this can't be right. We've only had one drink each."

"You've had one coffee each, but your friend has been parked on this table for hours, drinking coffee and working his way through the cakes. It all adds up."

"So I see." Dan took out his wallet, poring over his credit cards and trying to remember which one had the lowest balance.

Alan plucked the bill from his fingers. "I'll get this."

"I'll fetch the card machine," Nikki said, then she headed for the counter.

"Blimey!" Alan muttered. "That's a hell of a lot of coffee. No wonder Brian was on a short fuse. And all those cakes. If he's telling the truth about his heart, the man must have a death wish."

"He's rattled about something," Dan said. "And the way he flew off the handle when I mentioned Edward…"

"You think it's a case of he doth protest too much?"

"Could be." Dan lifted his gaze to look past Alan. "Here comes Nikki. Best behaviour. And make sure you add a tip. I'd quite like to come here again, and as things stand, I think we might be barred."

Alan sighed. "The other day, I was thinking that it's been quite some time since we were thrown out of an establishment, but I should've known. It was far too good to last."

"Yes, but on the plus side, the places we're getting thrown out of are improving rapidly. If we keep this up, we could be getting kicked out of Michelin-starred restaurants before Christmas."

"Any more jokes, and you can pay the bill," Alan said. "Grab your coat. As soon as I've paid, we're leaving."

Outside, Dan and Alan loitered on the street.

"Where next?" Alan asked. "Back to the hotel?"

"No, I thought we could head along the coast, see if we can find that bar and track down the disappearing waitress."

"Fair enough," Alan said. "But somehow, I don't think she'll be pleased to see us."

"There's only one way to find out."

A few minutes later, they rejoined the coastal path, but they hadn't gone far when Dan's phone rang, and he stopped to answer it: "Dan Corrigan."

"Hello, Mr Corrigan. It's Detective Constable Kulkarni here, Devon and Cornwall police. We met last night at the Regent hotel."

"Yes. Would you like us to come over to have our fingerprints taken?"

"Thanks, but there's no need," Kulkarni replied. "It turns out that the typewriter at the hotel hasn't got anything to do with the case, so it's not necessary to take your fingerprints at the moment."

"Right. Thanks for letting me know." Dan hesitated, his mind racing. "I hope you don't mind me asking, but how do you know that the typewriter isn't important?"

"Mr Corrigan, I'm sure you appreciate that, in any serious investigation, we tend to keep a tight rein on the information we release."

"Yes, but I was the one who suggested that you look at the typewriter, so surely it would be okay to let me know why I was wrong." He lowered his voice, making his tone gentle. "Naturally, I've been distraught about what happened to Mr Rudge. So if there's anything you can tell me, it would really put my mind at rest."

"It's nothing that need concern you, Mr Corrigan. But if it helps, I can tell you that we checked the typewriters in the hotel basement, and they both took a standard ribbon. But that didn't match the one that was used to tie Mr Rudge's hands."

"Oh? What size ribbon was used?"

"Er…"

"I find the details help me to deal with my… anxiety. They give me something to focus on."

"Well, the ribbon used on Mr Rudge was three-quarters of an inch wide. Quite an unusual one by all accounts. Very old."

"I see. Thank you, that's very helpful. And what about Roz? Is she still with you?"

"After helping us with our enquiries, Ms Hammond wanted to go home. I drove her there myself last night. It was quite late by the time we got there, but she was in good spirits when I left her. Again, nothing for you to worry about, Mr Corrigan."

"Does that mean she's not a suspect?"

There was a pause before Kulkarni replied: "As I say, Ms Hammond is helping us with our enquiries. Those enquiries are ongoing, so that's all I can tell you at the moment. Thanks for trying to help, but if we need to talk to you again, we'll give you a call. In the meantime, if you remember anything that might prove useful, please get in touch. Goodbye."

The call was ended, and Dan pocketed his phone. "The ribbon didn't match the typewriter in the basement. The one used to tie Rudge was three-quarters of an inch wide. Much older, apparently."

"Okay. And how about Roz? What did they say?"

"She's at home. Officially, she's helping the police with their enquiries. More than that, they wouldn't say. But at least we know that she's not in custody. They took her home late last night."

"Thank goodness for that." Alan took out his phone, but he stared at it, forlorn.

"Are you going to call Roz?" Dan asked.

"I'm not sure. She might be resting, or she might not want to talk. And she might be angry, wanting to know why we didn't do more to help when they took her in. I won't know what to say."

"Send her a message. Let her know you're thinking of her and say that she can call whenever she wants."

"I could, but text messages always feel so impersonal." Alan looked to Dan. "Am I over-thinking it?"

"Understandably so," Dan said. "But believe me, Roz will be pleased to get a message from you. She'll be glad to know you're there for her." Dan smiled. "I speak from personal experience."

"All right." Alan looked a little happier as his fingers tapped across the screen, then, satisfied, he pocketed his phone.

"Well done," Dan said. "Now we can move on."

"Yes." Alan gave Dan a sideways look. "When you were on the phone just now, what was all that about you getting anxious? It's the first I've heard of it. Something you're not telling me?"

"Well, I had to spin her a line – otherwise she'd have given us nothing. But thanks to my little white lie, we have a valuable new clue. If we can find that typewriter, we can connect the notes with what happened to Rudge. And that will take us a great deal closer to catching the culprit."

"I'm game. But where shall we start? With the typewriter or the waitress?"

"The waitress. The bar isn't far from here, and maybe she plays there. She had her guitar case with her when she went in."

"We could certainly use a break," Alan said.

They started walking. Dan took deep breaths of the cold, salty air. And it did the trick.

"I've just remembered something," he said. "Her name was Florence. The waitress. Rudge started banging on about Firenze, remember?"

Alan nodded. "Well done. This is more like it. We've talked to Brian, and assuming we believe his story, we can eliminate him as a suspect. I can't see a man with a dodgy heart tackling Rudge on a clifftop, can you?"

"I'm not sure. It could be argued that Brian has nothing to lose. He's facing an uncertain future, so he plans on going out in style, overeating, smoking, drinking and settling old scores. And you saw the erratic way he behaved. One minute he's wallowing in self-pity, the next, he's furious. He's an intelligent man, capable of engineering a murder, but has he got it in him? Does he have the drive to carry off such a terrible crime?"

"I don't have him pegged as the criminal type, but I finally feel as though we're getting to the meat of the matter. Who has the guts to want Dominic dead, and why?" Alan rubbed his hands together. "We're just getting started, but before long we'll get somewhere. I'm sure of it."

CHAPTER 21

Despite the board standing outside the bar, claiming it was *Open All Day*, the Drowned Sailor looked very much as though it was closed for business. Permanently. But the sign also advertised live music, so Dan and Alan pushed their way in through the heavy front door and stepped into the gloomy interior.

The temperature inside the bar was not much higher than that outside, and it smelt damp: the aroma of wet laundry mingled with the scent of stale beer. The carpet stuck to the soles of Dan's shoes as he walked, and casting an eye over the room, his heart sank. This wasn't the kind of place where you'd find answers; problems, yes, but never their solutions. Not even in the bottom of the badly washed glasses.

At the back of the room, a door swung open and a man appeared, one hand massaging the knuckles of the other. In his fifties, he was built like a beer barrel: squat and markedly wider around the middle. His hair was cropped short, almost to the scalp, and his watery blue eyes were anything but friendly. He let the door swing shut behind him, then he stood his ground. "You're early, gents. We don't open for half an hour."

Dan fought the urge to turn around and walk out. He stepped closer to the man, glad to have Alan at his side. "We were just wondering about the live music. Is that a regular thing?"

The man shook his head. "No, mate. No music."

Dan gestured toward the door. "There's a sign outside…"

"Yeah, I never got around to changing it." The man sniffed. "We had a few bands in summer, but not now. And like I said, we're closed."

Dan hesitated. The man had rings on every finger of both hands, and a poorly drawn tattoo traced its irregular path down the side of his neck: a chain, perhaps, or a length of barbed wire. Dan had faced down plenty of alpha males in the past, but they'd all been dressed in bespoke suits and handmade shoes; this was different.

"Okay," Dan said. "We could come back later, but maybe you can help. We're looking for someone who can play the guitar, and we heard there was a young woman who might be available. Her name's Florence."

The man's expression did not alter. "Why?"

"We want to hire someone," Dan said. "It's for an event. A Christmas party. If we leave you a number, could you ask her to call us?"

"No."

"Thanks anyway," Alan said. He tapped Dan's arm. "Time to go."

But Dan stayed where he was. "She was here. I saw her the other day. She came in at around this time."

The man narrowed his eyes. "You what? Are you calling me a liar?"

"No," Dan said, keeping his voice level. "I'm just trying to get in touch with a young woman called Florence. It's all above board. I just thought she could use the work."

"Get out." The man didn't raise his voice, he didn't have to: his meaning was abundantly clear.

"We're going," Alan said. "Come on, Dan."

Alan made for the door and, reluctantly, Dan followed. Outside, Dan shook himself. "Ugh. What a dump. I dread to think what Florence was doing in there."

"Looking for work?" Alan suggested.

"Then why wouldn't he tell us anything?"

"Because he had no idea who we were, and in a place like that, suspicion is the default setting."

"I don't like it," Dan said. "We're wading into darker waters."

"I hope not. But maybe you're reading too much into it. There could be a simple explanation. Maybe he hired Florence to work behind the bar, but her wages aren't on the books. Or she might've popped in for a drink, or for any number of reasons."

"Hm. Wait here."

"Why? What are you going to do?"

"I won't be a sec." Opening the door as quietly as he could, Dan slipped back inside the bar. The barman had appeared very quickly last time, so perhaps there was CCTV or some other way for the man to monitor the door, but Dan was sure of one thing: he wouldn't have much time.

Striding across the carpet, Dan searched the walls. Yes. There was a noticeboard, its surface littered with scraps of paper, their edges curling in the damp air. Hurrying to examine it, Dan heard a door open across the room, but he didn't stop to look around.

"Oi! I told you. Bugger off!"

"One second." Dan scanned the scattered notices: handwritten offers of items for sale, homemade flyers advertising a range of services from cleaning to website design, a couple of business cards. And there, a postcard-sized photo of a girl with a guitar. Dan grabbed it from the board, plucking it from its drawing pins. But as he turned the card over, the barman appeared at his side.

"I warned you," he growled, snatching the card from Dan's hands.

"But, she's looking for work," Dan protested. "She's advertising, and I'm ready to pay. Where's the harm in me having her number?"

The man thrust his face close to Dan's. "Out. Now."

Dan swallowed. "I'll go. But if you see Florence—"

"She doesn't come in here."

"But she did," Dan insisted. "You've got the evidence in your hand."

"Once. She asked if she could put the card up, and I felt sorry for her, so I said all right. End of."

"It's important. I don't know if you've heard, but a man was killed here last night."

For the first time, the man's expression betrayed him, a muscle twitching in his cheek. "What do you mean *here?*"

"In Newquay. He was pushed off a cliff."

"And what's that got to do with you? You're not police."

"No, but a friend of ours is in trouble," Dan said. "She's innocent, but the police are giving her a hard time."

"And what's that got to do with this girl?"

"We think she might know something. All we want to do is ask her a couple of questions. I swear."

"Why didn't you say all this in the first place?"

"You didn't give me much of a chance."

"Yeah, well." The man took a breath, like a dog raising its snout to sample the air. "She plays in town. Busking. She's there most days."

"Thank you." Dan tried for a smile. "And why didn't *you* say *that* in the first place?"

"Because I don't like your face. Now, bugger off."

"Happy to." Dan turned and started walking.

"And don't come back," the man called after him.

"I'll try to resist the temptation," Dan replied, then he

barged out through the door and greeted Alan with a broad smile.

"Success?" Alan asked.

"Success. Let's head into town. Florence is a busker, apparently, so at this time of day, there's a good chance we'll find her at work."

"Good. And I shan't be sorry to see the back of the Drowned Sailor."

"Amen to that," Dan said, and he set off at a brisk pace.

DAN COCKED AN EAR. "Do you hear that?"

Alan furrowed his brow, but then he smiled. "Someone playing the guitar. It could be her."

"Capital, Watson," Dan said. "Follow that sound."

They strode along the pavement, and when they turned onto the main street, they spotted Florence at once.

Standing alone outside a branch of WH Smith, she was singing her heart out to a haunting melody, strumming her guitar with a fierce passion, her eyes almost closed.

She can certainly sing, Dan thought. *So much emotion.* Florence had the kind of voice that carried, cutting through the background noise. Her words echoed from the shop fronts to reverberate through the wintry air, and the strolling shoppers slowed their pace, watching her as they passed. But Dan saw no one stop to throw money into the guitar case that lay open on the ground beside her. Instead, people veered away from her as if frightened of straying too near.

Perhaps the mournful song wasn't to their taste. But more likely, they kept their distance for another reason.

An aura of intense melancholy emanated from the young woman. It wasn't just the way her voice cracked as she poured her heart and soul into the song. It was in her posture, the way she stood, her chin held high, defying the world. And it was in the way she gripped her guitar, hugging it to her body and channelling all her energy into every chord, her pink fingers poking out through the tips of her fingerless gloves.

But although no one stopped to listen or to offer a handful of change, she didn't care. She wasn't playing for them; she was playing for herself.

It's as if she isn't here, Dan decided as they drew nearer. *She sings to escape. But where does she go?*

They halted in front of her, but Florence didn't notice until she reached the end of the song.

She eyed them warily, and Alan stepped forward, producing his wallet. "That was excellent," he said, slipping a five pound note under the few coins in her guitar case. "Wonderful." Alan stepped back, keeping a respectful distance.

"Thanks." Florence glanced at Alan's contribution. "Thanks very much. Very kind."

"I didn't recognise the song," Dan said.

"You wouldn't. I wrote it myself." She held Dan's gaze as if expecting a challenge, ready to defend herself.

Flattery and warm words would be no use here, so Dan got straight to the point. "We bumped into one another at the coffee shop earlier. Sorry about that."

"*You* ran into *me*, you mean." Florence shrugged. "It doesn't matter. Forget about it." She looked Dan up and down, her eyes lingering enviously on his warm coat. "Are you going to throw some money in as well, or is your friend the generous one?"

"He can afford to throw money around," Dan said. "I can't."

She snorted. "Yeah, right."

"I'm serious," Dan insisted. "Okay, I'm not broke, but I'm looking for work, trying to get by. Just like you." He paused. "Maybe I should ask around at a few restaurants.

They're always looking for waiters, aren't they. I could try that Thai place. The Temple Garden. I hear they're short staffed."

A flash of alarm lit her hazel eyes, but Florence kept a straight face. "I've had enough of this pitch. I'll try somewhere else." She pulled the guitar's strap over her head, then scooped the money from the guitar case before laying the guitar in its place. There was a label beside the guitar case's handle. A single word: *Flo*.

"Do you go by Flo or Florence?" Dan asked.

She looked up sharply. "I didn't tell you my name."

"No, but there's a label on your guitar case."

"All right, I'm Flo. You got me. I can't stand that other name. No one calls me that."

"Except for your employer," Dan said.

"Ex-employer. Stuck-up cow."

"Is that why you left the restaurant?" Dan asked. "A disagreement with your boss?"

Flo didn't reply.

"We saw you there, at the Temple Garden, but only for a few seconds. You took one look at our table, then you disappeared. Why was that? Why did you run away?"

"Had to go. Got to go now." Flo sorted through her scant takings, stuffing them into a small fabric bag she wore across her body.

"How much would you normally earn, busking for an hour?" Dan asked.

Flo didn't look up. She fastened her guitar case, struggling with a catch that refused to stay closed. "Bloody thing!" she muttered. "It's knackered."

"It was a serious question," Dan went on. "We just wanted to ask you a couple of questions. And maybe, if we gave you, say, twenty pounds, you could pack up for an hour, go somewhere warm, buy something to eat."

The catch finally snapped shut and Flo stood, guitar case

in hand. "Back off. I know what kind of *questions* blokes like you want to ask. And I'm not interested."

"You misunderstand," Dan said. "I only want to know why you ran out of the restaurant the other night."

"Cos I felt like it." Flo started walking.

"Who did you recognise?" Dan called after her. "It could be important. A man has been killed. Murdered. Dominic Rudge."

Flo froze in her tracks, then slowly, she turned to face them. "What?"

"Do you recognise the name?" Dan asked.

For a moment, Flo didn't react, but then she nodded.

"I'm sorry if this comes as a shock," Alan said gently. "But Mr Rudge is dead." He sent Dan a disapproving glance. "We shouldn't have sprung it on you like that. It was unforgivable. I'm sorry."

"Nothing to be sorry about." Flo took a faltering step toward them. "Are you taking the piss? Because if you are…"

"It happened last night," Dan said. "It'll be on the news today."

Flo shook her head in disbelief. "The Grudge. Dead. Bloody hell."

"His name was Rudge," Dan said. "He was there, at the Temple Garden. Are we talking about the same person? Is that who you recognised?"

"It's what we called him. The Grudge. It was kind of a joke. To get through it. But now he's gone." Flo let out a long breath. "Thank Christ for that. What happened?"

"He was found on the beach," Dan said. "He'd fallen from a cliff. The police are treating it as murder. They'll probably want to talk to you."

"Not me. I'm not talking to anybody."

Flo started to turn away, but Alan said, "Please wait. Just a second."

"Why? What do you want?"

"One of our friends is in trouble," Alan replied. "She's been questioned by the police. We're sure she had nothing to do with the murder, so we're trying to help her. If you have any information—"

"I don't. The first I knew about this was when you told me."

Dan opened his mouth to speak, but Alan laid his hand on his arm. "If Flo wants to talk to us, she can find us in her own good time." Alan rummaged in his pocket. "Flo. Is it okay if I call you Flo? I've got some cards in here somewhere." He took out a plastic case and removed a business card, offering it to her without closing the distance between them. "Please, take it. It has my mobile number, and if you want to talk, you can call me. But it will be just between us. We won't tell the police about you, not if you don't want us to."

Flo pursed her lips. Then, just as Dan was sure she'd walk away, she stepped forward and took Alan's card. "It says you're a writer."

"Yes. Children's books."

Her eyes darted to Dan. "And what about him?"

"He's out of work, as he said," Alan replied. "And I'm sorry if we've upset you. It wasn't our intention. It's been a difficult time."

"Isn't it always?" Flo tapped Alan's card against her fingers. "I'm not promising anything. I might call. I might not."

"Or you can find us at the Regent Hotel," Dan said. "My name's Dan Corrigan."

"Like that's going to happen." Her eyes rolled skyward. "Not dodgy at all."

"If you could call us, you'd be helping an innocent woman," Alan said. "Please, think about it." He smiled. "And I meant what I said about your music. It was great. I'd buy a CD, that's for sure."

Flo laughed, but it was a weary sound, born of hardship.

"Nobody buys CDs anymore. Streaming, that's the way to go. Or vinyl."

"Vinyl never went out of style," Alan said. "You can't beat it."

"Too right." Flo smiled at Alan. "You're all right. Shame about your friend."

"He's a philistine," Alan said. "But what can you do?"

"I don't know. Hopeless case." And this time, there was genuine warmth in her laughter.

She cast a disparaging glance at Dan, then she walked away, her slim frame bent by the weight of her guitar case, but her stride purposeful and determined. It was her against the world, and she wasn't about to go down without a fight.

"Do you think she'll call?" Dan asked.

"No, I don't think she will. But if she does, I'm afraid it won't be easy to deal with."

"What do you mean?"

"I mean that, whatever she has to tell us, it's not going to be good."

Alan stared down at the pavement, and Dan knew better than to ask what was going through his mind.

Already, Flo had vanished from view. That seemed to be the way of it with her: a fleeting existence, barely connected to the world. It was an odd contradiction, but for someone who went out of their way to perform in public, Flo seemed very keen to disappear.

I wonder why? Dan asked himself. But he didn't want to think about the answer to that question. He didn't want to think about it at all.

CHAPTER 22

A fter their encounter with Flo, Dan and Alan barely spoke as they trudged through the town. Then Dan said, "I've been thinking."

"Oh," Alan replied, his voice heavy with indifference.

But Dan soldiered on. "About typewriters. The thing is, the ribbon used on Rudge could've come from anywhere. The killer could have brought it with him, so the typewriter might be miles away."

"Hm." Alan drew a deep breath, rousing himself. "You've got a point. And now that I think about it, the ribbon might not have been taken from a machine at all. You can buy replacement ribbons easily enough."

"But this was a rare size. Three-quarters of an inch. That would make it harder to buy, wouldn't it?"

Alan shrugged. "You can get almost anything online. Still, it might give us an opening. I feel a burst of research coming on, but I should finish one job before I start another, and you wanted me to track down that journalist."

"He can wait. I want you to get stuck into the hunt for the typewriter, while I go back to the notes. They could be the clue to the murderer."

Alan frowned. "But they were to do with Edward, weren't they?"

"I wouldn't be so sure. Rudge had his hands tied with typewriter ribbon, and the notes were typewritten. That fact has been staring us in the face. It's a direct link between the notes and the murder. But there's more. You received your note after everyone else. What did it say?"

"From one explorer to another, and that Edward had nothing to fear. But I don't see what you're getting at."

"Two things. We've already established that the notes were written recently; that's the only way their author could've referred to Edward's disappearance. But there's a second implication. It's not quite so obvious, but it's much more significant." Dan paused. "The notes definitely had a target, but it wasn't Edward."

"But the only threatening note was sent to Edward."

"Was it?"

"Yes. It was pushed under his door."

"But the note didn't have his name on it," Dan said. "Think about it. Everyone received a note because someone wanted to deliver a threat, and they wanted to cover their tracks while they were doing it."

"I see. You think the culprit wanted to cause confusion and divert attention from what was really going on."

"That's right. But only one note mattered, and it was received by Edward."

"You've lost me," Alan admitted. "I thought you just said—"

"The threat was *received* by Edward, but it wasn't *intended* for him."

"My God! It was delivered to the wrong room."

"That's my theory," Dan said.

Alan clutched his arm. "No. It's a fact. You weren't there, but when Edward got that note, he stormed off. I was worried, so I asked Dominic for Edward's room number, and he gave me the number for Brian's room by mistake."

"Edward was in the Regency suite," Dan said.

"I know, but Dominic had it wrong on his spreadsheet. He said Edward had changed his room just before we arrived."

"What I wouldn't give for a peek at that spreadsheet."

"I can get it right now," Alan said. "Dominic sent it by email a few days before the retreat. Everyone had a copy." Alan stopped to take out his phone. "Give me a second."

Dan peered over his shoulder. "Yes, that's it. Tap the file to download it."

"I know how to do it. I'm not a total dinosaur, you know."

"Sorry. Can you open it yet? Why is it taking so long?"

"Rotten signal." Alan held up his phone and turned around on the spot, frowning. "That's better. Here we go." Lowering his phone, he slid his fingers across the screen to zoom in.

"Who booked the Regency suite originally?" Dan asked.

"Dominic. That figures. He would've given himself the best room, but if Edward made a fuss, Dominic would've bowed to his demands."

"It all fits," Dan said. "The murderer had Dominic in his sights, but first, he wanted to make him squirm. So he sent a threatening note, not realising that Dominic and Edward had swapped rooms."

"It's not that simple," Alan replied. "Brian said he'd changed rooms too. So he probably received the wrong note as well."

"I can't recall what each note said, can you?"

Alan thought for a moment. "Brian's note was something about receiving the acclaim of his peers."

"Suitably vague. That could be for anyone, but it fits Edward, especially since he has a film deal in the pipeline."

"Dominic's note was a reference to Hamlet," Alan said.

"When sorrows come, they come not single spies. And there was something about new horizons."

"Again, that's not specific to one person, but I can see how it could've been written for Brian. He's been down on his luck recently, hasn't he?"

"And he's working on something new," Alan replied. "That could be his new horizon."

"Right." Dan ran his hand through his hair. "I'd like to get all the notes together and look at them properly. I could look for patterns, draw a diagram to map out all the possible combinations."

"Back to the hotel?" Alan asked. "You could look into the notes while I do some research, then we could regroup for lunch and plan our next steps."

Dan sent him an appraising look. "You've got the bit between your teeth."

"This is nothing," Alan replied. "You should see me when I'm belting out a final chapter. Sparks fly."

"I'm sure they do," Dan said. "Okay, let's go back to the hotel. It's time to harness all that restless energy."

CHAPTER 23

S itting at the desk in his hotel room, Alan took a break to
stand up and stretch his back. He closed his eyes,
massaging his temples with his fingertips, and visions of
typewriter ribbons pranced through his imagination.

There were nylon ribbons, cotton ribbons, ribbons that
came attached to spools, and those that had to be wound on
by hand. Some had metal eyelets designed to trigger the auto-
reverse ribbon feed, and some did not. It was possible to buy
ribbon in a range of colours. As well as the regular monotone
or red and black, you could buy pink, green, brown, orange,
and even purple. *Why purple?* Alan wondered. *Why on earth
would anyone want to write in purple?*

He'd also learned that, over time, there'd been at least
twenty-six different types of typewriter spool for sale. Almost
all had been designed for the standard half-inch ribbon,
although maddeningly, many suppliers didn't quote the
ribbon widths on their website; they simply gave a list of
compatible makes and models of typewriter, and that meant
more searches, more checks, more work.

Alan went to the bathroom to splash some cold water on
his face, and as he towelled his cheeks, he began to feel

fresher. "Focus," he told his reflection in the bathroom mirror. Truth be told, he'd been much less efficient than usual. He'd long hankered after a vintage typewriter, and too many of his searches had resulted in prolonged trawls through online stores. *No more eBay*, he told himself. *No more getting sidetracked.*

Retaking his place at the desk, he began again, concentrating only on three-quarter-inch ribbon. Soon, he'd narrowed his research down to one typewriter manufacturer: the German company Adler. The company was now defunct, but it had created a few machines that took the wider ribbons, particularly a popular machine branded as the Wellington in the USA and the Empire Number One in Canada. These typewriters were antique rather than vintage. Used models were rare, and if they were in full working order, sold for significant sums. The machine, if he could find one, would be easy to recognise. But could they assume that the ribbon used to tie Rudge came from the typewriter used for the notes? It felt like a stretch.

Alan grabbed his phone, thinking to call Dan with a progress report, but he saw he'd missed a message from Roz: *Thnx. We'll talk later. Not today. Take care xx.*

How like Roz to tell *him* to take care, when she was the one under pressure. He had to try harder to help her. He had to do something, use his initiative. He couldn't always be hanging on to Dan's coat-tails.

And he could start by finding Charlie Heath. Dan had given him the journalist's name, and as Alan had predicted, it wasn't hard to find the man online. Charlie had profiles on LinkedIn and Facebook, and it was a short hop from there to his official website. Alan skimmed through the portfolio section, quietly impressed by the range and quality of the man's credits. Charlie Heath was no mere celeb-hunter; he was a serious investigative reporter with a handful of awards to his name.

The site offered a phone number, and Alan added Charlie to his contacts before placing a call. He half expected to hear only an automated reply, but the phone was answered straight away.

"Charlie's phone," a woman intoned. "He's out on a job, but I can take a message."

Her voice was dull with weary resignation, and Alan smiled to lighten his tone before he spoke: "Hello, I wonder if you can help me. I'd like to speak to Charlie directly. Are you his receptionist?"

A snort. "You'd think so, the way he carries on. But no, I'm his wife. And before you ask, I haven't spoken to him for days, but like I said, I can take a message."

"Ah, it would help if you could give me his number. It's really quite important."

"Sorry, but he doesn't like me to—" She broke off, and Alan heard children's voices in the background. Her voice grew faint as if she was holding the phone away from her mouth "Sh! Mummy's on the phone, darling, all right? You've got... yes I know. I know. Josie, let him have a go with the glitter. It *is* fair, darling. It's for both of you. You've got to *share*."

Alan grinned, and when the woman came back on the line, he said, "Let me guess. They're making Christmas cards."

The woman laughed. "How did you know?"

"I used to be a primary school teacher. I know what it's like. The build-up to Christmas starts earlier every year, doesn't it?"

"Tell me about it." The woman sighed. "It sounds awful, but I'll be glad when my two are old enough for school. They need something to keep them busy."

"The pre-school years are wonderful but exhausting," Alan said. "It sounds as though you've got your hands full."

"Yeah, they're good as gold really, but, you know..." The

woman left her sentence unfinished, but she sounded much happier now.

She's been cooped up with her kids for too long, Alan decided. Pouring as much charm into his voice as he could, he said, "I'm sure you're doing a wonderful job. And it must be hard, with your husband away."

"It's not so bad. But listen, it's been nice talking to you, er…"

"Alan. Alan Hargreaves. I'm calling from Newquay."

"Right, well… Newquay?"

"Yes. I've seen Charlie around, and I thought we could meet up, but I don't have his number with me."

"Oh, I see." The woman hesitated. "I suppose, since you know Charlie, I could give you his number."

"It would save you the bother of taking a message."

"That's true. All right then. Here you go, Mr Hargreaves." She reeled off the number and Alan scribbled it down.

"Thank you, Mrs Heath. You're very kind. And good luck with the Christmas cards. Cover the tables with plenty of old newspapers, that's my advice."

"Too late. The place looks like an explosion in Santa's grotto." She chuckled under her breath. "You know, the house is full of old papers, but will Charlie let me have them for the kids? Will he hell. Research material, he calls it. Background."

"I'd have thought it was all digital these days."

"That's what I keep telling him. But he doesn't listen. You wouldn't think it to look at him, but he's old school is my Charlie. A newspaperman. Give him a chance and he'd march around in a trench coat and a trilby."

"I might tell him you said that."

"Don't you dare!" Her laugh was louder this time, almost husky. "But I know you won't say anything. You sound a lot nicer than most of Charlie's mates, I can tell you."

"I'll take that as a compliment," Alan said. "Thanks again. Bye now."

He ended the call, taking a moment to get his thoughts in order, then he tapped Charlie's direct number into his phone and pressed the green icon to connect.

He didn't have to wait long for his call to be answered: "Yeah? Who's this?"

"Mr Heath, my name is Alan Hargreaves. I'm calling from the Regent Hotel."

"Oh." A pause. "Hargreaves. Ex-teacher, author of the Uncle Derek books. Listen, if you're calling about Rudge, you've got to be quick. I'm on a deadline."

"Actually, I wanted to ask you about Roz Hammond."

"What about her?"

"Roz is a friend. She was pulled in for questioning by the police, but we think she had nothing to do with Dominic's death. If she was coming to see you—"

"She'd be in the clear," Charlie interrupted. "But I can't help her or you. Sorry, mate. Now, about Rudge. How long have you known him?"

"No, I won't answer your questions unless you answer mine. On the night Rudge was killed, did Roz come to see you, yes or no?"

"All right, she came to see me. But it won't do you much good. We didn't talk for long, so she had plenty of time to slip off and do the deed."

"What did you talk about?"

"Uh-uh. Your turn," Charlie said. "How long have you known Dominic Rudge? Did you work together?"

"I first met Rudge about five years ago when I came on one of these retreats. But no, we've never worked together. Why do you ask?"

"You were both teachers. Thought you might have worked at the same school, that's all."

A sharp chill crept up Alan's spine. "I didn't know he was a teacher. He never mentioned anything about it."

"Interesting," Charlie said, his voice distant, as though he was concentrating on something else.

"Where did he teach?" Alan asked.

"Lots of places. Private schools mainly. And a stint abroad, working for a charity. *Cambodia.*" Charlie emphasised the last word, imbuing it with a dark significance.

"Are you…" Alan began. "Are you suggesting some kind of impropriety?"

"I don't know. Am I? You tell me."

"For the record, Rudge and I were not close friends," Alan said firmly. "My only connection with him was through these annual meetings, and if there was anything suspicious in his past, I certainly wasn't aware of it. Until you told me just now, I didn't even know he'd been a teacher. As I said before, he never mentioned it."

"So, the victim led a double life, keeping his past hidden. Thanks for that. It's always good to get a bit of corroboration, so I'll do you a favour. Yes, I met with Roz. She dragged me out to Fistral Beach. I was instructed to wait by the statue. You know, the one with the dolphins. The whole thing would've been very cloak-and-dagger if she hadn't turned up on her pushbike. That kind of spoiled the moment."

"Go on. What did she say?"

"She offered me a story. It was about Rudge but, at the time, I wasn't interested."

"Why not?" Alan asked.

"She was trying to do a hatchet job on him, spilling the beans. But that's not what I do, and anyway, it wouldn't stand up. She wasn't a credible source. Quite frankly, after her high jinks with Hatcher, I couldn't use any of the stuff she gave me. Any decent editor would just laugh in my face."

Alan furrowed his brow. "Are you referring to the disagreement between Roz and Edward's publisher? I don't see what that's got to do with it."

Charlie's laughter was hollow and without humour.

"Wake up, mate! This isn't some spat over a couple of scribbles. Roz and Hatcher were having an affair, sneaking into hotel rooms then creeping out at the crack of dawn, leaving lacy knickers in the bed. One whiff of that, and the tabloids would've been all over it. And my in-depth piece on Hatcher would've been spiked. I can't afford to take that chance. I've got a mortgage to pay, and a wife and kids to feed."

"I know," Alan said. "I spoke to your wife earlier. She was charming. She was making Christmas cards with the children."

There was a pause before Charlie replied. "You don't have kids, do you, Alan?"

"No."

"Thought not. Well, if you ever get around to it, you'll know what I'm talking about. When it comes to motivation, there's nothing like having a couple of hungry mouths to feed."

"I'm sure that's true," Alan said. "But nevertheless, I'd be amazed if Roz and Edward were engaged in any kind of relationship. And even if they were, I still don't see the connection between that and Dominic Rudge."

"Has anyone ever told you you're naïve, Alan?"

"Frequently. But I don't see it as a criticism. You may go through life seeing the worst in people, but I prefer not to."

"Hm. Not bad. Uplifting. I might be able to work that into my piece."

"You'll do no such thing," Alan said. "Your story isn't about me. And you still haven't answered my question."

"It's simple. Roz had a history with Dominic Rudge. A fling, we might call it. They were photographed together at various literary functions, and she was on his arm at a couple of award ceremonies. Quite the couple. The darlings of the literati."

"I didn't know that."

"But it's true," Charlie said. "And it paints Roz in an unfavourable light. You see, to the great British public, she's traded up, spurning Rudge, the literary prize-winner, so she can slide between the sheets with Hatcher: a man who's much older and a great deal wealthier. Hatcher is worth an absolute mint, and I should know. But his money makes Roz look like a calculating gold-digger, and that, my friend, means she's lost all credibility."

"That's ridiculous," Alan protested.

"It's a double standard, but so what? Have you read a newspaper recently? They're many things, but fair isn't one of them."

"Even so," Alan began, but Charlie didn't let him finish.

"Listen, according to Roz, Dominic was a bully, a nasty piece of work, but that doesn't mean she can use the press to sling mud at her ex. I wasn't interested in her story, so I fobbed her off, told her I'd think about it. Mind you, the situation has changed."

"Does that mean you're going to use Roz's story after all?"

"Yes and no," Charlie said. "I'm not interested in what she was up to with Hatcher, but unfortunately for Roz, she's still in the frame for shoving her old boyfriend off a cliff. The cops might've let her go, but officially she's still helping the police with their enquiries, and we both know what that means. Plus, she had a motive. The worm that turned."

"Oh, come on. You were with her that night. You admitted it. Would she have met up with a journalist and talked about Rudge, then turned around and killed him?"

"Hm. To be honest, I don't much like it. When she came out to meet me, she was spitting feathers, know what I mean? Furious. But, after she'd poured it all out, she went flat. She'd been keeping it all under wraps, and once she got it off her chest, the fight went out of her. By the time she left, she was tearful, shaky, all over the place. She could barely pedal her pushbike, never mind tackle a bloke Rudge's size."

"Have you talked to the police yet?"

"Yeah. I've told them the same story," Charlie said. "Not that it'll do much good for Ms Hammond. I couldn't tell them where she went after we talked. I told her to go and have a stiff drink, but by then she wasn't listening to a word I said. She could've gone anywhere."

"And what are you going to report? Are you going to make her look guilty, even though you know it's not true?"

Charlie sighed. "Listen, I'm not here to sensationalise things for the sake of it, Mr Hargreaves. I'm a serious journalist. I report the facts, but others won't be so generous. Rightly or wrongly, Roz is going to be in for a rough time in the press. People like to think there's no smoke without fire, but they also have short memories. As soon as someone else gets charged with the murder, Roz will be forgotten."

Alan stared at the wall. He wanted to argue with the man, tell him he was wrong, accuse him of being a cynic. But he couldn't. Instead, he said, "I'd better go."

"Yeah. But maybe we can help each other out. If you hear anything about the case, give me a heads-up, and I'll make sure you get the chance to put your side of the story."

"And if you find anything, will you share it with me?"

"Not bloody likely, mate. I've got a job to do."

"Goodbye, Charlie." Alan ended the call, and thought, *What do I do now?* He'd have to meet Dan soon, and he wasn't looking forward to their conversation. Rudge had a murky past, and the motive behind his murder was becoming clearer. But Alan didn't know if he had the courage to carry on asking questions. He felt like a man who'd pulled on a loose thread, only to find he was unravelling the carpet beneath his feet. He already had a handful of thread, but if he continued to pull, the carpet would eventually be destroyed. The only alternative was to cut the thread and walk away.

It was up to him to choose.

CHAPTER 24

F lo Walker strode along the clifftop path. She'd left her guitar at the flat, and she felt lighter without it; free to stand straight and swing her arms. And she didn't feel the cold. Not today.

She lost track of time, thought only of the rhythm of her footsteps on the path, the breath in her lungs. And soon, she was at the place.

It hadn't been hard to find; they'd shown it on TV. And the crime scene tape was a dead giveaway. It fluttered in the breeze, like a prop from a cop show. She'd never liked those crime stories, never seen the appeal. But now, a thrill ran through her. This was exciting. This was real.

As she walked up to the yellow tape, a policeman in a high-vis jacket strode toward her, a clipboard in his hand. "Can I help you with something?" he asked.

"Just curious," Flo said. "Is this where it happened?"

The policeman fixed her with a stern look. "If you have something to tell us, then we'll talk. If you witnessed the incident that took place here last night, we'll be glad to hear about it."

"No. I was in the pub last night." Flo offered a smile, but the policeman wasn't impressed.

"Listen, if you don't have a reason to be here, please keep walking. Otherwise, I'll need to take your name and address."

"Why?"

"Because that's our procedure. What's it to be?"

"Been a lot of people coming to look, has there?"

"Too many." The policeman raised his clipboard, his pen poised. "Right, miss. Your name, please."

Flo reeled off her details. Really, she ought to have told him to get lost, but she was in too good a mood to make a fuss.

The policeman waved her on, and Flo sauntered away. When she'd put a reasonable distance between herself and the cop, she stopped to admire the view out to sea. Leaning on the fence, she craned her neck to peer down to the water. The waves were small today, and she could hear them lapping against the cliff face below, but whether the tide was coming in or going out, she couldn't tell.

It doesn't matter, she thought. Either way, it was a long way down.

She pictured Rudge falling. Had he screamed in the moments before he'd hit the ground, or had he been paralysed by fear, his throat tightening until no breath would pass, never mind a shout or a scream or a sob? She knew what that was like.

On the TV, they'd said that his hands had been tied. *Helpless*, she thought. *Good*.

She stayed for a couple of minutes, letting her mind empty. Then she straightened and felt in her coat pocket for the journal. It was only a cheap notebook: a gift from a friend. But when you're eleven years old and away from home for the first time, you value each kindness, each friendly gesture, each gift.

The journal was held closed with a thick rubber band, and

that was fine, because she didn't need to open it. Many of the pages were blank, but not all. And for those she'd filled in, she could recall almost every word she'd written. She knew precisely what those clumsy sentences said, and what they didn't say, *couldn't* say.

She waited for the wind to drop, then she hurled the little book with all her might. It spun through the air, then it tumbled. A second later, she thought she heard a splash, but maybe that was her imagination. She'd always had a vivid imagination; everyone had always been keen to inform of her of that fact. It had been used to explain her nightmares, her fear of the dark, her anxiety about pretty much every damned thing. And those fears had defined her, held her down.

"Not anymore," she whispered to the wind. Those days had gone. She'd given her fears to the sea, and good riddance.

Flo took one last look at the sea, then she turned away and headed back to town, walking quickly. She didn't even glance at the policeman as she passed, and as the sound of the waves faded away behind her, a melody came into her mind. It was new. She'd learned to recognise these moments, and she let the tune play all the way through in her mind. *Not too shabby*, she thought. Now all she needed was some words. And they would come to her. It was time for a new song.

CHAPTER 25

D an knocked on the hotel room door, then he stepped back, waiting. He'd asked Alan to forward the spreadsheet of allotted room numbers, and mistakes notwithstanding, he'd tracked down and called on almost all the remaining attendees. Only Albert Fernworthy remained, and from the sounds of frenetic typing coming from within, he was hard at work.

Dan held his breath. Was that typewriter keys he could hear? He prepared to knock again, but the door swung open, and Albert thrust his face into the gap. "Yes?"

"I was hoping you could help me out with something," Dan began, but he was distracted by the clatter of keys still emanating from the room. He tried to peer past Albert's shoulder, but with little success. "I'm sorry to disturb you, but do you have a typewriter? Are you working with someone?"

"No. I'm here alone, but I am working, so unless there's something important, I'd like to get back to it."

"It is important. It's about Dominic Rudge." Dan gestured toward the door. "But I can hear someone typing."

"All right, if that's what's bothering you, I'll fix it." Albert tutted. "Honestly, it's not that loud. I don't know what people are complaining about. It's not my fault the damned walls are so thin." He turned away from the door, leaving it open. "You'd better come in."

Cautiously, Dan stepped inside. The room was similar to his own: sparse but functional. But in Albert's room, the bed was entirely covered with sheets of paper, magazines and at least half a dozen paperback books.

"Hey Google," Albert said. "Stop."

Dan spotted a Google Home Mini sitting on the desk beside a laptop. The smart speaker's lights pulsed, and abruptly the sound of typing stopped.

"Ambient sound," Albert explained. "It helps me work. Some people like rain or the buzz of a coffee shop, but I like the sound of typing. It seems right somehow." He smiled ruefully. "I'm sorry about the noise. I tried wearing headphones, but it wasn't the same. I need the sound to fill the room. The problem is, I've got so used to it, I can hardly do a damned thing without it. Writers, eh? We're a weird bunch."

"Certainly idiosyncratic." Dan glanced at the plethora of material on the bed. "I suppose, writing science fiction, you must need to do a lot of research."

Albert chuckled. "Yes, but probably not in the way you're imagining. When it comes to the science stuff, the Internet is my friend. But as for the meat of my story…" He crossed to the bed, plucking a thick paperback from the pillow. "That's where this kind of thing comes in handy."

He offered the book, and Dan took it. "*War and Peace*?"

"Part one," Albert corrected him. "The first instalment of the greatest novel ever written. What Tolstoy doesn't know about story isn't worth knowing." He picked up a much slimmer volume. "And this little beauty, *One Day in the Life of Ivan Denisovich*, it blows my mind. I read it once a year."

"Interesting. I wouldn't have had you down as a scholar of Russian literature."

"So, just because I write sci-fi, I'm a know-nothing lowlife who spends all his time watching reruns of Star Trek TOS, and moaning about the way Firefly got cancelled."

"No, not at all," Dan said, but he couldn't stop the colour rising to his cheeks. Albert had read his mind perfectly, and they both knew it. To cover his embarrassment, Dan said, "TOS? Terms of service?"

"The original series." Albert grinned. "To be fair, I do spend a fair amount of my leisure time enjoying the continuing journey of the starship Enterprise, but that's just for fun. When it comes to my work, I fall back on my first love, the classics. When you're planning a series that plays out over a dozen books, and you're building whole worlds, each with their own cultures, languages, technologies and traditions, you need to think on an epic scale. Not for nothing is it called space opera. Fortunately, I have a first-class honours degree in English literature, and that's always stood me in good stead."

"Now that really is interesting," Dan said. "I came to ask if I could see the note that was left in your room, but maybe you can shed some light on another little problem. We'll get to that in a minute, but do you still have that note?"

Albert regarded him from beneath lowered brows. "Sure, I still have the note. It's around here somewhere. Why do you want it?"

"I think it's connected to Rudge's murder. I'm almost certain of it. There's a good chance it was written by whoever killed him."

"Seriously? Then why haven't the police come looking for it?"

"They probably will, but they haven't got there yet. They're still stuck on the idea that Roz was involved. But I'm sure she's innocent, so I'm doing my best to figure out what really happened."

MICHAEL CAMPLING

"I see. So, in this scenario, you're playing Hercule Poirot. What does that make me, a suspect?"

Dan looked him in the eye. "Potentially, yes."

"I'm not sure how to take that. Should I be hurt or flattered?"

"I leave that to you. But if we look at that note, it might help you decide."

Albert smiled. He had an easy-going, lopsided smile, and Dan found himself warming to the man. "The other day, at the meeting, you said that you'd left the note in your bag," Dan went on. "You said it mentioned boldly venturing to new realms."

"So I did. Well remembered." Albert strode over to the desk and bent down to search beneath it. "You obviously have a keen ear for dialogue and a first-rate memory. I can see I'll have to be careful with you around."

Dan tensed. Albert's last remark struck him as odd; if the man had nothing to hide, then why would he need to be careful? Roz had said something similar when they'd first met. Was that a coincidence?

"Where the hell is it?" Albert muttered, his voice growing sharp with irritation. "I can never find a damned thing when I want it."

Dan tried for a casual tone. "There's no rush."

"Give me a minute," Albert said, but he was making heavy weather of the search. He'd dragged a small holdall from beneath the desk, and it sounded as though he was vigorously rifling through its contents with both hands, but he was hunched over the bag in such a way that his body shielded it from view.

Dan took half a step back toward the door. "I could come back later. It's no trouble."

"No, goddammit! I just need… one second."

"Seriously, don't worry about it," Dan said, but Albert straightened suddenly, wheeling around to face him, his hand held aloft, something long and thin protruding from his clenched fist.

Dan almost flinched, but the only thing in Albert's hand was a tightly rolled sheet of paper.

"Got it!" Albert offered the sheet of paper as though presenting a scroll. "I rolled it up so that it wouldn't get creased. It's not every day I get valedictory messages thrust beneath my door." His brow furrowed as he noticed Dan's expression. "Sorry to make a fuss. It's that damned bag. It's supposed to keep me organised, but it has so many pockets it drives me wild."

"Right." Dan took the proffered paper, unrolling it carefully. The sheet of paper was identical to the others and bore the Conqueror watermark. The typewritten text, too, appeared to be identical in layout to the other notes.

Be bold in your attempts to conquer new realms. If one is forever cautious, can one remain a human being?

"The last line is a quote from Solzhenitsyn," Albert said. "Whoever sent it, they obviously knew I'd appreciate it."

"Some of the notes are more personal than others," Dan mused. "But they've been cleverly written."

"How so?"

"There's an element of wordplay. It's as if the writer is teasing us, giving little hints. Most of the notes seem to be giving praise, but they can be interpreted in different ways. And that's why we didn't realise that some of you received the wrong notes."

"Oh. I didn't know that had happened." Albert went to Dan's side, squinting as he peered at the page. "Well, that note was certainly meant for me. I don't know anyone else here who would've spotted the Solzhenitsyn reference." He smiled. "Now that you've seen the note, what was the other problem you wanted help with?"

That's a very swift change in subject, Dan thought. But Albert appeared to be relaxed. If he was hiding something, he was doing an excellent job of it.

"Presumably you're well versed in the work of Charles Dickens," Dan said.

Albert gave a half shrug. "I'm not an expert, but I know his work better than most. *A Tale of Two Cities* is one of my all-time favourites. Genius."

"Did you know that Roz used the names of a lot of Dickensian characters in her books?"

"No, but it doesn't surprise me. I don't do it myself, but we all have our own little ways of finding names for characters. Some writers like to pick a theme and stick to it, others trawl through lists on the Internet. I believe Philip Pullman used a phone directory from Hungary or some such to find the names of his witches."

"I also think that Roz based some of her characters on real people. People she knew well."

Albert raised his eyebrows, but he didn't comment.

"What would you say," Dan went on, "if I said the name, King Hurlnot?"

"I'd say that I have absolutely no idea what you're talking about."

"It doesn't ring a bell? Nothing from Dickens?"

Albert shook his head. "How are you spelling that?"

Dan spelled the name out, but Albert's blank expression didn't alter.

"Can I have that back?" Albert gestured to the note, and Dan couldn't think of a reason to object, so he handed it over. Albert cast his eye over the note once, then he tossed it back into his bag. "I'll hold on to it for a while, in case it's needed for evidence or anything, but after that, it's going straight into the nearest bin. If it turns out to be connected with Dominic's death, then I certainly don't want the damned thing."

Before Dan could say a word, Albert snatched up a pen from the desk and began writing on a scrap of paper. "King

Hurlnot," he muttered. "I was going to say leave it with me. But now that I see it in front of me, it looks like an anagram."

Dan silently cursed himself for not thinking of that possibility himself. But none of the other names in Roz's book were anagrams; they'd hardly been changed at all.

Albert's deep frown suddenly morphed into a broad grin. "Got it! It's obvious really. Well, it would be to anyone who knew their Dickens."

"Who is it?"

"I've a good mind to tell you to work it out for yourself. I could give you the title of the novel, maybe, and then we could see how long it takes you to figure it out. That might be fun. You strike me as the kind of man who enjoys a challenge."

"Not in this case," Dan replied. "I'd much rather have the answer, if it's all the same to you."

"Such impatience." Albert chortled. "The name is Tulkinghorn. And he's from *Bleak House*, by the way."

"I don't know it. Who, or what, is Tulkinghorn?"

Albert sucked air from between pursed lips. "A nasty piece of work. Cruel. Manipulative. Misogynistic. One of the vilest villains of all time. Ebenezer Scrooge, or your namesake, Daniel Quilp, might be better known, but to some extent, they're cartoonish characters, larger than life. Tulkinghorn was the real deal. The Devil incarnate. Today, we'd call him a sociopath, and he'd strike fear into our quivering liberal hearts."

"What exactly did he do?"

"He was a legal type, a solicitor, but he liked to gain control of his clients. Dickens never really explained why, and somehow that makes Tulkinghorn seem even worse."

"And you said that he was a misogynist," Dan prompted.

Albert nodded firmly. "That's part of the picture. One of his clients, Sir Leicester Dedlock, had a wife, and she had a secret past. She had a child out of wedlock, and Tulkinghorn found out about it. It gave him a hold over her, and he tried to use it to control her."

"He was a blackmailer."

"Worse. It wasn't about the money for him. He simply wanted to torment the lady, to persecute her and make her life a misery, just because he could."

"My God." Dan's shoulders slumped as if a great weight had been lowered onto his back.

"Are you all right?" Albert asked. "You've gone white as a sheet."

"I've got to go. Thanks for all your help, but I really have to go. Things to do."

"Okay, but listen, take it easy. You don't look well."

Dan nodded, then he made for the door. Albert called something after him, but he didn't catch it.

In the corridor, Dan headed for his room, his mind spinning.

Roz was a passionate person who launched herself into life and into her work with reckless abandon. He'd seen her throw caution to the wind when she'd marched along the crumbling cliff edge, tempting fate, defying the elements. And he'd witnessed her uncontrolled outburst when DS Firth cornered her in the hotel.

At first meeting, Roz came across as a calm and well-adjusted person. But Dan had known there was something going on beneath the surface, something out of kilter.

Now, he was certain that she'd been treated badly by someone, and it had left her struggling with an inner conflict.

Had Roz used her work as an escape valve, an outlet for her anxiety? She'd told him that no one saw the world quite so keenly as an artist. She'd also said that, as an artist, she sought to understand her subject matter. But she hadn't been talking about woodland animals. The characters she'd created were very human, very relatable. Had she poured her personal experience into her work, portraying herself as the hapless Fox?

Dan could scarcely believe it, but the logic was inescapable. Her hidden allusion to an infamous villain had to be significant; it could not have occurred by accident.

Had Rudge been her tormentor, her Tulkinghorn? If so, how would she have reacted if he'd pushed her too far?

Dan reached his own door, but he marched past it. He stopped outside Alan's room and hammered on the door. He needed to talk to the one person who'd listen and understand.

Alan opened the door and ushered him inside. But before Dan could speak, Alan held up his hand.

"We need to talk," Alan said. "It's about Roz."

CHAPTER 26

Dan listened carefully as Alan recounted his conversation with Charlie Heath and in return he explained his theory based on Roz's book.

"It all fits," Dan said. "I think Rudge had some kind of hold over Roz, and he used it to bully her, to manipulate her."

"From what we're finding out about Rudge, that sounds plausible," Alan replied. "Poor Roz. She didn't stand a chance against a man like that. Now we know why she was so distraught after she met with Charlie."

"And do you remember when Kulkarni mentioned a victim? Roz said, 'Who's been talking about me?' I thought it was strange at the time, but now we can understand what she meant."

Alan hung his head and heaved a sigh, and when he looked back up, his face was pale and drawn. "I used to wonder why Rudge arranged the retreat here every year, and now I know the reason. This place is on Roz's doorstep. He came here to control her, to make her attend, to force her to dance to his tune. It's sick. It's psychological abuse."

"And there's that poor young woman. Flo. If she went to one of the schools where Rudge worked…"

"I'd like to think we could help her," Alan said. "But I honestly don't know what we can do. It's been a while since my child protection training, and besides, she's an adult and Rudge is dead. Whatever happened, she may not want to drag it up, and that's her right. If we go looking for her, I'm not sure how she'd react. We have to respect her privacy. If she calls me, I can suggest that she seeks out some support. But other than that…"

"I'm sure you'd deal with it more sensitively than I ever could," Dan said. "I wouldn't know where to start, but if there's anything I can do, tell me."

Alan nodded. "I will. And if I think of anything we can do, I'll give you a shout."

"Thanks, Alan." Dan hesitated. "Unfortunately, this doesn't look good for Roz. We don't know for sure what happened between her and Rudge, but it doesn't take much to imagine a scenario where she'd like to see him dead."

"Perhaps, but I still don't believe she could've done anything so brutal. Yes, she tried to smear Rudge in the press, but that was the extent of her revenge. And Charlie said she was in no fit state to do anything once she'd offloaded her story. He told her to go for a stiff drink."

"And did she, do you think?"

Alan shrugged. "I've no idea. Roz isn't much of a drinker. She'll have a glass of wine with a meal, but that's her limit."

"Remember how she looked when she came in that night? She was distinctly red around the eyes. I thought she was just cold, but she could've had a drink or two. And what about the way she yelled when Firth laid his hands on her?"

"I see what you're saying," Alan said. "The whole thing was wildly out of character. But to have a man taking hold of her like that… it must've been awful for her. It may have triggered all kinds of buried emotions. I've never heard her so much as raise her voice before."

"Where did she meet Charlie?"

"Fistral Beach. It's popular with surfers. There's a statue of some dolphins, and Roz had told him to meet her there." Alan managed a small smile. "Roz turned up on her pushbike, apparently. It must've been quite a scene."

"She arrived back here at around eight, didn't she?"

"Yes, I think so."

"And her hair was a mess," Dan said. "It was all over the place."

"Well, she'd been through a traumatic experience. I hardly think—"

"Don't you see?" Dan interrupted. "Roz wears a helmet when she rides her bike, but from the state of her hair, I'd say she walked back to the hotel. And that supports the idea that she'd been somewhere for a drink. If we can find out where, we might be able to give her an alibi."

"But she'll have told all that to the police. They must've asked her to account for her whereabouts, and I can't see why she wouldn't want to defend herself. Surely the police will check her story. They'll have access to CCTV and they can go knocking on doors. They're bound to follow up every lead, aren't they?"

"You'd think," Dan said. "DS Firth seems like a fairly energetic character, but you never know. I think we'll still have to do some digging ourselves."

"No one is going to show us their CCTV footage."

"Agreed. We need another avenue. What about having another crack at finding that typewriter?"

"Why not? Where shall we start?"

"Local shops."

"Really?" Alan asked. "But it could've been bought anywhere; online, even."

"An online purchase would need a credit card or an online account, and either way, it would leave a trail. I'd bet the murderer was careful enough to buy the machine with cash, and that means a small shop."

"Still, there's nothing to suggest it was bought here."

Dan paused. "My intuition says otherwise. This killer has a certain flair. There's a sense of melodrama about the whole affair. The antique typewriter, the ribbon around the hands, the anonymous notes, the expensive paper. They want everything to tie together neatly. And how fitting it would be if the typewriter came from the very place where the crime was to be committed. Very neat. No loose ends."

"Fair enough," Alan said. "I can run a search for antique shops, junk shops, flea markets. It shouldn't be a long list. Thankfully, the town centre is fairly small."

"Great. Let's hit the streets. We'll search as we go, and we'll get some lunch while we're out."

"Sounds like a plan," Alan said, and he grabbed his coat.

CHAPTER 27

DC Kulkarni was not a regular visitor to the Drowned Sailor. She'd been to the bar only twice before: once, on the trail of stolen goods from a spate of burglaries at local building sites; and once to meet an informant who'd promised to give her chapter and verse on a local drug dealer.

Both visits had been utterly fruitless. The first time, she'd run into a stone wall of silence. The customers and staff had simply refused to talk to her, and she'd left frustrated and angry, certain that most of the patrons would have suspiciously heavy-duty power tools in their sheds at home. And the second visit had been no better. The so-called informant had turned out to be a drug dealer himself, trying to corner the market by informing on his opposition.

There's no reason why today should be any better, she thought as she pushed open the door. But once inside the gloomy bar, her eyes went straight to the CCTV camera mounted near the ceiling in one corner of the room. That was more like it. And presumably the camera worked, because only a few seconds passed before a door opened at the far end of the room and Dave Bentley, the bar's illustrious proprietor, hove into view.

Kulkarni had her warrant card ready, but Bentley didn't

even glance at it as he marched toward her, a steely glint in his eye.

"Mr Bentley, I'm Detective Constable—"

"I know who you are, love," Bentley interrupted. "What do you want?"

"I'd like to ask you some questions in relation to the incident that occurred nearby on the evening of Tuesday, the eighth of December."

Bentley lifted his chin. "Bloke got murdered. What about it?"

"The death is being treated as suspicious. And as you may have heard, it occurred just before 7 o'clock that evening. You were open at that time, yes?"

"Yeah. It wasn't hardly worth bothering, but I was here."

"Business a bit slow?" Kulkarni asked.

Bentley managed a reluctant shrug.

"So, it shouldn't be too hard to recall how many customers you had at around that time."

"There were a few. But I don't recall any of their names, so don't ask."

"I wasn't going to," Kulkarni said. "Believe it or not, Mr Bentley, but on this occasion, I'm not interested in the handful of nameless individuals who make up your customer base. I'm trying to trace a particular person, and I doubt very much whether she's been in your bar before. I'm looking for a tall, slim woman with long red hair."

"That's what they all say, love." Bentley gave her a lascivious grin. "But this is a pub, not a knocking shop."

Kulkarni took out her phone and found the picture of Roz Hammond, then she turned it around to show Bentley. "Have you seen this woman before? Was she here on Tuesday evening?"

Bentley squinted at her phone. He kept his face impassive, but he couldn't hide the spark of recognition in his eyes.

"Well?" Kulkarni said.

"Maybe. I'm not sure."

"Look again. And this time, Mr Bentley, please remember that, very soon, this case is almost certainly going to become a murder investigation. We're going to be seizing the CCTV footage from every camera in the area, and if we find out that you've withheld information…" She left her sentence unfinished, her words hanging in the air while she locked eyes with him.

"All right," Bentley admitted. "She was in here. Satisfied?"

Kulkarni pocketed her phone and whipped out her notebook. "The woman you've identified is called Roz Hammond. What time did she arrive that night?"

"Sometime before seven."

"Was she on her own?"

"Yeah," Bentley said. "She came in by herself. She had a few drinks, and then she left."

"And how did she seem to you? How did she behave?"

Bentley hesitated. "She didn't do it, did she? She didn't push that bloke off the cliff?"

"That's what we're trying to ascertain." Kulkarni watched him carefully. "What makes you think that she might have been involved? Did she say anything about the incident? Did she mention being out on the coastal path?"

"No, nothing like that. But she was all pale and shaky. She didn't really talk to anyone while she was in here. She just stood at the bar, downing her drinks. But you could tell that something was up."

"When you say pale and shaky, do you mean that she appeared angry?"

Bentley screwed up his face. "No. I mean she was upset. More sad than anything."

"And what time did she leave?"

"I dunno. She was here for about an hour, maybe a bit less."

"Okay," Kulkarni said. "I'll need to see the CCTV footage from that night. You do still have it, don't you?"

Bentley paused before replying. "From inside, no. Sorry, but I don't bother recording in here."

"Seriously? Do you expect me to believe that?"

"Yeah. That camera's mainly so I can keep an eye on the bar when I'm out the back."

A familiar sense of frustration crept through Kulkarni's mind. Why did it have to be like this? Why were her efforts continually stymied by some little detail? It wasn't like this on TV. In the crime dramas she'd watched growing up, there were always fingerprints, footprints, witnesses with sharp memories and crystal-clear vision. In real life, there were greasy smudges, shapeless mud and witnesses who would probably be incapable of recognising their own mothers at twenty paces.

With a considerable effort, Kulkarni kept her voice neutral as she asked her next question: "You seemed concerned when I mentioned CCTV earlier. Does that mean that you have other cameras — ones that actually record properly?"

"One. Outside, at the back, in case of burglaries. If your lot did your job properly, we wouldn't need it, but there you go."

"Do customers have access to the rear of your property?"

"Yeah. It's just a little yard, for the bins and that, but we had to put a porch up. For the smokers."

"Did Ms Hammond visit your smoking area?"

"I don't think so." Bentley's expression brightened. "I wonder if it's her bike."

Kulkarni froze, her pen in mid-sentence. "Is it a Trek hybrid bike? Light blue frame?"

"It's blue. I don't know about the rest, but it looks like a woman's bike to me. It's been chained to the railings all day. And just now, with you talking about it, I figured it's probably been there since Tuesday night." He grinned evilly.

"I'd half a mind to take a pair of bolt cutters to that chain, flog the bike on eBay."

"That would be against the law," Kulkarni said. "But forget about that for a minute, because that bike almost certainly belongs to Ms Hammond. Did you touch it?"

"No."

"And you definitely have CCTV recordings from Tuesday night?"

"Yeah," Bentley said. "I just told you that."

"Yes, you did," Kulkarni replied. "But it's such good news, I can hardly believe my ears." She gave the landlord a broad smile. "Now, Mr Bentley, let's go and have a look at those recordings, shall we? I believe you're about to make my day."

CHAPTER 28

Standing in the high street, Dan stared at Alan in disbelief. "What do you mean, there aren't any?"

"I mean exactly what I say," Alan replied. "There are no antique shops in Newquay. Neither are there any flea markets or junk shops. I've rephrased the search in as many different ways as I can, but I'm coming up empty. If you think you can do any better, then you're welcome to try."

Dan blinked. He'd no reason to doubt Alan's results; if he said there were no antique shops, then he was probably right. But he'd been so certain that the typewriter had been bought nearby. "What about the nearby towns and villages?"

"If we widen the search, I can find several, but they're quite spread out. We could try phoning them."

"No, it has to be in Newquay. I'm sure of it." Dan turned, looking in both directions along the street. "Where else would you be able to buy an antique typewriter?"

"Charity shops," Alan suggested. "We've passed a few, and they sell all kinds of odd things."

"That's a good idea, but the machine we're trying to trace would've been quite valuable. Charities tend to sort through their donations, and if there's anything that could fetch a high price, they sell it online."

"Then I'm stuck." Alan pocketed his phone. "Look around you. Most of these shops you could find in any town centre. They're all fairly standard, and none of them sell second-hand goods." He paused. "I don't want to stop, but I got up early and I'm starving. Shall we break for lunch?"

"Why not? We need to have another think, and a hot meal might give us a boost."

"Do you want to go back to the Horizon Cafe, or shall we look for somewhere new?"

"Let's try somewhere else," Dan said. "I've rather gone off the Horizon Cafe. I'm still smarting from the memory of Brian's bill."

"Why? I paid it."

"I know," Dan replied. "That's precisely what's annoying me. I should have been able to cover it."

"I'll tell you what. You can make up for it by treating me to a pint. Let's find a nice pub and sit by the fire."

Dan considered Alan's suggestion, but not for long. "Go on then. You know the town better than me. Just so long as you don't want to revisit the Drowned Sailor."

"Oh, I think I can do better than that," Alan said. "Follow me."

The Rusty Saw was only a ten-minute walk from the town centre, but once Dan and Alan were ensconced in the corner by the log fire, they could've been sheltering from the wintry winds in the middle of Exmoor.

"It's a good find, this place," Dan said, casting an eye over the pub's interior. The pub had either been well maintained for decades or lovingly restored to its original splendour. Thick beams of dark wood crossed the ceiling, their stained surfaces gleaming warmly in the firelight, and the pub's stone walls were so thick they might've been built to withstand cannon fire. The chairs and tables comprised a fascinating collection of shapes, styles and sizes; all different, but somehow working together to create an effect of old-world comfort. And beneath their feet, the oak boards had been worn smooth by generations of customers.

"The beer's good, too," Alan replied.

"Hint taken." Dan checked he had his wallet. "What are you having?"

"I saw an intriguing stout on the way in. I wouldn't mind trying it. It's a pint-of-stout kind of day."

"I'll drink to that," Dan said. "I'll be right back. And I'll grab a couple of menus."

At the bar, Dan was greeted by a smartly dressed young man who gave off an aura of boundless enthusiasm. "Yes, sir. What can I get for you? Would you like the lunch menu?"

"Yes, please," Dan said. "And I've no idea how you pronounce it, but we'll have two pints of this stout, please." He indicated the black pump on the bar.

"Mena Dhu," the barman said, passing Dan two menus. "It means black hill, which was the name of the farm owned by the man who started the brewery. But it's a thoroughly modern beer. It's got an aroma of oak smoke, a hint of dark chocolate and a liquorice finish. You'll enjoy it."

"I'm sure I will."

The barman took his time filling the glasses, letting them settle, then examining each one before topping it up. "Perfect," he said, placing the pints reverentially on the polished bar. "Anything else?"

"Not unless you've got an antique typewriter." Dan chuckled as he tucked the menus under his arm and picked up his prizes. "Sorry, don't mind me. Just a joke."

The barman furrowed his brow. "I don't quite get it, but if you're looking for the typewriter, it's over there."

"Sorry?" If Dan hadn't had his hands full, he might've pinched himself.

"The old typewriter. It's on the bureau, in the alcove." The barman pointed, and when Dan turned to look, he saw an old writing bureau, its writing surface open to reveal several rows of storage compartments. And on its padded leather writing surface sat a vintage portable typewriter, its rows of circular keys edged with glittering steel, its black body pristine.

"Does it work?" Dan asked quietly.

"After a fashion," the barman replied. "Some of the keys don't seem to do anything. It's like they've got disconnected or something. You can have a look if you like, but we don't encourage people to use it. It's there for show."

"Right." Dan strode toward the alcove. "Alan, come and have a look at this."

Alan joined him as he reached the bureau. "My God," Alan breathed. "What are the chances?"

"Pretty low," Dan said. "The barman said it only works after a fashion."

"And it's the wrong make. Imperial." Alan bent over the typewriter to inspect it more closely. "That looks like a standard half-inch ribbon to me."

"Hold these." Dan thrust the two pint glasses toward Alan, and as soon as they'd been safely delivered, he strode back to the bar.

The barman glanced at the menus still tucked beneath Dan's arm. "Everything all right, sir?"

"Yes. But do you, by any chance, have another typewriter? An older one, bigger?"

"No, sorry."

"Okay, can you tell me where you bought that one?"

"Well, I didn't buy it myself. I only work here."

"Damn!"

The barman looked slightly alarmed by Dan's reaction. "Er, I can call the owner though. She takes care of all the decor, and she's always keen to help."

"Would you mind?" Dan asked. "We're collectors, you see. Very keen on typewriters."

"Right. I'll see what I can do."

"Thanks. I appreciate it." Dan headed back to his seat.

Alan had made himself comfortable and was already sampling his beer, but he lowered his glass and wiped the foam from his top lip as Dan approached. "What did he say?"

Dan placed the menus on the table and sat down. "He thinks the owner bought it. He's going to call and ask."

"That's what I call service," Alan replied. "Try your pint. It's fantastic."

"It would be rude not to." Dan took a long drink, the dark beer warming his stomach. "That's bloody good."

"It's like alcoholic treacle broth," Alan said. "Sweet and savoury at the same time."

"We'd better get something to eat. I think that beer is going to your head."

Dan skimmed through the menu, his mind elsewhere.

"I think I'll go for the steak and ale pie," Alan said.

"Right. I'll go and order." Dan took a hasty sip of beer then crossed to the bar. "Any news on the typewriter?" he asked the barman.

"You are keen, aren't you?" The barman smiled. "I'm afraid the boss hasn't got back to me yet. I left a message. Meanwhile, are you ready to order?"

"Yes. One steak and ale pie, and the vegetarian butternut squash risotto; there aren't any dairy products in it, are there?"

"We get asked that a lot. Only the Parmesan shavings, and we can serve it without if you prefer."

"Fine. Without the cheese, please."

"Certainly."

Dan paid the bill immediately, circumventing any objection from Alan, then he returned to his seat. "On its way," he told Alan. "Nothing else to report."

But it wasn't long before the barman approached. "Here

you go, sir." He handed a slip of paper to Dan. "Newquay Interiors. It's on Oakleigh Terrace. Not far from here."

"Thank you," Dan said. "I really appreciate it."

As soon as the barman retreated, Dan grabbed his phone and opened the map, tapping in the address.

"Of course," Alan said. "People buy all kinds of vintage stuff as ornaments. We should've thought of that."

"Yes." Dan looked up. "I've found it, and it has to be the place! It's near the hotel."

"Good. Should we forget about lunch?"

"No. We need to eat, and besides, I've already paid." Dan raised a hand to ward off any negotiation, then he took a gulp of beer. They could afford to wait another half an hour or so. At last, they were closing in on the murderer.

CHAPTER 29

The proprietor of Newquay Interiors rose from his seat behind the counter and strolled to meet Dan and Alan as they made their way through the door labelled *Showroom*. A middle-aged man, dressed in an immaculate three-piece suit, he gave them an appraising look before offering a smile. "Good afternoon, gentlemen. Would you like any help or are you just here to browse for inspiration?"

"Afternoon," Dan said. "Actually, I'm looking for something specific."

"Interesting. A piece of furniture perhaps? We have some lovely dining chairs at the moment. They're on display on our upper floor."

"Not today," Dan replied. "I want a vintage typewriter, and I've heard that you're able to supply them."

The man's smile faded a little. "Yes, we have one or two on display on the lower level. I can show you, if you wish."

"Erm, we're actually trying to find a particular typewriter," Alan put in. "An Empire Number One or a Wellington. They were made by Adler."

The man's expression said that he'd like to ask why but was too polite to enquire. "We have a very nice Olympia portable and an Olivetti. They're the kind of thing that people generally ask for." He hoisted his smile a little higher. "They're very attractive pieces. I'm afraid we don't have any brightly coloured machines at the moment. They've become rather hard to source since they became fashionable, especially the red models."

Alan took out his phone, and finding an image of the Empire Number One, he showed the screen to the proprietor. "We're looking for something exactly like this."

"Oh. I had one of those once, or something almost identical. Let me see, it must've been about this time last year."

"Who did you sell it to?" Dan blurted.

"I beg your pardon?"

Dan softened his tone. "I'm sorry. I know it sounds like an odd question, but I collect typewriters, and I really need to get hold of that machine. It's quite rare, and I think it might've been bought by a rival collector. If I could work out who has it, I might be able to make them an offer."

The man pursed his lips, thinking, but then he came to a decision. "Funnily enough, he said almost exactly the same thing. He said he was a collector, and he asked me to keep the whole thing under my hat. But then, he also promised he'd come back. He swore he was having his whole house remodelled, and he made all kinds of promises. But I haven't seen hide nor hair of him since."

"Shocking," Alan said. "Perhaps, in the circumstances, you wouldn't mind giving us his name."

"I'm not sure I recall. He paid in cash, you see, and he took the machine with him, so I didn't need a full name and address."

"Could his first name have been Edward?" Dan asked.

"No, no. It was something odd. Something short." He frowned.

"Albert?" Alan suggested. "Marcus?"

"Buzz," the man said. "No, wait a minute. Hang on. It was Boz. That's it. 'Call me Boz,' he said."

Dan stared at the man. "Boz? Are you sure?"

"Charles Dickens' pen name," Alan said. "Another piece that fits the puzzle."

"But it gets us no closer," Dan replied. "We'll have to go through some photos."

"I'll see what I can find." Alan busied himself with his phone.

"This seems like a lot of effort for a typewriter," the man said.

"It's a very important typewriter," Dan replied. "This Boz character, would you recognise him if you saw him again?"

"Probably." The man chortled quietly.

"What's so funny?" Dan asked.

"Pardon me, it was nothing really. It was just the way he typed. He wanted to try out the machine, and of course I let him. But he was hilarious. He was waving his hands around like this." The man mimed an exaggerated display of typing, flicking his fingers upward at the end of each stroke. "It was like he was playing the piano or something. I've never seen anything like it."

"I have," Alan said. He tapped out a search on his phone, then he turned the screen to face the shopkeeper.

"That's him!" the man exclaimed. "That was quick work. How did you know? Friend of yours, is he?"

"Not exactly." Alan showed the screen to Dan.

"It's Tim," Dan said. "Tim Kendall." He locked eyes with Alan. "We have to get back to the hotel."

"I'll call DS Firth," Alan said. "He needs to know about this."

Dan nodded once. "We can walk and talk. Let's go."

The shopkeeper watched them, bemused. "Are you phoning the police? Why?"

"Nothing for you to worry about," Dan said, "but you'll

need to talk to them later." He made for the door, Alan hard on his heels.

"But I haven't done anything wrong," the man called after them. "What's going on?"

"Thanks for your help," Alan replied, then he joined Dan outside.

"Come on," Dan said, and they set off at a jog.

CHAPTER 30

"Here she comes." At her desk in Bodmin HQ, DC Kulkarni paused the video playback on her monitor and checked the time stamp against her notes. "Six thirty-nine."

Behind her, DS Firth grunted. "Go on."

They watched the grainy image as Roz Hammond chained her bike against the railings behind the Drowned Sailor then walked out of view.

"That's it until..." Kulkarni forwarded the recording at high speed. A couple of figures flickered into view, one man smoking a cigarette before he disappeared. The second man inspected the bike and tugged at the chain. He took something from the handlebars, then he slouched away.

"What did he nick?" Firth asked.

"Cycling helmet."

"Little blighter."

"He'd have pinched the bike, but Hammond has a top-quality lock," Kulkarni said. "Just as well. I checked, and that bike wasn't cheap."

"How much?"

"About a thousand pounds. Why, do you think it might be significant?"

"No," Firth replied. "My eldest is after a new bike, but I'm not going to shell out a grand, I can tell you."

"Here she is." Kulkarni slowed the playback. On the screen, Roz went to her bike, but she seemed unsteady on her feet. Leaning against the railings, she paused for a moment, then she shook her head. She breathed out, sending a plume of misty breath into the air, then she strolled away without a backward glance.

Kulkarni stopped the recording. The time stamp read seven forty-one. "Looks like Ms Hammond is in the clear," she said. "We think Rudge was killed shortly before seven."

"Unless she killed Rudge, and then went for a stiffener."

"But Heath was with her at six thirty by Fistral beach, and they talked for several minutes. She must've gone straight from there to that pub. Heath said he'd told her to get a drink and calm herself down. I checked the route, and assuming she was on her way back to the hotel, the Drowned Sailor would've been the first bar she passed; the first one that was open at this time of year, anyway. She probably saw the sign and decided to follow Heath's advice."

"We don't know for sure she was inside the pub all that time," Firth argued. "She could've grabbed a taxi, nipped out, come back."

"Not according to the landlord. Bentley said she arrived before seven and she didn't leave for almost an hour. That ties in with the CCTV perfectly."

Firth scraped his hand down his face. "All right. Hammond was always a long shot, and that settles it. Even if she had an accomplice, and he picked her up as soon as she'd chained up her bike, I doubt whether she could've got across town, dealt with Rudge, then made it back in time. It just doesn't add up."

"Agreed, Sarge. What's our next step?"

"We'll go back through all the initial interviews and conversations. We need to collate all our notes and look for inconsistencies. Someone has lied to us, and we've missed it. That's not good enough."

His phone buzzed in his pocket, and he answered the call. "DS Firth." He listened, his expression unreadable, then he said, "Thanks, Mr Hargreaves, but—"

His eyes widened, and when he spoke again his tone had changed, grown more urgent: "We'll send a patrol. And I'll be there as fast as I can."

He gestured to Kulkarni. "Looks like we've got a lead on that typewriter ribbon. Believe it or not, Hargreaves reckons he's found where it was bought, and the shop's owner identified one of the writers from the hotel."

Kulkarni got to her feet. "Who?"

"Our suspect's name is Mr Tim Kendall." Firth grinned. "It's a shame he wasn't a doctor. And called Richard. I've always wanted to say that."

"Sarge, are you going for a reference to *The Fugitive*? Only that was Kimble, not Kendall."

"Close enough, isn't it?" Firth shook his head. "Come on. You can drive. I've got calls to make."

And pressing his phone against his ear, DS Firth stormed across the office.

CHAPTER 31

D an and Alan stood shoulder to shoulder outside Tim Kendall's hotel room. From within, the strains of opera could be heard, Tim singing along. But the sound ended abruptly when Dan pounded his fist against the door.

A moment later, the door opened fully and Tim stood before them, blinking blearily. "Ah, what a pleasant surprise. Unless, that is, you've come to complain about my music. I do hope it wasn't too loud."

"It wasn't the music," Dan replied. "Is it okay if we come in for a minute?"

"Well, I…"

Dan stepped forward, forcing Tim to retreat, then he marched inside, closely followed by Alan.

"Right, well, I suppose you'd better come in." Tim pulled a comic face, trying to make light of the situation, but his voice wavered uncertainly. He turned away to close the door, and Dan saw a flash of alarm in the man's eyes. But when Tim faced them, he'd composed himself, and he stood tall, his hands clasped in front of him.

Dan gestured to the open laptop on the desk, its screen filled with text. "Were you working?"

"Yes. As usual."

"And your music – do you stream it from your phone?"

"My laptop," Tim replied. "I have a playlist set up. I always like to listen to music when writing. But it has to be opera. I love the drama of it. It helps me to capture the mood."

"Albert does something similar," Dan said. "And like him, I see that you use a smart speaker."

"My trusty Amazon Echo," Tim replied. "It goes everywhere with me."

"Almost everywhere," Dan said.

"Pardon?" Tim plastered a bland smile across his features and turned his attention to Alan. "Your friend seems rather abrupt. What's all this about, Alan?"

Alan remained stony faced. "You'll see. We have a few questions."

"Oh. What about?"

"Little things," Dan said. "Idle curiosity. I've always been fascinated by the way writers work. What's your routine?"

Tim let out a nervous chuckle. "I'm afraid my process is rather mundane. I sit in my chair and I type. That's all there is to it."

"Really?" Dan asked. "Just now, you said you were working, but when we arrived, you weren't sitting at your desk."

"What an extraordinary thing to say."

"Is it?" Dan paced across the room to the bedside table. "You need reading glasses to work, and yet, here they are by your bed."

"I make the fonts larger on my laptop," Tim replied. "Honestly, what is this, the Spanish Inquisition?"

Dan smiled. "Far from it. But when we came in, I couldn't help noticing the puffiness around your eyes. You looked very much as though you'd been asleep."

Tim's fingers went to the corners of his eyes, self-consciously massaging his lower lids. "If my eyes look tired, it's because I haven't been sleeping well. With all the terrible things that have been going on, it's hardly surprising."

"No, it isn't." Dan picked up a small framed photograph from the bedside table. The image was black and white, professionally taken, and it showed a handsome young woman dressed in a formal gown, her neck bedecked with pearls, and her hair swept upward into an elaborate arrangement.

"That's my Cyn," Tim said. "My wife. It was taken before we were married. She was Lady Cynthia Kington back then, but it's my favourite photo of her."

"At the restaurant, you said you'd married well," Alan put in. "Now I see what you mean. But you didn't mention that you had aristocratic connections. Why is that?"

Tim shrugged modestly. "One doesn't like to boast. And you know how catty some people can be. There are those who will say I've only been successful because I've had certain privileges in life. But I've had to work damned hard for everything I've achieved."

"And what is that, exactly?" Dan asked. "What have you achieved?"

"I don't have to justify myself to you, Mr Corrigan." Tim bridled, his lips drawn tight, his nose uplifted.

"Indulge me," Dan said smoothly. "Tell me about your work."

"Very well. If you insist." Tim drew a haughty breath. "I've topped the bestseller charts, in both *the New York Times* and *USA Today*, on several occasions. In this country, my latest novel was selected as Book of the Month by *The Times*. I've won the Costa Book Award, and I've been shortlisted for the Man Booker Prize. My books are sold around the world and have been translated into forty-five languages. Is that good enough for you?"

Dan tilted his head on one side. "An impressive empire.

That's certainly something you'd want to protect if it were to be threatened in some way."

"I don't see what you're getting at," Tim said.

"No?" Dan let an uncomfortable silence fill the room.

Eventually, Tim said, "I suppose I've had my share of critics over the years. There are always those who snipe from the sidelines."

"So, how do you protect your reputation?" Dan asked.

"I have a good lawyer and broad shoulders," Tim replied. "I find that to be a winning combination. I can look after myself."

"But you've had others to consider, haven't you," Alan said. "Your father was a prominent man, and then there's your wife."

"Leave my wife out of this," Tim shot back. "Now, if I've satisfied your *idle curiosity*, perhaps you'd let me return to my—"

"Typing," Dan interrupted. "You're quite an impressive typist, so I hear."

"What?"

"And judging by your age," Dan went on, "it's safe to assume that you learned on a manual machine. An Olympia, perhaps." He paused. "Or maybe even an Empire Number One."

For a split second, Tim's features seemed fixed in place, like a photograph taken at an inopportune moment. But then he let out a snide chuckle. "I have absolutely no idea what the hell you're blithering about, but I think you've wasted enough of my time, don't you?" Without waiting for an answer, he opened the door and waved them toward it, flinging his arm wide. "Run along, gentlemen. You've seriously outstayed your welcome. Please leave before I have you thrown out."

"The shopkeeper at Newquay Interiors identified you," Dan said, his voice calm. "You made a mistake there, Tim.

Such an unusual typewriter, he was bound to remember it. And he remembered you; he was very clear about that."

"So what?" Tim demanded. "I bought a typewriter."

"Is it here?" Dan glanced around the room, his eyes alighting on a holdall in the corner. "We know you have it with you. It won't be hard to match the machine to the notes you sent." In three quick strides, Dan was across the room, and bending over the holdall, he pulled back the zip.

"Don't touch that!" Tim moved toward Dan, but Alan sidestepped, barring his way.

Tim glared. "Get the hell out of my way."

"No," Alan replied. "You're fine where you are. Stay right there."

"Let's have a look," Dan said.

Inside the bag, crumpled shirts were tangled together with socks and underwear. The bag looked full, but Dan reached inside, parting the thin layer of clothes to reveal a sheet of plastic bubble wrap. "What have we here?"

"Stop!" Tim snapped. "You have no right to touch that. No right at all." He tried to push past Alan, but Alan held him back, grasping his arm.

Dan didn't look up from his task. Unfolding the bubble wrap, he held his breath. And there it was. "Bingo."

The typewriter's sleek black body gleamed darkly in its nest of plastic. And picked out in ornate gold lettering across the metal were two words: *The Empire*.

"All right, I wrote a few notes," Tim spluttered. "So what? It was only a bit of harmless fun."

Dan stood. "Edward didn't think so."

"You can't blame me for that," Tim protested. "He's highly strung. He's always been like that. He can't take a joke."

"But the threat wasn't meant for him, was it?" Dan said. "You didn't know about the room changes, so your plan went awry. But it wasn't hard to figure out the intended target for your poison-pen letter. You wanted to make Rudge squirm, so you planned to send him a threat. And you came up with a scheme that appealed to your sense of melodrama. Writing a note to everyone, including yourself, was a nice touch, but I did notice that your own note was particularly complimentary. Your vanity came to the fore, even as you planned to destroy Dominic Rudge."

Tim tutted in contempt. "Nonsense. The notes were a practical joke, a bit of theatre. Yes, my note to Edward was a bit over the top, but I'd fallen out with him, so I wanted to give him a fright. How was I to know he'd fly off the handle?"

"Oh, you're good," Dan replied. "He's good, isn't he, Alan?"

"Compelling," Alan said. "But he slipped up when he used that ribbon. He must've skimped on his research. Frankly, I'm surprised at him. As a historical writer, he should've known better."

Tim's lips curled in a sneer. "How dare you. You're nothing but a teller of bedtime stories for half-witted brats. I'm a historian, a respected authority in the field. My knowledge of the nineteenth century—"

"Does not include the development of the typewriter ribbon," Alan interjected. "I can see why you wanted the Empire. It was first made in 1892, so that fits with your interest in the nineteenth century. But perhaps you didn't know that its three-quarter-inch ribbon was never popular, and apart from the Adler thrust-action machines, it wasn't widely adopted."

Tim opened his mouth, but he seemed to be having difficulty choosing his first word.

"Still, that nice thick ribbon must've been perfect for tying Rudge's hands together," Dan said. "There's only one thing I don't know for sure, and that's why you did it. We know Rudge had a history of mistreating women. Was that the reason, Tim? Was that why he had to die?"

Tim's expression hardened, and he found his tongue. "You know nothing. You've got nothing. You have no proof whatsoever. But I was working when Rudge was killed. I was in here, on my own, the whole evening."

Dan smiled. "About that. Bear with me for a second, because there's one more piece of the puzzle to put into place. You see, when we arrived, I believe I was correct when I said that you were asleep until I knocked on your door."

"Dan," Alan began, "he can't have been asleep. We heard him singing. And on the night of the murder, I heard him then too. He must've been in this room when Rudge was killed. We've made a mistake."

"Ha!" Tim shook his head, enjoying his moment of triumph. "You see! You've made a fool of yourself, Corrigan."

Dan held up his hand for quiet. "Alexa," he said, "resume."

The speaker's light pulsed blue, and a moment later the room was filled with the sound of opera. And with the unmistakable sound of Tim singing along.

"You recorded yourself and played it on that evening to conceal the fact that you weren't in your room," Dan went on. "Just now, you were listening to it when you fell asleep. It took me a while to figure it out, but it all came together in the end."

Tim backed toward the door. "You bloody idiots. You have no idea what you're talking about."

"We'll see soon enough," Alan said. "The police are on their way."

"Oh, bollocks to this!" Tim growled, and then he was out the door and away.

Dan dashed forward to follow him, and he heard Alan fall in behind.

Tim was already halfway along the corridor, moving fast, and Dan gave chase. "Stop!" he called out, but Tim gave no heed. He ran on, his clumsy footsteps thumping on the thin carpet.

At the end of the corridor, Tim halted beside a plain wooden door. Glancing back at Dan, his eyes wild, he jabbed at the door's combination lock, and then he was through.

Dan put on a burst of speed, and just in time he caught the door before it swung shut. On the other side, an unlit stairwell offered two choices: up or down, both disappearing into darkness. Dan almost headed down, guessing Tim would make for the street, but he could hear him staggering upward, and he followed, feeling his way.

Behind him, Alan called out, "I've found the switch." And the stairwell was flooded with light.

Dan's eyes hadn't yet adjusted to the dark, but even so, he squinted against the harsh glare of the fluorescent overhead lights. Ahead, Tim stumbled, but he carried on, his wheezing breath unnaturally loud in the confined space.

"Tim, you've got to stop," Dan shouted.

But Tim did not slow. He was at the top of the stairs now, and already scrabbling at another keypad. He pushed the door open, and a gust of wind yanked it from his hands, then he disappeared.

Dan dug deep, powering up the last few stairs. The open door swung toward him, slowly closing, its sluggish spring fighting against the wind. If the door closed before he got there, if the lock had time to engage, Tim would escape.

The door was within millimetres of meeting its frame, and Dan hurled himself against it, barging it open with his shoulder. A jolt of pain shot through his arm, but the heavy door juddered open, and he was outside.

Dan staggered to a standstill. In front of him, a low stone balustrade was all that separated him from a dizzying drop. Behind him, the grim slope of the hotel roof stretched upward, its dark slates worn smooth by the salty air.

Dan stood on a narrow walkway, its stony surface slick

with damp. At the far end of the walkway, Tim stood, looking down, his hands on the balustrade.

Dan froze.

Above them, a seagull wheeled through the air, shrieking as if affronted at having its territory invaded. It swept past Tim, and he turned to watch its flight.

Catching Dan's eye he said, "A European herring gull. Nothing special."

Dan swallowed. "Do you like birds?"

"I used to, as a child." Tim shrugged. "It was a long time ago, but you never forget."

Dan took a small step closer. "They all look the same to me. Seagulls."

"Oh dear." Tim tutted. "There's no bird called a seagull. Not all sea birds are gulls. It's a common mistake to lump them all together."

"I'll remember that." Dan edged along the walkway as he talked, keeping his gaze on Tim.

Behind him, someone hammered against the door. *Damn!* He'd let it swing shut, and now Alan couldn't open it. But perhaps that was just as well. Tim was putting on a brave front, but his eyes were wild, his mouth twitching. His nerves were already strained to their limits; the presence of another person might be enough to make him do something stupid.

Tim had heard the noise too. "Poor Alan. Never mind. We're on our own. Just you and me and this most excellent canopy the air."

"Hamlet."

"Bravo." Tim mimed a round of applause. "You're not quite the philistine I thought."

"I had to learn that speech at school," Dan said. "I can't say I fully understood it."

"Ah, I should've guessed." Tim's expression soured.

Thinking quickly, Dan said, "Tell me more about the birds. I saw a huge one the other day. It had a pointed beak and a long neck. Dark feathers. It stood on a rock and stretched its wings out. It was like something from a David Attenborough programme."

"A cormorant." Tim smiled. "The common cormorant or shag, lays eggs inside a paper bag. Christopher Isherwood. Do you know it?"

"No. Another childhood memory?"

"Yes. I always loved nonsense poetry. Edward Lear, Hilaire Belloc, Ogden Nash. I must've known dozens of them by heart before I'd reached the age of seven."

"Did your parents read them to you?"

Tim let out a burst of laughter so bitter that Dan stopped in his tracks.

"Read to me?" Tim said. "My parents scarcely knew I existed." He shook his head. "Books were my only friends, my companions. They were all I had."

"I know what that's like."

Tim gave him a sharp look. "Do you?"

"Yes. I was sent to boarding school at a young age. It wasn't easy to be separated from my parents."

"Hm. I didn't mind school. In some ways, I was happier there than at home. At least my intelligence was recognised." He sighed. "You've kept me talking admirably, Corrigan, but you can stop right there."

Dan did as he was told. If he pushed his luck, he wasn't sure how Tim would react. And he was nowhere near close enough to make a grab for the man. "So, what happens next?"

"I jump. Get it over with."

"No, don't do that. Please." Dan glanced over the balustrade. He had no problem with heights; he could race up a climbing wall or abseil down a cliff. But this was different. The vertical sides of the building plummeted to the car park below, and the drop played games with his sense of depth. The thought of someone hurtling to the ground unnerved him. But Dan clenched his stomach to calm the fear squirming in his gut. No one was going to fall; not today.

He locked eyes with Tim. "You have a wife waiting for you. Cynthia."

"I think she'd prefer a corpse to a convict, don't you? I can't imagine her coping with the knowledge that her husband was a murderer. I can't do that to her. Better to leave her a widow. Let her think I lost my marbles. She'll be devastated, but she'll get over it. And besides, she always looked good in black."

"You're talking nonsense," Dan said. "Whatever you've done, you love your wife. I could see it when you looked at her photograph."

Tim pushed out his lower lip. "I've let her down."

He hung his head, and Dan seized his chance to creep closer. "Give her a chance, Tim. Cynthia might rally round, support you in your hour of need."

Tim didn't reply.

"Would you say she was a strong person?" Dan asked, trying to keep his voice steady as he inched closer and closer.

Tim looked up. "Stop." He said it calmly, but there was authority in his voice. "Move a muscle, and I'll jump."

"Okay, okay." Dan took a long breath, releasing it slowly. He risked a peek over the edge. At last, the police were putting in an appearance, a patrol car rolling to a halt in front of the hotel. Two uniformed officers leaped from the car and hurried inside. A moment later, another car swerved into the car park, stopping behind the patrol car. A man and a woman climbed out, and Dan recognised DS Firth and DC Kulkarni. A faint hope stirred in Dan's mind, but what could the police do? By the time they climbed the stairs, it could all be too late.

"Tim," he began, "let me help you."

"How? What are you going to do, wave a magic wand and bring Rudge back to life? Don't bother. No one would thank you. The world is a better place without him."

"You could be right. But if you explain it to me, if you tell me *why* you killed him, I might be able to—"

"You don't know?" Tim interrupted. "After everything you said, after all your tinkering about with typewriters and... and..." Words failed him. He shook his head, incredulous. "But you didn't understand *why?* Do you really not know why that bastard had to die?"

He stared expectantly.

Dan's mouth was dry, but he swallowed and said, "Was it because of the way he treated Roz? I know he had some kind of hold over her."

"Well, I suppose you're halfway there." Tim's face fell, his cheeks sagging, his eyes growing dull. "Roz is very special. She always has been. And years ago, when we were both young and foolish, we... we were lovers." Tim's shoulders rose and fell, and although he fought to control it, his voice cracked. "When she fell pregnant, I acted shamefully. I abandoned her. I was just becoming successful, and back then I couldn't afford the scandal."

"You're the father of her child?"

Tim nodded.

"But Roz's daughter is a teenager, so this can't have been all that long ago. I can't see how it's a scandal, unless..."

"I was already married, and my wife moved in the highest of circles. On her arm, I was welcomed into the ranks of the elite. For the first time in my life, my father was actually proud of me. Can you imagine?"

Dan shook his head, but Tim hardly seemed to notice.

"I wanted to help Roz, I really did," Tim went on. "I sent her money, but she threw it back in my face. She wanted something more precious than that. She needed commitment, trust, love."

"So you walked away." Dan couldn't keep the contempt from his tone, and Tim flinched.

"I couldn't give her what she needed, and I couldn't turn

my back on the life I'd always wanted, the life I deserved. You've got to remember, my career hung in the balance. If you're a rock star, you can get away with just about anything, but when you're that genteel author who writes the kind of sweet stories people chat about while they're having their hair done, forget it."

"I'm not sure that people are so judgemental," Dan said.

"Ha! You never met my father. And there are plenty of people in the literary world who are every bit as bad. My publisher would've dropped me like a hot brick. I told you I was big in the States, and my readership over there is extremely conservative."

"So, Rudge knew he could cause trouble for you."

Tim snorted in disgust. "Oh yes. But he wasn't man enough to come after me directly. No, he threatened Roz. He said he'd use her to take me down a peg or two. He convinced her she'd be dragged into the dirt along with me, her private life exposed to the world, her daughter's innocence shattered."

"Does the girl know you're her father?"

Tim shook his head. "Roz wanted it kept from her until she was older. She built a stable home for Shona, gave her all the love and care I couldn't provide. But Rudge said he'd tear all that apart. You can't know what that did to Roz. She's a fragile person, and Rudge can smell a victim from a mile away. He tormented her at every turn, made her life a misery. All Roz wanted was to protect her daughter, *our* daughter."

"She came to you for help."

"No, she would never have done that," Tim replied. "Rudge told me himself. He took great pleasure in telling me how he'd made her suffer. So I had to make him stop. The man was a monster. What else could I have done?"

Tim looked past Dan's shoulder. "Here they come."

Dan fought the urge to turn, but he heard the door opening slowly, and then DS Firth's voice: "Mr Kendall, you remember me, don't you? I'm Detective Sergeant Firth. It's time to come inside."

"Stay back!" Tim took his weight on his arms and hoisted himself up so he sat on the balustrade.

"No," Dan said. "Tim, get down."

"It's all right, Dan," Tim replied. "You can stay. But the rest of you can bugger off. Go on. Get back inside or I'll do it."

"I can't do that," Firth said. "I'm staying."

Tim grunted in exasperation. "Typical. Bloody pleb." He gave Dan a weary smile. "Ah well, it's all over. Funny it should end like this, all the way up here. You know, this is the very spot where I was going to push Dominic off the edge. I had the whole thing planned. But then Edward did a runner, and I got rattled." He thought for a moment. "Everything's connected. It was Edward who showed me how to get up here. He…" Tim clamped his lips shut.

"What were you going to say?" Dan asked.

"It doesn't matter. The point is, it was Edward who worked out the code for the doors. Good old Edward. He can find his way around any problem — almost. It's the way his mind works. Not sneaky, exactly. Resourceful. He's had to be."

"Because of his time in the intelligence service," Dan said.

"That's part of it, but there's something else. I won't tell you why, but Edward is a very private man. So when he got that damned note, it was a disaster. He assumed the threat was meant for him. He must've been furious. Distraught."

"Edward told me he was worried on account of his film deal," Dan said. "I'm guessing that wasn't true."

"There's only one thing that could shake Edward, and I made him think the cat was out the bag, quite by chance. I was such a fool. I should've been more careful, double-checked the room numbers."

"There's no point dwelling on past mistakes," Dan said.

"But perhaps you can help to put things right. Do you know where Edward is now?"

"I won't betray his confidence. I've done enough damage." Tim lifted one leg over the balustrade.

"Don't do that," Firth called out. Dan heard the policeman moving forward.

"Tim, wait," Dan said. "You haven't finished your story."

"Yes, I have. It's all wrapped up, and that's just how a final chapter should be. Neat."

"But what about the epilogue?" Dan asked. "What about the funeral scene, the grieving widow with all her questions unanswered? Won't that make a mess of your plot?"

"I've never been a fan of epilogues. Better to make a clean end." Tim lifted his other leg onto the balustrade.

And Dan lunged forward.

CHAPTER 32

D an flung his arms around Tim's upper body even as the older man slid from the stone rail. Dan locked his arms around Tim's chest, but even so, he felt him slipping through his grip, plunging downward. Dan held tight, but Tim dangled in the air, a dead weight, pulling Dan closer to the edge, dragging him down. Dan's feet lost their purchase on the smooth walkway, and his chest thudded against the stone railing, but he hung on for grim death, closing his eyes, willing himself to stay anchored to the spot.

And it worked.

Dan opened his eyes, and wished he hadn't. He was bent over the balustrade, staring downward, Tim's body trapped in his arms, the man suspended over the void like an ungainly puppet. Dan had managed to hook Tim beneath the armpits, but he couldn't hold on much longer. He could scarcely breathe, and already his grip was growing looser, his arm muscles burning.

Tim let out a moan, a wail of despair, and then, against all reason, he started to struggle.

"Don't bloody move or you'll take me with you," Dan growled.

"No, he won't," someone said. And then there were people at Dan's side, arms reaching down to grab hold of Tim. Firth stood on Dan's right, Kulkarni on his left, and together they hauled Tim back onto the walkway.

Firth manhandled Tim into a standing position, and Kulkarni took hold of Dan's upper arm, concern in her eyes. "Are you all right, Mr Corrigan?"

Dan straightened his back, brushing himself down. He drew a deep breath, and though a sharp pain needled him between the ribs, he said, "Yes. I'm fine."

"That was quite something." Kulkarni let go of his arm. "It was very brave of you."

"I don't know about that," Dan said. "I'm just glad you helped when you did. I'm not sure how much longer I could've held him."

"Right," Firth said. "Homilies over. Tim Kendall, I'm DS Firth, Devon and Cornwall Police, and I'm arresting you for the crime of murder. You do not have to say anything, but it may harm your defence if you do not mention when questioned something which you later may rely on in court. Anything you do say may be given in evidence. Do you understand?"

Tim nodded meekly. He glanced at Dan, but he didn't speak until Kulkarni produced a pair of handcuffs, and then he said, "Oh, will those be necessary? My hands... they're how I make my living."

Kulkarni hesitated, but Firth sent her a reproving look. "Cuff him," he said. "You're being arrested for murder, Mr Kendall."

Kulkarni applied the cuffs and Tim watched, crestfallen. "The shame of it," he murmured. "I don't know what my wife will think. I'll have to call her. She mustn't hear about this from anybody else."

"We'll sort that out when we get to the station," Firth

replied. "We'll take you to Bodmin, but before we go, do you need any medical attention?"

"No. I'm all right." Tim cleared his throat. "I could do with a large brandy, but I don't suppose…"

"We'll get you a mug of sweet tea at the station," Firth said. "Mr Corrigan, we'll need a statement from you. There are a couple of officers inside, and they can bring you and Mr Hargreaves over to Bodmin. Are you good to go?"

"Yes, we may as well get it over with. Will I get tea too? It suddenly sounds wonderful."

"I think we might be able to manage it." Kulkarni smiled. "I might even be persuaded to nip out and fetch a decent cup of coffee."

"Even better," Dan said.

"If you're ready…" Firth gave his colleague a sardonic smile.

"Yes, Sarge." Kulkarni stepped back smartly, giving Firth room to lead Tim past.

Tim shuffled along, dragging his feet as though he didn't trust his legs. As he passed, he stopped for a moment, turning his watery gaze on Dan. "I'm sorry," he mumbled. "I shouldn't have put you through that."

"I'll survive," Dan replied. "But if you want to make amends, tell me where Edward is."

"I can't do that," Tim said. "That wouldn't be right at all." He looked down and let Firth lead him away. A uniformed constable was holding the door open, and Firth took Tim through.

"Ready?" Kulkarni asked Dan.

"Yes."

At the bottom of the stairs, Alan was waiting with a uniformed officer. "They wouldn't let me go back up," Alan said. "Are you okay?"

Dan nodded.

They didn't talk much on the way to Bodmin, and once

they were inside the brightly lit police station, the time passed in a flurry of bewildering procedures.

At one point, Dan was left sitting on his own in a corridor. Surrounded by the hubbub of a busy office, he felt strangely disconnected, cast adrift in a sea of bustling officialdom.

It gave him time to think, and surprisingly, his thoughts returned to his cottage in Embervale. Was Jay progressing well with the work on the floorboards, or would he have uncovered new problems that would have to be dealt with? It would be good to get back there and find out; good to light the wood burner and sit back to enjoy its warmth; and even better to lock the door against the outside world.

After a while, Kulkarni strode toward him, bearing a couple of large paper cups. Offering one to Dan, she said, "I forgot to ask, but you look like a man who takes his coffee black."

"Thank you." Dan took the cup gratefully and removed the plastic lid, inhaling the heady aroma as he sipped the hot coffee. "Perfect."

"You're welcome."

"How's Tim doing? And Alan?"

"Mr Hargreaves has finished giving his statement, so he'll be here in a minute, and then we'll run you back to your hotel."

"And Tim?"

Kulkarni hesitated. "I can't say much, but let's put it this way: I don't think you'll be needed as a witness."

"He's admitted everything?"

"He's co-operating, so it looks as though the whole case will be tied up very soon."

"Good," Dan said. "Thanks for letting me know."

"No problem. But I have a lot of work to do, so I'd better get back to it." Kulkarni smiled then she hurried away.

Dan drank his coffee, and just as he drained the last drop, Alan arrived.

"Have you given your statement?" Alan asked.

"Yes. All done."

"Thank goodness." Alan glanced enviously at Dan's cup. "They gave me a mug of tea you could stand a spoon up in, but I drank it happily. I needed it."

Dan stood. "Shall we go? DC Kulkarni said they'd give us a lift."

"I think they'll come and fetch us when they're ready."

"Fair enough."

They stood in the corridor, unsure what to do. After a few seconds of silence, Dan said, "Unofficially, they told me that Tim's co-operating. Hopefully, that means he'll plead guilty."

"That would probably be for the best," Alan replied. "So what now? I don't know about you, but I'm ready to head for home."

"I can pack my bag as soon as we get to the hotel. But when we get back to Embervale, there's something I want to do."

"What's that? Collapse on the sofa with a whisky?"

"That does sound appealing," Dan said. "But after that, I want to find Edward."

CHAPTER 33

Before heading down to check out of the Regent Hotel, Dan prowled the corridors. And finally, he found who he was looking for.

A laundry trolley stood beside an open door, and Dan leaned against the wall and waited quietly. A moment later, Daphne emerged, a bundle of crumpled sheets in her arms.

"Good morning," Dan said, and Daphne jumped.

"Mr Corrigan! I didn't see you there. Are you... looking for something?"

"You." Dan moved away from the wall to stand in the centre of the corridor, his arms folded.

"Oh?" Daphne tipped the sheets onto the top of the bulging bag of laundry. "Is there something I can help you with, only I'm rather busy this morning."

"Lots of people checking out today."

"Yes. Everyone." Daphne's lips tightened, and she looked past Dan as though eager to get away.

"This will only take a minute. I'd like to ask you about a couple of things."

"Such as?"

"Tim told me that he learned the combination for the

doors to the roof from Edward Hatcher. Was that true, do you think?"

"I've no idea."

"Did either of them get the combination from you?"

"Of course not. I've never been up there. Why would I?"

"Good question," Dan said. "But someone must use those doors."

Daphne thought for a moment. "Matthew would know. And I suppose Dennis might go up there. He does all the maintenance. He comes in now and then to fix a dripping tap or bleed the radiators. That sort of thing."

"Ah. I'm guessing that Dennis is quite a tall man."

"Yeah. He's about your height," Daphne said. "Was that all you wanted?"

"Almost. What do you know about Charlie Heath?"

"Who?" Daphne tried too hard to make the question sound innocent.

"Come on, Daphne," Dan said. "I think you know that he's the journalist who was hanging around outside."

"No. The name doesn't ring a bell."

"Really. That's interesting, because he told Alan that an item of underwear was found in Edward Hatcher's bed."

Daphne shrugged. "First I've heard of it."

"I don't believe you. There's only one person who could've been rifling through Edward's sheets, and that's you."

"No, we have lots of people cleaning rooms. They come and go."

"Not at this time of year with half the hotel empty," Dan said. "I checked. I asked Matthew. Your uncle."

"Matthew's my uncle. So what?"

"So, he's very proud of you. When I mentioned your name, he boasted about what a hard worker you are, cleaning all the rooms on your own."

Daphne looked down at the floor.

"What size were they?" Dan asked.

Daphne looked up. "What?"

"The underwear you found. What size was it?"

"Oh, I don't…"

"There's no need to be coy. And you won't get in trouble. You can tell me in confidence. Were they size eight?"

Daphne looked around as though fearing she might be overheard, then she shook her head. "Bigger. A lot bigger."

"And you thought they belonged to Roz. Why?"

"I saw her in the corridor one morning," Daphne said. "I was going down to help with breakfast when I spotted her. It was very early, so I thought she must've stayed the night."

"But Roz is quite a slim person, isn't she?"

Daphne's eyes clouded with doubt. "Yes. I suppose she is."

"So the underwear probably didn't belong to her. And anyway, I happen to know that she goes home every night. She has a teenage daughter, and she likes to be there for her; to make sure she has a good meal, does her homework and gets a good night's sleep."

"That's nice," Daphne said, a hint of sadness creeping into her voice.

"But Roz does like to get up very early in the morning," Dan said. "She likes to ride her bike when there's no one around and the roads are quiet. So when you saw her, was she coming from someone's room having stayed the night, or was she going to make an early call on a friend?"

"She…" Daphne lowered her brows in concentration. "Now that I think about it, she might've had that helmet with her. But if she'd just arrived, Matthew would've seen her come in."

"Would he? You seem very short staffed. You and Matthew seem to do almost everything yourselves. Can we be sure that someone was at the reception desk for every minute of the day?"

"No. Matthew tries, but there's too much to do. And the owners won't take on any more staff, not while it's so quiet."

"There we are, then. You put two and two together and made seventy-three."

Daphne frowned at him. "I'm not stupid."

"No. But you have jumped to an unfortunate conclusion. You see, I checked. I asked around, and it seems that Lucille, or should I say Ms Turner, also likes to rise early, although in her case it's to meditate."

"Really," Daphne said, unimpressed.

"Yes. And when Ms Turner learned that Roz is a highly experienced practitioner of tai chi, they agreed to meet early in the mornings and practise together. Roz was helping a friend, that's all. That's the sort of person she is. Kind. Helpful. But you and your uncle, you thought you could exploit her."

Daphne pursed her lips. Her cheeks coloured.

"Listen carefully," Dan went on. "If I see one word of gossip about Roz or Edward in the press or on social media, I'll know exactly where it came from. It took me about fifteen seconds to find a name and address for the company that owns this hotel, and I'll make sure they know the way you and your uncle have been conducting your affairs. Am I making myself clear?"

Daphne nodded.

"Good." Dan was severely tempted to say more, but he walked away. He'd seen more than enough of Daphne and the Regent Hotel. It was time to go home.

SUNDAY

CHAPTER 34

EMBERVALE

After a few days spent getting his house back in order, Dan made the call.

It was ten o'clock in the morning, but when Charlie Heath answered the phone, he sounded tired: "Hello, who's this?"

"It's Dan Corrigan, Charlie. We met in Newquay."

"Oh? Hang on." His voice went quiet. "No, don't do that, you'll spill — oh hell! Never mind. Daddy will wipe it up in a minute." A sigh. "Sorry about that. You'll have to remind me. Newquay was last century."

"I was retained by Mr Hatcher. You were following him, and it was my job to... discourage you."

"Ah! Got you. Tall bloke. Pushy. Bloody nuisance."

"That's me," Dan said. "Anyway, as you probably know, Mr Hatcher has dropped off the map, and I was hoping you might be able to help me find him."

Charlie chuckled. "What happened? Did he bugger off without paying you?"

"Actually, yes. That's exactly what happened."

"Oh dear. How sad."

In the silence, Dan fancied he could hear Charlie's smirk.

"Come on, Charlie," Dan said. "Like you, I was doing a

job, trying to earn a few pounds. Surely you wouldn't mind helping me out?"

Charlie sniffed. "You know, I'm not surprised Hatcher stiffed you. It's typical of your rich and famous types. Oh, they'll give a few grand to charity if it gets their faces on TV, but when it comes to paying their way, they suddenly realise they've left their wallets in their other Armani trousers. And Hatcher could afford to pay you, believe me. The guy is loaded."

"Unfortunately, he's also difficult to track down."

"You're telling me, mate. I worked on him for weeks, but I can't help you. Wherever he hides away, I couldn't find it."

"You must have some clue," Dan insisted. "An investigative journalist such as you must've found something."

A pause. "Listen, I've got to go. Good luck with finding Hatcher. And if you see him, tell him I want to talk. I'll give him a good write-up if he gives me an exclusive on his nervous breakdown, or whatever it was that made him do a runner, so long as we can talk about the film deal as well. Bye."

"Wait! Please!"

The line hissed, and then Charlie said, "All right. All I know is that he can't be too far outside London. He used to come in on the train and travel back on the same day, usually at peak times. It was like a commute for him. He only ever carried a shoulder bag."

"What station did he use? Paddington?"

"Waterloo. Always. I tried following him a few times, but he always clocked me, and he was very good at losing himself in the crowd."

"Do you have notes of the days and times when he arrived?"

"Somewhere," Charlie said. "I keep everything."

"Could you send me a list? A text would be fine."

MICHAEL CAMPLING

"I suppose so. But after that, Mr Corrigan, do me a favour and leave me in peace, all right?"

"Definitely. Thank you," Dan said, but Charlie had already hung up.

Dan pocketed his phone and headed for the small downstairs room at the back of the house. There was no sense in sitting and waiting for Charlie's text, and anyway, he'd set aside part of the day to tackle the tiny room. He fancied it as a kind of study, but with all the work going on in the rest of the house, the room had become a dumping ground for anything that was in the way.

A set of dumb-bells vied for floor space with plastic crates of cables and stacks of battered paperbacks. There were cardboard boxes that he hadn't unpacked since moving in, and he was starting to wonder whether he'd ever get around to them. Whatever was inside, if he hadn't needed it yet, perhaps he never would.

But that decision could be left for another day. A few weeks earlier, he'd bought a flat-packed desk from Ikea, along with a high-backed office chair, and both were already assembled by the window. Picking his way through the clutter on the floor, Dan sat at the desk and began setting up his desktop computer. The machine was a good one; he'd built it himself, spending weeks poring over the specs of every part of the system, and it ran like a greyhound on steroids.

He spent an enjoyable half hour arranging the tower unit, the pair of twenty-four-inch monitors and the associated peripherals, squaring the cables away tidily to leave the desk as clear as possible. The PC booted up at the touch of a button, the tower making scarcely a whisper thanks to his careful selection of a sound-insulated case and quiet components. Dan ran through a few system checks, updating his anti-virus software and cleaning up the computer's registry, and time passed quickly.

It seemed as though he'd only been at his desk for a few minutes when his phone buzzed, and he picked it up, frowning at the display.

The text was from Charlie and he'd listed several dates, each with a departure time from the station. Dan took the first item from the list and pulled up a website with live departure boards from Waterloo. It didn't take him long to discover that the time matched a regular train from Waterloo to Bournemouth, and he scribbled down all the stops. After leaving Waterloo, it called at Clapham Junction, Woking, Basingstoke, Winchester, Eastleigh, Southampton Airport Parkway, Southampton Central, Brockenhurst, New Milton, Christchurch and Pokesdown, before arriving at Bournemouth a little over two hours after leaving London.

Dan scribbled the list onto a scrap of paper, but then he was interrupted by someone knocking on the door. He hurried through to the kitchen, the list still in his hand, and found Alan peering in through the window. He waved him inside and waited, eager to share his news.

But Alan spoke first, waggling his phone in the air as he came in: "I've got something to show you."

"Me too," Dan said. "I've had a word with Charlie Heath, and he's given me some possibilities for Edward's hideaway."

"That's good, but I think you'll like this. I've had an email from Tim, and it's all very cryptic. It's going to take some serious brain work. Any chance of a brew?"

"Can't you just tell me what it says?"

Alan held up his phone and squinted at the screen. "Hang on. I've closed it. You make the tea and I'll retrieve it."

"All right. Take a seat."

Alan made himself comfortable at the kitchen table, and a couple of minutes later Dan set a mug of tea in front of him. Sitting opposite Alan, he said, "Right. When did you get this email, and what does it say?"

"It came a few minutes ago. I came straight over to show you, but…" Alan made a show of sniffing the air. "I can still smell insecticide. Are you sure it's safe to be in here?"

"It's fine. Jay gave me the full health and safety lecture, and there's nothing to worry about. But tell me about the email."

"Well, it's from Tim's email address, but it's a weird message."

"Let me have a look." Dan held out his hand and Alan passed him the phone.

The message was short, and it took only a few seconds to read. "I see what you mean," Dan said, "It's cryptic all right. More like a crossword clue. But this is interesting; he's signed himself as Timothy the Toad. Do you think Roz named her character after him?"

Alan shrugged. "It's possible, but I'm not sure it's important. Anyway, we can't ask her. She's still not returning my calls."

"She'll let you know when she's ready." Dan turned his attention back to the email. "Why would Tim send you such a cryptic clue?"

"I think he meant it for you. He didn't have your email address, but he knows we're neighbours, so he sent it to me. And I think he might've guessed that you'd be looking for Edward."

Dan nodded. "I asked him about it when we were on the roof."

"There you are, then. You saved Tim's life, and he wants to return the favour." Alan smiled. "Did you see his wife on the news last night?"

"Oh yes. Lady Cynthia is quite something. You know, I told Tim he should give her a chance. Looks like I was right."

"Definitely." Alan adopted a strident upper-class accent. "My husband has been the victim of a cruel sociopath, but he remains strong, and we shall fight this terrible injustice together."

"I can't see him getting away with it," Dan said. "But who knows? He might pull it off. Tim is a schemer. And that makes me think twice about this email. What's he trying to achieve? I mean, if he wanted to help, why didn't he just give us Edward's address in plain English?"

"It's the way his mind works," Alan said. "Either that, or he's deliberately tugging your chain for his own amusement. Anyway, there's no harm in us taking a crack at the clue. Give it here, and I'll have another look. And we're going to need a pen and some paper."

Dan passed the phone back to Alan, then he stood and crossed to the kitchen counter, retrieving a pad of A4 paper and a handful of biros. "That should be enough, but I've got plenty more."

Alan nodded, pulling the pad toward him and grabbing a pen. Then he studied the email before reading it aloud: "The cart drew on without a virtual hero, but the miniature edition of Pip's adventures makes a home in Hammond's woodland." He thought for a second and then began scribbling. "We know that Hammond's woodland is a reference to Roz's books, and we know she used Dickensian names for her characters. By Pip's adventure, he must mean *Great Expectations*. That could give us the letters G and E, or it could be more literary."

"This is Tim we're talking about. It'll be literary."

"Right," Alan said. "So which of Roz's creatures are named after characters from *Great Expectations*?"

"There's Pippa the pied wagtail, of course, but I don't think that's the answer. It's too obvious."

Alan nodded. "There must be another. Roz has written at least a dozen Freddie the fox books, and I don't know all the characters. Do you have your laptop handy?"

"I'll get it." Dan hurried from the room and returned a

couple of minutes later with his sleek Microsoft Surface laptop and its power supply. "It needs plugging in," Dan said as he trailed the cable across the room to the nearest socket. "It won't charge properly for some reason, and I haven't been able to get to the bottom of it."

"You should get a new machine."

Dan almost laughed "Have you any idea how much these things cost?"

"No. Sorry, that was a bit tactless." Alan hesitated. "You know, I upgrade my Dell pretty regularly. Maybe next time, you could take the old one off my hands. If you don't mind having a cast-off, that is."

"Er, thanks. I'll think about it."

"There's nothing wrong with it," Alan said. "It's just that I like to have something reliable to work on and my current machine's getting a bit slow."

"I expect it only needs a few tweaks to optimise it."

Alan shrugged. "Maybe, but I can't be bothered with all that tinkering. It's not worth it."

"I could give it a spring clean for you. Bring it over sometime, and I'll take a look. If I can speed it up, you can buy me a pint. How's that?"

"Okay. It's a deal." Alan thought for a second, then added, "Don't say no immediately, but if you're still looking for work, I can't be the only one who could use some technical help with a computer."

"Are you suggesting that I offer my services? Put a postcard up in the village shop window?"

"It couldn't hurt. With Christmas coming up, and the sales in January, there'll be lots of people with shiny new computers and no idea how to set them up properly."

"And they'll have old machines that could be refurbished and reused," Dan said.

"Definitely. You'd be doing your bit for the environment, and you'd be providing a much-needed service to the community. As far as I know, there's no one in the village who fixes computers."

Dan shook his head. "There are plenty of twelve-year-olds with better technical skills than me."

"But would you trust your computer to a youngster? Most people wouldn't. They want a professional job done by a professional person, and you look the part."

"I'm not sure how to take that."

"As a compliment," Alan said. "But you don't have to decide right now. Mull it over while we unravel Tim's email."

"Mm." Dan opened a browser on his laptop. "Okay. We need a list of Roz's characters so we can cross-reference it with *Great Expectations*."

It didn't take Dan long to find Roz's website, and there was a section dedicated to Freddie the fox and his friends, complete with illustrations. Making a quick count, Dan said, "Roz has more than thirty characters across the series." He opened a new tab and quickly retrieved a list of Dickensian characters. "Oh. There are at least twenty names in *Great Expectations*. We could do with narrowing it down a bit."

Alan clicked his fingers. "We're missing something. We should be treating it more like a crossword clue. The word *miniature* must be significant. We might have to shorten a word or—"

"It's not just *miniature*," Dan interrupted. "It's *miniature edition*. So what would a shorter edition be called? Condensed? A digest?"

"Pocket-sized." Alan thumped the table. "There's a character in *Great Expectations* called Herbert Pocket."

"So there is. Unfortunately, he's not the only Pocket. There's also a Belinda and a Matthew."

"Could that be a reference to the Matthew who worked at the hotel?"

"He wouldn't be in Roz's books though." Dan switched tabs and studied Roz's website. "Anyway, Roz doesn't have a

Matthew or a Belinda. Oh, and there's no Herbert. But hang on. There's a Bertie the beaver, and that's short for Herbert, so it could fit."

"And a beaver's home is called a lodge." Alan made a note. "I think we're getting somewhere. Now for the first part. The cart drew on without a virtual hero."

"The word 'without' often means you've got to remove some letters," Dan said.

"Of course! I don't know why I didn't see this straight away, but take some letters from *cart drew on* and you get *Cardew*. Edward's pen name was staring us in the face." Alan scribbled on his pad. "And the letters you have to remove, are *T*, *R*, *O* and *N*. Tron. And there's our virtual hero."

"Cardew Lodge," Dan murmured as he pulled up Google maps and started a search. "There's a Cardew near Carlisle. It's a hamlet. Edward said he lived in the countryside, but according to Charlie, Edward's hideaway is somewhere between London and Bournemouth."

"Do you remember when we met Edward in Newquay?" Alan asked. "He was going on about living in the countryside, and he said something about a train chugging along and church bells."

"That's right! It's coming back to me now. But did he say chugging? I thought it was chuffing."

Alan furrowed his brow. "What's the difference?"

"Chugging could be a modern diesel, but chuffing might mean a steam train."

"Unlikely," Alan said. "There are only a handful of working steam railways in the country."

"That's why we need to remember exactly what he said." Dan closed his eyes for a second, summoning the memory of the first time he'd met Edward. "The church was called Saint... James'. At least, I think that's right."

"That's a common name for a church," Alan replied. "But

he also said something about the scent of lavender, didn't he?"

"That's right." Dan's fingers blurred across the keyboard, and as the results appeared, he grinned. "There's a steam railway in Hampshire: the Mid-Hants Railway, also known as the Watercress Line. It's not far from Winchester." Dan checked his list of stations. "Edward took a train that went through Winchester. If I search nearby for Saint James's church." He looked up. "There's a Saint *John's* church in a place called Alresford. It's close to Winchester, there's a station for the steam railway, and guess what! There's a place where they grow lavender. That has to be it."

"Is there a Cardew Lodge?"

"Not listed, but Edward knows how to go to ground. He's hardly likely to hang out a sign."

"It could be what they call a cherished address," Alan said. "Like this place. It wasn't always called the Old Shop."

"I know. The first time I tried to order something online, the address was rejected. It took me a while to work out it was officially Number Two, Fore Street."

"So, what's our next step?" Alan asked. "We can't very well drive all the way over to Hampshire and wander around looking for a house called Cardew Lodge."

But Dan's only reply was to raise an eyebrow.

MONDAY

CHAPTER 35
ALRESFORD

Dan parked his Toyota RAV4 on the main road that ran through the small Hampshire town of Alresford. Sitting next to him on the passenger seat, Alan checked his watch. "Three hours it's taken us to get here. I hope it's going to be worth it."

"Only one way to find out," Dan replied. "Let's stretch our legs. If nothing else, we can find somewhere to grab a coffee."

"Or an early lunch," Alan said hopefully.

"Possibly. It depends how we fare in our search for the lodge."

Alan looked doubtful, but he kept his thoughts to himself, and they set off, strolling through the town, admiring the Christmas decorations adorning the eclectic range of shops. Soon, they discovered what they were looking for.

The distinctive oval sign advertised the presence of a post office within the Co-operative supermarket, and Dan and Alan headed inside and went straight to the post office counter.

From the other side of the glass screen, a young woman looked at them inquiringly and said, "Good morning. What can I do for you today?"

Dan summoned a warm smile and checked the woman's name badge. "Good morning, Beryl. I was hoping you could help me."

Beryl tilted her head to one side. "In what way?"

"I have a Christmas card I want to deliver, but I'm having trouble finding the address."

"You could always post it," Beryl said with a smile. "It's what we do."

Dan chortled. "Yes, but I really wanted to deliver this by hand. It's for an old friend."

"Show me the address, and I'll see if I know it." Beryl indicated the slot beneath the screen. "Pop your card through. I can tell you by the postcode."

"I don't have it with me," Dan replied. "Alan, do you have that card?"

Alan held out his hands. "No. Perhaps you left it in the car."

"Yes. That's right. It's in the car. And it wouldn't have been much help, anyway. I don't have the postcode."

"Okay, so do you have the address?" Beryl asked.

"Yes. It's Cardew Lodge, Alresford."

Beryl blinked. "No street name?"

"No, I'm afraid not. That's all I have."

"Then there's not much I can do to help. I've never heard of a Cardew Lodge. There's a Cardew House, could that be it?"

"No, I've already tried there," Dan said. "I called them on the phone."

Beryl frowned. "You called someone to ask if they were the person you want to send a Christmas card to."

"I know it sounds silly," Dan replied, "but, you see, erm…"

"He's delivering cards for his mother," Alan put in. "And I'm afraid she's getting a bit forgetful. She's made rather a muddle of her Christmas card list, bless her, but she's very keen not to leave anyone out. I'm sure you understand."

Beryl's smile was back. "I see. Well, I'll try and help. As I say, I don't know of a Cardew Lodge, but give me a second. My senior colleague is busy in the store room, but he's lived here for a long time. If he doesn't know where it is, it probably isn't there anymore."

"Thank you," Alan said smoothly. "That's very kind of you."

"No problem." Beryl sauntered away from the counter, disappearing through a doorway at the far end of the shop.

"If my mother could hear what you just said about her," Dan muttered to Alan, "you'd soon discover that she's still as sharp as a tack."

"I had to say *something*," Alan protested. "If you hadn't blurted out that you'd already called that other—"

"Sh!" Dan nodded toward the doorway. "She's coming back."

Beryl had a spring in her step as she returned to the counter. "You're in luck. Trevor knew all about it. He's drawn you a map." She slid a slip of paper across the counter. "You can't miss it. It's a big place, but it's fairly new. That's why I didn't know the name." Beryl wrinkled her nose. "Mock Georgian according to Trev, and it's got a stone wall all around it. Must've cost a fortune."

"Yes, probably." Dan took the paper and studied the simple map. "Thanks for this. You've been very helpful. Is it in walking distance?"

"I'd drive if I were you," Beryl replied. "It's a little way out of town."

"Right. Thanks again." Dan gave Beryl a grateful smile, then he and Alan headed for the door.

"She was nice," Alan said.

Dan grinned. "Yes. Prompt and efficient. You can tell we're that bit nearer to London."

"What are you talking about?"

"Back in Devon, that conversation would've taken half an hour, and we'd have been forced to listen to Beryl's life story. And then we'd have been introduced to Trevor, and unless I'm much mistaken, he'd have given us a lecture on Georgian architecture and the evils of gentrification."

"Nonsense," Alan protested, but he knew when Dan was joking, and he chuckled.

Back in the car, they'd only driven for ten minutes when Alan pointed through the windscreen. "There. That must be it. It's the only entrance."

Dan spotted the open gateway set into the high stone wall, and he guided the Toyota between the gate's twin pillars. A tarmac driveway took them on a winding path through a series of neat flower beds, the soil punctuated by rows of short bare branches.

"Roses," Alan said. "It'll be a picture in the summer."

"The grounds are certainly on a grand scale," Dan replied. "I feel like I should be wearing a tie and driving a Jag. Edward must've done well for himself."

"We'll see. This might not be his place, after all."

The drive brought them to a curved area beside a large house, and Dan parked next to a dark-blue Range Rover.

"It looks like someone might be home," Dan said. "Let's go and say hello."

Climbing from the car, Dan paused to admire the house. Even from the side, the place seemed to have been built to impress. Constructed from mellow brick, the house was impressively tall, with large windows ranged across three storeys. A neatly trimmed creeper clung to a wooden trellis, but the twisted vines were bereft of leaves.

Dan and Alan made their way to the front of the house.

"Wow," Alan murmured.

"Quite." Dan didn't know if the architecture was Georgian, mock or otherwise, but the front aspect of the house called to mind a time of opulence. The porch was picked out in white, its triangular pediment supported by two pillars of smooth stone, and the great wooden door was painted in flawless gloss black. Dan pointed to the brass plaque mounted beside the front door. Its highly polished surface was etched with two words: *Cardew Lodge*. "At least we've found the right place."

"Yes," Alan said. "But if this is Edward's house, you were wrong about him hanging a sign."

Like the plaque, the doorbell was made from gleaming brass, and Dan gave the button a firm push.

Inside, a dog barked, and Dan and Alan shared a look. But when the door was opened, they saw that there was nothing to fear. The red setter that squeezed its way into the widening gap studied them with a soft eye, then it raised its nose and sniffed hopefully, as if they might have brought food.

"Really, Clarence, have some manners," someone said, and the door opened fully to reveal an immaculately dressed woman in her fifties. Wearing a long tweed skirt, accompanied by a pale-green cardigan over a white blouse, the woman looked every inch the refined country lady, complete with a string of pearls and matching earrings. Her hair was medium length and stylishly silver-grey, and she peered down at them through spectacles framed in tortoiseshell, the thick lenses magnifying her eyes.

"Oh, hello," she said, her tone polite rather than unfriendly. "How did you get in? Was the gate open?"

"Yes, it was," Dan replied. "I hope we're not disturbing you."

"Mm? Well, yes, as a matter of fact I am working. I really must have a word with the gardener. He's forever leaving the gate open. It really is too bad. Now, whatever it is, I'm not interested, so if you could leave by the way you came in, that would be appreciated."

"This will only take a second," Alan said. "We're looking for Edward Hatcher."

The woman froze, then slowly, she removed her glasses, letting them hang from a slender chain around her neck.

"My God!" Alan breathed. "Edward?"

Dan looked from Alan to the lady in front of him, his mind filled with a jumble of competing sensations.

The woman shook her head. "He's not at home." Her voice was unsteady, but she cleared her throat and replaced her glasses, regaining her composure. "Please leave."

"I'm sorry, but I know it's you, Edward," Alan insisted. "I don't want to upset you, but we came to find you, to check if you were all right."

The woman sighed, and this time, when she removed her glasses, it was as if Edward appeared before them. "I should remember to take my reading glasses off before I open the door," he said, his voice sounding unnaturally deep now that it had returned to its regular register. "I can't see beyond the end of my nose when I've got them on. But my mind was elsewhere." He paused. "You'd better come inside." He stepped back from the door, and Alan led the way, Dan following meekly behind.

"Come along, Clarence," Edward said, marching through the elegantly appointed hallway, heels tapping on the parquet floor. "Let's show our visitors to the front lounge."

Clarence trotted happily alongside its owner, and Dan and Alan trailed along behind.

They followed Edward into a spacious lounge, the centre of the room dominated by a tan leather sofa and a pair of matching armchairs. Edward took an armchair and gestured toward the sofa. "Please, make yourself comfortable." Then, as they sat down, he added, "If that's at all possible." He offered them a weary smile. "I know this must all look very curious to you."

"No," Dan and Alan said at the same time.

"How you live your life is entirely up to you," Dan added. "We're just glad that you're okay. When you disappeared from Newquay, we were worried. But now, perhaps, we can understand why you left in such a hurry."

"You think you have all the answers, do you?" Edward said. "How clever you must be."

"Forgive me," Dan replied. "That sounded condescending. All I really meant to say was that I can understand why you were so upset by the note you received. It said that your secret was about to be revealed, and presumably you were keen to keep your private life to yourself."

Edward's eyebrows flickered upward. "You've got that part right, I'll admit. But you don't understand. You can't."

"You don't owe us an explanation," Alan said, but Edward shook his head.

"I shouldn't have been so hasty to disappear. But old habits die hard, and for too many years I lived on my wits. When you're undercover in the field, you learn to smell trouble, to fear discovery. When you walk into a room, you check the exits, and you always have an escape route in the back of your mind. *Always.* As soon as you get an inkling that things might go wrong, you do a disappearing act. It's the only way to stay alive."

Edward sighed, his gaze losing focus. "But it wasn't until after I left the service that I realised there was another side to my character, another way I could live my life. I started writing, and the first character I created was myself. You see, to me, Max Cardew has always been female. Her identity and the work go hand in hand. The arrangement has served me well, but it's always been private. There's simply no need for anyone else to know about it."

"Tim knows?" Dan asked.

Edward nodded. "Tim and I go back a long way. I knew he'd never deliberately tell anyone about me, but when I got that note, I assumed he must've let something slip. I was sure that Brian had cottoned on and sent that note to taunt me. We've often quarrelled, and he can be very childish."

"Brian spoke up for you when you disappeared," Alan said. "He was upset. And he has a heart condition. Did you know that?"

"Oh dear." Edward's shoulders slumped. "Poor Brian. I owe him an apology. But after everything that's happened…"

"You must've heard about Dominic Rudge," Dan said. "The note you received was intended for him. Tim sent it to the wrong room."

"Ah! It all begins to make sense." Edward's eyes clouded. "I was sorry to hear about that business with Tim on the roof. When I heard the news, I felt dreadful. I'm partly to blame; I showed him how to open the doors. I shouldn't have done it, but I was showing off, making a point. On my first night at the hotel, I had a drink with Tim in the bar, and he got me talking about my days in the service. Looking back, I can see that he led me by the nose, but at the time it seemed harmless enough. He asked about opening locked doors, and I bragged about how easy it was. He challenged me to prove it."

Alan was on the edge of his seat. "What did you do?"

"I simply watched one of the staff opening a door off the lobby, and I bet Tim that all the combinations in the hotel were the same. People are lazy, you see. But Tim insisted that we try it out, and by then I was in high spirits, so I agreed. I don't know what possessed me." Edward shook his head, smiling. "We were like a couple of schoolboys sneaking out of the dorm after lights out."

"He showed you the door that led to the roof," Dan suggested.

"Yes. If only I'd known what he was planning, I'd never have gone along with it, but it's a little late for regrets. I should've known better."

"And the same combination would've been used for the hotel's store rooms and broom cupboards." Dan said.

"Presumably."

"So when you left the hotel, were you, by any chance, dressed in overalls?" Dan asked.

"I was sorely tempted," Edward replied. "No one ever notices the maintenance man, but I saw him, and he's about my height. I could pass for him any day of the week, but the truth was much simpler. All I had to do was slip into the guise of my female alter ego. If I'm away from home for more than a day or so, I generally carry a few things with me. It's a nuisance to carry so much luggage, but for me it's a necessity."

"And no one noticed you walking out?" Alan asked.

"I was cautious. From the first floor landing you can see the front desk. I waited until that buffoon sloped off to play online poker, then I marched out of the front door and no one gave me a second glance."

"Incredible," Alan murmured. "Not even the journalist?"

"He ignored me completely."

"But why did you throw your jacket over the fence?" Dan asked.

"I didn't. The bags were too heavy, slowing me down, and I felt too conspicuous. So I ditched one bag and the suit carrier, then I went on my way. When I'd put enough distance between me and the hotel, I took a cab to the station and grabbed the next train out of there."

"Someone must've found the suit carrier and rifled through it," Dan said. "When they didn't find a wallet, they threw the jacket over the fence."

Edward nodded. "Well, now you know the truth, what are you going to do?"

"Your secret is safe with us," Dan replied. "There's no need for us to tell anyone, although you may want to contact the Devon and Cornwall Police. I'm afraid we filed a missing person's report."

"I've taken care of that already," Edward said. "Friends in the Home Office come in handy once in a while."

"Good. That's all right, then." Dan caught Alan's eye. "We should be leaving. It's a long drive back to Devon."

Alan nodded, but he kept his attention on Edward. "If you don't mind me asking, what should we call you?"

"That's kind of you, Alan, but I'm still Edward. Max serves her purpose, but she's just one aspect of who I am. This is how I choose to live when there's no one else around. There's only Clarence, and he doesn't care what I wear. I have no neighbours, no one overlooks the property, and hardly anyone knows this address. I'm free to do as I please, and I spend most of my day at the keyboard. But, whenever I want, I can change into a collar and tie and go out into the world as Edward Hatcher."

"You mentioned a gardener," Dan said. "Doesn't he notice?"

"He only comes once a week, less often in winter. He potters around outside, but he likes to keep to himself. He prefers plants to people, and he's too shy to look me in the eye." Edward stood, smoothing down his skirt. "I'd offer you a cup of tea, but I have a schedule to keep, and I really must get back to work. I'll see you out."

Dan and Alan stood.

"Thanks for seeing us," Alan said. "We'll leave you in peace."

Edward led them to the front door and held it open for them, but as they stepped outside, he said, "Hold on a second, Dan. I believe I owe you for services rendered."

"Oh, not at all," Dan replied. "Forget about it. I hardly did anything."

"But I've put you to all this trouble," Edward protested. "I feel awful."

"There's no need," Dan insisted. "You're in one piece and that's all that matters."

"And you can rely on us to be discreet," Alan said. "Bye, Edward. All the best."

"Goodbye," Edward replied. "And thank you."

"Bye." Dan waved, then he and Alan turned away and headed back to car.

"So, the underwear that was left in the hotel bedroom…" Alan began.

"I'd have thought that was obvious," Dan said.

"Yes. I suppose it is." Alan's expression brightened. "Lunch?"

Dan nodded firmly. "Lunch and then home. And I don't know about you, but I need to finish putting my Christmas decorations up."

EPILOGUE

NEWQUAY

W hen it was all over, Roz took a long walk, and found herself drawn to the coastal path.

It was good to stand and watch the wind whisk the wavetops, and the breeze brought a revitalising tingle to her cheeks. The ocean swelled and roiled, seething with uncontrollable power. And yet, twice a day, every day, the tide crept in gently to wash the sand clean and leave the stones glistening in the sunlight.

Once, Roz had looked to the ocean and seen only oblivion; now, she saw renewal.

After a while, when she felt strong enough, Roz walked to the place where it had happened. Had Rudge been afraid? she wondered. Had he begged Tim for mercy even as the cliff's edge had crumbled beneath his feet? Or had he been resigned to his fate, knowing he'd been beaten, the bully finally cowed?

Roz could hardly comprehend the dreadfulness of Rudge's final moments. But there was one question she'd asked herself more often than any other: was it her fault?

She replayed the phone call over in her mind for the

thousandth time, and she could almost feel the damp mist that had seeped into her bones on that dreadful night.

Tim had answered her call straight away.

"Toad," she'd said. "I need to talk to you."

"Roz? What's the matter? Where are you?"

"Outside. Near Fistral beach."

"Why? What's happened? Roz, you sound terrible."

"I don't know, Toad, I…" Her voice had failed her.

"I wish you wouldn't call me that," Tim had said. "Why don't you come to the hotel? We can talk in person."

"But Toad, I mean, Tim, I've done something."

"What? Are you hurt? Do I need to call an ambulance?"

"No. I'm all right." Roz had hesitated, but then it had all come spilling out. "That reporter who was hanging around the hotel, I've talked to him, told him all about Rudge, how he harassed me, how he took advantage of me, how he… he…"

Tim had groaned. "Roz, you poor thing. You shouldn't have done that. I had it all worked out. I told you I'd stop him. You know I'd do anything to take care of you."

"But you could never *be* with me. So I've taken care of him myself, Tim. I had no choice."

"You've made a mistake, Roz. You shouldn't have talked to the press. Now I'll have to change my plans. I'd better go. I haven't much time."

"But, Tim—"

"Come back to the hotel," Tim had said. "No, wait. Go somewhere public. Find a restaurant or a pub or something. Make sure they can see you the whole time."

"Why?"

"Just do it, Roz. Please. Don't come back here for at least an hour. That should give me time."

"Time for what?" she'd asked. But Tim had ended the call.

She'd known that Tim was up to something. The letter she'd received had been from him. He'd meant it to appear anonymous at first glance, just like the other typewritten notes, but to Roz's eyes, he'd given himself away. It had read:

In the space between reality and imagination, your work illuminates the darkness within.

Let not thy divining heart
Forethink me any ill;
Destiny may take thy part,
And may thy fears fulfil.

She'd recognised the last lines immediately. He'd taken them from a song by the poet John Donne. It was called *Sweetest Love, I do not go,* and more than once, Tim had read it aloud to her as they'd snuggled together in bed. Their time together had been punctuated by intervals of loneliness and separation, but their shared love of Donne's songs and poetry had provided a thread of continuity that bound them together. So she'd known he'd written that letter, and that meant he'd sent all the notes. But she couldn't have known what he was going to do. No one could've predicted that.

Now, Roz watched the tide rise over the rocks where Rudge had breathed his last. The cold gnawed at her fingers and toes, but she stayed until the tip of the last rock had slipped below the surface.

No, she decided. *It wasn't my fault. It wasn't my fault at all.*

Roz turned away from the sea and walked into town. As she passed WH Smith, she stopped to listen to a busker. The young woman was good, playing her heart out, her strong voice filling the street and banishing the bitter chill of winter.

Searching through her purse, Roz gathered together all her notes without counting them, and laid them in the girl's guitar case, sliding them under the handful of coins that were already there.

Without missing a beat, the busker smiled and slipped the words *thank you* into her song.

"Thank *you*," Roz said. And then, her heart feeling lighter than it had for a while, she strolled through the town with a sense of purpose. There was a little shop that sold art supplies, and she had a sudden impulse to stock up. There was work to be done, and stories to be told, and one thing was for sure: from now on, her stories would be filled with light and colour, but most of all with joy.

Than you very much for reading Murder Between the Tides. I hope you enjoyed it.
Keep Reading for your Bonus Short Story:
Mystery at the Hall

Or dive right into the next full-length novel in The Devonshire Mysteries:
Mystery in May

Find it on your favourite store
Mystery in May
Visit: books2read.com/mysteryinmay

AUTHOR NOTES

Is the Regent Hotel a real hotel in Newquay?

As with all the Devonshire Mysteries, places are used in a fictionalised way. There are some big old hotels in Newquay, and I stayed in one of them, immediately realising that it had to feature in a mystery. The staircase was grand, the halls wide, and there was plenty of polished wood panelling. The hotel I stayed in was Victorian rather than Regency, but some of its features have made it into the book, albeit on a grander scale than reality.

Similarly, I have played fast and loose with the geography of Newquay, while trying to evoke a sense of the place. I always feel that there's something intriguing about seaside towns out of season; it's almost as if you shouldn't be there. You feel as though you're trespassing, peeking behind the scenes, and I tried to bring some of that sensation to the story.

There is a coastal path in Newquay, and there's also a statue of dolphins at Fistral beach. The Horizon cafe was inspired by a vegan cafe tucked away in a side-street, but you'll be glad to know that The Drowned Sailor exists only in my imagination. Also, the delightful pub called The Rusty Saw was purely fictional.

What about Arlesford?

I visited Arlesford, a small town near Winchester, and it does have a steam railway, a church and a lavender farm, and so on. The post office counter is even inside the co-op. But Cardew Lodge is purely fictitious. I invented the name Max Cardew right at the beginning of the first draft, long before I thought of using Arlesford as his hideaway. I was horrified to discover that there is a Cardew House in the town, but by then I was writing the last chapter and it was far too late to go back and change the name, so I soldiered on. To avoid confusion, I made a fleeting reference to Cardew House, and I hope the residents don't mind.

Is the Empire Number One a real typewriter?

Yes. I researched this quite a bit, and you can get a flavour of my progress by reading about Alan's attempt at research. The typewriter I wanted had to be distinctive in some way, and I discovered that almost all typewriter ribbons are the same width, except for a few older models. Also, the Empire Number One fitted the bill in that it was small enough to be concealed; unlike some of the big old office machines which were enormous. The typewriter Dan and Alan discovered in the pub was based on an Imperial portable machine that I've owned for many years, and like Alan, I own an Olivetti Lettera 32. I bought it at an auction when I was still at school, because even back then, I wanted to be a writer. I still covet such machines, and one of these days, I hope to find an Olympia SM4 at a reasonable price.

Some of the writers play games with character names; do you?

Just between ourselves, I can tell you that many of the character names have been borrowed from members of my extended family. But I won't tell you which ones, and I must stress that borrowing a name is not the same thing as basing a character on someone! In fact, I invent characters first and then give them names afterwards. For me, characters have to be imaginary; if I felt they were based on real people, it would hold me back.

I think a lot of writers play games with words for their own amusement because we tend to spend all day in our heads, and our brains need a little light entertainment. Sometimes, I'll imagine a certain actor playing the part, and then I might base a name on that actor to remind me. I've always admired 'character actors': those talented individuals who seem to disappear into a part. In this book, I realised that Dr Brian Coyle could be played by the actor Brian Cox. My little joke here is that the actor shares his name with the scientist and TV presenter, Dr Brian Cox. I've heard the actor say that people are sometimes disappointed to discover that they're not about to meet the scientist. And so, my fictional character insists on people using his title, even though he's washed up as an academic. It's not hilarious, but it kept me entertained.

More beer?

Yes, the brands of beer mentioned are authentic, and no, I'm still not receiving anything in return for mentioning them. Not so much as one drop.

Can we see some of the sources you used for research?

Certainly. Here you go:

michaelcampling.com/murder-between-the-tides-sources

Keep Reading for your Bonus Short Story:
Mystery at the Hall

MYSTERY AT THE HALL
A DEVONSHIRE MYSTERIES STORY

SATURDAY

October 31

CHAPTER 1

S itting at a table in Embervale's only pub, The Wild Boar, Dan Corrigan cast his eyes around the room as he waited for his neighbour, Alan Hargreaves, to return with their drinks.

Since the summer, the pub had been redecorated, and the new manager, Samantha Ashford, known to all as Sam, had brought a homely touch to the old place. There were new curtains at the windows, the walls had been repainted, and the shelves had been swept clear of dusty knick-knacks; the space filled instead with a collection of venerable hardbacked books. But wisely, Sam had steered clear of anything too trendy, and The Boar was still every inch a country pub. The polished oak bar was centre-stage, and the great stone fireplace shared the billing, its slate hearth gleaming darkly in the glow from the logs crackling lustily in the grate.

It's a good thing she hasn't gone overboard, Dan thought. *The locals would never have stood for it.* Dan pictured the pub remodelled in the style of a fashionable city watering hole, and he smiled to himself at the thought of the locals perching uncomfortably on brightly coloured plastic bar stools.

"What are you grinning at?" Alan asked, sliding a pair of pint glasses onto the table.

"Nothing much," Dan said. "I was just wondering where everyone is. The place is half empty."

"The village hall, probably. There's a Halloween party." Alan took a sip of beer. "I got you a pint of Gun Dog, but I'm trying the Reel Ale. It's not bad."

"Right. Thanks." Dan tried his pint, but for some reason, he didn't savour the taste as much as usual. It was hard to relax when the bar was so quiet. Without the background buzz of boisterous conversation, his voice seemed unnaturally loud and his London accent out of place. "I suppose this party is for the kids, right?"

"Mainly, although there'll be lots of grownups there too. It's a family-friendly kind of event." Alan eyed him for a moment. "Why, do you fancy taking a look?"

"No. It's fine. I was just curious."

In the corner, a couple donned their coats before heading for the door, and Dan stared balefully at the vacant table.

Alan stood. "Come on. Grab your pint. We'll go across to the hall and poke our noses in."

"What? But we can't just—"

"It's only over the road," Alan interrupted. He smiled over at the bar where Sam was watching him with a raised eyebrow. "Sam, you don't mind if we nip over to the hall, do you? I want to show Dan our barbaric pagan rituals. We'll be back in a few minutes."

"Just mind you bring those glasses back," Sam replied. "And don't be too slow if you want to find a seat. They'll all be trooping back over here when they've finished their fun and games."

"Definitely." Alan made for the exit, his glass in one hand and his coat in the other, and Dan followed uncertainly. He sent Sam an apologetic smile, but she'd already turned her attention to her few remaining customers, watching them intently as though defying any of them to leave.

Outside, the crisp night air nipped Dan's cheeks, and the chill roused his spirits. Walking away from the pub with their drinks was a strangely transgressive act, like sneaking out of school, and Dan found himself smiling as he crossed the road.

"Really, we ought to be in fancy dress," Alan said.

"Oh. Will we be allowed in?"

"Yes. I don't think we'll be the only ones in mufti, but there's a prize for the best costume. A couple of years ago, I won a bottle of wine."

"What did you go as?"

"Guess," Alan said.

"Something traditional, something old school. I know. Count Dracula."

"Nope. I was a wicked wizard. I've still got the false nose somewhere."

They halted in front of a stone building, its upper storey rendered and painted white between a framework of dark timbers, and its roof topped with a neat thatch. The door stood open, and from within the ancient walls, the strains of pop music crept out into the night, the rhythm mixed with the squeals of overexcited children.

"Are you sure about this?" Dan asked.

"It'll be fun," Alan insisted, and he marched inside.

CHAPTER 2

Inside the village hall, the lights were low, and a swirling mob of children dashed around the room, forming good-natured scrums and taking turns to frighten each other. Mummies waved their bandaged arms, zombies lurched, and witches and wizards twitched their fingers to cast complex curses. The adults had been relegated to the hall's perimeter where they chatted amongst themselves while keeping a watchful eye on their little monsters.

Alan indicated a quiet corner, and Dan followed him along the edge of the temporary dance floor, both men receiving a few nods of acknowledgement and a word or two in greeting. Some parents were in costume and some were not, but all looked faintly harassed, and Dan's drink attracted envious glances.

Raising his voice, Alan said, "It's certainly buzzing. What do you think of it?"

"It's very… lively," Dan replied. "But you promised me pagan shenanigans. This is more like a school disco."

"I think we've missed the party games. Ah well, the kids are having fun. It's good to see them active instead of being cooped up with their games consoles."

"I'm not sure the parents would all agree," Dan said. "A few of them look like they'd happily swap anything for a bit of peace and quiet right now."

Alan chortled, content to sip his drink and watch the fun.

Dan spotted Marjorie Treave across the room, but though he tried to catch her eye, she didn't notice him. She was fussing over a girl of nine or ten, perhaps a relative. From what Dan knew, the Treave family's roots ran far and wide in the area.

Close by, someone cleared their throat, and Dan turned to see a middle-aged man smiling at him and nodding enthusiastically. Dressed in a dark suit and white shirt, the man's face had been painted to resemble a vampire, his brow a sickly white and his cheekbones emphasised by carefully applied make up. The effect was amplified by his dark eyes, which danced as if at some private amusement, and his mop of thick black hair had been plastered with gel and combed into an elaborate bouffant quiff.

"It's you, isn't it," the man said.

"Erm, yes. That is, it depends on who you think I am." Dan tried for a careless chuckle, but it somehow turned into nervous laughter.

"You're Dan Corrigan. The one who figured out what happened when that poor man was killed."

Slowly, Dan nodded, and from the corner of his eye, he saw that Alan had registered the arrival of the newcomer.

"Hello," Alan said. "Can we help you with something?"

"We were just talking about that terrible business back in the summer," the man replied. "A murder in a place like this. Who'd have thought it?" He shook his head, but his dismay only lasted a second. His expression brightened, and he thrust out his hand. "Where are my manners? I'm Martin Crowe. That's Crowe like the actor, not the bird. I'm the chair of the parish council and the village hall committee, and I'm the treasurer of the allotment association, and the secretary of the summer fayre committee, so one way or another, we were bound to cross paths sooner or later. Pleased to meet you."

Dan and Alan took turns to shake hands with Martin. "Of course, we've met before," Alan said. "I didn't recognise you underneath all that face paint."

"Face paint?" Martin touched his cheek in mock horror. "That's not face paint. I've just seen the price of beer over at The Boar." He laughed, and Dan did his best to join in.

"Speaking of which," Martin went on, "I'll see you over there in a bit. You seem like a pair of public-spirited guys, so I'll buy you a pint, and we'll see if we can't rope you in."

"For what?" Dan asked.

"Oh, I hardly know where to begin," Martin replied. "Don't worry, I'm not asking you to join some awful committee. But whenever we hold an event like this, we always need foot soldiers to help out on the day. Most people enjoy it."

Dan tried to look as though he was considering the idea. "Mm, it sounds interesting, but I'm not sure I'll have the time."

Martin simply patted him on the arm. "We'll fix you up with something light, to begin with. We'll talk in the pub. See you over there." Martin winked, then he strode into the melee, still smiling.

Dan watched him go. "Interesting character."

"Yes. At least, he thinks he is," Alan replied. "Well, have you seen enough, or do you want to stay for the judging of the costumes? There's a raffle too."

"There's *always* a raffle. I only moved in to the village a few months ago, and already, I've bought more raffle tickets than I care to remember."

"You do exaggerate," Alan said. "The question is, have you won anything yet?"

"Not really. I snagged a bar of soap once. Lily of the valley. I donated it to the next person who came asking for prizes for *his* raffle. But before he left, he made sure to sell me a strip of tickets, so I'll probably win the damned thing back."

"Stranger things have happened." Alan nodded across the room. "Our new friend is spreading the word about your exploits. I really think this might be a good time to leave."

Sure enough, Martin Crowe was addressing a small knot of people, and when he paused to point in Dan's direction, they all turned to stare.

"Lead the way," Dan said. "I'll be right behind you."

Back in the pub, Alan and Dan picked up where they'd left off, chatting about nothing in particular and enjoying their beer. The heat from the fire turned the pub into a cocoon of warmth, and within minutes, Dan forgot all about his strange encounter at the Halloween party.

But eventually, the quiet was shattered by an influx of parents, some with children in tow. Most of the adults were still in their Halloween costumes, and all of them had a certain thirsty glint in their eyes.

"Here come the satanic hordes," Alan said. "There goes the neighbourhood."

"Still, at least the kids aren't allowed in the bar," Dan replied. "They'll have to go into the back room, so we should be safe from trick or treaters for a while."

"Ah, they're only having a bit of fun. Don't be so grumpy."

They watched the crowd at the bar for a minute, enjoying the spectacle of grownup wizards and witches vying to be served. But then Alan leaned close to Dan, and in a stage whisper, he said, "You spoke too soon. I don't know if we're in for a trick or a treat, but your new pal is heading this way, and he's brought his gang with him."

Sure enough, Martin Crowe was making a beeline toward them, a couple of friends tagging along in his wake. "Mind if we join you?" Martin boomed. "The promise of a pint still stands."

Alan gestured to the empty seats at the table. "Help yourselves. But there's no need to buy us drinks."

"Nonsense. It'll be my pleasure. What's everybody drinking?"

Alan was the first to give in. "Well, if you insist, I'll have a pint of Reel Ale. Thank you very much."

"Same for me," Dan said. "Thanks." He turned his attention to Martin's friends, a man and a woman who were both in their forties, and both made up to resemble Frankenstein's monster. "I'm Dan, and you probably know Alan already."

The monsters nodded in unison, and the female creature extended her hand for a shake. "Tamsin. Tamsin Pettigrew."

Dan half rose from his seat to shake her hand. "Nice to meet you, Tamsin."

"And I'm John Simmons," the other monster said. "A pleasure to meet you, Dan. And always nice to bump into you again, Alan. Hopefully, we'll be on friendlier terms tonight."

"What's this?" Dan asked. "Is there acrimony in the air?"

Alan chuckled. "Not at all. John's team has beaten mine into second place many times at the quiz night. He's a demon when it comes to general knowledge, so we're bitter rivals, aren't we, John?"

"Only on quiz nights," John said. "And I haven't made it to the quiz for quite a while. I'm always driving the kids somewhere or picking them up. As soon as they hit their teens, I became a one-man taxi service."

"Anyway, sit down, you two," Martin insisted. "I'm off to the bar. Tamsin, John, what are you having?"

"Orange juice for me," Tamsin replied as she and John sat down.

"And I'll have a half of whatever you're having," John chipped in. "I've got to collect the kids later."

Martin rubbed his hands together. "A cheap round for me, eh? Marvellous. I'll be back in a jiffy. Talk amongst yourselves."

He marched toward the bar,- and an embarrassed silence settled over the group.

Tamsin fussed over the beermats, arranging them neatly on the table, then she said, "What did you think of our little party, Dan? It must seem very provincial to a city man like yourself."

"Not at all," Dan replied. "It was charming. It was nice to see the adults getting involved too. Your face paint must've taken ages. Did you do it together?"

Tamsin laughed nervously, and John said, "Oh, no, it's just a coincidence. We didn't arrange it that way. My daughters did mine—I've got two girls—and, er, Tamsin, I think you did yours yourself, didn't you?"

"Yes. Isn't it funny?" Tamsin replied. "People have been remarking on it all night. What are the odds?"

"Pretty good, I expect," Dan said. "Most people seem to have gone for the classic Halloween staples."

John looked pleased with himself. "We like to keep the party as a fairly traditional event. If you'd come over earlier, you'd have seen the games. It was hilarious."

"Maybe next year," Alan said. "Ah, here comes Martin with the drinks."

The atmosphere around the table lightened as drinks were dispensed and appreciative comments were murmured. Martin pulled a chair up to the table and sat at its head as if presiding over a meeting. "Now," he began, "tell us, Dan, how are you finding life in the village? Are you settling in all right?"

"Yes, I'm enjoying it. The house is shaping up, and now that the decorating is almost finished, the place looks good."

"Not too quiet for you?" John asked. "Some people find the rural way of life takes some getting used to. Apart from the events we organise ourselves, there's not a lot going on."

Dan weighed his words before replying. In truth, he was at something of a loose end, and there were times when he'd found the time passing far too slowly. He needed paid employment, but although he'd been casting around for opportunities, he still had no idea what he was looking for. "I'm adjusting. I'm sure it'll all work out in the end."

Martin grinned, the smile made sinister by his face paint. "I'm afraid we can't offer murder and mayhem every five minutes just to keep you occupied."

Tamsin delivered a playful slap to Martin's arm. "Oh really, that's in very poor taste. Very poor indeed."

"You must forgive, Martin," John said. "He likes to tease people."

"That's all right," Dan replied. "I know I made a certain impression on my arrival in Embervale. Believe me, I'd rather not have been involved in a murder case, but it happened, and I'd rather have people joke about it to my face than whisper about it behind my back."

Martin clapped. "Bravo! Quite right. So no more beating about the bush. I must admit, I have an ulterior motive in bringing us all together tonight."

Dan and Alan exchanged a look, and for their part, John and Tamsin looked distinctly uncomfortable.

"You're not going to go into all that business again, are you?" John asked.

"Helen's untimely demise, you mean," Martin shot back. "And yes, I would like to talk about it, and I think that our newest resident might enjoy hearing about it too. I think he'll find it diverting."

"What's this?" Alan asked. "Helen who?"

"It was probably before your time," John replied wearily. "There was an unexplained death. In the village hall, actually. It was—"

"Seven years ago to the day," Martin interrupted. "On Allhallows Eve, Helen Beecham went to the children's party, and she never left it again, not alive at any rate."

"That's terrible," Alan said. "The poor woman. What happened?"

Martin smiled triumphantly. "You see! I knew they'd be interested."

John pushed his chair back from the table. "Well, I'm not. I really don't want to talk about this, Martin, so if it's all the same to you, I'm going to head off. I need to collect the kids. They say they're too old for the village party, so they're at a friend's house watching scary movies. I expect they're full to the brim with pizza and popcorn by now." He offered a smile around the group, but before he could stand, Martin laid his hand on John's arm, pressing it against the table.

"You don't want to do that, John," Martin said. "It would be very rude if you were to dash off like that. I've just bought you a drink."

"But—"

"Don't be a spoilsport," Martin insisted. "Your kids are having fun, so stay with us a little longer. After all, we need you to complete the tale."

It looked as though John was going to argue, but Tamsin said, "I suppose we can talk about Helen. It was a long time ago and there's nothing to hide. Helen was my friend, and I'm sure she wouldn't mind. It saddens me when I think she might be forgotten."

"Exactly. I couldn't have put it better myself." Martin sat back, releasing John's arm.

"All right," John said. "We can discuss what happened, but you'll have to keep it respectful. I hope that's understood."

"Naturally." Martin smiled, satisfied, and Dan watched him carefully. There was something odd about Martin's demeanour, something that wasn't quite right. The man came across as likeable enough: he was friendly and outgoing, open and cheerful. At the Halloween party, he'd made an effort to welcome Dan, and he'd made a point of introducing himself as the chair of various committees. He clearly saw himself as a central figure in the community, a friend to all. But his congeniality only went so far, and from the way he'd talked down to John, it seemed that Martin didn't care to be contradicted.

"Perhaps we should change the subject," Alan said. "I think there'll be a frost tonight. The sky was certainly clear enough."

Martin shook his head. "No. We'll tell you the story of how we lost our dear friend, Helen, and we'll see what you make of it. Obviously, we know what happened, and the matter was all dealt with properly at the time, but it'll be interesting to see what you think, Dan. It'll give you an insight into what it's like to live in the village. You'll be able to see what makes this place tick."

There was silence around the table, then Dan said, "All right. You've piqued my interest. You're going to have to tell us now, or we'll be on tenterhooks all night."

"Exactly." Martin took a drink of his pint, then smacking his lips, he began.

"In those days, the Halloween party was a small affair, and all very traditional. We had apple bobbing contests, toffee apples, and plenty of sweeties and such for the kids."

"We did have some music and dancing as well," Tamsin interjected. "This isn't the fifties we're talking about."

Martin waved her interruption aside. "Yes, yes. I should know. I was the one who organised it. I'm *always* the one who organises it, aren't I?" He shrugged. "Someone has to do it. Anyway, where was I? Oh yes. John was helping out. As the secretary of the village hall committee, he was there to make sure everything was done properly. He kept an eye on the health and safety, you might say."

MICHAEL CAMPLING

"I help with most of the events at the hall," John said. "The only thing I don't like is when the burglar alarm goes off in the middle of the night, but that hardly ever happens."

"You're the key holder," Dan suggested.

John nodded. "For my sins. I'm also a trustee of the village hall fund, and a few more things besides. It's important to give something back to the community."

"I don't know how you find the time," Tamsin said. "You do so much, and you look after two children, all on your own." She turned her gaze on Dan. "It's a shame John's girls weren't there tonight. They used to like dressing up in wizard's robes, you know, like from Harry Potter. Adorable."

"Moving on," Martin said, "we get down to the details of who was doing what seven years ago. I was looking after the refreshments. Soft drinks for the kids, tea and coffee for the grownups. John was in charge of the raffle, so he was stationed just inside the door, trying to catch everyone when they came in. And Helen and Tamsin were in charge of the snacks and sweets."

"And where were they positioned?" Dan asked.

"The food and drinks were next to each other," Tamsin replied. "We always used to put the tables in an L-shape in the corner, on the far-left as you go in."

Dan nodded thoughtfully.

"I see what you're thinking," Martin said. "And you're right. Tonight, when I came over to meet you, you were standing on the very spot where Helen was helping on the day she died. In fact, that's what put me in mind of that night."

"These days, we put the tables at the other end of the hall," Tamsin said quickly. "It seems to work out better."

"And it's further away from the toilets," John added, wrinkling his nose.

"Right," Martin said. "But back then, we had a winning formula, and we stuck to it. At first, everything was just as normal. The party was in full swing, the kids were running around playing…" He glanced at the others.

"Musical statues," Tamsin said. "The kids run around while the music's playing, but when it stops, they have to stand stock still. It was noisy, and it was getting hot in there. I remember I was wearing a thick black cloak—I was dressed as a witch—and I had to take it off. Anyway, it was during the game that Helen started complaining of a headache."

"A migraine," John chipped in. "I believe she suffered from them quite a lot."

Tamsin nodded. "Yes. Sorry. I meant that she felt a migraine coming on. I told her that she should go home. I said I'd be able to manage the food on my own, but she wouldn't hear of it. She said that the clearing up would take ages, and she knew that we had to leave the hall clean and tidy."

"There was an event the next day," John said. "The local history group were having a talk on something or other. I can't recall what it was going to be about, and of course, it never took place, on account of what happened to Helen."

"And what did happen?" Alan asked.

"Well, Helen wouldn't go home," Tamsin replied. "So I suggested that she at least take a break for a few minutes to get away from the noise. I said that she could always come back later and help to clear up—if she was feeling up to it, that is—and she agreed."

Dan gestured toward Martin. "You said she never left the hall, so where did she go?"

"There are a few rooms at the top of the village hall," Martin said. "There's no heating or anything upstairs, so we just use it as a storage area."

"We keep the trestle tables upstairs," John explained. "There's not much else we can keep up there—it would get too damp. But I suppose Helen must've thought she'd get some peace and quiet, because that's where she was found."

"Dead." Martin leaned forward. "In a locked room with no windows, and the key was still in the lock, on the inside."

"How dreadful," Alan said. "What happened? How did she die?"

"They said it was an accidental overdose," Tamsin replied. "When the police came, they found some pills in her handbag. They think she meant to take her migraine medication, but for some reason, she took these other pills by mistake. They were painkillers, prescribed for her husband, but he…" Tamsin broke off, her gaze lowered.

"His name was Jack," Martin said. "He died of cancer. That must've been about two years before Helen passed away. Ah, Jack was a good friend. It was terrible to see him brought so low. Toward the end, he was on some very strong medication, and Helen must've kept hold of it. We'll never know why."

"I've always thought she was intending to take those pills back to a pharmacy," John suggested. "That's what you're meant to do, isn't it. But I suppose it must've slipped her mind."

Dan thought for a moment. "I don't like to ask, but do any of you know what kind of painkillers we're talking about?"

Tamsin shook her head, but Martin and John avoided eye contact, both men studying their drinks.

"It doesn't matter if you don't know," Dan said. "It's just that, you wanted to hear what I made of the case, and as far as I know, deaths from an overdose of painkillers are quite rare. People are usually hospitalised first, unless there are other factors." He paused. "Was there something else? Something you're not telling me?"

Tamsin looked as though she wanted to say something, but before she could speak, Alan said, "Hang on a minute. How come nobody found her in time. You must've known that she was upstairs, didn't you?"

Tamsin nodded. "She told me where she was going, but

when she didn't come back, I assumed she'd changed her mind about staying to help. I thought she'd probably gone home. I remember asking after her when I was getting ready to leave. I'd left my cloak on a coat hook in the porch, and when I went to collect it, I popped my head into the kitchen and asked if anyone had seen her." She looked at the others. "You were both there when I asked about her, and we decided she must've gone home. That's right, isn't it?"

"Definitely," John said. "I knew she'd gone upstairs earlier, because she'd passed me on the way. I was right beside the door, and I thought she was looking a bit peaky when she went by. I remember, I asked her if she was all right, and she said she'd be okay in a few minutes, and she was just popping upstairs for a tea break. She had a mug in her hand. I can see it like it was yesterday." He sighed. "I should've gone up to check on her, but with all the noise and the activities, I must've lost track of time."

"Apart from the main entrance, does the village hall have any other doors?" Dan asked.

"Certainly," John replied. "There's a fire exit in the far-right corner. But it wasn't used that night. I checked it when I locked up. It's one of my responsibilities." He frowned. "Why do you ask?"

"I'm just trying to build up a picture," Dan said. "I like to get all the facts straight. For instance, were you beside the entrance all night, John?"

"Yes. Most people bought a few strips of raffle tickets as they came in, and I had to separate all the individual tickets and fold them up so they'd be ready for the draw. That took me quite a while, and I had to keep an eye on the prizes."

Dan almost laughed. "Why? Were they particularly valuable?"

"No. But there were some bottles of booze to be won, and with all the kids running about, we didn't want to end up with broken glass all over the place."

MICHAEL CAMPLING

"Fair enough," Dan said.

Martin grunted in disapproval. "You weren't there *all* night, John. One of your daughters hurt herself, didn't she?"

"Oh yes, I'd forgotten about that. Minnie tripped up and grazed her knee. She's a teenager now, but back then she was only small. She was very brave about taking a tumble, but as usual, I made a fuss. I insisted on fixing her up, so we went down to the kitchen. There's a first aid kit in there, and I cleaned Minnie's knee and popped a plaster on. After that, she was as right as rain, so she went back to run around with the other kids." John smiled fondly. "They've always been tough, my girls. I suppose they've had to be."

"Are you divorced?" Dan asked.

"John's a widower," Tamsin said quietly, then she flashed him an apologetic smile. "Sorry, John, I didn't mean to answer for you. Anyway, your poor wife passed long before any of this happened, so there's no need to drag her into it. Let's stick to the subject, shall we?"

"Tamsin is a stickler for getting to the point," Martin said. "She keeps the parish council in line, that's for sure. And it's just as well, or we'd waffle on all night about the weather and the state of our vegetable plots."

Tamsin looked quietly pleased. "I do my best." Turning to Dan, she added, "I'm the clerk for the parish council. I keep the minutes and things, that's all. Martin is just flattering me, as usual."

"Why was Helen helping at the party?" Dan asked. "Were her kids there?"

"No, Helen didn't have any children of her own," Tamsin replied. "She was incredibly good with the little ones, though. They all loved her. She was such a lively character. She could be very playful, almost like a child herself. She loved to help with parties and fairs and things like that."

"It sounds as if she was very community-minded," Dan said. "Was she a member of the parish council as well?"

302

Tamsin shook her head, but Martin and John chuckled.

"She had too much life in her for that," Martin said. "Helen would do anything for anybody, but there was no way she'd have put up with our committee meetings and suchlike. She wouldn't have wanted to sit around listening to old duffers arguing over litter bins and parking spaces. She was a free spirit."

Tamsin sat up a little straighter, a deep breath flaring her nostrils. She remained silent, but Dan knew exactly what she was thinking: *What does that make me?*

Helen had clearly been a vivacious character, so perhaps Tamsin had lived in her shade. But Dan hadn't detected any trace of animosity. Tamsin had described Helen as a friend, and she'd spoken of her with genuine warmth.

This is all just speculation, Dan thought, and a flash of irritation sparked in his mind. His evening had been hijacked, and there was no doubt that Martin would insist on them all sitting tight until he'd reached the end of his tale.

As if sensing his friend's frustration, Alan caught Dan's eye, then he smiled. "Why don't we go over to the village hall and take a look? It might give us a better perspective."

"There's really no need," John replied. "Anyway, I've locked the place up."

Martin slapped his palm on the table. "Nonsense! We can soon open it up again."

"Honestly," Tamsin said. "What will you think of next, Martin?"

"It wasn't my idea. Alan thought of it, but I reckon it's a sound plan. So come on. Finish your drinks. We'll show Dan around the village hall. Where's the harm in that, John?"

"Oh, all right," John said, though his sour smile said that he was far from happy. "But I can't be long. The girls—"

"Yes, yes. We'll keep an eye on the time." Martin stood, draining most of his pint in a few long gulps, then he slammed the almost empty glass onto the table. "Let's go."

John and Alan took a few hurried slurps from their drinks, but Dan had lost interest in his, and he left it untouched on the table. Tamsin pushed her orange juice aside and stood stiffly, her back straight.

Then Martin shepherded them toward the door, and they made their way, once more, into the cold night air.

CHAPTER 3

S tanding at the village hall's entrance, John fussed over a
bunch of keys. When he finally unlocked the front door,
he held up his hand. "Give me a second before you come any
further. I need to disable the alarm."

Crossing the enclosed porch, he opened the inner door
and disappeared inside. Meanwhile, Martin took the
opportunity to deliver a short lecture on the history of the
hall. "Over three hundred years old, this place," he began,
and Dan tuned out, focusing his attention on the outside of
the building.

There were no windows upstairs, and no hatches or other
openings that could provide access to the upper floor. The
situation could be completely different at the back of the
building, but he'd find out soon enough.

In the hall, the lights flickered on, and John emerged,
smiling hesitantly. "Okay, you can come in," John said, then
he ducked back inside.

Martin extended his arm toward the doorway. "After you,
Dan. You're the guest of honour."

"Thanks." Dan stepped over the threshold and passed
through the porch which boasted nothing more than a row of

coat hooks on the wall. Beyond the inner door, the building was a little more interesting, but not by much. John was waiting in the short hallway, and though there was a noticeboard and a couple of faded photographs in wooden frames on the wall, there was little else to brighten the place except for a bright red fire extinguisher that sat on the floor. Directly ahead, four shallow stone steps led up to the main room where the party had taken place. On Dan's right, a plain wooden door stood open, revealing a basic kitchen, and on his left, a narrow flight of concrete stairs led upwards.

The others filed in behind Dan, and the hallway rapidly became crowded. "Do you want to go upstairs?" John asked, then he lowered his voice. "Because if you don't, that's fine. Don't let Martin pressure you. It's just his way."

"What's that?" Martin called out. "What are you muttering about, John?"

"Nothing." John looked at Dan and Alan hopefully. "Well?"

"Now we're here, we may as well go upstairs," Alan said. "No point in coming otherwise."

Dan nodded. "I don't want to put you out, John, but I'd like to see the room."

"All right. It's no trouble. Watch your step." John trudged up the stairs and Dan followed, the others trailing behind him.

At the top, they gathered on a landing made from bare floorboards, and they were faced with a row of three doors. But only one of them bore a steel security bolt, its handle secured by a sturdy padlock.

John had apparently come prepared with the correct key, and he unlocked the padlock and drew back the bolt.

"That bolt looks as if it was fitted relatively recently," Dan stated.

"Yes. After everything that happened, we wanted to make sure it could only be locked from the outside." John pushed the door open and stepped inside, fumbling along the wall for a light switch. "Come in. There's not much to see."

They trooped into the room, and Dan cast his eyes around the place. Folding wooden chairs were stacked against one wall, and several careworn trestles stood to one side, the tabletops standing on their edges and leaning against the wall.

"We hardly ever use those old tables anymore," John said. "We bought some new ones last year. Plastic. Much easier to keep clean." He tutted under his breath. "I should've stowed them in here tonight, but Martin lured us all over the road with the promise of a free drink."

Dan paced across the room, examining the place in as much detail as the dim ceiling light would allow. The walls and ceiling had been given a coat of white emulsion, but the floorboards were bare save for a layer of dust. All in all, it was a grim little room. Dan had never had a migraine, but he could only imagine that Helen must've been in quite a bad way before she'd willingly have chosen such an unpromising place for a rest.

"What was she doing in here?" he wondered aloud. "Was there some other furniture in here, something she could lie down on?"

"No, but she'd used one of the chairs," Tamsin said. "It was over there, by the wall."

"And where was Helen found?" Dan asked.

Tamsin raised a hand to point to the centre of the room. "She was... she was right there. Lying on the floor. On her back. They said, if she'd been on her side, you know, in the recovery position, she might've been okay, but..."

Tamsin's voice trailed away, and a silence filled the room as they all pictured the scene.

"Wait a minute," Dan said. "Tamsin, were you the one who found her?"

Tamsin nodded, and a chilling sense of disquiet stirred in

Dan's gut. He glanced at Martin and saw that the man's eyes were hard. Something was going on here. Martin wasn't just throwing his weight about, indulging in a bit of fun at the expense of the newcomer; he'd deliberately opened an old wound, forcing his friends to relive a night they'd much rather forget. But why? Did Martin suspect that one of them was complicit in Helen's death? Or did he have some darker motive? Perhaps Martin had been involved himself. Killers had been known to flaunt their deeds, defying others to catch them, even calling the police to gloat over their crimes.

Either way, Dan's instincts told him that there was something untoward in the manner of Helen Beecham's death, and he couldn't let it lie. Not now.

Dan locked eyes with Tamsin. "Take me through it. Tell me everything that happened from the moment you arrived at the hall on the day after the party, right up to finding the body."

"There's not a lot to tell," Tamsin began. "We hadn't put the tables away, so I came along in the morning to take care of it."

"By yourself?" Dan asked.

"Yes. It was about eleven o'clock or thereabouts. I'd taken the front door key from the cupboard in the kitchen the night before, so I let myself in, and I set about taking the tabletops from the trestles. Then I grabbed one of the trestles and carried it upstairs."

Dan glanced over at the wooden tabletops and trestles. "You were going to carry all those by yourself? Not easy when the stairs are so narrow."

"No. John was going to come along and help later."

"Wouldn't it have been better to wait for him?" Alan asked. "If you'd decided to clear the tables together, why did you go to all the trouble of taking the key the night before?"

Tamsin shrugged. "I don't know. It's just what we'd agreed. John was doing something with his girls that morning, so I said I'd go ahead and make a start." She paused. "Are you going to pick holes in everything I say? Only, I'm not here to be interrogated."

"No one's interrogating you," Martin said. "But we persuaded Dan to take an interest, so we can't complain when he asks a few questions."

Dan gave Tamsin a smile. "I'm just keen to know what happened. When you got to the top of the stairs, you found the door locked, is that right?"

After a moment's consideration, Tamsin said, "Yes. We just had the old mortise lock on this door back then, but the key wouldn't fit. I realised there was a key already in the lock, on the inside, and that's when I knew something was wrong." Her hand flew to her chest. "I'll never forget that moment, not as long as I live."

"What did you do next?" Dan asked.

"I kneeled down and tried to look through the keyhole, but of course, I couldn't see anything." Tamsin hesitated. "And there was... I don't like to say it."

"Go on," Dan said. "What did you see?"

"It wasn't so much what I could *see*." Tamsin wrinkled her nose. "There was a smell. A powerful smell of strong drink."

The phrase *strong drink* struck Dan as curiously prim, and he recalled that Tamsin had only ordered orange juice in the bar. There were plenty of good reasons for someone to abstain from alcohol, but equally, some motivations were borne of necessity.

Tamsin noticed the way Dan was looking at her, and her cheeks flushed a little. "I'm not one to gossip, but when we managed to get the door open, the place smelled like a distillery. Helen's mug was on the floor, lying on its side, so I suppose that whatever she had in there, it wasn't just tea."

"How can you say that?" Martin demanded. "We don't know what she was drinking, not for sure. And God knows, Helen can't defend herself."

"Come on, Martin," John began. "It was no secret that Helen liked a drink. No one blamed her. It was awful the way she lost her husband. She put a brave face on it, laughing and joking with everyone, but underneath it all, she was still hurting. For all we know, she didn't swallow those pills by mistake. She was at a low ebb, and—"

"Don't you dare," Martin interrupted. "Helen would never have harmed herself. I don't believe it for a second."

"But think about it," John said. "She'd carried those pills around with her for a long time. It was almost like she was preparing herself. Then there's the drink she washed them down with. We never did find the bottle, but it smelt like rum to me, and she must've swallowed a fair amount. As Tamsin said, the placed reeked of it."

"You were there too?" Dan asked.

John nodded. "Tamsin called me, and I came over straight away. I tried the key, but it wouldn't fit into the lock. So I kicked the door in. It took me a few tries, but in the end, I got it open. And we found her. Just lying there."

"I called for an ambulance straight away," Tamsin put in. "John was very good. He tried to revive her."

"I'd had some CPR training at work, but it was all a bit hopeless," John said. "I did my best, but I knew it was too late. She was gone."

"I arrived soon afterwards," Martin said. "Tamsin had called me as well, and I told them we had to step back, to get out of the way and wait for the authorities to arrive. There was nothing else we could do. It was all over. A life snuffed out, just like that."

Alan let out a tiny sigh and said, "Tragic."

Everyone nodded sadly in resigned agreement, and once again, the room was silent. But watching the individual reactions of John, Tamsin and Martin, Dan found himself clenching his jaw. There was something in the way they'd recounted their experiences that didn't tally with their reactions. It was true that several years had passed, and time had a way of distorting memories, but it was as though all three were not entirely convinced of their stories, like amateur actors who'd learned all their lines but still failed to convince the audience.

There was an aura of pretence in the room, and that could only mean one thing: someone present had played a part in Helen's death. The guilty party wouldn't be easy to unmask; they'd had years to perfect their cover story. But all Dan needed was a way in, a weakness in their combined narratives, then he could tease apart the facts one thread at a time, working at the fabric of events until the truth appeared.

Dan gazed down at the floor, studying the dusty boards, and he knew where he could start. Looking at John, he said, "When you opened the door, was the key on the inside of the lock as you'd thought?"

"No. It must've fallen out when the door swung open. The key was lying on the floor."

"Where?"

John pointed to a spot that lay on a direct line between the door and the centre of the room. "It was right there."

Dan stared at him. "Are you sure? That's more than a metre away from the door. Think carefully, John. It's important."

"Yes. I'm as sure as I can be." John looked to Tamsin. "I've got it right, haven't I?"

"Definitely," Tamsin stated. "I saw it too."

Dan strode across to the doorway. "Is this the same door or has it been replaced?"

"It's the same," Martin replied. "The door was undamaged. It was only the frame that had to be repaired. The mortise took a chunk out of the wood."

Dan ran his fingers along the doorframe, searching out the joints that showed where a new piece of wood had been inserted. "In that case, it would be true to say that the gap between the door and the floor hasn't changed."

"That's right," John said. "There's never been a carpet up here, so there's not much of gap. In fact, the door tends to scrape across the floorboards."

"Yes, I can see the marks." Dan turned on his heel to face them. "Imagine the door being kicked violently. Now, if the key had simply shaken loose, it would've dropped right in front of the door. In that case, it's likely that when the door opened, it would've pushed the key to one side. On the other hand, if the key had stayed in the lock until *after* the door had been forced open, it could've shaken free, but again, it would've been dropped to one side of the doorway. It certainly couldn't have landed as you've described. There's no way it could've travelled that distance."

"So, how did it get there?" Alan asked. "What are you saying?"

"Isn't it obvious?" Dan looked at each of them in turn. "The key couldn't have landed there, so it must've been placed by the person who killed Helen Beecham."

"Steady on," Martin began, but Dan didn't give him the chance to protest.

"You see, the murderer knew that the door would be forced open, and they wanted to make sure that the key was spotted immediately afterwards. They needed everyone to believe that the door had been locked from the inside."

"But, the door *was* locked," John insisted. "I tried to open it myself, and I bent down and looked into the keyhole. There was a key in the lock."

"There was *something* in the lock," Dan said. "It's safe to assume that nothing was found, otherwise you'd have told me about it. So..." He traced an imaginary arc with his finger from the door to one side, then he took a few steps and kneeled down, lowering his head to study the floorboards. "The killer would've been careful. Whatever they left in the lock, it had to be something innocuous, something that wouldn't look out of place if it fell out and was spotted. And they'd have planned to retrieve it as soon as possible, knowing that the discovery of the body would cause a commotion. With everyone distracted, the killer could remove the incriminating evidence without anyone noticing. But there's always a chance that things didn't go quite to plan. The object might've fallen out of the lock, and with these old floorboards, it could've slipped out of sight." Dan fished in his coat pocket and produced a small black torch. "This tactical light is brilliant, literally." Switching on the light, he placed it against the gap between two floorboards and began sliding it along, his face close to the floor. "There's a whole lot of dust and grit down there. Hang on. That could be something."

"What is it?" Alan asked. "What have you found?"

Dan didn't reply, but after a long second, he looked up with a wry grin. "Nothing. It's just an old nail, one of those flat ones you use for nailing down floorboards."

"A brad," Martin said. "But keep looking, Dan. I think you're on to something."

"This is becoming ridiculous," John muttered, his voice taking on an edge of restrained anger. "Martin, I really don't know what you're hoping to achieve by raking all this up. But are you seriously expecting us to stand around while you accuse us of... of murdering our friend?"

Martin held out his hands. "If the cap fits."

"For God's sake," John shot back. "What happened that night was a tragedy, a terrible accident, but you're not the only one who was hurt by it. Helen's death touched all of us."

"Some more than others," Martin growled, then he bit back his words, his lips tight.

"Enough!" Dan stood, raising himself up to his full height. "There's no point in squabbling. Arguments will get us nowhere, and anyway, it's all academic now. I know exactly what happened, and tomorrow, I'll have the proof I need."

They all stared at Dan, their eyes wide.

"Are you serious?" Alan asked.

Dan nodded. "I caught a glimpse of something metallic beneath the floorboards. I'm not sure what it is, but there's definitely something down there. We'll need to lift the boards to retrieve it. I suggest that we come back here in daylight and do the job properly. We'll need to be very careful. Obviously, we'll have to involve the police, but that can wait. I don't want to call them out until we have something concrete to show them. In the meantime, we should all leave. I want this room and the hall kept securely locked until the morning. No one must be allowed to come in. Can you handle that, John?"

"Yes. Yes, of course," John said uncertainly. "If you're sure…"

"One hundred percent." Dan gestured to the door. "Martin, if you'd lead the way, we'll all follow. I'll come down with John so that I can check everything's locked properly, and I'll need to collect all the keys."

John bridled. "There's really no need for that."

"Yes, there is," Dan said. "Now, let's go."

John didn't look happy about it, but he trudged down the stairs, and the others did as they were told. Alan sent Dan a questioning look, but he kept his thoughts to himself, and soon, the group reassembled outside.

"John, what time can you meet me back here?" Dan asked.

"Well, it's a Sunday, so the girls won't thank me if I leave the house too early. I can pop over here by, say, nine o'clock?"

"I suppose that'll have to do," Dan said. "It depends on Alan."

"Does it?" Alan asked. "I mean, I'm happy to come along, but why does it depend on me?"

"Because you're a practical sort of person, and I'm willing

to bet you have some kind of crowbar that we can use to get the boards up."

Alan nodded. "As it happens, I do have a nice little pinch bar. It's just the thing for floorboards, and nine o'clock is fine for me."

"That's settled then," Dan said. "Nine o'clock, it is."

Martin shifted his weight from one foot to the other. "I think I should be there too. After all, I am the chair of the village hall committee."

"You feel that gives you a certain jurisdiction, do you?" Tamsin said archly. "Honestly, Martin, if this is really going to become a police matter, then I don't think anyone is going to be impressed by your credentials."

Martin recoiled from her words as though stung. He was obviously upset, but he did his best to hide it. "Maybe so, but I'd like to be there. I was the one who raised this painful issue, so I really feel I ought to see it through to the end."

"That's fine," Dan said. "Tamsin? What about you? Do you want to come along?"

Tamsin pursed her lips. "I'll see. I'm usually getting ready for church at that time, and that's very important to me. I don't miss a Sunday service unless absolutely necessary, and I'm not convinced by all this intrigue and melodrama. I can't help but feel that you've all got caught up in some kind of silly game. It isn't seemly, and it has no basis in reality." She looked at each of them in turn. "John, I'm surprised at you, and Martin, I thought you'd know better. At any rate, if I'm not there, I'm sure you'll carry on without me. But now, I'm going home, so I'll bid you all a good night."

Tamsin made to turn away, but Dan called out, "Wait a minute. I have a question I'd like to ask you."

"Not now," Tamsin replied without looking back. "Perhaps we can catch up tomorrow."

"Yes," Dan said thoughtfully.

After a brief silence, John said, "You know, she's got a point. This has gone too far."

"I don't know." Martin ran his hand across his mouth. "Maybe we just need to pause for a minute, take a breath. Why don't we repair to The Boar and talk about something else for a while, what do you say?"

"I've got to go and pick up my girls," John replied. "But don't let me stop you."

"I'm going to head home," Dan said. "I'll see you tomorrow. I think we ought to swap numbers, then if any of us can't make it on time, the others won't be kept waiting."

Martin took a phone from his pocket. "Good idea."

They exchanged numbers, then the small group broke up, and Dan and Alan headed back along Fore Street.

"Do you really think that poor woman was murdered?" Alan asked.

"I'm certain of it," Dan said. "Tomorrow, we'll know for sure."

Alan hesitated. "Are you laying a trap? Are we going to wait and see if anyone comes back in the dead of night to lift the boards?"

"No. That won't be necessary. The murderer has kept out of sight for seven years. They aren't going to blow their cover now."

"I can see the logic in that," Alan admitted. "But what if we don't find anything under the floorboards, or it turns out that all you saw down there was another old nail?"

"Funnily enough, it hardly matters." Dan lowered his voice. "I'm afraid I haven't been quite honest with you, Alan. I've been doing some thinking, and there's something I have to tell you."

"Let me guess. You've seen the error of your vegan ways, and you've been secretly frying bacon in the dead of night."

Dan sighed. "This is serious, Alan."

"Okay. You have my undivided attention."

"That's good because, with what I've got in mind, I'm going to need your help. Is that all right?"

"Do you have to ask?" Alan said.

Dan glanced at Alan, taking in his earnest expression. "No. I know I can count on you."

Alan smiled. "Right, let's hear the plan of action."

"It's not so much about action," Dan began. "It's all about presentation."

The two men bent their heads together, and as they marched along the quiet street, Dan did most of the talking, his words little more than a hushed murmur.

SUNDAY

November 1

CHAPTER 4

A t seven o'clock in the morning, the sun had not yet risen in Embervale, and there were very few people up and about. But on Fore Street, one figure strode through the village alone, head down, face shielded by the peak of a black baseball cap. A pickup truck trundled past, and the lone pedestrian flinched but kept walking, shoulders hunched, gaze averted.

Outside the village hall, the figure halted, looking back along the street as if to check whether they were being observed. But the road remained empty, and apparently satisfied, the figure stepped up to the village hall entrance and tapped on the door. In the next instant, the door was opened from within, light flooding out, and Dan appeared in the opening.

"Good morning," Dan said. "That's an interesting outfit, Tamsin. Is that the hat you wear to church? Times have changed."

Tamsin frowned, her hands going to the straps of the small grey rucksack she was carrying on her back. "I thought I may as well do some cleaning whilst I'm here. I don't know why you insisted on changing the time, but I'm here now, so

I'm going to make the best use of the morning. Once you've finished mucking about with the floorboards, I'm going to clean the hall. After the party, it's going to be a dirty job. I've spoiled enough good clothes while looking after this place, and I'm in no rush to ruin any more."

"So what's in the bag? Dusters? A bottle of Flash?"

"Since you ask, I've brought some rubber gloves and a couple of scouring pads. The kitchen sink needs a damned good scrubbing." Tamsin paused. "Let's go inside and get this over with. It's freezing out here."

"Be my guest." Dan stood back and Tamsin bustled inside.

"Are the others here?" she asked.

"Alan and John are upstairs, waiting."

Tamsin halted at the foot of the stairs. "What about Martin?"

Dan shook his head firmly. "I didn't tell him we were coming here early."

"Oh. Why is that?"

"You'll see. We'll talk about this upstairs."

Tamsin narrowed her eyes and looked ready to argue, but she seemed to change her mind. She huffed in irritation, and when she climbed the stairs, her movements were stiff and uncertain.

Dan caught up with her on the landing. "We're meeting in the storeroom. Go ahead."

"All right. There's no rush, is there?" Tamsin opened the storeroom door slowly, then she made her way inside.

Five wooden folding chairs had been arranged in a circle in the centre of the room, and John and Alan had already taken their places.

"What's this?" Tamsin asked, her tone a little too bright. "Are we going to play musical chairs?"

"Please, have a seat," John said.

"Very well." Tamsin glanced around the room, then she

took her place. "I thought you were going to pull the floorboards up. Have you changed your minds?"

"We've already done it," John said. "We've put them back."

"And look at what we found." Dan sat down opposite Tamsin, then he leaned forward, extending his arm to show her the small strip of metal that he held between finger and thumb. "Do you recognise this, Tamsin?"

Tamsin squinted at the object. "It's one of those springy hair clips. I don't use them myself." She patted the back of her neck self-consciously. "I know the bob doesn't do me any favours, but it's practical, and…" She broke off, her lips forming an *O*. "You think that, just because it was under the floorboards, it must've been jammed into the lock."

"I'm sure it was," Dan replied. "The spring clip has been bent backwards to keep it open, and that would've kept it in the lock for a while. Clever, wasn't it?"

"*If* you're right," Tamsin said. "On the other hand, it might just be a hair clip that someone dropped at any time during the last few years."

John nodded. "That's what I said."

"But look at the way it's been bent," Alan chipped in. "That was deliberate. It hasn't been stepped on or snapped. It's been carefully reshaped."

"All right," John said. "Let's say you're right. Someone placed it in the lock on purpose. But what if the clip hadn't fallen out? It would've looked strange for the keyhole to be blocked with a hair clip when there was a perfectly good key lying on the floor."

"Strange, but not impossible to reconcile," Dan replied. "A hair clip is a perfectly reasonable thing for Helen to have carried. The police would've assumed that she'd jammed the door deliberately. All it really would've told them was that, for whatever reason, she didn't want to be disturbed. She knew that there was another key to the room, and she didn't want it to be used."

"I suppose that would cover it." John folded his arms and shrugged, resigned. Then he turned his baleful gaze on Tamsin.

"John?" Tamsin began. "What are you looking at me like that for? I don't even—"

"Stop!" Dan interrupted. "That night, you were dressed as a witch, yes?"

Tamsin's brow furrowed. "Yes, that's right. But I wasn't wearing hair clips. I just made a pointy hat. It stayed on with a strap that I tied under my chin."

"And what about Martin?" Alan asked. "What was he wearing?"

"He… let me see now. On that year, I think he went as a sort of mad scientist."

"Doctor Frankenstein," John intoned.

"Yes, that was it." Tamsin smiled. "He had this fantastic white wig with the hair sticking out in all directions. He did look a sight."

"But Martin's natural hair is quite thick," Dan said. "So how do you think he would've kept it tucked underneath the wig?"

"Oh. Yes, of course, he would've used clips to keep his hair flat." Tamsin hesitated. "Are you trying to imply that Martin had something to do with Helen's death? Because that's nonsense. He was the one who persuaded you to look into all this. He'd hardly do that if he was guilty. I'd have thought that was obvious." Tamsin made a disapproving noise in her throat, then she gathered herself as if about to stand.

"Wait, Tamsin." John gestured for her to remain seated. "Hear him out. I didn't want to believe it either, but Dan makes a very compelling case, and I really think you should listen to what he has to say."

Tamsin hesitated, then she said, "All right."

"Thanks," Dan said. "But first, there are a few points I'd like to clarify. If you could help me out by answering a couple of questions, I'd appreciate it."

"Very well. What do you want to know?"

Dan sat back. "Firstly, you told us that while John was in the kitchen, you stayed in the main room because you were looking after the refreshments. But I believe that you followed John out of the room. He didn't pay much attention to you, because he was busy tending to his daughter, but you went out to the porch for a while, and perhaps you cooled down for a minute, taking a short break from the heat and the noise before you went back to the party."

Tamsin's face fell. "I'd forgotten about that completely, but you're right. I did take a breather. But how did you know about it?"

"You said that you removed your cloak during the game of musical statues," Dan replied, "but you also said that you collected the cloak from a coat hook in the porch before you went home. Martin was by the door for almost all of the evening. He would've remembered if he'd seen you leave the room, so you must've nipped out at the one time when he was occupied."

Tamsin nodded slowly. "Well, you certainly got that right. I'm sorry I forgot about it. I didn't intend to deceive anyone, it was just one of those tiny things that you do and then forget instantly."

"Don't worry about it," Alan said. "We understand."

Tamsin sent Alan a grateful smile. "Still, I don't really see the significance."

"It means that Martin was left to his own devices for a while," John said. "I was in the kitchen, and you were getting a breath of air."

"Tamsin, how long did it take you to hang your cloak and cool down?" Dan asked.

"Only a few minutes," Tamsin replied. "Do you think Martin had time to… to do something to Helen?"

"He didn't need long," Dan said. "Martin had prepared carefully. He had everything planned out in his mind. He's a man who knows how to seize an opportunity. He took a bottle of rum from the raffle prizes, then he dashed upstairs. He tempted Helen with a generous measure of rum, then perhaps he persuaded her to lie down, and he offered to fetch her a pill from her handbag. Migraines can leave people feeling fuzzy and disorientated, and the rum wouldn't have helped. He probably gave her a much bigger shot than she was used to, and that accounts for the fact that it still smelled strongly of alcohol the next morning. At any rate, she accepted the pill. It wouldn't have taken long for her to feel out of it. After that, all he had to do was lay the key on the floor and leave the room. He'd brought his own key, and that was one of the things that gave him away."

"I see," Tamsin said. "Martin has been the chair of the village hall committee for as long as I can remember, so it would've been easy for him to obtain a key."

"Exactly," Dan said. "He locked the door with his key, bent a hair clip into shape and jammed it into the lock, then he headed downstairs. John is pretty sure that he was in the kitchen for about fifteen minutes, and that gave Martin plenty of time to put his plan into action."

"But I wasn't out the room that long," Tamsin protested. "It doesn't add up."

"It does if you admit the whole truth," Dan said. He locked eyes with Tamsin. "Did you have a nice time with John in the kitchen? Was it just a cosy chat or was there more to it than that?"

John sat up straight in his chair. "Now hold on a minute! I don't much like your tone, Dan."

But Dan kept his eyes on Tamsin. "It doesn't take long to

hang up a cloak, Tamsin. So what did you do after that? You can't have been in the main room, or you'd have known that Martin was missing, so you must've been in the kitchen with John."

"Hold on a second." Tamsin paled. "I... I must've... no, that's not right. Maybe I—"

"Come on," Dan interrupted. "You were with John. You're both adults and you spent some time together. Where's the harm in that?"

Tamsin stared at John for a second, then she let out a sigh. "Oh, what's the use? I can't do this anymore. I just can't." She looked down at her hands, twisting her fingers in her lap. "All right. I admit it."

"Admit what?" John asked. "Tamsin, I don't understand. You weren't in the kitchen with me. Not at all."

"I know that," Tamsin said, "and so does Dan. He's just been toying with me, leading me along. He threw me a line, knowing that I'd grab onto it, and now, I can't stick to my story without implicating you. My version of events doesn't make sense unless I was with you. Maybe there was a way to make it work, but I can't see it, and it's no use pretending anymore."

John stared at her, his face pale and his expression pinched. "What are you saying?"

"Dear John, you're such an innocent, but can't you see what all this is about?" Tamsin asked. "Dan has caught me out. For a minute, I really thought the whole thing could be pinned on Martin, so I went along with it. I insisted I was only gone for a few minutes, so the only way for me to have an alibi was if you'd be prepared to lie and say we were together. But anyone can see that you'd never do that. You're far too honest." She gazed at John, her eyes dark with longing. "I wanted us to be together, John. I've been carrying a torch for you for years, but you've never even noticed. What chance did I have? Helen was so much more attractive than me. She was bright, and she was pretty, and she was fun to be around. She could wrap any man around her little finger. When she set her sights on you, I knew I had to do something. I had to stop her. It was the only way. Otherwise, she'd have got you, and she'd have kept hold of you. Oh, I know she picked up men and tossed them aside. I saw the way she treated Martin. She led him a dance, but he knew his precious reputation would be ruined if he gave in to temptation. He had his wife to keep him grounded, but with you, there'd have been no stopping Helen. She'd have taken you, heart and soul, and then you would've been lost to me forever. I couldn't face that, John. I couldn't stand a lifetime of loneliness. Anything was better than that. Anything. Even the ultimate sin."

John's whole body sagged. "No," he whispered. "No."

Alan patted John on the shoulder. "This wasn't your fault."

"No, it was all down to me." Tamsin took a deep breath then let it out. "Strange, but you don't realise what a weight you've been carrying until it's gone." She smiled sadly. "I've tried to atone for my sins, but all these years, I've lived with the burden of what I did that night. It was almost as you said, Dan. I waited until John was in the kitchen, then I told Martin I was going to hang my cloak on the coat hooks. To be honest, I don't think he was even listening. He only pays attention to people who can be useful to him, and as far as he's concerned, I'm a useful minion but nothing more."

"He underestimated you," Dan said. "But you proved him wrong that night, didn't you."

Tamsin managed a wry smile. "It wasn't as hard as you might think. I'd worked it all out in advance, you see. Living on my own, I have a lot of time to think, and I've always been good at taking things step by step. In my mind, I'd played the whole thing out in a number of different ways. All I needed was a chance, and the party fitted the bill. First, I removed my cloak and told Martin I was going to put it away. With the cloak draped over my arm, it was easy for me to take a bottle from the raffle table as I passed."

"You were lucky that John was away from the table," Alan said. "You couldn't have known about that in advance."

"Couldn't I?" Tamsin glanced at John. "I shouldn't have tripped little Minnie up, the poor thing. She was so small back then, but children are resilient, aren't they. And when I comforted her, I'm afraid I pinched one of her hair clips as well. She'd dropped it on the floor, and I thought it would give me an excuse to talk to you later, John. I'd return it, and you'd be grateful, and everything would be fine. I know I shouldn't have done it, but Minnie wasn't seriously hurt, and I knew she'd be all right with you to look after her."

John's hand went to his chest, but he didn't reply.

"When I left the party, I hung the cloak in the porch, then I sneaked into the kitchen and took the spare storeroom key from the hook," Tamsin went on. "You were busy with your daughter, John, and neither of you noticed me, so I slipped back out and dashed upstairs. Helen wasn't pleased to see me, but she soon perked up when I showed her the bottle. I poured a good measure into her cup, and I pretended to take a drink, then I topped it up even higher. Considering she was a drinker, the rum made her tipsy very quickly. Perhaps she'd already had a few before the party. After that, it was easy to persuade her to take a couple of pills and have a lie-down. Her breathing became very shallow, and I knew she was on the way. I splashed a bit of booze around the place to make it seem as though she'd been drinking heavily, and I tipped the mug over."

"It didn't matter that your fingerprints were on the mug," Dan said. "You were helping out with the food on the next table, so it would've been easy to claim you'd handed her the drink. But I must admit that the absence of the bottle of rum made me very suspicious."

Tamsin shrugged. "I had to take it with me. It had my fingerprints all over it, but John had handled it too, and I couldn't take the risk that he might be implicated. I took off my pointed hat and hid the bottle inside it. It meant I couldn't wear the hat again, but nobody noticed I was carrying it. When I was sure Helen was fading, I left, locking the door and putting the hair clip into the keyhole." She smiled. "That was a bonus. I'd planned just to lock the door and walk away, taking the spare key with me. But I remembered I had the hair clip in my pocket, and the idea came to me in a flash. I suppose I was trying to be too clever. Anyway, once the door was secured, I went downstairs and took my place at the food table. Martin didn't know how long I'd been; he didn't care. After that, all I had to do was watch and wait. Much to my surprise, no one went to check on her. They were all too wrapped up in their own families. When the party was over, I went into the kitchen and made sure I mentioned Helen before I left. It put me in the clear, and if you ask a question in the right way, you can make people give any answer you want. I said, 'Helen went home with a migraine, didn't she?' and they all nodded and agreed. That done, I replaced the spare storeroom key while making a show of taking the key for the front door, saying that I wanted to come back the next day to do some tidying up. Everyone was happy with that, of course. When I arrived home, I cleaned the empty rum bottle, then I took a stroll and threw it into a ditch."

"I should've noticed that there was a raffle prize missing," John said. "I can't believe I missed that."

"There were lots of prizes that year," Tamsin replied. "Back then, we just pulled out the winning tickets and let people choose anything they wanted from the table. It was all a bit of a muddle, and it went on for what felt like ages."

"Meanwhile, Helen was up here, slowly slipping away," Dan said. "I don't know how you could've gone through with it. You must have ice in your veins."

Tamsin looked down, staring into space. "No, I'm just an ordinary person. But when you want someone, when you really *need* them with every fibre of your being, then you'll do anything to try and bring them closer to you. Honestly, it didn't even feel like a choice."

John let out a groan. "There are always choices, Tamsin. Always. But you chose to end the life of a warm and wonderful human being. Helen wasn't perfect, and she had her demons, but she deserved a chance of happiness, and so did I. I knew she didn't want me in the right way or even for the right reasons. I think she cared for my girls more than she cared for me. But we might've made a life together. You took that away, Tamsin, and I can't forgive you for that. Never."

Tamsin gave no sign of having heard John's heartfelt words. She looked up at Dan. "What will you do?"

"What do you want me to do?" Dan asked.

"I… I wish I could beg for forgiveness or understanding, but the truth is, I don't deserve that. If you want to call the police, then please, go ahead. I'll stay here until they arrive. I won't try and wriggle out of this. I'll tell them the whole story."

"I'll make the call." Dan stood. "I'll take it outside. John, I think you'd better come with me. Alan, if you don't mind, would you keep Tamsin company for a few minutes?"

"Of course," Alan said. "Are you going to call DS Spiller?"

"Yes. I need someone who'll hear me out, and I think he'll listen. He owes me one."

John rose, unsteady on his feet. "I have to get out of here."

"That's fine." Dan ushered him toward the door. "I know this can't have been easy for you, John, but you've been a great help. You can go home now."

"Thank God for that." John cast a fleeting glance at

Tamsin, then he allowed Dan to lead him from the room. They headed outside, and the fresh morning air brought the colour back to John's cheeks. They said their goodbyes, then John hurried along the street without looking back. Dan watched him for a minute, then he took his phone from his pocket and made the call.

CHAPTER 5

Dan and Alan stood side by side on the pavement, watching as DS Spiller installed Tamsin in the back seat of his Volvo saloon. Behind the wheel, DC Collins stared straight ahead, studiously ignoring his surroundings.

"He doesn't look happy," Alan said.

Dan smiled. "I get the feeling that DC Collins is rarely satisfied with his lot. You'd think he'd be pleased, but… hang on, Spiller's coming over."

DS Spiller's expression was inscrutable as he approached, and he came to a halt in front of them, regarding them in silence, his hands in the pockets of his long coat.

"There's no need to thank me," Dan said.

"I wasn't going to," Spiller replied. "I just wanted to ask whether this kind of thing is going to become a regular occurrence."

"I hope not," Alan said firmly. "With a bit of luck, once this has blown over, life will return to normal."

"Define *normal*," Dan replied. "I'm sure DS Spiller's normality is distinctly different from your own."

"Sometimes, there's no talking to you," Alan said. "You

know what I meant, and for my part, I'm happy to settle for a peaceful life."

"Quite right, sir." Spiller fixed Dan with a look. "You'd do well to take a leaf out of your friend's book. There's enough trouble in the world; there's really no need to go looking for it."

"I agree," Dan said. "But I didn't ask for any part in this. I was happily minding my own business, but unfortunately, this case was presented directly to me. I was asked to give it some thought, so what was I supposed to do, turn them away?"

Spiller raised his eyebrows. "*Case?* I think you're in danger of overstepping the mark, Mr Corrigan. If you're unlucky enough to come across a crime, leave it to me and my colleagues. We're professionals. We're trained to deal with such things. We might ask the public to come forward with information now and then, but that's as far as it goes. There's a line between people like you and people like me, Mr Corrigan, and you'd better not cross it. Am I making myself clear?"

"Very," Dan said. "But if I'd called you at the outset when I had nothing more than my suspicions to go on, would you have listened? Would you have reopened the case and sent a team to investigate?"

Spiller pursed his lips.

"I thought not," Dan said. "Enjoy the rest of your day, Detective Sergeant. Tamsin's confession won't take long, but I'm sure the paperwork will keep you occupied for a while."

Spiller sent him a mocking smile, then he turned on his heel and marched away.

"You shouldn't antagonise him," Alan said. "You're lucky he turned up, otherwise we'd have been in a pickle."

"I knew he'd come running. We just handed him a ready-made murder. Again. At this rate, they'll make him an inspector."

"You've been watching too much television. I think it's a tad more complicated than that." Alan glanced at the village hall where the door was still hanging open. "We'd better call Martin and tell him to come and lock the place up. You'll have to break the news to him. He still thinks we're meeting at nine o'clock."

"That was a necessary part of the plan. I had to put someone else in the frame; it was the only way to draw Tamsin in. Martin was the obvious candidate, and I have to say, your idea of putting an empty chair in his place was brilliant, a really good piece of stage management."

Alan acknowledged the praise with a bow of his head. "You did all the hard work. I'm still amazed you managed to put it all together so quickly."

"To begin with, it wasn't easy. I misunderstood Martin's reasons for bringing the case to me. There was a fire in his eyes, a kind of suppressed rage that seemed almost like madness. But then I realised he'd been in love with Helen, and his emotions became easier to understand. He wanted justice for her, but he couldn't do much about it himself, because that would've meant admitting his feelings for her. Martin is well known in this village, and that's important to him. When he fell for Helen, he didn't want the rumours to start flying, so he pushed his feelings underground, and he's tried to keep them buried ever since. Once I was certain of that, the dominoes fell one after another. I watched Tamsin and John carefully, and it was clear that she yearned for him, but he didn't think of her in the same way."

Alan nodded. "The matching Halloween costumes were a bit of a giveaway."

"That was a clue, but I was more interested in the scores of little things that passed between them. When Tamsin thought no one was watching, she stole little glances at John, and whenever we were forced together, like in the entrance of the village hall, she always stood closer to him than she needed

333

MICHAEL CAMPLING

to. And in the pub, did you see what she did with the beermats?"

"I saw her fiddling around with them, but I didn't think much of it. She was just being neat and tidy, wasn't she?"

"No. She was placing a beermat in front of John so that it would be ready for his drink. It was almost as if she was laying the table for him, perhaps in the way she'd dreamed of doing for years. In her mind, she was playing house."

Alan's face fell. "What she did to Helen was truly terrible, but somehow, I can't help but feel sorry for Tamsin. She must've been deeply unhappy, disturbed even. And it's not as if her plan had the result she wanted. I have the feeling she's suffered a great deal of remorse over the years. I suppose that's what made her confess."

Dan let out a dismissive grunt. "She wouldn't have admitted a thing if we hadn't found her out."

"You're probably right. You discovered her pressure point, and you used it against her."

"Yes and no," Dan said. "It was a little more subtle than that."

"I'll take your word for it. The way your mind works is a mystery."

"You should see it from this side," Dan said. "But let's not get into that. I don't know about you, but I'm ready for a coffee. Come on, I'll brew you an espresso that'll set you up for the rest of the day."

"Sounds good, but what about the village hall? We can't just leave it unlocked."

"I'll call Martin, but I don't feel like waiting for him to show up. Pull the door shut, and we'll leave it. I'm sure it'll be fine." Dan smiled. "After all, nothing much happens here. This is Embervale."

Thank You for reading Mystery at the Hall
I hope that you enjoyed it.

The next case for Dan and Alan is:
Mystery in May

Find it on your favourite store
Mystery in May
Visit: books2read.com / mysteryinmay

AUTHOR NOTES

Is Embervale based on a real place?

Embervale is a fictional village, and although it isn't based on any one place, it is inspired by the small villages in Dartmoor where I've been lucky enough to make my home for over twenty years. We live in the beautiful Teign Valley, and Embervale is located at an imaginary point somewhere nearby. In the adventures of Corrigan and Hargreaves, I have used real places to provide the surrounding towns and villages, but these places are, to some extent, fictionalised.

Are the brands of beer real?

Yes. I like to include locally made products, so Reel Ale and Gun Dog are real beers, brewed by Teignworthy Brewery. I don't receive anything in return for mentioning brands, and the references do not constitute any kind of endorsement.

Will there be more adventures for Corrigan and Hargreaves?

I sincerely hope so. People seem to like them, and I enjoy the challenge of coming up with new mysteries. In my youth, I was a precocious reader, and since YA books weren't much in evidence at the time, once I'd graduated from children's stories, there was nothing for it but to march into the adult section of the library and start browsing. I discovered Agatha Christie at an early age, and I've always admired the way that she could lead her readers down the garden path. Many years passed before I dared to try a mystery story myself, but while the whole process is daunting and certainly has its perils, I'm finding the experience rather wonderful. It feels, I should imagine, like compiling a cryptic crossword for others to complete. The answers must be in there somewhere, but they can't be too obvious or there'll be no fun in trying to find them.

Thank you for reading this far

I hope I've kept you entertained, and thank you for taking the time to read my work. You'll be needing something else to read now, so I'd better get back to my keyboard and start tapping the keys.

If you'd like me to hurry up and complete another mystery, then please consider posting a review of my mysteries online. Also, a great way to encourage any author to write more in a series is to tell your friends about the books you've enjoyed. These days, readers have millions of books to choose from, and so word of mouth recommendations are very valuable.

Whatever your next reading adventure, have fun.

Take care and best wishes,

Mikey C

BECOME A VIP READER

MEMBERS GET FREE BOOKS,
EXCLUSIVE CONTENT AND MORE

Visit: michaelcampling.com / freebooks

ABOUT THE AUTHOR

Michael (Mikey to friends) is a full-time writer living and working on the edge of Dartmoor in Devon. He writes stories with characters you can believe in and plots you can sink your teeth into. His style is vivid but never flowery; every word packs a punch. His stories are complex, thought-provoking, atmospheric and grounded in real life.

You can start reading his work for free with a complimentary starter library when you join Michael's VIP Readers' Club. You'll receive free books and stories plus a newsletter that's actually worth reading. Learn more and start reading today at: michaelcampling.com/freebooks facebook.com/authormichaelcampling

x.com/mikeycampling

instagram.com/mikeycampling

amazon.com/Michael-Campling/e/B00EUVA0GE

bookbub.com/authors/michael-campling

ALSO BY MICHAEL CAMPLING

One Link to Rule Them All:

michaelcampling.com / find-my-books

The Devonshire Mysteries

A Study in Stone

Valley of Lies

Mystery at the Hall

Murder Between the Tides

Mystery in May

Death at Blackingstone Rock

Accomplice to Murder

A Must-Have Murder

The Darkeningstone Series:

Breaking Ground - A Darkeningstone Prequel

Trespass: The Darkeningstone Book I

Outcast — The Darkeningstone Book II

Scaderstone — The Darkeningstone Book III

Darkeningstone Trilogy Box Set